SNIPER
A THRILLER

VAUGHN C. HARDACKER

Skyhorse Publishing

Skyhorse Publishing books may be purchased in bulk at special discounts for sales promotion, corporate gifts, fund-raising, or educational purposes. Special editions can also be created to specifications. For details, contact the Special Sales Department, Skyhorse Publishing, 307 West 36th Street, 11th Floor, New York, NY 10018 or info@skyhorsepublishing.com.

Skyhorse® and Skyhorse Publishing® are registered trademarks of Skyhorse Publishing, Inc.®, a Delaware corporation.

www.skyhorsepublishing.com

10 9 8 7 6 5 4 3 2 1

Library of Congress Cataloging-in-Publication Data

Hardacker, Vaughn C.
  Sniper : a thriller / Vaughn C. Hardacker.
   ISBN 978-1-62636-557-5 (pbk.)
   1. Snipers—Fiction. 2. Serial murderers—Fiction. 3. Criminal behavior, Prediction of—Fiction. 4. Criminal investigation—Fiction. I. Title.
   PS3608.A72518S65 2014
   813'.6—dc23
                        2013036198

Printed in the United States of America

I

ONE SHOT; ONE KILL

"The sniper is the big-game hunter of the battlefield, and he needs
all the skills of a woodsman, marksman, hunter, and poacher. He
must possess the field craft to be able to position himself for a killing shot, and he
must be able to effectively place a single bullet into his intended target."
—Charles Henderson, *Marine Sniper*

"There is no weapon in the US military arsenal more deadly
than the marine and his rifle . . ."
—Lesson taught at Marine Corps Boot Camp

PRELUDE TO THE KILL

"Before operations in an area, a sniper should study the terrain, vegetation and lay of the land to determine the best possible type of personal camouflage."
—*US Marine Corps Scout/Sniper Training Manual*

He stood in the middle of Boston Common, paying particular attention to possible shooting positions: monuments, building entrances and exits. He turned his attention away from the geography to the indigenous people who strolled, lounged and played there. August meant baseball season, and many people wore Red Sox attire of one type or another. His next stop would be to a local discount store to purchase the appropriate clothing.

Without trying, lines of fire, direction of the wind and shooting lanes flashed through his mind. Satisfied that he had learned all he could from the present location, the man moved to the perimeter of the kill zone. He circled the park, stopping on each intersection, and decided that the corner of Charles and Beacon was the ideal location. To the left the shooter saw a crowd of tourists lined up in front of the *Cheers* bar and beyond it, the golden dome of the Massachusetts State House. *Yes,* he resolved, *this is my hide . . . lots of targets of opportunity.*

The shooter turned and walked along Charles to Chestnut Street where he stopped beside a double-parked white van. The driver's window dropped, and his co-shooter and spotter, dressed in a New England Patriots jacket, stared out at him. "Well?"

"Tomorrow . . ."

1

"...I decided that the best way to get the attention ...was to simply
go out and kill a whole bunch of people."
—Gunnery Sergeant Jack Coughlin, USMC

Detective Mike Houston surveyed the carnage around him. The area around the bodies was cordoned off with yellow police tape. Teams from the crime scene unit and medical examiner's office carefully crossed under to begin their work. What had started as a beautiful late summer day on Boston Common had ended with the caustic sounds of rifle fire . . . it looked more like Mogadishu after a skirmish between rival warlords than New England's most famous park.

"This," Houston said, "is going to turn into a real shit sandwich . . . and fast."

Anne Bouchard, his partner, stood silently beside him. "I've never seen anything like this," she said.

Houston mentally blocked out the sight of the devastation around them and instead studied Anne. Her complexion was pallid. A normal reaction for someone who had never experienced a crime of this magnitude. They had been partners for five years and were as close as two people could get without being "in a relationship." Cops probably knew more about their partners than they did their significant others. But, Houston kept these thoughts to himself.

"I have—but not here . . ." When he spoke, it brought him back to the present, away from a time and place he had thought he had put behind him forever. "Time to go to work." Houston approached the perimeter, stopping beside a uniformed cop. One glance was all Houston needed to know that he had never met this cop and he flashed his identification. "What do we have here?"

"Looks like a drive-by . . . the shooter pulled up at the corner." The uniformed officer pointed toward Charles Street. "From what we've been able to piece together, it took him less than a minute to put four people down."

"Anyone get a license plate?"

The cop looked at Houston. "You're kidding, right?"

"Just answer my question."

"We should be so lucky. Apparently it went down so fast nobody saw shit."

"Looks like we're in for a long day." Houston clipped his ID to his chest pocket and pulled on a pair of latex gloves. The uniformed cop lifted the tape, and Houston and Anne stepped into the kill zone. They continued along the periphery of the crime scene, watching where they placed their feet. Walking a few steps ahead of Anne, Houston surveyed the Common. In spite of the throng of curious spectators who lined the police barricades, it was unnaturally quiet. The only sound was the murmur of the low voices of cops and investigators as they moved about performing their duties. Even the forensics team seemed reluctant to break the silence as its members gathered evidence and photographed the area from every angle.

Houston had dealt with violent death for most of his adult life and over the years had learned to control his emotions so that no matter how repulsive the act, he could analyze the facts objectively. Jaw clenched and eyes narrowed, Houston vowed to bring in whoever had perpetrated this butchery.

"I've never seen anything anger you this much," said Anne.

"What really pisses me off is that from now on the Common will be just another damned crime scene."

"Yeah," Anne said, "nothing is sacred to scumbags—sooner or later, everyplace in the city is going to be one . . ."

"I wish I could think differently . . . but I agree with you."

Anne scanned the area, paying particular interest to the throng gathered along the Common's periphery. "You think the perp is watching us?"

"It wouldn't surprise me. Perpetrators of crimes like this love to hang around and watch the aftermath—their way of confirming their kills."

"Well," Anne said, "we better get to it."

They headed toward the victims.

The four bodies lay within a few yards of each other. This told Houston that the shooter had probably picked his targets at random, concentrating on people who were in close proximity to one another. When Houston reached the geometrical center of the kill zone, he stopped and looked toward the corner of Beacon and Charles Streets, the location from which the uniformed officer had said the killer had attacked. Experience and the position of the victims told him that was correct—all four shots came from the same spot. Houston pictured the shooter as he calmly peered through his telescopic sight—ensuring that his sight alignment and sight picture were correct—and once he was satisfied all was in order, selected his targets.

The first victim was a woman. She lay on her back, head and torso obscured by a lush flower bed filled with radiant red and yellow flowers. Her skirt was hiked up, revealing her thighs, blood-splattered legs and lacy white thong. As hardened as he was to scenes of devastation, the sight of her scanty, intimate garment served to bring home to him the senselessness of this act. "Death doesn't give a damn about modesty."

They were silent as they continued through the kill zone.

The second victim was a white male. He laid on a sparse patch of grass, beneath the spreading branches of a gigantic maple tree, an ideal place for sitting in the shade and watching people as they strolled through the Common. It was a place for lazing about—not for dying.

"If he didn't have a bullet hole in his forehead," Anne said, "you could almost believe he was taking a nap."

Number three was a large black man who lay on his side in the middle of the paved walk, one arm thrown up as if he were passing a football, the other tucked under his massive belly.

Victim number four was facedown in front of the park bench where he must have been sitting. A crumpled and bloodstained street map of Boston lay beneath him and an expensive camera was at his side, lying in a puddle of his blood; its strap was still looped around his shoulder. "Probably a tourist," Houston said.

Outwardly, it appeared that these people shared only one thing. They had all stopped to enjoy a warm late-summer afternoon in the park. A few fateful minutes later, each lay dead in a dark crimson puddle of blood.

He visualized tomorrow morning's headlines. They would all read some variation of *COMMON SITE OF SECOND BOSTON MASSACRE!* The *Tribune* would try to be tactful (if such a word could be used to describe a newspaper) and downplay it, but other papers would sensationalize the story to boost their flagging circulations. He paused and looked back at the woman, wondering which one would run a picture of her with her thighs and panties exposed on the front page. He noticed Tom Lukasic, a member of the crime lab, walking in his direction and motioned for him.

When the forensic scientist reached his side, Houston could see a shocked expression on his pallid face. "T-they never covered anything like this in school," Lukasic stuttered.

"Don't think about it. Just do your job." Houston nodded to the female victim. "Take care of her first. Okay? Try to get her body covered up before some press vulture photographs her."

Lukasic swallowed and some color returned to his face. "I'm on it . . ."

Houston stared at the cluster of forensics people, who were gathered around the spot from which the shots were fired. "Tom."

"Yeah?"

"How far you think it is from here to where the furthest vic is?"

Without rising, Lukasic looked toward the corner. "Three, maybe four hundred yards—why?"

On a summer afternoon, the Common was always crowded. Why had the shooter targeted victims so far out? Why not pick closer, easier-to-hit targets? Was this shooter leaving a message?

"Either way, if he hit what he intended to hit, he knows his way around weapons. Pretty stiff breeze today."

Exactly what I thought, Houston mused. It was time to look at the scene from the shooter's perspective. He watched until Lukasic knelt at the victim's side and then searched the area for Anne. When he found her, he motioned for her to meet him at the corner from which the killer had struck.

The brim of the tall man's Red Sox cap rested on top of his dark glasses, obscuring much of his face. He stood among the herd of gawkers and couldn't help but feel like a celebrity, which, in a way, he was. Without him, there would be no throng crowding the periphery of Boston Common like jackals around a ripe carcass.

He threaded his way through the herd of sensation-seekers until he reached the cordon of yellow tape. He watched the cops and smirked as they moved through the kill zone like hounds seeking a scent. Cops, like military intelligence, were clueless.

He rested his hands on his hips and watched. The cops performed their duties much like soldiers did after a terrorist attack—it was as if they worked from the same manual.

The two in street clothes were detectives, a woman and a man. The male cop, Houston, was the reason he was here. In truth, he was the reason for this entire show. The man studied the male detective closely, trying to determine if he had changed any. The man's eyes followed the cop's every move, taking in everything and paying attention to the smallest of details. A good sniper (which he defined as a live sniper) was always aware of several things: the environment, the behavior and the habits of his target. He committed his target's every move and mannerism to memory—one never knew when the enemy would unwittingly reveal a weakness. The man in the hat wondered if Houston was still the officious bastard he remembered.

Houston paused beside the female victim and said something to another man, who nodded and then quickly walked to the woman. After a minute or so, number two lowered the woman's skirt. The shooter grinned, twisting his mouth into a ghoulish smile. "You always were a compassionate piece of shit, Mikey."

He was unaware that he had spoken aloud until a woman next to him jerked her head and gave him a stern look.

He removed his hat, revealing a face so hideously scarred that it resembled a wax statue that had melted and then cooled. She recoiled at the sight of his damaged skin. Before she could apologize, he scowled at her and almost laughed when her disapproving look fled like a doe before a forest fire. He could have left things at that, but he had long since lost tolerance for the cretins of the world and their petty bullshit. "What's the matter, lady . . . you got virgin ears or something?"

The sniper leered at the woman, closing in on her until his scarred face was only inches from her pallid one. He grinned, and her eyes opened with fear. He laughed a deep, condescending laugh as she scurried away, pushing her way through the crowd.

2

"When a bad guy hides deep in a building or mixes in among civilians,
he cannot be readily seen and identified . . ."
—Gunnery Sergeant Jack Coughlin, USMC

Houston perused the crowd that had assembled along the periphery of the crime scene. He felt sure that the shooter was among them. He studied the faces of the audience and saw nothing out of the ordinary, a lot of Red Sox attire and faces depicting shock, revulsion and disbelief that someone had perpetrated such a dreadful crime in their city.

A news van pulled up as close to the crime scene as possible and drew Houston's focus away from the throng. A petite brunette wearing a business-like top and cut off dungaree shorts jumped out of the truck while it was still moving. Houston immediately recognized Amanda Boyce, a local celebrity. She surveyed the area, no doubt looking for a broadcast position that would frame the activity on the Common behind her.

A few moments later, a man carrying a large camera got out of the van. The technician lifted the camera onto his right shoulder and placed his eye to the reticule. He slowly moved around, keeping the camera positioned so that her blue denim shorts would not be visible to the viewing audience. Boyce seemed to quickly assess the situation and then looked over her shoulder once again. When she seemed satisfied that the camera framed the scene as she wanted it, she turned back to face the lens, raised a wireless microphone to her lips and performed a quick sound test. As Boyce spoke, the camera operator tracked her like a smart bomb homing in on its target, moving in a circle as she squared herself in front of the action on the Common. She smoothed her blouse and shaped her hair with her free hand. Houston heard her ask the camera operator, "How do I look?"

The cinematographer replied, "You're ravishing . . . get ready to go live. Three . . . two . . . one . . . and . . ."

"This is Amanda Boyce, WBO news, live at the Boston Common where a short time ago an unidentified number of people were gunned down in an apparent drive-by shooting . . ." Although she spoke in a professional, yet subdued voice, in the unnatural quiet of the space her words seemed as loud as if they boomed from a loudspeaker.

Houston didn't want the media cornering him so he turned away.

"Now the media circus begins," Anne said.

"They're like vultures . . . as soon as they hear of a body they flock to it." He tried to filter the disgust out of his voice but was not completely successful.

"I don't think I'd characterize Amanda that way," Anne said.

Houston turned to her, a question written on his face. "You sound as if you know her. Do you?"

"Yeah, we knew each other in college."

Houston saw Barry Newton, head crime lab technician, straighten, place his hands on the small of his back and arch backward, stretching his taut muscles. He lifted the yellow tape and motioned Houston inside.

When he was inside, Houston asked, "What'cha got, Barry?"

Newton dropped the tape. "What we have here is a stellar example of a Chinese fire drill."

Barry Newton was as good a crime scene tech as there was anywhere in the country. He had a reputation for being no-nonsense and up-front. Houston knew that Newton wouldn't string him along. If he had something, Houston would get it. On the other hand, if he had nothing he would come right out and say so. At this early stage of the investigation, Houston felt certain that the latter was the case.

"We got about what you would expect," Newton said. "Nothing, nada, zip."

"Well," Houston commented, "whoever this shooter was, he definitely knew his business. This wasn't haphazard—it was planned, right down to the location and time." He brought his arm up and moved his hand from side to side. "From here they have any number of escape routes. They could have taken I-93 north or south, crossed one of the bridges into Cambridge or disappeared into the city."

"We did find one thing." Newton held a plastic bag with a single expended cartridge in it.

Houston took the bag and inspected the cartridge.

"It's a .308," Newton said.

"Same caliber as the rifle I used in the Marines . . ."

"As well as a million hunters."

The sniper watched the female cop as she sat beside a crying woman dressed in a nurse's light-blue scrubs. *Another compassionate idiot,* he thought in disgust. Whatever happened to the cops he knew as a kid in Louisville? Like Wilcox—that bastard would bust your head and place a size ten up your ass as he sent you on your way.

He turned his mind to other things. Without intending, he started computing distances, wind velocity and direction. His palms were moist with sweat as the need to feel the loving caress of a trigger's resistance against his finger swept through him. It would be so easy. . . .

Houston surveyed the Common, looking for Anne. After a few seconds, he saw her sitting on a bench beside a grief-stricken woman. Although he was the senior officer, Anne was more adept when it came to dealing with distraught witnesses. As was their routine, he left her to do what she did best. Turning back to Newton, he asked, "You got anything else?"

"I won't have anything definite until we get to the lab."

"When can you get me a report?"

"I'll be here the rest of the day—how about the day after tomorrow?"

"I could use it sooner than that, if that's possible. Like, first thing in the morning."

Houston saw mock disgust in Barry's face when he heard the unreasonable request. Nevertheless, Houston knew he had been expecting it; if it had not come from him, it would have come from someone else. The murder of four people in the middle of one of Boston's biggest tourist attractions at the height of the season was certain to create a lot of heat fast. Every politician, from the most junior city council member to the governor, would be hot for a quick resolution to this case. He wouldn't be the only person putting in a lot of overtime to solve this one. "I'll do my best."

"That's one of the reasons why I like you." Houston scanned the surrounding area—the brownstones, Beacon Hill and the *Cheers* bar. In the near distance the gold dome of the state capitol shone in the sunshine. "You know, Barry, it wouldn't surprise me to learn that this site was chosen and this was staged and choreographed down to the second."

"Staged?"

"Yeah, maybe our shooter was looking for maximum shock value. Not to mention publicity. I'd expect something like this to go down at a gang turf war in Dorchester or Mattapan, one of the more crime-prone neighborhoods."

Anne broke away from the gathered cops and met Houston beside their car. "It looks as if our shooter may have some redeeming qualities," she said.

"Oh?"

She indicated the distraught woman, whom she had interviewed before turning her over to a group of uniformed cops. "Yeah, he had that nurse in his sights, but changed his mind at the last minute."

"Are you sure?"

"That's her story. She saw the rifle aimed at her, and then he seemed to think differently and chose another victim. Maybe he realized it was a woman."

"That's interesting. But I don't think her being a woman had anything to do with it." He pointed to the flower bed. "If that was the case, *she* wouldn't be dead."

"Well," Anne asked, "what do you think?"

"I'd rather keep my opinions to myself for a bit."

Anne gave him a quizzical look; it wasn't like him to hold things back from her.

In a manner that made Anne think he spoke to himself, Houston said, "I think he has his own code of ethics."

"A mass murderer with a code of ethics? I find that hard to imagine."

"Who knows what motivates an asshole sick enough to do this?" Houston nodded to his left. "There's the captain."

"A crime of this magnitude is bound to attract all the brass. I wouldn't be surprised if the mayor showed up."

They walked over to Capt. William Dysart, who stoically studied the activity around the crime scene. He inhaled smoke from a cigarette, then looked at it as if it suddenly tasted foul. Houston and Anne stopped beside him. "This is gonna be a real clusterfuck," Houston said.

"Ain't no *gonna be* about it. Five minutes after this went down the commissioner was on my phone—she'll be here soon."

"She's not one to miss an opportunity for a photo-op."

"Photo-op or no, it would be professional suicide for her if she didn't show up." Dysart tossed his cigarette into the gutter and turned to his detectives. "You guys got the lead on this. I don't have to tell you that we need a quick resolution."

"We're on it."

Dysart pulled a fresh cigarette from the pack and lit it as Houston and Anne walked away.

"Where do we go from here?" Anne asked.

"We visit Jimmy O'Leary."

"Jimmy O may be a weasel, but I don't think he's this low. Why do you want to talk to him?"

"Anyone planning something like this won't want any records of an ammunition purchase. If someone wants to buy ammo on the down-low, Jimmy will either know about it or can find out who sold it."

"There's also the other possibility . . ." Anne said.

Houston completed the thought for her. "Or he sold it to them."

The sniper watched the cops walk out of the kill zone. When they were about ten meters from him, he called out, "Hello, Mikey, it's been a long time." He chuckled as Houston scanned the throng, trying to see who had called to him. He resisted speaking again and lost himself in the crowd.

3

"Hell, anybody would be crazy to like to go out and kill folks..."
—Gunnery Sergeant Carlos Hathcock, USMC

Jimmy O'Leary and Michael Houston grew up together, fighting to survive adolescence on the tough, mean streets of South Boston. They were best friends throughout high school, but when O'Leary dropped out in their junior year, their lives took different paths. Houston stayed in school while Jimmy walked the dark streets and alleys of Southie. He started by boosting cars and later moved on to crimes that were more lucrative as well as more serious in nature—he became a member of Whitey Bulger's Winter Hill Gang.

To the average citizen, Jimmy O was a successful businessman who owned a popular Irish pub and ran a profitable commodity-trading business. Ask anyone in Southie about O'Leary and you would hear a glowing testimonial of a disadvantaged kid who made good. On the other hand, Boston PD knew that the commodities he dealt in covered a wide spectrum. Jimmy O was purported to be involved in any form of graft from which he could derive a tax-exempt living—from the protection racket to weapons and, albeit unproven, murder. He was reputed to make the bulk of his money shaking down bookmakers and drug dealers and through illegal gambling. Jimmy O was also the self-appointed protector of Southie. If someone had a problem, that person could get a faster response from O'Leary than from the police. The BPD had been unable to break Southie's code of silence when Jimmy exercised his unique form of justice on any criminals or gang members stupid enough to venture onto his turf.

Houston enlisted in the United States Marine Corps shortly after graduating from high school. After his release from active duty, he became a member of the BPD, with his childhood friend on the other side of the fence. When they promoted him to detective, Houston immediately informed his boss, Capt. William Dysart, of the background that he and O'Leary shared. Dysart made it a practice to avoid even a hint of a conflict of interest by never assigning Houston to any case that directly involved O'Leary.

Over the years, O'Leary had become big enough to cover himself with several layers of expensive criminal lawyers and had accrued enough wealth to ensure that any charge his attorneys couldn't handle was dropped for lack of evidence or some procedural issue. Houston and BPD believed that when Whitey Bulger disappeared, most of Whitey's enterprises came under O'Leary's control. Nevertheless, they couldn't prove anything.

The Claddagh Pub sat dead center in a block off Broadway. The street was so narrow that driving down it was a challenge. Parked cars, many of which were illegally double-parked, created an obstacle course for driving. Three-storied tenements, known as triple-deckers to Bostonians, were so close together that sunshine only touched the street during the noon hour. The weary houses were fronted by stoops that sagged as much as the tough, tired-faced people who sat on them drinking and glaring at any strange cars that passed.

Houston and Anne found a vacant spot across the street from the pub and parked. Anne studied the flashing sign above the front door of the tavern. "What does it mean?"

"What does what mean?"

"Claddagh. What does it mean in English?"

"It means Claddagh. It's not a thing; it's a place. At one time, it was a fishing village near Galway in western Ireland. During the twentieth century, Galway grew to be so large that Claddagh became a neighborhood in the middle of the city." He chuckled. "If you were gutter Irish from Southie instead of a French aristocrat from Wellesley, you'd have known that."

"I've heard of the Claddagh ring," Anne said, "and always wondered what the word meant. You seem to know a lot about it. Is Houston an Irish surname?"

"Nope, it's Scottish, but there are a lot of us in Ireland. My mother's maiden name was Byrne—you don't get any more Irish than that. Either way, Irish or not, you don't grow up in Southie and not learn about things Irish."

They entered the tavern and stood by the door until their eyes adjusted to the dim light. Within seconds, the cop detector in the head of every occupant of the bar was flashing warnings and sending alarms. In Southie, people knew when the Man arrived—it was almost instinct. Every set of eyes in the room turned in their direction. Without looking away, Anne whispered, "I feel like a Jew visiting Mecca during Ramadan . . ."

"Being a cop in Southie isn't a hell of a lot different." Houston returned the hard stares as they moved deeper into the pub's interior, angling toward the bar.

When they slid onto stools at the bar, the bartender stopped wiping glasses, tossed the towel into the sink with considerably more force than necessary and sauntered toward them. He threw a pair of cork coasters on the bar. "You lost?"

Houston made a point of studying the tavern's clientele. "From the looks of these assholes, maybe we oughtta spend more time in here. How you bin, Gordon?"

Gordon Winter, O'Leary's right-hand man and supposed manager of the pub, shrugged. "Can't complain."

"I'm sure Jimmy's glad to hear that."

"Probably . . . then again it wouldn't change nothing if I did," Winter said. "Nobody wants to listen to anyone piss and moan."

"Jimmy around?"

"That depends . . ."

"On what might it depend?" Anne asked.

"It would most likely depend on *why* you want to see him."

Houston looked over Winter's shoulder at one of the TVs in the corners of the bar. Amanda Boyce was still broadcasting from Boston Common.

Winter followed Houston's line of sight. "No way Jimmy had anythin' to do with that mess."

Houston took his eyes away from the screen. He swiveled the bar stool until he was facing Winter. "That's what I thought when I walked in here, but you being so goddamned defensive makes me have second thoughts."

"*Second* thoughts? The next thought one of you cops has will be your first. B'sides, you can have all the thoughts you want, it don't change the fact that he had nothin' to do with it."

Before he could respond to Winter's slight, movement in the deepest recesses of the tavern attracted Houston's attention. He swiveled his seat and saw Jimmy O walk out of the darkness. O'Leary had not changed much in the three years since he and Mike had last seen each other. He was of above average height and thin as a rail. If not for his thinning hair and the absence of the raging acne that plagued him in high school, he looked pretty much the way he did as a kid. A chain smoker since he was twelve, he had a cigarette dangling from his lips.

O'Leary slid onto the stool beside Houston, leaned back and studied Anne with a scrutiny that bordered on perversion. "Get me the usual, Gord."

Winter slid a shot glass across the bar, grabbed a bottle of Jameson Irish Whiskey and filled the glass. He set the bottle on the bar and stepped back. Jimmy O raised the glass and toasted Winter. "Here's hopin' that you're in heaven ten seconds before the devil knows you're dead." He downed the shot and refilled his glass. To Houston he said, "You, on the other hand, I hope you're burning in the fires of hell before the good Lord knows you're dead."

Houston ignored his childhood friend's insult. "How you doin', Jimmy?"

"I'd be doing a hell of a lot better if I didn't expect one of you cops to jump out of my shitty undershorts every time I take them off."

"Then keep your shorts clean and you got nothin' to worry about."

O'Leary's scarred face cracked into what Houston knew he thought passed for a smile. "You always had a way with the words, Mike. If you was ever to kiss the Blarney Stone, it'd crack."

"We *need* to talk."

"So talk."

"Not here. What I got to say isn't for public ears."

"Gord, go out back and ask Lisa to watch the front. Then come to my office."

Houston placed a restraining hand on O'Leary's arm. "It might be best if we talked alone."

Jimmy O stared down at Houston's hand as if its presence there would contaminate him with a social disease. Houston met the visual challenge by maintaining his grip for several seconds. When Houston dropped his hand, O'Leary said, "What . . . and have every asshole in Southie think I'm your stoolie? Since word got out that Whitey was a rat bastard, informing for the feebies, people around here are a bit sensitive about anyone who has private meetings with the Man. Either Gordon joins us in my office or we talk here. Or you get your ass out of my place." He nodded toward Anne. "If it makes you feel better, bring the dish."

Anne refused to react. She kept her eyes forward, maintaining eye contact with the gang boss via the mirror that backed the bar.

A young woman appeared. She tied a white apron around her waist and glared. Houston thought she would be beautiful if not for the hard cast to her eyes. At one time or another, everyone in Southie had run afoul of the cops. Houston couldn't help but wonder what the source of her dislike was. Maybe she had been rousted or one of her relatives was doing time.

"We shouldn't be long." O'Leary slid off his stool. With a curt gesture, he motioned for them to follow.

Houston and Anne followed him through the common area and down a short, unlit corridor, past the restrooms. At the end, O'Leary stopped beside an open door and let the entourage precede him inside. The first thing Houston noticed when he stepped across the threshold was the overwhelming stench of stale cigarette smoke. He believed everything in the office was coated with a brown film of nicotine and tar. It reminded him of his mother's house. When she died, his father wanted her favorite set of prayer beads placed in her hands and buried with her. He asked his son to clean the ugly brown beads. The surface coating dissolved and revealed the true color of the beads—green.

When O'Leary indicated that they should sit, Houston and Anne perched on a couch facing an old wooden desk. Gordon Winter dropped into an easy chair. O'Leary walked around and sat behind the desk. No sooner had he settled into the chair than he lit a cigarette. "This ain't no public area, it's *my* office and I'll goddamn smoke if I want."

Houston sat back. Anne took her cue from him and leaned back.

"What brings you here?" Jimmy asked. "Things ain't like they was when we was kids. The onliest times I see you anymore is when you're tryin' to bust my ass over somethin' or another."

"It's about the shootings on the Common this afternoon—"

O'Leary cut him off. "If you think I was involved in that, then things really have changed."

"I didn't say you had anything to do with it. Nevertheless, you've been known to deal in . . . shall we say . . . off-the-record ordnance."

O'Leary broke out in a loud horselaugh. "Shit, Mike, come out and say it. You think I sell illegal guns."

"Don't you?" Anne asked.

O'Leary shrugged. "If I do, how come I ain't making license plates in Walpole or Bridgewater? Both you guys and the Feds been trying to bust my ass for twenty years and ain't never proved nothin' yet." He sucked on his cigarette and leaned back in his chair. "That all you wanted to ask me?"

Smoke drifted through the air like a ground fog. Suddenly, Houston stood up and walked through the door.

He heard Anne dart after him. She overtook him in the corridor. "What happened?"

"The smoke was driving me nuts." Houston stared back into the foggy office. "I'm not through with him yet. But, I want to be alone with him."

"I need to go to the ladies room anyway." Houston smiled when she said, "If it's not clean I'm calling the Board of Health . . ."

"It's probably clean. Jimmy's female employees would make sure of that."

"I'll be right back."

"Okay, listen, if I'm not here when you come out, wait for me in the bar."

"Be careful. He's not the same kid you grew up with."

"The problem is that he *is* the same kid I grew up with."

When the door of the women's room closed behind her, Houston returned to the office. He entered without knocking and found O'Leary and Winter in deep conversation. As soon as they saw him, they stopped talking.

"I want to talk, Jimmy." He looked at Winter. "Alone."

O'Leary nodded, and Winter left the room, giving Houston a piercing look as he passed.

Houston reached back and shut the door behind him. He flopped into the chair Winter had vacated. "First of all, I *do not* believe that you would ever be involved in something like this afternoon's shootings . . . it's a psychotic act and there's no profit in it. You never were one to do anything that didn't profit you."

"That didn't stop you from running over here like a dog that pissed on an electric fence."

"Because you hear things that I'll never hear and can get close to people that I can't get within thirty yards of. This is a real ass-kicker, Jimmy—possibly the worst Boston has ever seen. Right now, we have no ideas, no motive, no clues as to the identity of the shooter. Not that that's unusual, but this is bullshit . . . and unnecessary. This perp took out four innocent people for no apparent reason."

"Your perp has reasons—even if they're nothin' more than doin' this because he can. Either way, we're living in some fucked-up times. Seems like the whole city is goin' goddamned nuts," O'Leary said. "Used to be when someone got whacked there was a purpose behind it. Now, even kids are carrying iron and hittin' people. Like, life's a damned video game or something."

He lit a cigarette from the one he held and then ground the butt in his ashtray. It didn't completely extinguish and sent a column of smoke spiraling into the already foul air.

"Jesus, Jimmy, how in hell do you breathe in this smog?"

"You reformed smokers are ballbusters, you know that? I remember when we was kids and we'd steal smokes from your ol' lady and smoke 'em behind the garage out back of the apartment house."

"That was a long time ago, in a different time and world."

"World ain't no different, Mike. It's still the largest cesspool in the universe, but we changed, didn't we?" A wistful look came over O'Leary's face as he inhaled another lungful of smoke. "Together we coulda bin something else, you know? Only you went over to the other side."

"Yeah, but think of it this way—now, rather than being in jail and taking it in the ass by some punk, I put the assholes in jail."

O'Leary bristled, rose up and leaned over his desk, his weight resting on his clenched fists. His cigarette hung from his mouth. "Did you just call me an asshole?"

"If the shoe fits . . ."

After several tense seconds, O'Leary's laughed and he sat back.

"You got any idea what woulda happened if anyone else talked to me like that?"

"I'm not anyone else."

"No, you ain't. But don't get to thinking that just because we got a history you can get away with saying anything you want to me."

"I'll remember that. But, you keep this in mind too. You haven't seen heat until you see what's gonna come down on you if you ever pop a cop. So, can I count on a call if you learn anything?"

"Maybe . . . maybe not."

"What's that mean?"

"Just that, I might call or I might not."

"You haven't changed a hell of a lot over the years, Jimmy."

"You haven't a clue how much I've changed. There was a time anyone talked to me like you just done . . . well, it would be a long time before anyone saw them again. By the way, your partner . . ."

"What about her?"

"She's a real looker. If I had a partner who looked like her, I'd be all over her like a dog. Your relationship more than professional?"

Houston felt his face flush with anger. "Strictly professional. Let's just say that I'm not her type and leave it at that."

"I doubt that, Mike. But then when it comes to women you were never the sharpest tack in the bulletin board."

"Like you are?"

O'Leary laughed. "Compared to you, I'm a Casanova."

Houston turned to the door. "I'll be expecting your call."

"Don't hold your breath while you do—it could kill you."

As Houston walked down the corridor, O'Leary's laughter echoed behind him. When the guffaws turned into a spasm of deep bronchial coughing, he muttered, "Choke, you bastard, choke."

4

"O divine art of subtlety and secrecy! Through you we learn to be invisible,
through you inaudible; and we can hold the enemy's fate
in our hands."
—Sun Tzu Wu, *The Art of War*

After Houston and the dish left, O'Leary sat at the bar. Winter was tending bar again, and he placed a bottle of Jameson and a glass in front of his boss. O'Leary scowled at Winter, letting him know that the last thing he wanted to do was talk.

O'Leary was on his second drink when the pub door opened. A black woman walked a couple of steps inside the barroom and stopped. She appeared nervous and cautious, like a deer entering a meadow during hunting season. He knew what was going through her mind as she studied the bar's patrons. The faces turned toward her were not only blatantly hostile but all were white. When her gaze circled the room and settled on him, he thought she looked familiar. It only took him a few seconds to recall her name. She was heavier than he remembered and her face showed the ravages of trying to make it in one of the most expensive cities in the country on minimum-wage.

His memories took him back more than forty years, to the busing riots of the 1970s. The city had bussed him—along with hundreds of lower-class white Irish kids whose parents could not afford the tuition at a parochial school—from Southie to the predominantly black schools in Roxbury, Mattapan and Dorchester. At the same time, they brought black students into Southie, and the resulting riots were among the worst in Boston's history. It was while he was a student attending grammar school in Roxbury that O'Leary met Marian Stokes and her brother, Rasheed. He motioned for her to join him.

His action gave her the impetus to walk across the barroom until she stood before him. "Mr. O'Leary?"

"How are you . . . Marian?" When she nodded he knew that she was indeed his old acquaintance. "Sit down, please. It's been a long time."

She remained standing, her hands twisting the soft clutch bag she held. She cast another nervous look around the room, noting that the customers clustered in small groups ignored her presence now that O'Leary was talking with her. "I need help."

"Let's go where we can talk in private." He swept his arm toward the corridor that led to his office. "This way, please." He turned to Winter and said, "I'll be back in a few—stick around in case I need you."

Winter nodded and kept wiping glasses.

O'Leary led the woman to the office and guided her to the couch that faced his desk. "Please, sit down, Marian." He circled his desk, dropped into his chair and took his cigarettes out of his shirt pocket. He shook one from the box, put it in his mouth and then offered the box to Marian.

O'Leary lit his as Marian took a cigarette. When she placed the cigarette in her mouth, he noticed that her hands shook. He held the lit Zippo toward her. Marian leaned forward to touch the end of the cigarette to the flame. Her head was shaking so violently that he had to track the end of the cigarette with his lighter.

O'Leary sat back, forming a steeple in front of his face with his hands. "You want a drink?"

"A glass of wine be nice, Mr. O'Leary . . ."

"Marian, we've known each other for over thirty years. Call me Jimmy."

"Yes, sir." She inhaled deeply and held the smoke in her lungs. It was clear to him that she was struggling to keep from crying.

Jimmy picked up the phone and punched a single number. "Gordon . . ." He covered the microphone with his hand and turned to Marian. "Any particular type of wine?"

"Anything red."

O'Leary removed his hand. "Bring me a glass of Merlot." He placed the phone on its receiver. "So what can I do for you?"

Suddenly, Marian's resolve broke. Her tears left watery trails down her cheeks, and she swiped at them with her fingers. He knew that life in the 'Bury, as locals referred to Roxbury, was hard and it took a tough woman to survive there. There was only one thing he knew of that would upset a woman from there this much—someone had done something to one of her kids. O'Leary took a box of tissues from his drawer and slid it across the desk to her.

Marian snatched a couple of sheets and wiped her cheeks. Her head bent back and she stared into the smoky air. She took another deep drag on the cigarette. She exhaled sharply, sat back and for the first time since she had come to him, made eye contact.

O'Leary leaned back in his chair. Once again, he steepled his fingers.

"My daughter, Latisha . . ."

He dropped his hands, took the cigarette from his mouth and leaned forward. Marian could not have said anything that would get his undivided attention more than those three words.

There was a light knock at the door, but he didn't move. He knew it was either Lisa or Gordon. Without waiting for permission to enter, Lisa walked in, placed the wine next to Marian and then left without saying a word.

"What about your daughter?"

"They killed her, Mr. O . . . Jimmy."

"Who killed your daughter?"

"Them gang bastards filled my baby up with junk, then raped and killed her."

"You'd better start at the beginning."

"To make ends meet, I work two jobs. When I was at work, Latisha stayed with my momma. She was a good girl, Jimmy, never no bother." She leaned forward and ground out her cigarette. He offered her another.

"Go on."

"Two week ago, my baby was found in an alley. She all torn up."

"You reported this to the cops obviously."

"Cops don't care what happen to no black girl in the hood. They too busy keepin' white people safe." She looked sheepish, as if she had only then realized that O'Leary was white.

"It's more about money and power than race, Marian . . . if you got either, no matter what your color, then the cops care, if you got no money or political clout, then you ain't shit."

"Don't matter, do it? Either way, we fucked."

"Do you have any idea who might have done this?"

"I got no way of provin' nothin', but I 'spect that Watts boy, Jermaine, who live across the hall, know something. He always be hitting on her and acting cool when she come by. She only thirteen, too young to be knowin' what a nineteen-year-old boy really after . . . 'specially one who belong to the Devs."

"The Devs—I didn't think they would do anything like this."

"Maybe Watt's an a couple a his homies do it alone?"

"Where can I find this Jermaine Watts?"

"On the street. They calls him Razor. I heard it said he like using a straight razor on people. I hear he hang out on Martin Luther King Boulevard, by Malcolm X Park."

O'Leary wrote down the address Marian gave him and then picked up his phone. "Gordon, would you come in here?"

———————————

Anne picked at her salad. She pushed a piece of tomato around with her fork, her eyes averted.

"What's on your mind?" Mike asked.

"What was it like growing up in Southie?"

"Every day was a war between the gangs and the Irish mob. Someone was always after you."

"Is that what made O'Leary the way he is?"

"It probably had a lot to do with it. Doesn't matter where you live, you grow up with a drunk who uses his wife and kids for punching bags . . . you either get tough or you die."

"Why didn't you turn out like him?"

"Luck of the draw. My old man was no saint, but he gave us the best he could. He worked himself to death unloading baggage at Logan. He'd work sixty, seventy hours some weeks for not much more than minimum wage, but no matter how hard he worked there was always something that kept him from puttin' any money in the bank. Still, he gave us the most important things, as much of his time as he could . . . and his love."

"We come from two different worlds. I've never known anyone like Jimmy O—at least not personally."

"Our differences are what make us a good team. We complement each other." Houston waited for her to continue.

"People like Jimmy O anger me. I want to throw him and everyone like him into a hole and bury them forever. You, on the other hand, seem to be able to ignore what he does."

"I grew up with him, Anne. When I got out of high school I was poised to become what he is today."

"Why didn't you?"

"Back then we had hope and the belief that we could rise above the neighborhood. Something that doesn't appear to be true any longer . . ."

"That's no excuse for what Jimmy is."

"I'd be Jimmy if I hadn't left the neighborhood for the Marines."

"Why didn't he do the same?"

Houston made an effort to objectively explain what happened, rather than defend O'Leary. "When we were in high school, Jimmy was in and out of trouble for boosting cars and even had a couple of possession busts. Once he had a rap sheet, the services wouldn't touch him and he figured that only left him one avenue to follow. He may be a hood, for want of a better word, but he does have his code."

"That's twice today that's come up, first a mass murderer and now a thug with ethics."

"I know that sounds nuts, but we all have some line that we won't cross. Jimmy remembers where he came from. As far as the people of Southie are concerned, he does more good than harm. He doesn't trust cops. In Southie, most people never have and never will. They do the best they can and take care of their own. That's what guys like Jimmy do for them. As bad as his reputation is—and don't get me wrong, he's earned that rep— they trust him. If for no other reason than that he's one of them."

"In many ways, you're still one of them."

"No, not anymore—I'm a cop and that makes me the enemy. At best, they think that like all cops, I don't give a damn about them. As I said, they see Jimmy as one of their own who made it big."

The server returned and placed their meals on the table. "Can I get you anything else?"

"We're fine." Houston waited until he was gone. "We've discussed this before and have always agreed to disagree on our differences. I know you'll never truly understand my background, no more than I'll ever be able to imagine what it was like growing up in Wellesley."

"That isn't fair . . ."

"It's every bit as fair as you bringing up my background."

She paused for a second. "You're right."

"Now," Houston said, "what you say we cut to the real issue?"

"This afternoon bothered me more than I ever could have imagined."

"Anne, we may be cops, but that doesn't mean we stop being human. It bothered me too."

She pushed her plate aside. "I know it did . . . you think you hide your feelings. And to anyone who doesn't know you as well as I do, you do. But I'm your partner. We spend more time together than some married couples, and I can tell when something gets to you."

"Do you know what truly gets to me?" he asked.

She waited for him to continue, but after several seconds without him saying anything further, she asked, "What?"

"That in another time and place, I perpetrated scenes as horrific as this one."

"Are you talking about Somalia?"

"Yes."

"But, that was twenty years ago and you were in a war. What would drive anyone to do something like this?"

"Power, bloodlust, who knows? You can be sure that when we bring this asshole, or assholes, down—and we will—I'll make it a point to ask. Until then, despite my unsavory background, we'll keep working together. We're too good a team not to."

Anne smiled. "And, contrary to my privileged, pampered upbringing and all my worries, I'll do the same." She settled back and took a drink. "But I'm still concerned about the different ways you and I view the world."

Houston picked up his fork and moved several french fries around his plate. "I know you are."

They finished their meal, paid the check and walked to their car. "What's that?" Anne asked.

"What's what?"

She pointed to a piece of paper held against the windshield by the driver-side wiper blade.

"Some ambitious rookie must have ticketed us."

"That's no ticket." She reached into the pocket of her jacket and took out a pair of latex gloves. Once her hands were covered, she took the slip of paper and read it. "You need to see this."

Houston circled the car and said, "I haven't any gloves. Read it to me."

"It says: *Hey, Mikey. Long time no see . . .*"

"That's it?"

"Well, not quite. There's some sort of drawing . . ."

"Drawing? Show it to me." She turned the slip of paper so that he could see it.

"What is it? It looks like some sort of military patch."

"That's exactly what it is. The eagle, globe and anchor are obvious, except the globe resembles a skull and, if you look around the edge, there's a sniper scope as well. All that's missing are the words *SNIPER SCHOOL QUANTICO*. This is a picture of the scout/sniper patch that we wore on our jackets."

"I've never seen patches on a marine's uniform . . . that's something the army does."

"We all had leather flight jackets. We sewed unit patches on them and wore them when we were off duty."

"Do you think . . ."

"That it's from our sniper? I don't know, but it's too much of a coincidence."

Anne was silent.

Houston said, "This sonuvabitch must be someone who knows me."

5

"Urban sniper movement can be a bitch to solve . . ."
—Gunnery Sergeant Jack Coughlin, USMC

After a miserable night filled with tossing and thrashing around the bed, Houston glanced at the clock—4 a.m.—and got up. Frustrated from his restless night, he decided to go to the precinct early. Houston always had trouble sleeping the night before an important event. Even as a child, there was not a single birthday or Christmas when he had slept well. While in the Marines, he would be up all night before a deployment—it made for some very long days. He knew what the source of his excitement was; he wanted to read the crime scene reports as soon as possible. After a quick shower, Houston bolted out the door.

By the time Houston reached the Homicide Unit office, his body screamed for a kick-start of caffeine. His first stop was at the urn in the break room for a cup of strong black coffee. Surprised to see that someone had already made a pot, he filled a disposable cup and walked out of the coffee mess to his desk, which was occupied. Barry Newton sat in his chair, feet resting on the open right-hand top drawer. A visitor's chair stood beside the desk, and Houston dropped into it. "You're in early."

"I've been in the lab all night. I knew you'd be in a rush to see my preliminary report, so I figured what the hell, may as well drop off copies for you and Dysart." A manila envelope lay on the desktop to his right. "There's your copy. I put Dysart's in his mailbox. He'll want to distribute it at the morning muster."

Houston noticed the puffiness around Barry's eyes and the red lines running through them. "Trying to get a jump on the screamers, huh?"

"You betcha. There won't be a shortage of people clamoring for a quick solution on this one. The heat—and I'm not referring to the weather—will be scorching by noon. Did you and Anne catch lead on this?"

"I don't know yet. We'll probably find out at the morning muster. So now that you've spent all night on this thing, what've you got?"

"Squat."

"What do you mean *squat*?"

"All things considered, the scene was clean. Other than the single shell casing I showed you, we don't have a hell of a lot of physical evidence. But I think we can forget about terrorists—they'd be falling all over themselves telling everyone that they did this. Is that enough *squat* for you? I can go on."

"So you're saying that we're starting from scratch on this? All we really know is that there's a shooter who's popping people because he or she can?"

Barry dropped his feet to the floor and picked up Houston's coffee. "That summarizes it. From now on, it looks like this one belongs to you guys. I'll get the final forensics report to you as soon as we get something back from the labs." He stood up and waved. "See you around. I'm going to get some sleep." He pointed at the thick envelope. "There's your preliminary report." He walked away with Houston's coffee.

"Hey, that's *my* coffee!"

"And a mighty fine cup of coffee it is." Without looking back, Barry raised his left arm in farewell and disappeared around the corner.

Houston heard the exit door slam behind Newton and then returned to the break area and poured another cup of coffee. Back at his desk, he opened the file.

Barry had been busy. The report was twenty pages long—a lot of work to show they had squat. Houston believed that only two types of organizations on Earth could use twenty sheets of paper to say they have nothing—police departments and the military. He read the prelim crime scene reports, paying close attention to what little physical evidence the crime scene technicians had found, which mostly consisted of rubber samples from the van's tires.

He was still reading when Anne walked into the squad room two hours later. She flopped into the visitor's chair and picked up the pages he had stacked facedown on the desk. "You're in early."

"Couldn't sleep . . ."

"Me either."

"Save me some time." She held up Barry's report. "What we got?"

"To quote Barry: *squat*."

"Great. So where do we start?"

"The usual place, the eye witnesses."

"When did you get a witness list?"

"I didn't, but I'm sure Dysart will hand one out during the morning muster."

She stood, picked up his coffee and sipped on it as she carried the preliminary report to her desk.

"Hey, that's *my* coffee!"

She looked over her shoulder and grinned while holding the disposable cup in a mock toast. "And a mighty fine cup of coffee it is."

Houston and Anne were the last people to enter the muster room. Uniformed and plain-clothes cops filled the chairs, so they stood against the wall at the back of the room. Anne nudged him. "Think one of Boston's finest will be gentleman enough to give a lady his seat?"

Houston smiled and bent over so his head was close to her ear. "That would open them up to a sexual harassment suit."

"There are times when equality isn't all it's made out to be."

Capt. William Dysart stopped talking and looked at Anne and Houston. "Are you two finished playing footsie?"

Anne blushed when Houston said, "Sorry, Captain, she just can't resist my animal charm—you know how it is."

"No, I'm afraid I don't. But I'm sure you'll explain it to me one of these days." Everyone in the briefing room laughed.

When Dysart turned away, Houston settled against the wall and folded his arms.

"Okay, people," the captain ordered, "settle down. I don't have to tell you that someone has handed us a ball of fire. The mayor, the city council, and the press have been all over me since yesterday afternoon. I think the politicians hope some whacked out terrorist group will take credit for this. That way they can bring pressure on the top cop to turn this over to the Feds. If she knuckles under, so be it. Until that time, this is our case and we need it closed PDQ, understood?"

A murmur of agreement rolled through the room.

"I've assigned Houston and Bouchard lead on this one, but I expect everyone in this room to be in on it. The mayor has threatened to castrate somebody if we don't solve this before his upcoming reelection campaign, and that begins in a little over a month. The mayor was very clear on one point: if he goes down over this, he ain't going alone. Needless to say that made the brass as scared as a rat in a room full of pythons." Dysart held up the morning edition of the *Boston Daily Liberal*. The headlines were large and bold enough to read from the back of the room: SECOND BOSTON MASSACRE! SNIPER KILLS FOUR!

"I don't have to tell you that the sharks in the media smell fresh meat. Let's ensure that we don't become chum for them, okay?

"So, let's look at what we have here. An unknown perp, or perps, pulls up beside the Common and in less than two minutes we have four dead or dying. Forensics says the weapon was a .308 caliber, at least a cartridge of that caliber was the only one found at the scene. The van was a white Chevy, Ford, or Dodge, which is no help at all. If you aren't aware of it, in the US white is the most popular color for commercial vans. So to sum it up, I figure our suspect pool is roughly equivalent to the adult population of eastern Massachusetts. Solving this one should be a piece of cake." Dysart turned to the watch commander. "Hand out the witness lists and copies of the prelim forensics report and then they're all yours."

As he passed abreast of Houston and Anne, Dysart beckoned them to come with him. Once they were inside the captain's office, he closed the door and, while walking to his desk, said, "I'm going to get to the point. I want you two to drop everything else on your plate and run this case—for a couple of reasons. First, you're the most relentless detectives I got. No matter what, you two won't back off, not from the mayor, the brass, or the press. My second reason is you, Mike. Because of your military background you know how these goddamned shooters think . . . possibly better than anyone on the force. I want a quick close on this, but don't blow up half the city doing it. I'm counting on you to bring this shooter, or shooters, down. I'll never admit this outside this room, but if the phrase dead or alive ever applied to a situation, this is it. Am I clear?"

Houston started for the door. "We'll get him. Now can we get on the street and earn our keep?"

"Yeah, get out of here, but I want daily updates."

Houston knew the order was directed to Anne.

"Twice daily and three times a day on weekends and holidays," she said.

"I knew I could count on you. Now take this scurvy burnout and get to work."

———————————

Houston and Anne's first stop was the Marriott Long Wharf on the waterfront. Because he hated city traffic, Houston let Anne drive. She parked in front of the hotel and waved her badge under the valet parking attendant's nose.

"It better be here when I come out," she warned.

Houston suppressed a grin. He knew she got a charge out of flashing her credentials at parking attendants and beating the outrageous downtown-Boston parking fees.

According to information collected at the scene, one eyewitness—Peter Blackman—was registered there. What the report did not say was which room.

The front-desk clerk was reluctant to release any information and vacillated. Houston waved his identification. "Are you ready to face the consequences of obstructing a murder investigation?"

The clerk suddenly relented. "Mr. and Mrs. Blackman are in room 512."

Before Houston and Anne took the elevator to the fifth floor, he cautioned the clerk. "If you call them, I'll take you in . . . understood?"

"Y-y-yes, sir . . ."

During the elevator ride, Houston saw Anne grin.

"What?"

"You sure are a tough guy. I thought he was about to crap himself."

Houston was still chuckling when they reached the fifth floor and the door opened.

Anne knocked on the door. "Boston police." The door opened as far as the security chain allowed and a portly man with unruly hair peered through the gap between the door and the frame. Either they had awakened him or he had not been up very long.

In a parody of Houston's actions at the front desk, Anne flashed her credentials before the man's eyes. "Peter Blackman?"

The fat man nodded.

"Boston police. We'd like to talk to you about yesterday," Anne said.

"I already told the other officers everything I saw," he said.

Anne's cheeks flushed and her left eyebrow twitched. A sure sign his reluctance to open the door was not going well with her. Houston tried to suppress a smirk and failed. If Blackman didn't open the door soon he was going feel the full force of Anne's temper. However, she kept her cool. "Yes, sir, I'm sure you did. But after the initial interview, witnesses often remember small things that may help."

Houston wasn't sure whether it was her badge or the *don't give me any crap* tone in her voice that convinced Blackman to let them inside. As soon as he removed the chain and opened the door, Houston charged in. He strode across the room to the sliding glass door and pulled the drapes aside. The room had a superior view of the waterfront; across the plaza people crowded in front of the New England Aquarium as they waited for the doors to open. Houston wondered what a room with this view cost per night.

A voice from the bathroom broke his reverie. "Who's here, sweetheart?"

Blackman started like a surprised cat. Houston glanced at Anne.

"The police . . ."

"Ask her to come out," Anne said.

"She may not be decent."

Anne yanked the bedspread from the unmade bed. "Give her this."

Before Blackman could take the spread from Anne, the bathroom door opened and a beautiful blonde wearing a terry-cloth hotel robe stepped out of the bathroom. Her freshly washed hair was wrapped in a towel, and her face was rosy from the shower.

Houston thought that she looked nothing like someone who would call Blackman sweetheart. There was no way the young beauty was married to him. He gave Blackman a knowing look.

The woman stopped abruptly with a worried look.

"This is Carolyn."

Houston doubted that was her real name; most likely she was one of Boston's more expensive escorts. When a woman works her way up to the thousand-bucks-a-night range, she is an escort—no longer a hooker.

"Mike," Anne said, "why don't you take Mr. Blackman downstairs for coffee while Carolyn and I have a chat?"

Blackman took a rumpled Hawaiian shirt from the back of a chair and pulled it over his head, hiding his cherry-red face for a second.

After the men departed the room, Anne sat in the vacant chair. She said nothing, but maintained unyielding eye contact with the young woman. Finally, Anne spoke. "Want to get it out on the table?"

The blonde stared at her for a second. "Are you referring to the fact that Peter and I aren't Mr. and Mrs.?"

"Among other things."

The woman sat and searched through her purse and took out a pack of cigarettes. "Do you mind?" she asked Anne.

"Even if I didn't, in Massachusetts it's illegal to smoke in a hotel room. Nevertheless, if you can afford the $250 the hotel fines, go ahead and light up."

"Like I give a damn, Peter's paying for the room . . . and he's loaded." Carolyn's hands shook as she fumbled a cigarette from the package. "Besides, I have a feeling I'm in deeper shit than an illegal smoking beef." She took a cigarette from the pack and slid a book of matches out of the cellophane wrapper. She pulled one free and struck it. The match ignited with a loud hiss. Carolyn inhaled deep as the flame touched the cigarette.

"Let's get one thing straight right now, shall we? I'm here investigating a mass murder, I don't give a damn about any working relationship you may have with Peter Blackman."

Carolyn visibly relaxed. "How can I help you?"

"Tell me what you saw."

"Nothing. I was supposed to meet Peter at a bar. I arrived early and decided to have a drink. Then I saw half the cops in Boston racing toward the Common."

"You can prove that?"

"Prove it? Are you implying I had something to do with this?"

"No, I'm just covering all possible angles."

Carolyn sucked on her cigarette. "I think so. The bartender should remember me. A guy kept hitting on me and he intervened."

"Okay, we'll check it out. Where was the bar?"

"Statler's Lounge, in the Park Plaza on Arlington Street."

"I know it well . . ."

Houston led Blackman to the hotel's restaurant. They got a table next to the window and ordered coffees. When Houston took out his notebook and pen, Blackman started to whine. "I don't know why I got to go through this all over again."

"Look, Blackman, if you work with me there won't be any reason for us to have to go through the hassle of getting subpoenas and bringing you and your *wife* back to town."

When he heard the words *wife* and *subpoena* in the same sentence, all the blood drained from Blackman's face.

"She's a real looker, quite the knockout."

"Who is?"

"Mrs. Blackman. Who'd you think I was talking about?"

"Look, detective—"

"Houston."

Blackman bent forward, as if breaking a sacred trust or revealing an international secret. "Officer Houston, I got a bit of a situation here—Carolyn isn't my wife."

"*No!* You don't say?"

"If word got back to my wife—"

"You should have thought about that before you started screwing around with a high-priced hooker. If you tell us everything you remember about yesterday, we'll do our best to keep your love trysts out of our report."

Blackman knew he was screwed. He stared into his coffee mug and nodded. Houston always admired a man who could lose gracefully and, unless he missed his guess, Peter Blackman was experiencing the first of many losses. "Now, who's the hooker?"

"Her name's Carolyn McGuire. She's from an escort service. I make business trips to Boston two, sometimes three times a year, and we have an arrangement."

"If it's any consolation to you, you needn't worry about being busted on a prostitution or solicitation rap—either of you. My partner and I got bigger fish to reel in than some john and his expensive hooker. Are we straight on that?"

Blackman nodded again. "Does that mean my wife won't learn of this?"

"Not from me or my partner."

When Blackman sipped his coffee, his hands shook so much that he spilled half of it. "What do you want to know?"

"Let's start with when you were at the Common."

"I got there at a little past eleven yesterday morning." He paused for a heartbeat and then said, "I've always enjoyed walking on the Common.

I'd just finished my last business appointment for the day and I called Carolyn and arranged for us to meet.

"I was standing near the corner of Charles and Boylston Streets looking at some of the old headstones in the Central Burying Ground, when a white van drove by real slow. It stopped on the corner of Charles and Beacon, quite a ways from me. Seconds later, I heard three pops, one after another, then a brief pause and a final one. I thought a car had backfired until I heard people screaming and saw everyone running. The driver floored it and took off—he really mashed the accelerator too."

"When the van drove by, did you see the passengers?"

"Well, even though the windows were tinted, the passenger window was partially open and I got a quick look at one of them. He wore a Red Sox cap and was disfigured."

"Disfigured? In what way?"

"His face was covered with burn scars . . ."

Houston made a note.

Once again, Blackman looked bewildered. "Will I have to testify in court?"

"I don't know. That depends on a number of things."

"Like what?"

"Like if we catch this guy and a grand jury wants your testimony. On the other hand, if someone else can better identify the shooters, they probably won't bother bringing you back from—"

"Illinois. I live in the suburbs, west of Chicago."

"Illinois." Houston verified the address he had provided to the officer on the scene. It checked; Blackman had given a home address in Naperville, Illinois. "What about the hooker? Did she see anything?"

"I don't know. She wasn't with me at the time. As I said, I was going to meet her near the *Cheers* bar."

"*Cheers* bar? Are you talking about the Bull & Finch Pub?"

"Yes, that's the place. She saw all the cops and for obvious reasons didn't want to get in the middle of things. She called me on my cell phone."

Houston drank the last of his coffee. "Is this number your cell?" He read the phone listing from the crime scene report.

"Yes, you can reach me on it anytime."

Houston saw Anne walk into the restaurant and waved to her. "All right, Mr. Blackman, if there's anything else I'll be in touch. When are you leaving Boston?"

"I have an early flight to O'Hare the day after tomorrow."

Houston slid a business card across the table, stood up and shook hands with Blackman. "Well, I hope you enjoy the rest of your stay."

Houston started to leave, but stopped when Blackman said, "I'm sorry I can't help you more."

"Every little bit helps." Houston nodded and left him sitting there. As Houston walked away, he knew Blackman was more worried about the little woman in Naperville learning about his expensive friend than he was being a witness to a mass murder.

When they were back in the car, Anne asked, "Did you get anything?"

"Maybe. He reinforced the fact that we're looking for a white van and he said one of the people inside had burn scars on his face. What did you get from his friend?"

"Nothing. She was killing time in a bar before meeting him. When she saw all the cops and commotion, she decided to stay put. She called him on his cell."

"That's what he said. Either they're telling the truth or they got their story straight before we got here."

"I believe them," Anne said. "First of all, none of the officers on scene mentioned her in any report. Second, I thought he was going to cry when he realized he'd been caught with his pants down."

"Yeah, for some reason I don't think he's heard the last of this."

"Where to next?"

"Copley Square. There are two witnesses staying at the Plaza."

The Marriott desk clerk hesitated when the badly scarred man approached the front desk. He made an ineffective attempt to keep from staring at his hideous burns. The scarred man opened his wallet and flashed his identification card at her. He closed the small wallet before he was able to read anything other than *FBI* in large letters.

"The two police officers that just left," he asked, "who did they talk to?"

The clerk hesitated. The last thing he wanted to do was to hinder a police investigation, let alone an FBI agent asking for information. "Mr. Blackman." He pointed toward the coffee shop. "That's him over there, the heavy-set man wearing the wrinkled Hawaiian shirt."

The FBI agent turned and looked at Blackman, seeming to commit him to memory. "Thank you."

The clerk stood dumbfounded when he left without speaking to Mr. Blackman. He noted that the agent limped as he departed through the revolving door. The clerk would never have thought that anyone so badly disfigured could get into the FBI. He shrugged his shoulders and turned back to his work.

6

"Certainly there is no hunting like the hunting of man and those
who have hunted armed men long enough and liked it, never really care
for anything else thereafter."
—Ernest Hemingway

"Nobody is saying anything, Tony," O'Leary said into the phone. "I just want to know if you've heard of anyone looking for or buying a .308 rifle and ammo under the table." He ignored the irate tone of the loud voice on the other end and slowly rotated his cigarette back and forth between his thumb and index finger as he listened.

Finally, he had listened to enough of Tony Petrano's caustic remarks. O'Leary cut him off. "All right, enough of the bullshit. If the cops are looking at my organization for this, then you better fuckin' believe they're lookin' at you guys too. You hear anything, the next goddamned person you talk to is me. You got that? Because if I find out you're holding back, there'll be hell to pay." He slammed the phone into its cradle and felt it flex in his hand. He turned it over and saw a crack running across the keypad. He held the broken phone up so it was visible to Gordon Winter. "Remember when we were kids and shit didn't break every friggin' time you looked at it cross-eyed?"

"Sounds like you're getting the runaround?"

O'Leary ignored the way Winter had discounted his comment about the fragility of modern appliances.

For several seconds, O'Leary stared at the broken phone. Then he yanked the cord from the wall and tossed it in his wastebasket. He turned his attention back to Winter. "This one has me by the balls. No one has heard anything about this whack-job. It ain't natural that some asshole is shooting the city up and nobody has a clue about who it is."

Winter contemplated his response for a brief moment. "Are the cops really tryin' to lay this bullshit at our feet?"

"I don't know about the rest of the cops, but I don't think Houston believes we had anything to do with it. He knows me better than that. He should know that I ain't never hit no one that didn't give me reason to. Shit, there's any number of buttheads walkin' around that I probably should have whacked years ago."

"Want me to check around?"

"Yeah, but before you do that, I got something else for you."

"Name it."

"You recall the woman that came in here yesterday afternoon?"

"Are you referring to the black broad?"

"Yeah, seems some local gangbangers raped and killed her thirteen-year-old daughter."

Gordon's face turned hard. "This city is fuckin' out of control. The kid was only thirteen?"

"Yeah, she was still a goddamned baby."

"You get a name . . . someplace for me to start?"

"A local shithead who uses the street name Razor may be involved. The name his mother gave him is Jermaine, Jermaine Watts." O'Leary held out a scrap of paper. "He hangs out in the 'Bury, around Martin Luther King Boulevard, near Malcolm X Park. Here's an address for his grandmother—she's raising him. I suppose 'supporting him' is more accurate."

Winter stood, took the slip of paper and, after memorizing what was written on it, tossed it into the wastebasket with the now useless telephone. "Consider it done. How you want it handled?"

"Bring him to the usual place and then call me. I'll talk to him there."

The smile on Winter's face was the one that made women grab their kids and scurry across the street. When Jimmy saw it, he knew the job was, for all intents and purposes, done.

"You got a picture of this asshole?"

"No, but he shouldn't be hard to find. Marian said he has spider webs tattooed around his eyes, like the damn Lone Ranger's mask."

"Once I get Watts, what we going to do about this sniper thing?" he asked.

"Since nobody wants to talk, we'll just have to go bust a few asses. Get me anything you can."

Winter leaned against the fender of his Lincoln Navigator, sipping coffee from a takeout cup. To a casual observer, he appeared relaxed; however, his eyes were in constant motion, studying everything on the street and missing nothing. If O'Leary's information was accurate, Jermaine Watts hung out in this neighborhood and it was only a matter of time before he would be roaming around. Winter believed that, as a rule, gang-bangers were as territorial as a pack of dogs and spent most of their time patrolling their turf to protect it from other gangs. Winter also knew that it was unlikely that a white man was going to learn much asking questions in the hood, so he did what he had learned to do as an army ranger; he observed and he listened.

Ten minutes passed before his quarry appeared. Jermaine Watts was still a quarter of a block away when Winter identified him by his tats. The kid bopped along, carrying an MP3 player with an earphone stuck in his right ear. Probably playing an incomprehensible rap song, Winter thought. He acted as if he were king of the streets. His baggy black jeans hung down exposing the top half of a greasy-looking, shiny pair of floral-print designer boxers. He wore a black Celtics cap, coated with enough hair gel to make it glisten in the sun. The cap's brim pointed three-quarters of the way toward the back of his head. Winter knew the angle designated the gang to which Razor belonged. There was nothing Winter hated more than people who wore hats backward—he believed that only catchers were supposed to do that and this punk was no ballplayer.

"Could you spare some change?"

Winter turned toward the voice. A grubby tramp stood beside him holding his soiled hand out. Winter made no effort to hide his loathing and said, "Change? What you need is to take a fuckin' bath in sheep dip and scour your cruddy carcass with a wire brush. Now get out of my goddamned face before I do something about it."

The tramp's eyes widened with fear and he scurried away.

Winter downed the last of his coffee, crumpled the cup and tossed it into a nearby trash can. He returned his attention to Jermaine, who was still shuffling and dancing his way toward him. As the gangbanger closed with him, his spider-web tats became more defined. The idiot had no idea that his life was about to turn to shit. Winter thought about what lay in Jermaine's near future and smiled. "Ignorance is bliss . . ."

7

"To the enemy, who knows the real capabilities of a sniper, he is a very feared ghostly phantom who is never seen, and never heard until his well-aimed round cracks through their formation or explodes the head of their platoon commander or radio man."
—*US Marine Corps Scout/Sniper Training Manual*

After leaving the Plaza, Anne and Houston stopped for lunch. There was a time when lunch had meant a couple of beers to Houston. But he had learned the hard way to be careful around booze. He looked across the table at Anne, toasted her with a frosty glass of lemonade and said, "I'm bushed. I must be getting old."

Anne leaned forward and looked into his eyes. "Mike, when was your last physical?"

"What has that got to do with anything? Don't start in on me, okay?"

"It's not even one o'clock and you look like something the cat dragged in and the dog was afraid to drag back out."

"Christ, Anne, I'm just tired, that's all. I didn't sleep worth a damn last night."

She sat back, her delicate hands slowly turned her glass and she softened. "Fatigue is our greatest enemy—you know that. It causes us to fail to see what we should and to see what we shouldn't and also increases our reaction time."

"I've operated under those conditions most of my life . . . I'll make it."

"I understand all that," Anne said. "It's just that you're my best friend and I worry about you."

"We *have* come a long way together, haven't we?"

She smiled. "Mike, you've come a lot further than I have."

"Maybe so, but without you I don't think I'd have survived the trip. How long have we been partners now?"

"Over five years."

"I was a mess back then," Houston said.

"Well, you had just gotten over a very traumatic divorce."

"There's something that I have to confess to you."

"Oh?"

"If I didn't agree to taking a partner—namely you—Dysart was about to shit-can me for being half-drunk all the time."

"I don't think they'd throw you off the force that easily. After all, you did have the highest rate of cleared cases."

"Oh, he wasn't going to throw me out . . . just make me a parking meter attendant."

Anne smiled.

"What?"

"I just got a mental picture of Mike Houston, meter maid."

He too smiled. "Yeah, with my legs, I'd look like hell in a skirt."

The sniper stood back in the shadows of the door and studied Houston and the woman. They were at ease, sitting like a couple of love-struck teenagers. He glanced at his watch and wondered if he had overestimated Houston. How could he be so stupid as to sit at a table next to a window where they were perfect targets? But there was time for Houston later; first he had another mission to complete. He saluted. "Be seein' yah, Mike."

Houston and Anne stood on the sidewalk, basking in the midday sun. Houston stretched. "Every time I eat lunch I get like a bear and want to hibernate."

Anne smiled at him. "So where do we go now?"

"We need to check out the victims' families."

"I'm not looking forward to that," Anne said, her eyes locked forward as she drove.

"Me neither. Still, it has to be done."

"Who should we see first?" Anne asked.

"Stephanie Leopold's family."

"Okay, but why is she first? She lives in Reading, the furthest away of all the vics."

"No particular reason. I thought I'd relax and take a ride while I let my lunch settle."

"Okay, you're the lead detective."

Anne drove onto I-93 and headed north to the junction of I-95/Route 128. Since they were heading out of the city and it was a couple of hours before afternoon rush hour, traffic was light and in no time, they turned off the expressway and onto Route 28. Mike had been silent for most of the drive. But when Anne stopped at a red light, he said, "One of DeSalvo's vics lived here."

"Albert DeSalvo, the Boston Strangler?"

"That's what's generally believed. Lately there've been questions raised. I know several people who think he wasn't capable of that level of violence or smart enough to elude capture as long as he did."

"But he confessed," Anne said. Her demeanor and tone said that was all the evidence of his guilt she needed.

"Wouldn't be the first time some mentally defective fool, looking for attention, fessed up to something he didn't do."

"But as soon as he was caught, the killings stopped."

Houston shrugged. "Makes you think, doesn't it? A perp smart enough to elude capture for two years is certainly smart enough either to stop or change his or her MO once the cops thought they had their perp. It's kind of like this case."

"How is it like this case?"

"Both are high profile and generate a lot of political heat."

Anne stared through the windshield, studying the slow-moving traffic ahead. "You know what scares me the most?"

"That I'm right?"

"That too, but what scares me most is that there are times when I think they were wrong when they told me you weren't the sharpest crayon in the box."

Charles Leopold was an impressive man. He stood a couple of inches over six feet and his biceps rippled under the sleeves of the form-fitting golf shirt he wore. When Houston and Anne identified themselves, he stepped back and allowed them entrance to the living room. It was immediately evident that a woman had decorated the house. The room was tasteful and everything seemed to be carefully placed so each item complemented the others.

"Your home is nice," Anne commented.

"Thank you, but I can't take the credit. My wife . . ." His eyes became shiny with tears. ". . . Stephanie did the décor. She had a talent for interior decorating. I don't know why she didn't pursue it as a career . . ." He took a deep breath and motioned toward a couple of easy chairs. "Please, sit down. Can I offer you something to drink?"

"I'm fine," Houston answered.

Leopold turned his head slightly and looked at Anne.

"I'm fine too."

Houston and Anne glanced at each other, looking for a cue as to who should start the questioning. Knowing Anne's skill with people, especially bereaved people, he gave a slight nod to her.

"Mr. Leopold, I'd like express the Boston Police Department's deepest sympathy for your loss."

"Thank you." Leopold's lips formed a straight line and his eyes narrowed. "All I want the Boston Police Department to do is catch the son of a bitch who murdered my wife . . ."

"That's why we're here. Can you think of any reason why someone might want to target Stephanie?"

"Not one. Hell, she was a grammar school teacher, third grade. All the students loved her. She was *that* type of teacher . . . you know the one that all the kids cluster around during recess."

"Why was your wife in Boston that day?" Houston asked.

"She loved going into the city. On warm summer days, she liked nothing better than to walk on the Common. School starts in a couple of weeks and she thought that this might be her last chance to do it." The irony of the statement hit him and he swallowed hard, choking back a sob.

Houston and Anne said nothing. The last thing the grieving husband wanted to hear was platitudes.

"When can I have her body?" Leopold's eyes started tearing again, leaving streaks on his cheeks. "I have . . . arrangements to make."

"Unfortunately," Houston answered, "we don't know. The medical examiner has control of the . . . your wife. But, I'm sure they won't keep her long." He wondered how Leopold would react if he knew of the indignities his wife's body had probably received on the medical examiner's table. There is no nice way to perform an autopsy. He recalled the image of her lying in the flowers with her skirt hiked up, exposing her thighs and underwear. He was thankful he had intervened and hoped that if any photographers had gotten a picture of her in that state that they would refrain from ever releasing or publishing it.

The silence became oppressive. When Anne's cell phone vibrated, Houston was grateful for the interruption. He remained stoic as she answered the phone and listened for several seconds. He knew something had happened when she suddenly stood and said, "I'm sorry we had to disturb you, Mr. Leopold." They shook the grieving man's hand in turn and left him standing in the middle of his immaculate living room, looking like an overgrown child.

Once they were in their car, Houston said, "That was a pretty abrupt end in there."

"That was Dysart. He wants to see us."

8

"The sniper is able to select his targets with care so that it will do the greatest possible damage to their morale and fighting ability."
—*US Marine Corps Scout/Sniper Training Manual*

The van sat far enough from the house for him to observe without being observed. He had been careful and moved the truck every hour, driving around the block and parking in a different location. He hoped the white van and his nondescript work clothes would make him appear as an appliance repairman. The last thing he wanted was for some nosey neighbor to call the cops and report a suspicious vehicle parked in front of their house for a long time.

During the third hour of his vigil, she appeared. He had checked and double-checked the address because of all the targets, this was the most important. The woman was petite, with flaming red hair that told of her Irish heritage. She had a terrific figure for her age, which by now must be her early to mid-forties. She threw some stuff into the back seat, got in her car and drove away. He followed her north on Waltham Street. When they turned onto Route 2 to Boston, he sighed in relief. It was a major thoroughfare and there was always a great deal of traffic. He relaxed, ceased worrying that she would realize he was following and let the traffic serve as camouflage.

He kept the distance between him and her car constant and wondered if he should have brought his driver. It was risky doing both the shooting and the driving. Besides, it wouldn't have hurt to have someone familiar with Boston traffic patterns. He blew through his lips. It was too late to worry about that. He would just have to make the best of the situation.

The woman left Route 2 at the Alewife Rotary and turned onto Fresh Pond Parkway, toward Memorial Drive, and crossed the Charles River toward Kenmore Square at the Harvard Bridge. Traffic began to slow due to the proximity of Fenway Park and he felt frustration and impatience creeping in. When she pulled into a gas station on Commonwealth Avenue, he exhaled in relief. She stopped alongside the pump closest to the street and got out. At least that worked in his favor. He spied an open area across the street and couldn't believe how lucky he was. Rather than making an illegal U-turn, which would attract attention, he drove past. He turned at the next corner, sped up as much as he dared and then returned to Commonwealth Avenue. He hoped she was still at the station and that no one had taken the open parking spot across the street while he had circled the block.

His luck held—the slot was still vacant. He looked toward the gas station. She stood beside her car, pumping gas and ignoring her surroundings. She didn't even glance up when he slid into the open space.

Commuters stood on the sidewalk, chatting loudly over the din of the city while waiting for their bus. One of the commuters tapped on the passenger door glass and shouted, "Hey, you dumb or something? This is a freakin' bus stop, for crying out loud." He knew the nosy interloper couldn't see into the van and was thankful for the tinted windows. Still he knew he had little time, a bus could come along at any moment. He lowered the street-side window. The heavy flow of traffic passing between him and the target meant that his timing had to be precise. The shot had to be taken at the exact instant or he might hit a passing car, allowing his target to escape.

His rifle sat on the floor on the passenger side, propped against the seat with the muzzle up. He snatched it up and leaned back so the rifle's short barrel remained within the confines of the vehicle. He quickly pulled the stock tight into his shoulder. He held the weapon firm and waited for his eye to acclimate itself to the scope's magnification. It almost exaggerated everything too much. A gigantic gas pump moved across the crosshairs and then the hood of her car appeared. He stopped sweeping and shifted his aim slightly, centered on the passenger window of her car. He smiled when he saw that, rather than use her air conditioning, she had rolled down all of the car's windows. The scope made her breasts seem huge, as if they were too large for the constraints imposed on them by the thin summer-weight T-shirt. Nice rack, he thought, too bad . . .

He waited until two cars, one in each direction, passed through the scope, blurring his sight picture. A horn blasted and he glanced at the outside mirror; a bus was pulling into the stop and the driver laid on the horn again. The bus driver honked a third time, holding it longer, and he ignored it, focusing on the reticules of the scope. The target was clear and centered in the crosshairs; he pulled the trigger. The blasting horn muted the rifle's bark to all but the passengers waiting at the stop. He heard the interloper shout, "What the hell was that? It sounded like gunfire!"

Someone else said, "Gunfire? This ain't the 'Bury . . . it's Comm Ave. It was probably a backfire."

The sniper glanced in the passenger-side mirror and saw a burnout with a ring in her nose pointing at his van. "I think it came from that van," she said.

The sniper knew it was time to exit the area. The shot had been taken and now it was time to haul ass. He took a last look at the gas station, but did not see the target. However, he was not concerned and was certain that even if he hadn't killed the target, his shot had scored. Throwing the rifle into the passenger seat, he pressed his foot down on the accelerator, suppressing his impulse to stomp hard on the gas pedal, making the tires scream, and attracting everyone's attention. He pulled out of the bus stop and drove away, gradually increasing speed as he left the bus behind. He sped toward Brookline and glanced in the rearview mirror, where he saw the burnout standing beside the curb, gesturing to him. The sniper put his left arm out the window and raised it to the sky with the middle finger extended. He laughed. "Now, Mikey, maybe you'll get the message."

Houston and Anne left I-93 at the former Boston Garden—now the TD Garden—and headed toward Storrow Drive. Traffic was horrible.

"Should I hit the lights and siren?" Anne asked.

"No. I'm kinda enjoyin' the ride. This case is getting to me."

"How many times has Dysart called you today?" she asked.

"More than he's called me in the last five years."

"What have you told him?"

"What is there to say? We got crap so far."

"Have you told him you talked to Jimmy O?"

"Hell, no. He'd go ballistic if he knew I was using Jimmy as a source."

Anne's cell phone rang. Since she was driving, Anne handed the phone to him. The caller ID listed the main number for BPD. He hit the speaker button. "Houston."

Dysart's voice said, "Mike? Why do you have Anne's phone?"

"She's driving."

"Where are you guys?"

"Storrow Drive, just past the Museum of Science."

"Good, you're close. Get your asses over to Kendall Square . . . the son of a bitch might have hit again . . ."

At times Houston believed Anne had been a cab driver in a previous life, because she handled city traffic better than anyone he knew. In spite of the late afternoon rush, she got to Commonwealth Avenue in less than ten minutes; a NASCAR driver couldn't have completed a practice lap easier. Nevertheless, by the time they arrived at the scene of the sniper's most recent kill, the crime scene unit was already on-site and several uniforms had the entrance to the self-service gas station blocked off.

Unable to get off the street without disturbing the scene, they double-parked beside one of the patrol cars. Anne and Houston hooked their badges to their belts as they approached the crime scene and stepped inside. The crime scene techs had finished most of their work and stood in a huddle about twenty feet away from a compact car that stood beside the outermost gas pumps. They were able to see that the victim was lying between the gas pumps and the Toyota Camry. Houston stared at the car—it was familiar. A woman's handbag lay on the ground nearby and for some reason he was reluctant to approach the body. His heart pounded so hard that it hammered in his chest and his throat constricted, making it difficult to breathe. He overcame his inertia and walked to the black sedan. Houston squatted beside the body and immediately bolted to his feet, cursed and spun around until he faced the busy street.

He tried to hide his reactions from Anne, but was unsuccessful. She asked, "What's going on, Mike? Do you know this woman?"

"Her name is Pamela."

"That's it? Pamela? Pamela *what?*"

"If she hasn't changed back to her maiden name, her name is Pamela Houston."

9

"I was taught to get in, get close, kill quickly, and get out, without ever being seen."
—Gunnery Sergeant Jack Coughlin, USMC

Anne's mouth was open with shock when she stood and said, "My God, Mike, are you telling me that she's—"

"My ex-wife."

Houston was so inwardly directed that he missed the fact that Anne was too surprised to know what to say. His face flushed with the heat of a blistering rage. Suddenly, his face cooled and he became worried. "Christ, how can I tell Susie?"

He couldn't remember another time in his life when he had no idea of what he should do. How could he tell his only child that her mother was dead? There was only one thing he believed would be worse—burying one's child.

"We haven't talked in a couple of years," Houston said. He faced Commonwealth Avenue and stared at something only he could see.

Anne ventured a response. "Well, you are divorced."

Houston turned his head toward her, as if he had forgotten her presence. "Not Pam—Susie." Houston turned back and seemed mesmerized by the crowd standing on the sidewalk across the street. "Now I have to find her and tell her this?" Houston's face had lost its color and when he clenched his fists, he reminded her of a World War II poster her grandfather had framed over his mantle. It depicted an angry man pulling off his jacket, with fists clenched for a fight. The caption read: TELL THAT TO THE MARINES!

Anne stepped to his side and placed a hand on his arm. "I'll help you. We'll talk to her together." She stepped in front of him, and he saw she was concerned for him. "Are you up to this, Mike? Maybe you should wait in the car."

Houston held up his hand to prompt her to stop fretting. "I can do my job, Anne."

"I didn't say you couldn't. I know you, Mike. You hide your feelings better than anyone I've ever known and that's fine in a poker game, but this is something else entirely. You've just looked at the body of someone who is important to you."

"Pam stopped being important years ago."

Houston heard Anne blow through her lips, a sound similar to a whale blowing water, and knew she was not buying his line.

"Who are you trying to convince—you or me?" she snapped. Anger elevated the volume of her words.

Houston inhaled sharply. His chest puffed out like a bird's feathers on a freezing day. "Either way, no matter who the vic is, we got a job to do." He walked back to the body.

Houston felt resistance as he squatted beside Pam's body and realized it was not physical but emotional resistance. Their life together flashed through his mind like a slide presentation. He remembered their wedding. Neither family could afford a big ceremony, so they decided on a private service—Pam, two witnesses and him.

The priest asked, "Pamela, do you take Michael as your lawfully wedded husband?"

Pam lost her place in the prayer book and frantically flipped pages, trying to find the correct one.

The priest smiled and gently said, "Pamela?"

She looked at him. "Yes?"

"Do you take Michael for your husband?"

She looked at him and then at Mike. She turned back to the preacher and rolled her eyes in a manner that showed how absurd she found the question. "Of course, that's why we're here, isn't it?"

As he inspected her body, Houston's hands brushed against Pam's cheeks. It was the first time he had touched her familiar body since their separation and divorce. Since the breakup, he had harbored the hope that someday they might mend things and get back together. He felt a profound sadness, caused by the sudden realization that now there was no way they could ever do so. His hands shook and he clenched them into fists to control it. He felt a light touch on his shoulder.

Without looking, he knew it was Anne. He also knew that she felt the tremors that racked him and hoped she believed they were a result of the situation and not the return of the damned shakes that he had been hiding from everyone the past year. Truthfully, he too was unsure whether the trembling was the result of whatever was going on within him or if Pam's murder rattled him more than he was willing to admit.

"Mike, let me do this."

He rocked back, folded his arms and hid his unsteady hands in his underarms. He looked skyward and rested on his heels. "She was a good woman, Anne—a far better wife to me than I was a husband to her. She deserved someone who could place her first . . ."

Anne gently guided him to his feet. "You sell yourself too cheap. It takes two to make a relationship and two to destroy it."

Houston allowed her to guide him away from the body. He walked a couple of steps to the side and stood there, feeling like a pressure cooker about to explode while Anne returned to the body. She squatted and brushed Pam's long red hair to one side, exposing her torso. Even though he stood several feet from her body, Houston saw the bloody smear on her left breast. Experience with wounds of this nature told him that based on the location of the bloodstain; the bullet had probably punctured her heart. Nevertheless, it would be up to the medical examiner to determine the exact cause of death. Of one thing, he was certain; if Pam had not died instantaneously, she was most likely dead shortly after she hit the pavement. The knowledge gave him no solace.

The air around Pam's body reeked of gasoline. Houston looked at the concrete beside the body bag and saw several places where gas had pooled. When Anne finished inspecting the body and stood up she motioned for the CSU people to bag the body. Unable to think of another way to assuage his anger and regain his objectivity, he stated the obvious. "It looks as if he hit her while she was gassing up."

Anne turned to the car and bent over, staring through the driver side window. "Was she going to school?"

"Not that I know of, why?"

"Look in the back seat." She stepped aside to allow him enough space.

Houston leaned in through the passenger-side window. He knew that touching the car was contaminating the crime scene, but he didn't care. He placed his hands on the windowsill and scanned the car's interior. Books and papers were scattered over the rear seat of the car and a Boston University T-shirt lay on the seat. Houston stepped back, stumbling as he did.

"What is it?" Anne asked.

As suddenly as the shaking had started, it stopped. Houston quickly recovered his composure. He avoided looking at the body bag when he spoke. "BU has buildings all along Comm Ave. and we're only a short distance from Kenmore Square. Even though it's August and the on-campus population is at its lowest, students take summer courses."

"Mike, what are you getting at?"

Houston wiped at the perspiration that soaked his brow. "Pam hated driving in Boston—the traffic drove her nuts. There's only one thing I can think of that would be important enough for her to drive here."

Anne suddenly made the connection. "Your daughter attends school in the city."

"Yeah, she's a freshman at BU."

Houston was unable to shake the feeling that the sniper was taunting him and would want to see his reaction to this personal attack. He stared at the crowded sidewalk across the street. Rage drilled a hole through his guts as he searched the faces of the gawkers, commuters, and baseball fans gathered there. He tried to concentrate on each face, hoping some supernatural power would suddenly take control and reveal the shooter to him.

He scrutinized the assembled throng, suspicious of every one of them. Until he had a specific suspect in mind, everyone he encountered would be considered a potential killer and he would trust few people, if any. Which one of the gathered crowd was his shooter? Which of them was thumbing a nose at him?

He didn't see Anne walk around the car and was surprised when she stood beside him. She too stared across the street at the spectators. "Are you going to be able to maintain your objectivity?"

"Yeah, I'll be okay."

Anne said, "This shooter is either a lot smarter or a lot luckier than the average criminal. He couldn't have chosen a better time of day."

"I was thinking the same thing. This crowd is gathering for the game between the Sox and the Yankees. If he'd waited an hour later, the streets from here to Fenway Park and Kenmore Square would be impassable." Houston turned to Anne. "I want this guy."

"I know you do. We all do."

"No, you don't understand. I *want* this guy. I'm not going to mess with Miranda rights, courts or due process, just him and me and Old Testament eye-for-an-eye justice. I want him in my sights."

He knew that she shared his anger—this case had taken on an entirely new dynamic. It had become personal.

They saw Barry Newton standing on the sidewalk across Comm Avenue, away from his crime scene team. He was talking with a couple of uniforms. Anne started walking to him and after a second, Houston followed.

"Anything?" she asked.

Newton looked at them and said, "Nothing . . . another crime scene devoid of any physical evidence. Which doesn't surprise me. The perp never set foot outside his vehicle. According to what witnesses told the first officers on-scene, a single shot was fired from a white van . . . at the bus stop. It was one hell of a shot . . . we haven't measured the distance yet, but I'd estimate it is over two hundred yards, through traffic."

"One shot, one kill," Houston said.

"What was that?" Barry asked.

"Nothing, Barry, I'm rambling. Let me know if you get anything else."

Barry looked into Houston's face. "You okay? You got the same look that was on my father's face when someone poisoned his dog."

"I know the vic. Her name is Pamela Houston. Or she may be using her maiden name. It's hard to tell what Pam would use."

Barry immediately made the connection. "Aw, hell, Mike, I had no idea—"

"No reason you would. We've been divorced for more than six years."

Houston walked a few steps away and then paused, pointing to one of the uniforms. The officer puffed on a cigarette and smoke encircled his head. "Barry, you happen to notice that there's a lot of gas on the ground?"

Barry looked up and saw the young cop and shouted, "Hey douse that damned thing! You want to blow us all to hell?"

Then he turned back to Houston. "Mike, as soon as I have something, you'll know."

Houston turned toward the unmarked police car and heard Barry say, "Jesus, I really screwed that up."

"How could you have known?" Anne replied. "I've been his partner for five years and I wasn't aware who she was until he told me a few minutes ago."

"Yeah, but knowing me and how I handle things, I'd have still messed it up somehow—I never know what to say at weddings and funerals."

"Don't worry. You handled it the best you could."

"I hope Mike understands."

"He does. Right now though, I'm concerned that he seems unable to understand how he feels."

"That's always the problem with male cops, isn't it?"

"What is?"

"Men, especially male cops, can usually deal with anything but feelings. I guess we don't want to be perceived as being soft . . ." He walked to the CSU van.

When Newton departed, Anne took her cell phone and hit a speed dial. "Captain? Bouchard. We're at the crime scene . . . there's been a complication."

Houston reached the car and realized that Anne was not with him. He turned and motioned for her to join him. She trotted across the parking lot.

"I need to locate Susie and tell her about her mother," he said, his voice lacking emotion.

"I know. I already called Dysart. They're calling BU."

"Thanks." Houston stared over the roof of the car as two EMTs picked up Pam's body, now encased in a black body bag, and placed it on a gurney. Mentally, he left the present for a place where he and his pain were the sole occupants. After several moments, he rubbed the back of his neck, trying to ease the tension. Realizing that it was all for naught, he got in the car. Anne settled in behind the steering wheel.

"Shit," Houston said, "this is going to be hard. There were some very bad feelings after the divorce and Susie blamed me for causing most of them."

"Well, no kid wants to see her parents get divorced."

Houston snapped his head around almost as if someone had doused him with cold water while he was asleep. "I know all that, but right now I wish I'd spent more time mending fences and less time burying myself in booze and this stinking job."

"It'll work out, Mike. It's been six years and she's older now."

Houston shrugged. "Either way, there isn't anything I can do about it now." He paused and then changed the subject. "If I wasn't sure before, now I'm beginning to believe that our shooter is military trained."

"Oh, what leads you down that road?"

"In Vietnam, in the late sixties, the Marines wanted to put some fear into the Viet Cong so they set up a sniper school. A marine named Carlos Hathcock helped found it. He had ninety-three confirmed kills in Vietnam. The instructors always emphasized that if a sniper was to survive they had to live by one basic rule—one shot, one kill. They pounded that into every student: get in, make your kill, and get out before the enemy learns what hit them. As far as we know, our shooter has followed the book and hasn't fired a second shot at any of the victims, if the sniper doesn't get it done with a single shot, the target gets to live."

"Do you think this Hathcock is our man? Lord, he'd be in his late sixties or early seventies now, not exactly a fit for the profile."

"No, it isn't Hathcock—he's dead."

"So where does this lead us?"

"At this point, I don't know. But it wouldn't surprise me to learn that this shooter has a military background."

"Do you think we'll get this guy?"

"Either I or someone will. Random killings are a bitch—there's no motive directly tying the shooter to the victim, only the killer knows what his or her reasoning is. Hell, look how long Bundy got away with it before he screwed up and they caught him. Our guy will screw up too. Eventually, he'll step on his own dick—they always do. When he does, I want to be there to shoot it off."

"Mike, this is *not* a random kill. Whoever this shooter is seems to have an agenda and I think I know what that agenda is."

"I do too. The voice calling me at the Common, the note on the car and now this, all tells me that I'm this asshole's agenda."

The radio came to life. There was a double shooting at Christopher Columbus Park. Anne said, "That's a couple of blocks from the Marriott."

"This shooter shows up every place we go. This guy is stalking us."

Anne turned on the emergency lights and sped toward the waterfront.

Anne parked the car in front of the small park that bordered one side of the Old Custom House, but she and Houston knew what they were going to find before they got to the bodies. Houston paused for a second and looked at the yachts moored in the Boston Yacht Haven before turning to study the crowd that had gathered along the sidewalk. He knew he was grasping at straws, but maybe he would recognize a face from one of the other shooting scenes. Once again, Houston studied each person in the crowd, looking for anything that might give the shooter away. He realized it was an exercise in futility, shrugged and accepted the fact that this shooter was a pro and was long gone by now. Houston walked toward the cordoned-off scene of the latest shooting.

An ashen-faced uniformed officer met them. Houston was still reeling from the afternoon's events, but he hid his exhaustion and anger behind a façade of professionalism. "What you got?"

"Two dead. Looks as if the shots came from across Atlantic Avenue."

"Any ID on the vics?"

The officer opened his notebook. "Guy's name is Blackman, Peter. The woman has a sheet—a hooker named Carolyn McGuire."

Houston stared across Atlantic Avenue. "You said the shots came from over there." He pointed.

"We haven't had a chance to get anyone up there yet, but I would guess they were fired from the top of the parking garage."

As he had done on the Common, Houston estimated the distance . . . it was at least five hundred yards.

The sniper stood at the edge of the top deck of the public parking garage, studying the scene across Atlantic Avenue through his range finder. He moved the instrument until the aiming box was centered on Houston and noted the distance—530 yards. *I could do you right now, Mikey.* He dropped the optical device into his pocket and kept his eyes on Houston.

Suddenly Houston seemed to look directly at him. When the detective began running toward his location, he waved and then made a hasty retreat from the building.

―――――――――

Houston began scanning the area around the park. When he looked at the top floor of the parking garage he spied a man who seemed to be observing them through some form of field glass. He froze, expecting to see the figure raise a rifle at any second. Fully aware of the futility of his action, he ran across the street hoping to get a better view of the perp.

He heard footsteps behind him and assumed it was Anne. His suspicions were confirmed when she called, "Mike, what are you doing?"

Houston raced inside the municipal parking garage and suddenly stopped. Anne halted beside him, panting for breath. "What . . . is . . . going . . . on?" she asked between gasps.

"You didn't see the bastard?"

"Who?"

"I think the shooter was on the top level." As he spoke Houston studied the building. In the center of each floor was the elevator, but when he saw the stairwells in each corner of the building, he realized the futility of his effort. The shooter could have taken any of them to make his escape. The loud bang of a door slamming in the northeast corner sent him racing. He opened the exit door to find an empty space with another door, this one leading outside. Stuck between the door and the jamb was another piece of paper.

He heard Anne say, "Mike, for crying out loud, it could have been someone getting their car—"

Houston snatched the paper from the door and handed it to her. "Still think so?"

Anne read the note and her complexion blanched.

"What's it say?" Houston asked.

She read: "*This is three times now . . . I can take you whenever I want.*"

Houston tightened his hands into fists and cursed. "The son of a bitch is playing with us . . ."

10

"The important thing is what happens when you are hard pressed.
The First Principle means you keep that clearly in mind, pay close attention
and make sure you do not get caught in a pinch, unprepared."
—Yagyū Munenori, *The Book of Family Traditions on the Art of War*

Houston and Anne stood in front of the entrance to the dormitory, waiting for the arrival of a campus police officer. Houston's patience was at its limit and his temper was showing. "Where the hell is this guy?"

"Mike, will you calm down?" Anne asked.

"What do you mean by that?" Houston stared through the glass in the heavy door. He fought against the desire to leave and let someone else take care of this onerous task.

"If you go busting in here like you're on a drug raid, all you'll do is make the rift between you and your daughter wider. She's going to have enough to deal with as it is. All your shitty attitude will do is make it harder."

Houston turned away from the building and looked both ways along the street. He glanced at his watch. "I don't think I've ever been this nervous before—not even on my first mission in Somalia, and that was in 1993, twenty years ago."

He turned back toward her, and she saw that, even though he tried to hide it, he was worried. She knew he fought with his emotions and that this was a battle he was not prepared for. She reached out and gripped his hand. "Mike, it's your daughter in there, not some armed nutcase hyped on drugs."

"That's the problem. I know how to deal with nutcases."

"Do you want me to do this for you?"

"No. I don't need you holding my hand like I was some kindergartner on the first day of school." Houston turned toward the building. "Well, this isn't getting it done, is it?"

"No, that's a fact." Anne took his arm. "I'm going with you, whether you like it or not."

"Anne, I *can* do this myself."

"I know that."

A campus police car pulled alongside of the curb and a female officer got out and walked to the entrance of the dorm. "Officers Houston and Bouchard?"

"That's us," Anne replied.

"Officer Beverley Justis. Could I see some ID, please?"

Anne held her badge and ID card open and Justis studied it for a few seconds. She nodded and then turned to Houston. "Sir?"

Anne gave him a reproachful look when he said, "Jesus Christ."

"Mike."

Houston displayed his credentials.

"Thank you," Justis said to him. "I understand that you're the father of one of our students."

"That's correct. Look Officer . . ." Houston glanced at the name plate she wore on her uniform blouse. ". . . Justis. I am not here in an official capacity. My daughter's mother has passed away and I want to be the one to tell her. So can we just get inside please?"

"Of course." A locked security door barred access to the building. The only way to gain entrance into the dormitory was via a call box on the wall to the left of the door. Justis leaned past Houston and entered a three-digit code to buzz the desired room. After several seconds a female voice asked, "Who is it?"

Justis leaned forward so her face aligned with the speaker. "BU Police."

The voice asked, "Is something wrong?"

"No, but I need to come up."

The door buzzed and Houston barged through. He rushed toward an elevator and punched the up button.

"Mike, don't go up there like you're storming a beach," Anne said.

He glared at her. "I'm all right."

"No, you're not. You're madder than hell and if you go in there acting like you were confronting a perp, how will she react? I don't know about Susie, but if it were me I'd never forgive you."

Justis gave him a look that told Anne the officer was having second thoughts about letting him have access to the dorm. The elevator arrived and they stepped inside. Anne took the initiative and pressed the button for the fourth floor.

She heard Houston inhale deeply and then exhale in a single explosive breath. "You're right," he said. "I can't handle this like a cop."

"No, you need to handle this like a father."

"Great . . . like I have a clue about how to do that."

Anne noted that Justis stood in the corner and silently studied them. It was evident that she was trying to decide just how close these two BPD officers were. Even Anne was aware that they communicated on a plane more personal than that of partners. She was relieved when the lift stopped and the door opened without any comment from the campus officer.

Susie lived in room 415. They exited the elevator and followed the arrow on a placard that indicated her room was to the left. Halfway down the hall, they stopped before a metal door with the appropriate number painted on it. Justis knocked on the door.

A petite blonde-haired girl wearing a lightweight BU shirt and cutoff blue jeans answered the door. The air conditioning was set low and it was evident she wore no bra. Justis said, "Susan Houston, please."

"She isn't here right now."

"These people are from the Boston police. They need to speak with her." She stepped aside as Anne and Houston showed her their credentials. The young girl's eyebrows arched with curiosity. "What has Susie done?"

"I'm her father." They were the first words Houston had uttered since exiting the elevator.

Anne answered the girl's question. "Nothing, we just need to speak with her."

"She's at the library. I can text her."

"Please do so," Justis said. "This is important."

"Don't," Houston interjected, "tell her that I'm here . . ."

The girl gave him a quizzical look, then shrugged. "Sure, whatever."

Anne thought Houston sounded disingenuous when he said, "I want to surprise her."

The coed turned from the door and picked up a cell phone. She spent a few seconds entering text into it and then put it down. In a matter of seconds the phone buzzed and she looked at the trio of adults at the door. "She's on her way back. I suppose it would be okay for you to come in and wait for her."

Once they were inside, Anne saw Houston studying the room. It was the first normal thing she had seen him do since they had departed the Comm Avenue crime scene. This was possibly the first time in many years he had been in a room in which his daughter lived and she wondered what was going through his mind.

It was a typical college dorm room, which contained two single beds, both in teenaged disarray with sheets and blankets twisted into formless piles and pushed inboard against the wall. Between the beds were two small desks, on which sat two laptops. Rap music reverberated from a nearby room and Anne tried to ignore it. She believed that the phrase "rap music" was an oxymoron. She had lost interest in popular music in the '90s. Compared to the angry pounding and violent, sexist lyrics of modern music, heavy metal seemed tame.

In one corner of the room a small television was tuned to the local news. Amanda Boyce was reporting from the waterfront shooting scene, informing Boston that the sniper had struck again . . . possibly twice.

The blonde girl interrupted her. "I'm Melissa Redfern, Susie's roommate.

"I'm Detective Bouchard," Anne said. "You've already been introduced to Detective Houston."

The girl looked at Houston with interest. It was as if she were checking him out to see if there were enough resemblance between him and Susie to name him in a paternity suit.

Houston felt his face flush. Who knew what Susie had told her roommate about their relationship? It wouldn't be the first time an angry child bad-mouthed a parent.

Houston went back to studying his daughter's half of the room. He walked to her bed and seemed to forget he was not alone. He reverently picked up a blouse that lay sprawled on the bed. He held it in his hands and studied it. He detected the faint scent of perfume and realized that his little girl was neither little nor a girl any longer. He replaced the blouse and looked at the small shelf mounted on the wall above the bed. Centered, and looking as if it were in a place of honor, was a picture of him standing next to Pam, an attractive and fit young woman. Susie, then a gangly girl, stood in front of him. He stood like a statue and stared at the framed photo. Houston stared, concentrating on Pam's image and realized that she had not changed much over the years.

Anne noted that Melissa was staring at them as if they had just arrived from another solar system. She thought there was a look of hostile disapproval when she looked at Houston. Ignoring the girl, Anne walked over and stood beside him. She looked at the picture that held his attention. "Pam was beautiful," she said.

Houston started. "Yes, she was. My sister took that picture on the Fourth of July. Susie was thirteen that year. Six months later everything went to hell and I left."

"You never tried to reconcile?"

"I didn't think there was any hope. I started drinking heavily and just lost my way. As long as I was a cop, Pam would never have considered reconciliation. She hated my job, almost as much as she came to hate me."

"I think you're being too harsh on yourself. I can understand how she may have disliked what you do, but I doubt she hated you. You are, after all is said and done, the father of her child, and for a woman that is something that always gives a man a special place in her heart."

"She'd probably have changed that if she could."

Houston went about his business in the only way he knew how. He needed to process things for himself, and part of the process he used was self-flagellation. For the time being she was thankful that she knew him well enough to restrict her role to that of an interested bystander.

She walked to the other side of the room, stood quiet and watched while he turned back to the desk and picked up one of Susie's textbooks. He flipped through the pages without actually reading them and returned the book to its place. He picked up a loose-leaf photo album, opened it and began looking at the pictures.

Curiosity got the better of Anne and she returned to his side and looked over his shoulder at the pictures. Ignoring her, he turned the pages slowly. The first page contained a portrait of Susie as a toddler and several that appeared to be early grammar school photos.

His face went through a number of emotions as he turned the pages. With each picture, he became sadder and on a couple of occasions grimaced as if someone had shoved a knife into his gut. He stared at an eight-by-five photo of a more mature Susie, dressed in a formal gown, standing between her mother and a healthy, athletic-looking young man. On the facing page was another of Susie and the young man alone, standing on a platform decorated with flowers and shiny banners.

"Mike, have you ever considered this? If Pam hated you so much, why didn't she remarry?"

Houston didn't want to address her statement and quickly changed the subject. He held the notebook up. "Looks like Susie's prom picture."

"She's beautiful," Anne said.

His eyes remained fixed on the photo album. "Something else I wasn't around for."

He valiantly tried to look casual as he flipped through the album. Suddenly he closed the book and spun around. "I'm only in one picture. I guess even when I was around—I wasn't."

Anne was shocked by the deep sorrow on her partner's face; he had never before shown this softer side. "Maybe you were behind the camera taking the pictures."

"I doubt that."

"This job places a lot of demands on a family."

"I screwed that up, didn't I? Instead of having a job to support my life I let it become my life."

"I don't think Susie is going to like you going through her things," Melissa said.

Anne felt her face flush with anger, but she held back the retort that was on her tongue.

The door opened and they stopped talking and turned toward it. A young woman walked in and immediately stopped, surprised by the presence of four people in her room. She held several books against her torso and her arms tensed, pulling them tighter. When she saw Houston, her face turned hard. She said nothing and closed the door behind her.

Houston stared at her. It was as if a younger Pam had walked through the door. Susie's hair was the same bright red as her mother's. Her green eyes had a classical shape and her complexion was flawless. She was tall and looked athletic. The only thing marring her youthful beauty was the dark, angry look she gave her father, which resembled the look on Houston's face when he was angry. She tensed, stiffened her back and demanded, "*What* are you doing here?"

Justis had been silently standing by the threshold of the door since they had entered. "Well, it looks as if my presence is no longer required. I'll be leaving."

"Thank you for your assistance," Anne said.

Justis nodded and left.

Melissa also took Susie's arrival as an excuse to exit. "I'm supposed to be studying with a friend," she said, making a hasty retreat from the room.

Tension filled the room and Houston's face reddened. Houston struggled, trying not to respond to his daughter's anger with his own. He was uncertain about what he should say. He stared at his daughter and said,

"Hello, Susie." His voice sounded gruff as he tried to hide the hurt, loss, and pain he felt.

Susie pushed her way past him and dumped her books on the bed. "That's it? After all these years, all you have to say is, 'Hello, Susie'? Why don't you do the one thing I know you're good at and leave?"

Houston's jaw clenched as he battled to control the anger that his self-recrimination fueled. He knew that he had to keep his cool, because anything he said in haste would only exacerbate the situation and then there would be one more thing for which he would have to atone. He remained quiet.

He realized that Anne tried to defuse the situation when she said, "Susie . . ."

His daughter spun and glared at her. "Who are you, his girlfriend? This is between my father and me—so butt out!"

The flush on Anne's face told Houston that she fought to keep from retaliating and lashing out at the younger woman. He debated whether or not he should intervene when Anne quickly regrouped, put on her professional face and said, "I'm your father's partner. We came here because something has happened that your father felt you should hear from him."

Susie seemed convinced it was all a ploy to get her to calm down. The venom in her voice startled Houston when she snapped, "Whatever it is, tell me and then get out!"

"It's about your mom," Houston said.

Houston saw Susie's mouth open with fear and her complexion pale. "Mom . . . what about Mom? Is she okay?" Despite her angry tone, her eyes darted between Anne and his. He knew that look all too well; he had seen it hundreds of times before.

"No, she isn't," Houston said.

"Has she been hurt?" Susie looked as if she were ready to bolt out the door and run to the nearest hospital.

"She's dead," Houston said. As soon as the words were out of his mouth he regretted how clinical and cold they sounded.

Susie's legs seemed to lose strength and she sat on the bed. "Mom . . . dead? No way!"

"I'm afraid it's the truth," Houston replied.

"Did she have an accident?"

"No." Houston offered nothing more.

Susie stared at her father as if the situation was beyond her comprehension. "If she didn't have an accident, how did she die?" Tears streamed down her cheeks, smearing her makeup and leaving black tracks across her cheeks.

"She was murdered." Houston's tone was devoid of any compassion.

Susie flopped backward, rolled onto her side and began to sob.

Houston was at a loss as to how he should handle the situation. Finally, he sat on the edge of the bed, reached out and placed his hand on her shoulder.

Susie recoiled from his touch and retreated to the far side of the bed, putting as much distance between them as the wall allowed. Suddenly she whirled around and launched herself at him, slapping at his arms and chest. As quickly as the attack started, it stopped, and Susie stared at her father through tear-filled eyes. "I want you to leave now."

Houston reached for her again and she kicked at him. "Just Go!"

"Susie . . ." Houston hated the pleading in his voice.

"Get the fuck out! I don't want you here!" She sat up and huddled with her back against the wall, her legs pulled tight against her torso and her arms wrapped around them. She dropped her head and buried her face between her knees.

Houston slid toward her and then checked his desire to embrace her, to help her deal with her shock. Suddenly he knew that his presence only made his daughter's loss seem deeper. It took all of his energy to maintain his composure and refrain from shouting at her. He did not resist when Anne gently pulled him to his feet and urged him toward the door. "Let me handle this, okay?"

He walked to the door and paused with his hand on the doorknob. He turned and looked back. Anne sat on the bed, Susie's face pressed into her shoulder. She looked at Houston in a manner that told him to go.

"I'll call your Aunt Maureen." Houston did not look back as he walked out.

Anne held Susie for several moments, letting her cry out her shock and grief. She felt awkward. Although holding Mike's daughter while she grieved for her mother seemed to be the natural thing to do, at the same time it felt unnatural. She had never before thought of herself as being a woman with a maternal instinct.

After a while, Anne felt Susie's sobs subside. Susie realized who held her and she pushed Anne away. She scrambled to the edge of the bed, reached over to the desk, grabbed some tissues from a box that was on the corner and began to dab at her eyes and cheeks.

"Susie, I know how hard this must be."

Susie's stare made Anne feel as if she had just arrived from some remote corner of the universe. "How can you know how I feel? You don't know me."

"No, I don't know you. But that doesn't mean that I don't know what it is like to lose a parent. I lost mine when I was a couple of years younger than you."

"I bet they weren't murdered . . ."

"Yes, they were, only not in the same way your mother was. They were killed in a car accident coming home from a Christmas party. A drunk driver ran a stop sign and hit them head-on. As far as I'm concerned, it was murder."

Susie stared at Anne for a few seconds. "That must have really sucked."

"Yes, it did—big time . . ."

Susie dabbed her eyes with a tissue. "Has anyone told Uncle Jimmy yet?"

Anne's head snapped back. "Uncle Jimmy?"

Susie looked at Anne as if the older woman was brain damaged. "Jimmy O'Leary. He's my mother's brother."

Anne walked out of the building a half hour after Houston. She saw that Houston sat behind the steering wheel and slid into the passenger seat.

She saw that Houston was in no mood to talk and she stared straight ahead. He started the motor and drove toward Kenmore Square. When he turned right onto Storrow Drive, she asked, "Where are we going?"

"I'm going to drop you at the precinct and then I have another stop to make."

"In Southie?"

Houston glanced at her. "As a matter of fact, yes."

"You're going to tell your brother-in-law, aren't you?"

He gave her a quizzical look. "How long have you known that Jimmy is . . . was . . . my brother-in-law?"

"Susie just told me."

Houston remained silent for a second. "It isn't something that either he or I advertise."

11

"Observation and perception are two different things; the observing eye
is stronger, the perceiving eye is weaker."
— Miyamoto Musashi, *The Book of Five Rings*

The Claddagh Pub was busy. Blue-collar types lined the bar, many of whom drank away their entire paychecks. The tables were full, only with a slightly more upscale clientele who actually made solid food an integral part of their diets. Every television in the bar was tuned to the city's most popular news broadcast, and the news team was split between the scenes of the two most recent sniper attacks. Houston looked at the shocked faces of O'Leary's customers and realized how close to hysteria the city was becoming. He heard bits and pieces of conversations and all amounted to the same thing . . . *What the hell are the cops doing about this psycho?* He moved through the room, refusing to react to the derogatory comments.

Houston noted that both Gordon Winter and the young woman O'Leary called Lisa were backing the bar. He ignored Winter's glare and walked past the bar, down the corridor and, without knocking, burst through the door of Jimmy O's office.

O'Leary was at his desk, eating a burger and watching the evening news while his ever-present cigarette smoldered in an ashtray beside him. When the door banged against the wall, he started and reached for the half-open drawer on his right. Seeing who the intruder was, he relaxed. "Nice entrance. Am I supposed to be scared or some shit?"

"We need to talk," Houston said, elevating his voice to drown out the news commentators.

"Again? It ain't like you to run off at the mouth this much, Mike."

From the corner of his eye, Houston saw the scene on the TV screen switch to the gas station on Comm Avenue.

O'Leary said, "You interrupted my dinner to talk—so what shall we talk about?"

Houston nodded to the TV. "That . . ."

O'Leary glanced at the screen. "I told you, I ain't involved in that shit. Why you back here bustin' my ass about it?"

"Because," Houston said, "you're involved now."

"Really, would it be possible for you to let me in on the fuckin' secret? Keep it slow and simple, okay? I ain't a high school grad like you."

"That vic was . . ."

"I hear it was some woman."

"Not just *some* woman . . . it was Pam."

O'Leary slammed his palm on the desk, and the ashtray and the plate on which the burger sat bounced off and exploded when they hit the floor. "What! How in fuck did that happen?"

Houston sat in the easy chair. "She was shot while filling her gas tank."

"And you think it was the same asshole?"

"Pretty sure. We'll know more when the ballistics report comes back. Nevertheless, I'm certain it's him."

O'Leary reached down to the floor beside his desk and when he sat up he held the cigarette and put it in his mouth. "You're right . . . I'm involved. In fact, me and my organization are all the way in now."

"I can't allow that, Jimmy. This is a police investigation . . ."

O'Leary sneered. "So investigate, but you can't stop me from lookin' for my sister's killer."

"Stay out of it, Jimmy. We'll get him."

"And then what? Put him up for the rest of his life? I know how the fuckin' law binds your hands. Well, I got my methods too—and believe you me, I'll get more information faster than you guys ever will."

O'Leary calmed down and picked up the ashtray. He stepped on the burning spot in the carpet, twisted his foot to put out the smoldering fire, and then ground his butt in the ashtray. "Susie bin told?"

"I just left her."

O'Leary picked up on Houston's body language. "Greeted you with open arms, did she?"

"You know better."

"I was you I'd get her out of that dorm and someplace where we can keep an eye on her."

"I thought about that too. She won't listen to me though."

"Well, she'll talk with her Uncle Jimmy. I'll call her and send someone to take her to your sister's place."

"I can get police security there."

"Hah! Cops as security? All the shooter has to do is wait until they're off someplace havin' a fuckin' donut. I'll put some of my best people on it."

"Jimmy . . ."

"The friggin' subject is closed. I'm in now and I ain't getting out until I see this sonuvabitch and anyone who's helpin' him on a slab in the morgue . . ."

Houston and O'Leary looked at each other without talking for the better part of a minute. Then Houston stood. "I guess that's about all there is to say, isn't it?"

O'Leary lit another cigarette and gazed into the smoke, ignoring his brother-in-law. Without speaking, Houston walked out of the office. When he closed the door he heard something crash against the wall.

12

"Power grows out of the barrel of a gun."

—Mao Tse-tung

Jimmy O'Leary walked into the warehouse, paused and waited for his eyes to adjust to the dim light. He saw Gordon Winter walk out of the office. "Where is he?" Jimmy asked.

"In the back. Billy is with him."

O'Leary tossed his cigarette to the ground, stepped on it and followed Winter inside. They wove their way through corridors of contraband, much of which was still in the original cartons, and stolen cars waiting for a trip either to Mexico or a local chop shop. In the far corner, next to a large tool crib, a young black man clad in hip-hop clothes sat in a chair beneath a single light. Duct tape had been used to bind the kid's feet to the chair legs and to secure his wrists to the armrests. O'Leary stood in front of him and lit another cigarette. "Billy, take his blindfold and gag off, then you can leave. Gord, I'd like for you to stick around."

"You think that's wise?"

"What, you staying here?"

"No, letting this piece of shit see you."

"Don't matter; he ain't gonna tell anyone."

Billy ripped away the duct tape they had used to blindfold Jermaine Watts. When he tore off the tape the adhesive pulled out eyebrows and eyelashes he ignored the gangbangers muffled screams. Billy used a finger to pick at one end of the tape that covered Watts' mouth. When he was able to get a grip on it, he yanked it free. He balled the tape up and arched it toward a fifty-five-gallon drum that served as a garbage can. The tape bounced off the lip and fell into the drum. Billy held his hands in the air as if he had just scored the decisive basket in a championship game. "Where are the fuckin' scouts when you need them?" He turned back and stopped goofing when he saw O'Leary's glare.

"Hey, Larry Bird, are you all done fucking around?" O'Leary asked.

"Sorry, boss."

"Go outside and keep an eye out, I don't want to be disturbed while me and Jermaine have a little talk."

Jimmy waited until Billy was gone before pulling a chair in front of the youngster. "Do you know who I am?"

"No, suh. I ain't never seen yo b'foe."

"My name is Jimmy O'Leary—most people just call me Jimmy O—and I'm the worst fuckin' thing that's ever happened to you"

The kid's eyes widened when he heard who was sitting before him. It finally registered that he was in serious trouble.

"How you been, Jermaine?"

"Hey, man, why you fuckin' roustin' me? I ain't done nothing to you." The young man's eyes were in constant motion darting from side to side as he tried to find a way out of his predicament.

O'Leary missed none of the telltale signs of fear. He knew it was just a matter of time before this gutless puke told him everything he wanted to know. Before he was finished, Jermaine would gladly sell his firstborn. "That's true, Jermaine, but what about Latisha Worthington?"

"D-don't know nobody named Latisha." Watts's breathing was labored and his voice quavered.

"Is that so? Let me refresh your mind . . . she was thirteen years old and lived across the hall from you and your grandmother. Seems she showed up dead a few weeks back, not far from where you and your homeboys hang out. Somebody introduced her to crack, then raped and murdered her. I think you know something about it."

"I tol' you, I don't know shit, man—" He made a last-ditch effort to sound tough. "Even if I did, no way I'd rat on my brothers to no cracker . . ."

"Well then, let's see what this cracker can do to jog your memory." O'Leary reached over and ground his cigarette out on the back of Watts' right hand.

Jermaine screamed and bucked against the tape that bound him to the chair arms.

O'Leary sat silent and stared at him until he calmed down. "You remember anything, Jermaine—or should I call you Razor?"

Sweat poured down Watts's forehead and he shook his head to get it out of his eyes. After several futile attempts, he raised his head to stare at his tormentor. "What you do that for? You ain't got no call to be doing shit like that."

"Son, you aren't in any position to be telling me what I can or cannot do."

O'Leary rose from his chair and walked to the tool crib. He pawed through it for a few seconds, removed several tools and then sat down again. "Let me tell you what I think, Jermaine. I think that if you didn't do her, then you know who did. As far as I'm concerned, either one makes you as guilty as the other."

He reached out and gripped Watts' left hand. "You got some real long nails, Jermaine." He gripped the index fingernail of the kid's right hand with a small vice grip and tightened the handle screw until the tool's jaws were tight and held the nail securely. "Once more, Jermaine; who did Latisha?"

"I don't know . . ."

O'Leary yanked back on the vice grip and ripped the fingernail from its place. Jermaine howled with pain.

"One down; nine to go," he said, removing his hand from Jermaine's chin. He loosened the tension on the vice grip, removed the bloody fingernail and studied it for a second—holding it before his prisoner's face as he did.

Watts's head dropped forward as if it had suddenly become too heavy to hold up. Sweat covered his face and dripped onto his lap. Blood poured from his mangled finger and splattered on the concrete floor.

His sobs were like music to O'Leary, who lit a cigarette. He glanced at his watch. "It's only ten o'clock, kid—we got a long night ahead of us ..."

An hour and eight fingernails later, later O'Leary wheeled an acetylene torch from the corner, placing it before the chair. He lit his lighter, opened the valve and held the flame to the torch's tip.

Watts's head snapped up when the gas ignited with a loud pop. O'Leary stood in front of him and made a big show of adjusting the flame until it was cobalt blue.

Watts's eyes widened and he began sobbing. "M-man, this ain't legal. You can't be doin' shit like this—I gots rights."

Winter watched his boss for a few seconds and then said, "I think I'll go outside and give Billy a hand—it looks like you got things here under control."

O'Leary dismissed him with a wave of his hand. He squatted in front of Watts. "What you think, I'm the fucking cops? What about Latisha's right to be a kid and grow up to have her own children? I'm goin' to keep hurting you until you tell me what I want to know." He swiped the torch across the boy's bloody fingertips, cauterizing the wounds. Watts bucked against his bonds screaming and cursing as the torch scorched and blistered his fingers. O'Leary grabbed the last of his fingernails and yanked. He smiled when Watts shrieked in agony.

"I hate guys who molest kids, Jermaine. You street punks think that once you're fifteen or sixteen you become men. Well, son, before I'm done with you, you'll wish you were still five years old."

"Man, you crazy!" Watts cried.

"Jermaine, you don't know the half of it ..." The torch swept across Watts's hands again and he screamed and bucked so hard the chair fell over.

Jimmy pulled the chair back onto its legs and squatted in front of his captive. The torch's angry hiss filled the warehouse. "Son, you better tell me what you know. I got a full tank of gas."

At two in the morning, O'Leary walked out of the warehouse and found Winter leaning against the wall. O'Leary lit a cigarette and inhaled deep.

"Is it over?"

"It is for Jermaine. I want you to get some of the guys and take care of a few things for me."

"Okay."

"Start by dumping that piece of garbage. Do it so word will get around. I want his goombahs to know what happened. Then find Jamaal Rooms and Shawnte Armstrong. Once that's taken care of, locate Andrew Sheets."

"You want them disappeared?"

"I don't care about Rooms and Armstrong, but Sheets is the leader. I want him. The others you can leave where any other drug-pushing, pedophiles will know the cost of molesting kids."

"You got it, Jimmy."

"Gordon . . ."

"Yeah?"

"Don't do it too fast, give the motherfuckers enough time to think about their sins and repent before they meet God face-to-face."

13

"It was the stalk that I enjoyed. Pitting yourself against another human being."
—Gunnery Sergeant Carlos Hathcock, USMC

Houston sat on the couch nursing a glass of iced tea. He was lost in thought and impervious to the sounds coming from the kitchen as Anne rattled the pan in which she cooked omelets. He used the few moments of solitude to reminisce about his life. Where had it all gone to hell? A kaleidoscope of memories came and left, vignettes of his marriage and Susie's early life racing through his mind. Never before had he been in a situation that made him feel so helpless.

Anne walked into the room and placed a plate in front of him. "You all right?"

"Lately that's all you seem to be asking me. No, as a matter of fact, I've never been further from all right . . ."

"Want to talk about it?"

"I don't know where to start." He picked at the food, spearing a chunk of omelet with his fork.

"How about the memory you're dealing with right now?"

"You'd think I was a sophomoric fool."

"Really? I know how memories can rip you up. I was a person long before I became a cop, you know."

"I was thinking about Susie. I remembered coming home after work and how she'd be waiting for me. As you know, a rookie doesn't make big bucks and back then we made a lot less. We rented a two-bedroom apartment on the ground floor. Our couch sat in front of the living room window and Susie had me timed. She would stand on the couch and watch out the window for me. I'll always remember how she looked. When she saw me coming up the walk, she'd get so excited that she'd jump up and down. The sight of that little red head bouncing like a curly-haired ball would instantly erase all the fatigue and frustration of my day . . ."

"It must have lit you up." Anne slowly chewed her omelet.

"Yeah, it did. Then I get to thinking . . . no, asking myself: Where did it all go wrong? What made me push all that aside for a job?"

"Mike, it wasn't entirely your fault—it never is."

"Then why do I feel like such a shit?"

"No doubt you carry your share of the blame. But you're not the sole cause of all of it. Pam had to be at fault too."

Houston sighed. "All I know is that she was a far better wife to me than I was a husband to her."

"You've always been your own worst critic, Mike. Maybe it's time you took the pity pot off your ass and stopped saying that."

Houston looked at Anne. His face went from angry to quizzical, as if her words were a great revelation. "You think I'm having a pity party?"

She smiled. "Yes, I think so."

"Anne, you're the best friend I've got . . ."

"Don't act grandiose, I'm the *only* friend you have. Nevertheless, I'm not about to let you flagellate yourself over what happened today."

"I know you're right, but knowing that doesn't let me off the hook." Houston took his mostly uneaten omelet into the kitchen. Halfway there, he realized that Anne might think he didn't like her cooking and he stopped. "No appetite."

Anne grinned at him. "Me either. You should be getting home. Are you going to be all right?"

"There's that damned question again . . . yeah, if I need you I'll call."

Anne walked to him and placed her hands on his arms and looked into his eyes. "Promise?"

"I promise."

"Come on. I'll walk you down."

The driver sat motionless, watching the apartment building. A normal person would have been half-crazy with boredom. He, however, had spent countless hours in a sniper hide. During those hours of immobility, the only thing active was his mind, and this time, as it did on many occasions, it took him back to where this had all started—Somalia.

The van's interior seemed to fill with the stench of burning flesh, his flesh. Black faces hovered inches above his face, looking at him like he was the football in a rugby scrum. They shouted at him in that gibberish they called a language, spit landing on his face. He recalled the inhuman pain of the burns that covered his body and remembered the smoke from his smoldering clothes forming a cloud around him.

Movement in the apartment building's vestibule broke his trance. He shifted in the seat and reached for his weapon.

Houston appeared from inside the building, followed by the broad who was his partner. The sniper smiled, twisting the scarred flesh on his face into a grotesque mask. He watched him open the door and walk down the steps to the sidewalk. Slowly, the sniper placed the 9mm Beretta pistol in his lap. His mind focused now, he watched and waited for his shot.

Houston settled into his car and Anne stepped back as he closed the door. When he rolled down the window, she said, "Get some sleep. We're going to be spending a lot of time on this one."

"Don't lecture me, I'm senior to you." He smiled at her.

"Watch your back, Mike. This perp is burning a torch for you."

"I don't deserve a friend like you. You know that, don't you?"

"Don't sell yourself short, Mike. You deserve a lot more than you think."

Unable to think of a suitable wisecrack, Houston settled for a forced chuckle.

"Mike . . ."

"Yeah?"

"Pam forgave you for everything."

"How could you possibly know that?"

"It's the way women are . . . we forgive easily. My mother always said that whenever my father messed up, she usually forgave him long before he forgave himself."

Houston pondered her words.

Anne placed her hand on his arm. "It's past the time when you should have forgiven yourself and moved on, Mike."

"Tell that to my daughter."

Anne took his hand. "She'll come around. You just have to give her time."

"I hate it when things take time—"

She reached through the window and gave him a quick pat on the shoulder. "I promise you that it will all work out. You just need to be patient."

She stepped back and watched as he started the car and put it in gear. She lifted her left hand in farewell as he drove away. She paid no mind to the van that pulled away from the curb and followed Houston's car.

Houston stopped before the bank of mailboxes in the foyer of his apartment building, retrieved his mail and browsed through it while climbing the stairs to his third floor walk-up. Halfway up the first flight of stairs a postcard caught his eye. The picture on the card was of the main gate at the Marine base in Quantico, Virginia. Who would be sending him a postcard from Quantico? He hadn't been there since—the epiphany made his eyes widen—scout/sniper school. He stopped walking, turned the card over and saw a message written in all caps:

HEY, HEY, WHAT DO YOU SAY?
IS MIKEY GOING TO CATCH THE SNIPER TODAY?

Houston stood on the steps and stared at the writing. The words brought to mind the familiar cadence of marines chanting as they ran. The rhythmic chant left his head as quickly as it had entered and he looked for anything that would give him a clue to the sender's identity. There was no return address, only a Boston postmark and stamp. Houston ran down the steps two at a time. He reentered the vestibule and saw the white van slowly cruising the street.

An arm appeared through the driver's window, a pistol gripped in its fist and aimed in his direction. Houston dove to the floor a second before the external glass door exploded, followed immediately by the angry snap of a bullet passing over his head. A deadly storm of glass engulfed him and he buried his face into his arms to protect it from the deadly shards that flew around the small lobby. The sound of the bullet passing was immediately followed by another loud snap as the interior glass door exploded sending yet more glass flying. He felt a tickling sensation on his forehead and realized that he was bleeding. The blood flowed down the side of his nose and dripped onto the floor.

He pulled his service pistol and scrambled across the floor on hands and knees, slipping and sliding through jagged glass and debris until he reached the base of the door. Broken glass cut through his trousers and razor-sharp pieces pierced his hands and knees. Ignoring the pain, Houston jumped to his feet and vaulted down the steps to the sidewalk. He raised his pistol and sighted at the truck. Suddenly a small face appeared in an apartment window behind the Chevy. Fearing a ricochet if he missed, he dared not shoot.

The shooter raised his arm in farewell and then stomped on the accelerator. The truck burned rubber and fishtailed as it sped away, filling the air with smoke and the screech of spinning tires. Houston stood in the middle of the street with his pistol pointed at the escaping truck.

Realizing that taking a shot at the fleeing truck would be stupid, Houston holstered his weapon and stared after the van. Never before had he felt so impotent. He concentrated on the license plate, but sweat and blood from the cuts on his forehead flowed into his eyes making the numbers illegible. However, he was able to note that the license plates were not green. The witnesses were either wrong or the sniper had switched plates, or this was a different truck.

Houston raced inside the building and vaulted the stairs three at a time until he reached his apartment. He bolted through the door and frantically searched for the phone. Spying it on the coffee table, he reached for it. Just as his hand touched the handset, it rang, scaring the hell out of him. Ignoring the blood that dripped from his lacerated hands and knees onto his carpet, Houston grabbed the phone. Not knowing who the caller was he shouted, "Get off the line!"

"Hey, Mikey, that's no way to treat an old buddy—especially one you fought skinnies with."

Skinnies? It had been years since Houston had heard the derogatory name the grunts in Somalia had used for the enemy. The voice was raspy and sounded as if the caller smoked as much as Jimmy O'Leary did.

"Who's this?"

"You don't remember? Shame on you, Mikey, how could you forget? Hell, you and me were comrades-in-arms together. Still, even after this afternoon's activity, I owe you from the Mowg."

Houston realized the caller referred to Pam and exploded with rage.

"Listen—"

"No, Mikey, you'd best listen and get with the fucking program. Because if you don't start coming up with answers to the right questions, I'll have to start leaving you more clues. Lethal and bloody clues. Remember our credo: one shot; one kill? Well, ol' buddy, let's change it to one shot; one clue."

Houston felt the small hairs on his neck stiffen. The sniper's phrase, "one shot; one kill," had him running a mental inventory of the name of every scout/sniper he remembered serving with in Somalia.

The sniper continued in a calm, almost teasing, tone. "Of course, you can stop it all right now, Houston."

"How can I stop it? That's up to you."

"Well, you're the hotshot detective—think about it. Either way, you can rest assured about one thing . . . I got special plans for you and me. I'll be in touch. Give my regards to Susie, will you?"

The line went dead.

As soon as he hung up Houston checked caller ID, hoping it had captured a phone number. The sniper was smart enough to block his phone. He pressed redial, hoping it would call the sniper back. Nothing happened.

He dialed 911, identified himself and told the dispatcher that he needed a crime scene team. Then he called Anne.

14

"Cities are sniper country."
—Gunnery Sergeant Jack Coughlin, USMC

Anne had finished taking a shower and was dressing when her phone rang. She glanced at the display and saw Houston's number.

"Hey," she said.

"I need you—"

"Mike . . ."

"The sniper just took a shot at me . . ."

Anne's stomach sank. "Are you all right?"

"He didn't hit me. In fact, I think he missed me intentionally."

"What makes you think that?"

"He called me after the attack. I just hung up with him."

"I'll be right there." She raced out of the apartment.

Anne walked through the door and immediately took control. A cursory glance at Houston's bloody, ripped pants and the wounds on his hands and knees was all she needed to determine what was in order. "We need to get you to the emergency room—"

Houston grunted. She knew he would never admit it, especially to her, but when it came to doctors and dentists, he was less than heroic. "I don't think I need medical attention."

"Michael Burnham Houston, I didn't ask what you thought," she said. "I told you what we *are going* to do. If you think I'm going to drag you all over the city while you whine every time you put pressure on a piece of that glass, you had better think again."

There were two telltale signs that always told Houston when Anne was truly angry: her left eye twitched and she used the full name of the object of her ire. When she turned to him and he saw her eye jerking as if she had a pebble in it, he knew she was really pissed. When she used his full name, *Michael Burnham Houston*, it was a definite sign that she was not going to back off. He stood silently by while she called in and told the dispatcher the address of the hospital where they would be. Finally, she pushed him out the door.

The emergency room was everything Houston had thought it would be. A sweet, little old woman took down his information and typed it into the computer. He admired her one finger technique and studied her arthritic hands as she hunted and pecked at the keyboard. In the course of the interview, she accidentally deleted his information three times and had to start over. It took every bit of his strength to keep his cool and patiently repeat the information each time she goofed. He even asked if they had ever met before—maybe at the Registry of Motor Vehicles.

"Do you want me to call Susie?"

Houston stared at Anne. "No, she's upset enough as it is. Besides, right now she'd just push the glass in deeper."

"Mike, she should be told."

"Anne, let it rest . . . okay?" He turned his attention back to the little old lady, effectively cutting off the discussion.

The admissions secretary finally got it right and a nurse led him to the real chamber of horrors, where a horde of psychopaths in green scrubs poked and dug into his tender flesh with lobster picks. When they swabbed the cuts with antiseptic, it hurt more than his injuries. They stuck him with a tetanus shot and then handed him a prescription for some antibiotics and pain pills. The doctor stepped back, turned the task of bandaging his knees and hands over to the nurse and left.

When they returned to his apartment, Houston took the CSI team through the sequence of events related to the shooting and watched with great interest as the lab people lifted a number of fingerprints from the surface of his mailbox. "I doubt anything will come of this," a petite blonde-haired crime scene technician said. "In the course of a day, mailboxes have more hands on them than the only hooker at a teamster convention." She smiled demurely, grabbed her equipment and bounced down the stairs.

"She must be late for a date," Anne said.

It was after midnight before everyone left and Anne and Houston were alone. They sat at the kitchen table drinking coffee and discussing Houston's first direct encounter with the sniper.

"I must know this guy," Houston said.

"It certainly looks that way."

"He knows a lot more about me than I know about him. He knows my address, phone number and even my military history."

"Maybe you know more about him than you think."

"What do you mean?"

"I believe that when we learn this shooter's identity, you're going to remember him. It's obvious that he's someone from your past."

He watched Anne while she sipped her coffee and remained silent. She was intelligent enough to leave it up to him whether or not to continue. If he opened up, she would listen and not be judgmental. On the other hand, if he decided to clam up, she would accept that too.

"When we find this guy I know it will be someone from Somalia. He as much as said so when he mentioned the Mowg."

"The Mowg?"

"That's what we called Mogadishu. Only someone who was there would use that term."

"We need to get the military to do a search of their records to see if they can provide us with the names of everyone who has been through that training."

"I may be able to help there. I know a guy, Danny Drews. He and I met when we were in scout/sniper training at Quantico. He's kept contact with many of the guys over the years."

Anne glanced at the clock and stood up. "It's past one in the morning. I need to get home and you need to get some rest."

Houston tossed and turned, unable to find a position in bed that didn't hurt. He took two of the painkillers the doctor had prescribed. He was convinced that the word was an oxymoron, the pills didn't kill pain; they merely postponed it until the wee hours of the morning when you were alone and feeling shitty. Each beat of his heart sent a throbbing pulse of pain through his hands and knees. He hurt so badly that rather than sleep, he turned on the television and tried watching an old mystery on one of the classic movie channels.

Houston stared at the TV. George Raft had just solved the mystery and all was well. Houston dialed his sister's number. The phone was answered on the second ring.

"Hello?"

"Maureen? It's Mike."

When she heard her brother's voice, Maureen's groggy voice softened. "I'm glad you called—even if it is at a ridiculous hour. Not to mention that the whole neighborhood is probably wondering why I have cop cars parked in front of my house."

"Do you think she'll talk with me?"

"She's asleep, Mike. She's angry with you right now. The first time that you come near her since the divorce is to tell her that her mother was murdered. Have you any idea what it's been like for her to have to deal with this? Why didn't you call me and wait until I got there?" Maureen sighed. "But then, that's usual for you, isn't it? You're the first to rescue a perfect stranger, but the last to do what your family needs."

Maureen's words struck him like a five-pound hammer. He'd been an absentee father for most of Susie's life and it was only natural for her to resent him for showing up now. "Mo, she all but threw me out. I didn't know what else to do . . . besides my partner, Anne, was with her."

"Susie told me about it. That's the one good thing that came out of this. She made the most of a bad situation."

"Yeah, Anne's a true friend."

"Don't hurt her like you did Pam."

"What are you talking about?"

"It's obvious to everyone but you that she cares a great deal for you."

"Don't be crazy. She's my partner . . . nothing more."

"Are you sure that she feels the same?"

Houston paused and for several moments said nothing. Feeling uncomfortable, he switched the subject. "Mo, I called to talk about Susie. If she'd had a weapon in her dorm, I think she'd have used it on me."

"Well, you have to admit that you really mucked this one up, brother."

"C'mon, Mo, give me a break here. I got a full plate as it is without you busting heavy on me. Do you think Susie will see me if I came by later?"

Maureen's voice softened. "I don't know. You two have a lot to work out. Even if she doesn't want to see you, I think she needs to."

"Tell her I'll be by around noon. Maybe we can go to lunch together."

"That would be nice, Mike. I think deep down, she needs you now, even if her actions don't show it. I'll talk to her in the morning and if there is any problem, I'll call you."

"Thanks, Mo. How are Lee and the kids?"

"We're all fine, Mike. You just take care of yourself, okay? We're your family, we care about you. Call or come around now and then, okay? You know, after all is said and done, all we have is each other."

A lump filled Houston's throat. "Yeah, I know . . . love you, Mo. Good night."

"Good night, Mike."

Anne lay in bed, thinking through the evening's events. She couldn't stop thinking about how close she had come to losing Houston. Thinking about the prospect of a life without him in it left her feeling scared and empty. Old self-doubts returned. Why couldn't she allow Mike in? She had wanted to for the past two years. The taboo against workplace relationships was a factor. Was being a cop more important to her than letting everyone know who she was? The thought made her pause. Her thoughts turned to her father, the one man in her life that she had truly loved more than life itself. She remembered how devastated she had been when he was killed. It was not that she didn't miss her mother too, but she had been a daddy's girl and adored her father and everything he did. For years she had known that her father wanted a son, but he had never let on to her that that was the case. If anything, the opposite was true—he was the most dedicated and understanding father a girl could ever hope for. The abandonment and loss she felt when he was killed returned and swept over her like a heavy fog. Had his death and her loss left her incapable of giving her heart to a man? She thought of the men she had dated over the intervening years and how none of them met her standards. *Maybe,* she wondered, *I never let them.* Did she hold them to a standard even God couldn't meet? Just as she felt she was close to a decision, the job got in the way. She loved being a cop, but there was the dangerous aspect of the job. Then she realized what the real roadblock was. Houston was the only cop who accepted her as a partner and it would ravage her if they were separated. She burrowed down into the bed and tried to turn her mind off. Shortly she dozed off.

15

Jimmy O hung up the phone and ground his cigarette into the ashtray. Before it stopped smoldering, he lit another. He stared into the smoke for several seconds and then picked up the phone and banged a number. "Gordon? Get your ass out of bed and come over here. We're going to rattle a few cages and see if we can't stir up a rat."

The Escalade turned the corner and crept up the street. The driver stayed on the dark side of the thoroughfare, staying close to the empty warehouses and avoiding the few lights in the abandoned industrial park. O'Leary stood back from the alley's entrance—hidden in the shadows— and glanced at his watch. Right on time, he thought. Being predictable is a very stupid thing for a drug dealer; but what the hell, if they were smart they would be doctors or lawyers. Jimmy tossed his cigarette to the ground and watched the wind tumble it end over end deeper into the alley. He nodded to Gordon.

O'Leary and Winter watched the SUV until it reached the end of the block and coasted to the curb. A man stepped out of a dark doorway and looked both ways, checking for unwanted observers. Satisfied the street was empty, the pusher approached the car.

They waited until they were certain that the pushers felt safe and then walked out of the alley. Even though he saw no weapons, O'Leary knew the dealers had guns hidden from sight. The street pusher stood on the sidewalk and leaned so close to the Escalade's tinted window that his face almost touched the glass. The driver lowered the window. A nickel-plated revolver appeared through the window, sparkling in the amber light of a nearby streetlamp. The pusher held his hands up so they were visible and backed up a step. Whoever was in the car appeared to be ready to shoot if the face belonged to anyone other than his expected contact. Their voices carried in the quiet early morning air.

"Whoa, motherfucker," the street dealer said, "ain't any call for the gun, man."

"How yuh doin', Jamal?" the man in the car asked. He had a Latino accent.

O'Leary and Winter closed with the SUV. At the last minute, the one named Jamal noticed them. O'Leary shoved him out of the way and grabbed the revolver. On the other side of the truck, Winter pushed a 9mm pistol against the driver's temple before he could stomp on the accelerator.

O'Leary looked at Jamal. "Take a hike, douchebag. I got business with Ricky and it ain't got nothin' to do with you.

The pusher gave the gun O'Leary held a nervous look and, like a wraith, disappeared into the night.

"Let's put the hardware aside, shall we?" O'Leary said. "I wouldn't want anyone gettin' hurt for no reason."

The drug dealer knew he had no chance and held his weapon up. O'Leary took it.

"Hey, Jimmy, since when you ripping off bidnezzmen?"

"I got no interest in your cash or the goods you sell." O'Leary opened the door, grabbed him by his shirt and yanked him onto the pavement.

"Damn, man, what's with you?"

O'Leary grabbed the man called Ricky by the back of his shirt collar and lifted him until his tiptoes barely touched the ground. He kept a tight grip on him and high-stepped the Hispanic along the sidewalk and into the alley he and Winter had just left. Once they were safely in the shadows, O'Leary slammed him against the brick wall so hard that the dealer's head bounced against it. "Talk to me, Ricky."

"I been tryin' but you actin' all postal and shit . . ."

Jimmy slammed the dealer's shoulders and head against the bricks again.

"Okay, okay. What you want to know? Jeezus, that fuckin' hurts—stop it, will ya?"

"The Common shooter . . ."

"Hey, man, I got nothin' to do with that. You know me Jimmy. I ain't never offed nobody 'less it was bidnezz."

"You know people who know people, Ricky. I want to know what you know about this guy." He thumped Ricky's head against the wall again.

"Okay, man. Shit, no reason for you goin' all fuckin' crazy about this. What happen, this dude do you wrong or sumptin?"

"Ricky, I'm getting tired of your bullshit act."

"All right." The ghetto dropped out of his voice. "The only thing I know about this shooter is that he's one whacked-out motherfucker. I've been told he looks like he's made of silly putty."

Jimmy leaned closer to Ricky, his eyes shining in the ambient light. "Silly putty?"

"Yeah, that stuff we had when we were kids . . ."

"I was never a kid . . ."

"Anyhow, this guy is burned so bad that he looks like he walked out halfway through his cremation."

O'Leary stepped away, released Ricky's shirt and took out his cigarettes. He lit a smoke and offered the pack to Ricky. The dealer pulled one out and lit it from O'Leary's lighter. He rubbed the back of his head. "Jesus, Jimmy, you like to busted my damn head."

"You got a name for this cowboy?"

"Nope, but I hear he's got a crib in Mattapan somewhere."

"I want that address."

"I don't know where it is, man. Like I said, this dude isn't put together normal. He's not like you and me. We're businessmen—we take people out only when it's necessary. This guy does it because he likes it."

O'Leary stepped out of the alley and motioned to Winter. He turned back to Ricky. "Put the word out, I want this guy. I'll make it worthwhile to anyone who leads me to him. And Ricky . . ."

"Yeah?"

"If you want to stay in *bidnezz*, you better stop being so goddamned predictable. You need to vary your routine a bit, know what I mean? Hell, I knew down to the minute when you'd be here."

Ricky stared at him as if he had no idea that he was stuck in a routine. Jimmy shook his head; some people just never get the concept. "You know, Ricky . . . what you lack in intelligence, you more than make up for in stupidity . . ."

When they were back in his Lincoln Navigator, Winter asked, "Where to next?"

"I want to hit a couple of places, one in Charlestown and another in Southie."

"It's four in the morning."

"The places we're going don't close."

Charlestown was a square mile in size and divided into two different and distinct cities. The title of Dickens's novel *A Tale of Two Cities* would have been ideal for a book about the city. The south side, around the Bunker Hill Monument and extending to Rutherford Avenue was the domain of the upper-middle class—called Tunies by the longtime residents—complete with successful small businesses and exorbitantly priced condominiums. On the other hand, the north end was where the working and non-working poor, the people known as Townies, were crammed into triple-decker apartments and low-income housing projects. This was where Jimmy O and Gordon were headed.

O'Leary and Winter parked alongside a hydrant on a street so narrow that a single car could barely fit. They walked down an alley between two of the triple-decker apartment houses that lined the street. The passage was barely wide enough to hold the garbage cans that filled the air with a ripe aroma. In the absolute dark Jimmy stumbled into one of the metal cans and cursed.

"You okay, boss?"

"Yeah." Jimmy circumvented the remaining obstacles, rounded the building, turned left and entered the back door of a seedy bar. To outsiders, the tavern was closed, but the Townies knew that the action had merely moved to the back room, which was in reality a private club.

O'Leary felt at home in Charlestown and was one of the few non-Townies with access to everywhere. He walked to the bar and slapped a heavyset man on the back. "How's it goin', Bobby?"

The man spun on his stool, ready to punch the interloper. When he recognized O'Leary, he smiled a broad smile that revealed a missing canine tooth. "Not bad, Jimmy. How 'bout you?"

"I'm doin' okay."

"You get the dough I sent?" Bobby asked.

O'Leary slid onto a bar stool beside Bobby and glanced around the room. He saw no one who was not known to him and felt secure enough to talk openly. "Yup, was that my cut from the armored car in Andover?"

"Yeah."

"You want some advice, Bobby?"

Bobby downed his shot of whiskey. "Depends. What's it gonna cost?"

"Nothin' . . . you know me—I charge for information. Advice, on the other hand, is free. But I'm lookin' for some info."

"Okay," Bobby said, "it's your dime."

"First, the advice: lay off the rolling banks for a while. I heard the Feebs have moved a task force into the city. They believe all the robberies are bein' done by a gang of Townies."

For a few seconds, Bobby pondered O'Leary's advice. "How long you figure we should lay low?"

"Shit, I was you guys, I'd get into a whole new line of business. It's hard to know who to trust anymore. Take Whitey, for instance. No way in hell anyone would have expected him to be a rat bastard informing to the Feds." Once again, O'Leary scanned the room. "It's getting to the point where you can only trust your blood relatives—and you better keep a close watch on them."

Bobby nodded his agreement. "Ain't like the old days, that's for fuckin' sure."

"Nope, the whole friggin' world has gone nuts. If the Feebs bust you, call me. I got a real good lawyer. It'll be on my dime, no charge."

"Thanks."

"Shit, you're almost family. Over the years you bin' loyal and I appreciate that."

"What can I do for you?" Bobby motioned for the bartender to bring him a refill. "And get Jimmy whatever he wants."

"Coffee," O'Leary ordered. He turned back to Bobby. "Talk to me about these shootin's goin' on all over the city."

"Jesus, Jimmy, you don't want to get in the middle of that. Street talk is that this guy's a fuckin' psycho with an agenda . . ."

"You got any idea what that agenda might be?"

Bobby's eyes widened as if he had just had an epiphany. "The woman that got popped over on Comm Ave. was . . ."

"My sister."

"Aw, damn it all to hell, Jimmy, I'm sorry. Pam was a good kid . . . that sucks big time."

"Yeah. So you see, this is personal. That's why I want anything and everything you know."

Like O'Leary had done moments before, Bobby glanced over his shoulder. "There's somethin' fucked up about this . . . you didn't get this from me, okay?"

"Sure. Now tell me what you got."

"The shooter's agenda is your former brother-in-law. He has a major hard-on for him, one that goes back years . . ."

16

"The sniper must always take maximum advantage of the terrain by occupying positions which offer good observation, fields of fire, concealment and cover, and which control enemy avenue of approach into the defensive position."
—*US Marine Corps Scout/Sniper Training Manual*

After hanging up the phone, Houston tried going to sleep again. It was a futile effort. Finally, at five o'clock, he got up, made coffee and poured a cup. He sat at the table going through his notes and running a mental inventory of every scout/sniper with whom he had ever served. If, indeed, someone from his past had an issue with him, there was not a single clue as to who it was. However, he was going to find out. Once the shooter's identity was known, they were going to settle this one-on-one. It might cost him his shield, but he didn't care. What really ate at him was that for the first time in his life, he was the mouse and not the cat.

By six o'clock, the caffeine had made him jittery and he decided to get busy. He opened his address book and looked up Danny Drews's phone number. He hoped Danny was still an early riser; if not—too bad. The information Danny could provide was too important to worry about something as trivial as his sleeping habits.

When Drews answered on the second ring, his voice sounded as if he had been awake for a while. "Hello."

"Danny, Mike Houston, what's up?"

Drews laughed, "I'd say nothing good if you're calling. What's it been, two years since we last talked?"

"Something like that, but who's counting?"

"I am, not that you care. You were always an independent son of a bitch, Mike."

"Hey, let's do breakfast."

"Sure, anytime."

"No, I mean this morning . . . now. Meet me at Andy's—say in an hour?"

"Yeah, sure, that'll be okay." Drews sounded suspicious of Houston's motives. Their relationship was not of the *let's get together for a couple of beers* variety.

"Hey, Danny, you still got that list of guys from the old days?"

"Do you mean my scout/sniper roll call?"

"Yeah, that's it. Bring it with you."

Danny said nothing for several seconds and Houston knew he was giving his next words serious thought. "Mike, is this about the sniper killings I been following in the news?"

"Yeah, Bucko, I'm afraid it is."

"You think the shooter is one of us?"

"Not only do I think it is, I'm certain of it. We'll talk over some eggs."

Andy's was a small local diner wedged in between rows of aging brownstones in a neighborhood that was in flux. Once the domain of the middle class, many of the brownstones had been purchased and converted into offices and classrooms by the myriad small colleges that filled Boston's Back Bay and west end. Cruising past the Common— site of the first shootings—Houston was cognizant of how fast time was passing. They were coming up on the end of the crucial first forty-eight hours after the crime and they still had little if anything to lead them to the shooter.

Houston got to the restaurant early, bought a newspaper and took a booth in the back. He flipped over the paper and saw a full-page picture of the Blackman/McGuire crime scene with a huge headline that read: *SNIPER STRIKES AGAIN: Death Toll Now 7.* On a wall-mounted television a local news anchor was interviewing the police commissioner. Even though the volume was low, the hysteria was clearly reaching extreme levels and all of the city's politicians were catching hell—especially those affiliated with the BPD. Opening the paper, Houston read the lead article, which pointed an accusing finger at the incompetence of the police when it came to bringing in the sniper.

Houston ordered a couple of mugs of coffee and the waitress placed them on the table as Danny Drews walked in. Drews had changed a lot during the two years since they had last seen each other. The years had not been good to him. Houston had to force himself from commenting on Drews's balding pate and the growing paunch that hung over his belt.

"You haven't changed much," Drews said.

"I don't know about that. I feel as if I've been rode hard and put away wet a few times too many. How've you been?"

"As you know, I got married—our first child is due in two months." Drews was jovial and smiling. It had to be the result of living a normal life, one that didn't make you deal with violence and guns on a daily basis. Houston wondered if he would ever feel like that again.

"You're expecting a baby already?"

"You know how it is . . . my mother always said the first one comes anytime—after that it takes nine months," Drews said.

Drews's joke had brought back memories and Houston felt nostalgic. Pam had been pregnant with Susie when he and she got married. "Now I remember—you sent me an invitation."

"You didn't come."

"Yeah, I got no excuse."

"Aw, hell, you would have been bored to tears anyhow. What fun is a wedding if you can't get shit-faced, huh?"

They sat in silence for a few moments, and then Drews settled into his seat, took a sip of coffee. "Here's the stuff you asked for." Drews slid a manila folder across the table. "Those are yours, I made copies of everything I got: names, addresses, and phone numbers. What makes you think it's one of us?"

"These kills have been planned with military precision . . . as if whoever did them is following the scout/sniper training manual. As a matter of fact, they remind me of the ops we did in the Mowg. Whoever this shooter is, he's either been through sniper training or he's working with someone who knows scout/sniper tactics. One thing is for certain though—somebody who knows search-and-kill procedures and tactics is involved in this somehow."

Drews shook his head. "I can see how you might come to your conclusion. It does sound as if this shooter is a trained sniper. But you got to get with the times, Mike."

"Oh?"

"Yeah, this is the Internet age. Hell, if you go online and search 'one shot; one kill' or sniper, you'd shit at how many hits you'll get. If you want to learn how to be a sniper, I can give you the names of some people who run camps and train anyone with the money. We're living in some fucked-up times, Mike. Goddamned terrorists have got the world paranoid. The NRA even had an actor in charge who said he'd only give up his gun when somebody pries it from his dead hands. Anybody with the money who wants to be a sniper can be. As for knowing about Hathcock and Burke—hell, Henderson's book, *Marine Sniper,* sold so many copies he used the pages his editor cut out of the first edition to write a sequel. Hathcock himself did a video interview you can buy on the Internet."

"Yeah, I know I may be jumping to conclusions. But this shooter made it personal when he shot my ex. He also called me and said we were in the Mowg together."

Drews's eyes widened. "Jesus, he shot Pam?"

Houston nodded. "Yeah, it's in the morning papers. There's more to it though. He sent me a warning last night. Had me dead in his sights and didn't hit me. Everything he's done so far indicates that he's too good to have missed unless he meant to. Immediately after that, he called me and referred to the Mowg."

"That's scary. Still, you can't eliminate the guys you've put away as a cop. They could be saying some of this shit to throw you off track."

"I hope so, Danny. That would mean I'm chasing an amateur. Unfortunately, nothing this perp has done so far says anything but that he's a trained and experienced professional."

They talked about old times for about an hour. Houston needed to ask one more question and finally threw it on the table. "Danny, during our time in the Corps, do you remember anyone who walked around with a major hard-on for me?"

Drews sat back and Houston visualized wheels turning in his mind. "I can only think of one guy who even comes close."

"Who was it?"

"Edwin Rosa."

"Rosa? Christ, I haven't thought about him in years. You're right about one thing though, he wouldn't spit to save me from dying of thirst. There's one major problem with that theory though—he died over there. I know—I was with him."

"That's not what the official record says. It lists him as MIA."

"That's bullshit! I was involved. There was no way he lived through that."

"Really?"

"He and I were on a mission and the enemy ambushed us. During the fight Rosa got hit through both legs and couldn't walk. We holed up in an old tenement and held them off for a couple of hours. Since Rosa was unable to walk, I decided one of us needed to go for help. Once it was dark enough for me to leave, I moved him to a window where he'd have a clear field of fire, gave him my rifle and headed back to the base camp. After I left, the skinnies burned the building to the ground. By the time we got back, it was just a pile of rubble. It must have burned faster than a paper house on a windy day—there was no way he could have made it out." Houston paused and took a drink of his coffee.

"Now I remember. But, I also know that they never found his body in the rubble."

Houston settled back, slowly turning his coffee cup. "Rosa was one bloodthirsty bastard. He and I butted heads several times over his indiscriminate shooting of noncombatants." Houston paused, staring into his mug of coffee, and looked like he was a million miles away. "Still, nobody deserves to die like he did."

Drews stood. "Well, some of us are gainfully employed. I hope the file helps you get this guy before someone else gets killed."

"Me too—it's been good seeing you, Danny."

"Same here—see you around."

The sniper had been on-site and in position for half an hour. He had broken into an under-renovation brownstone and climbed the three flights of stairs to the top floor. He was pleasantly surprised to find the door to the roof unlocked. He stepped onto the roof and checked his line of fire to the front door of the building across the street—it was unobstructed and only about a twenty- or thirty-meter shot. For a shot that short, he didn't need to worry about the wind or difference in elevation having an effect on the bullet's flight; for these reasons he had opted to use his 9mm pistol.

He made a quick survey of the roof's perimeter. The next building was separated by no more than six or seven feet. He backed up a couple of steps and easily vaulted across the narrow chasm. Once again he studied the roof and found a fire escape leading down to the narrow service street behind the line of buildings. Satisfied that he would be able to take his shot and exit the area, he jumped back to the partially renovated brown-stone. He returned to his shooting position and settled down behind the roof's parapet. Now there was nothing to do but wait for his target to appear. He glanced at the sun as it crept over the top of the city's skyline and felt the early-morning warmth on his ravaged skin. Gonna heat up quick—in more ways than one, he thought.

Houston and Drews shook hands.

"We should do this more often," Drews pulled a twenty from his pocket.

Before he could throw it on the table, Houston waved him off. "This is on me—for old times."

Houston counted out two singles as a tip for the waitress and tossed them on the table.

Drews nodded and headed for the exit. Drews opened the door and turned to wave good-bye. His arm was still in the air when his chest exploded. A microsecond later, a sharp crack broke the morning stillness. Blood and tissue flew everywhere, splattering a woman in a white business suit.

Houston ran forward, hoping to catch Danny as he fell. He didn't get there in time. Drews hit the floor with a muffled smack.

Houston took his pistol from its shoulder holster, held his badge up, and ignored the pain in his lacerated hands and knees as he slid across the floor, stopping beside his fallen friend. "Police, everyone get down!"

Houston knelt beside Drews; a cursory look told him that all a doctor would be able to do was pronounce him dead. His head was turned to the side, blood was smeared across his face from the nose and facial bones that had broken when he hit the restaurant's industrial tile floor. The leg of Houston's trousers was soaked with blood from the gaping exit wound in Drews's chest and his own ripped-open stitches. Houston's fingers were slippery with blood when he pressed them against Drews's carotid—there was no pulse. He left the body, duckwalked to the door and ventured a look outside.

The sniper ignored the ejected cartridge and concentrated downrange. He saw Houston's head appear around the doorjamb. He adjusted his aim until the pistol sights were centered a couple of inches beside the cop's head and squeezed the trigger.

A bright light flashed from the roof of the building directly across the street, and then something slapped into the doorjamb next to Houston's head. Wood splinters exploded and tore into the side of his face. Houston ducked, hiding behind the door, and belatedly raised his arms to shield his eyes from the sharp splinters. He paused for a few seconds, trying to decide what course of action he should take. He looked at the diner's patrons. The waitress knelt on the floor. She and the sobbing businesswoman clutched each other, one arm wrapped around the other woman and their other arms folded over their heads as if warding off falling debris.

Houston took a deep breath and burst through the door. He dashed between parked cars and raced across the street toward the building from which the sniper had fired. He felt as if he were a halfback running end zone to end zone on an endless football field and no matter how fast he ran, the entrance to the building seemed to remain at a fixed distance.

After what seemed an eternity but was only seconds, Houston vaulted up the six concrete steps leading to the entrance and slammed into the door with his shoulder. The door burst open and he faced a dark unlit stairwell. Ignoring personal safety, he ran up the old warped stairs. As he climbed, his feet hitting the aging wood sounded like a stampeding elephant. He was certain the sniper could hear him. Yet Houston pushed on, taking the steps two at a time. Intent on reaching the top floor, he gave no thought to the fact that a bullet could end his ascent at any second. He raced upward, ignoring dark doorways and landings in his determination to get to the roof. If the sniper were inside the building, rather than on the roof, Houston was a dead man, yet he didn't care. The chances of getting to the rooftop before the sniper fled were slim enough and taking precautionary procedures would reduce them to nil.

The sniper saw Houston dash out of the diner and race across the street. He was tempted to shoot again, ending the game once and for all. He lowered his pistol. "Not yet, Mikey . . . I have other plans."

He ran toward the adjacent building, vaulted across the narrow alley and hid behind an air conditioning compressor, waiting for Houston to appear.

Houston was gasping when he reached the door at the top of the four flights of stairs. He forced himself to pause before charging through. Blood mixed with sweat on his face and it stung as it dripped to his chest, staining his shirt. He stood before the door, steeling himself against the almost-certain probability that a bullet awaited him on the other side. Houston took a deep breath, trying to get his labored breathing and heaving chest under control. He opened the door and cursed when the brilliant light hit his eyes. Everything on the roof was concealed in the intense sunlight and would be until his eyes adjusted. The brilliant light burned and he blinked numerous times, trying to clear his vision. After a few seconds, his sight cleared enough for him to discern shapes and he burst out of the stairwell. He sighted along the top of his pistol and spun around as he checked left and right. The roof appeared to be vacant. Squinting his eyes in a vain attempt to minimize the pain, Houston slowly walked to the edge of the building and for the first time heard the wail of sirens approaching from several directions. The reflection of the sun hitting something metal caught his eye. He walked over to the object and bent down over it. He studied the cartridge casing left behind by the sniper.

The sniper watched Houston explode through the door and once again placed his sights on him. He waited for the most opportune moment to send his next message. The cop bent over and looked at one of the shiny cartridges he had intentionally left behind. He pulled the trigger. At the exact instant that bullet began its supersonic journey, Houston dropped onto his stomach.

Houston's peripheral vision detected movement on the roof of an adjoining building and he dove forward, losing his pistol as he hit the deck. The summer sun had already heated the tar to a semisolid state and his damaged hands burned as they slid through the soft, gooey roofing. Unable to support himself on the superheated surface, he went down on his face. A bullet passed near his head, marking its passage with an angry snap. Ignoring the pain in his damaged knees and hands, Houston was oblivious to the blistering tar and scrambled through the thick glaze. He hugged the deck, smearing his clothes with a mixture of black grit and roofing tar. He tensed and waited for the next bullet.

After several seconds passed without another shot, Houston scrambled to cover behind an air conditioning compressor unit and pulled a .380 caliber backup pistol from his ankle holster. He curled into a ball, trying to present as small a target as possible. Once safely out of sight, his attention turned to his burnt and lacerated hands. Cursing and picking at the congealing roofing material, he sat up and rested his back against the compressor unit, placed the pistol in his lap and studied his wounds. Houston groaned when he saw that he had ripped open some stitches and blood seeped from the newly opened cuts. He picked and tugged at the loose end of the sutures, but the pain soon stopped him. Blood mixed with sweat, staining the cuffs of his shirt and stinging. Shaking off his pain and discomfort, he concentrated on his predicament.

Evaluating the situation, he became more convinced than ever that the shooter was playing with him. On two occasions, the sniper had had him at a distinct disadvantage yet failed to follow through.

Houston looked for his service pistol and saw it lying in the open. Time for him to make a decision; there were only two courses of action open and neither was appealing. The first option was to wait and hope the sniper had had enough sport for one day. The second was to go for his pistol, which would once again present the killer with a clear target. Houston settled back against the compressor and listened for footsteps. The only sound breaking the morning silence was that of sirens. After several long moments, he decided to take a chance and stood, leaving the protection of the air conditioning unit. Knowing there was no one else on the roof, he breathed a sigh of relief.

Houston retrieved his service pistol before putting the hideaway back in its ankle holster. He quickly inspected the weapon to ensure that the action was free of tar and grit. Satisfied that all was in working order, he scanned the roof. "What do you want . . . what is your game?"

A car door slammed in the rear of the building and Houston ran to the back of the roof. The soft surface of the roofing tar pulled at his shoes, almost tearing them from his feet and slowing him down. As he moved, he double-checked his pistol. He reached the edge of the building and peered over the abutment into the fire alley below. The white van raced down the narrow street. The speeding vehicle was out of pistol range and shooting at it would only endanger innocent people. He holstered his pistol and then, realizing he was hyperventilating, sat on the roof's parapet and inhaled deeply until he regained his wind.

He felt the exhaustion brought on by several nights of fitful sleep and the abatement of his adrenaline rush, and he let his head hang. He looked at the mess on the front of his shirt. Tar, mixed with his and Danny Drews's blood, mired his chest and stomach. He shook his head, slid off his perch on the roof's edge and felt the tar shift under his buttocks as he sat in it. "Houston," he muttered, "you sure are fucking everything up . . ."

He was still there when three uniformed cops reached the roof.

17

"When you want to attack, you remain calm and quiet, then get the jump
on your opponent by attacking suddenly and quickly."
— Miyamoto Musashi, *The Book of Five Rings*

Anne and Houston left the crime scene shortly after noon. He carried Danny's file to his car; the last thing he wanted was for the department to confiscate it as evidence, tying it up before he could make a copy of it. He would turn it in as evidence once he had a chance to review the database in depth. They drove their individual cars to the police station where Houston parked his car and got into Anne's. He tossed the file on the seat.

"What's that?"

"It might be the reason the sniper targeted Danny."

When Anne didn't comment, he elaborated. "It's a roster of scout/ snipers who have stayed in touch with each other, most of whom have attended one of their reunions."

"They have reunions?"

"Yeah, a lot of military units have them."

"I never would have guessed. What do they do at them?"

"Never having attended one, I don't have firsthand knowledge. I assume they tell lies about their time in the service and get drunk—just like any reunion or convention."

"Sounds like every man's idea of a good time."

"It's a strange thing about military service. It seems that the older we get—the better we were."

"So that's what the reunions are about? Telling each other how great you all were?"

"More or less. It sounds boring to me. Then again, what do I know about having a good time? I'm just a cop."

Anne smiled. "Well, if you ever do decide to check one out let me know so I can have a hangover remedy on hand when you get back."

Anne pointed at his shirt. "I think that we need to get you cleaned up."

"Why? Isn't this what every well-dressed cop wears?"

"Our next stop is your place so you can get a change of clothes and a quick shower. Quite frankly, you're ripe. You look more like a homeless person than a cop."

"I'm shocked. I put my best cologne on this morning."

"Just what every woman wants to smell on a man, eau d'tar with an ever-so-slight dab of BO."

"If it's so alluring, I'll bottle it."

"Don't bother."

Houston opened the file and scanned its contents. If nothing else, Danny was organized. The database was extensive. The names were alphabetized, creating a master roster, cross-referenced by their years of service and the state in which each member currently resided. Houston flipped to the page containing Edwin Rosa's information. Beside Rosa's name, Danny had written *MIA, Mogadishu, Somalia, 1993.*

Anne had been driving for fifteen minutes, allowing a now clean Houston time to be alone with his thoughts. She saw him staring out the side window. "So where to? You want lunch?"

"Oh, hell."

"What is it now?"

"I was supposed to be at my sister's at noon. Susie and I were going to do lunch."

Anne turned on the car's emergency lights and performed a tight U-turn. She handed him her cell phone. "Call them and explain that you got tied up."

"My car is still at the station."

"Not a problem, I'll have you back to your car in no time."

Maureen saw Mike's car pull up and shook her head. It was *so* like him to be over two hours late. She turned and walked upstairs, stopped before the guest room door and knocked. A muted voice invited her in.

She opened the door and stood in the threshold for several seconds, watching her niece. Susie had pulled her hair into a ponytail and could have passed for fourteen. It had been over a year since Maureen had last seen Susie and, while she had matured into a beautiful young woman, she still clung to certain little girl habits. Maureen wondered how Mike had dealt with seeing his daughter as a grown-up rather than an awkward young girl.

Susie sat in front of the dresser, staring at a picture. Maureen's heart caught in her throat when she saw that it was a photo of Pamela and Mike on their wedding day. The picture was one she had seen before. "Your father is here."

"So?"

"Susie, dear, this is hard on all of us."

"Must be really hard on him. Why else would he bring some stranger with him to tell me about Mom?" Anger temporarily pushed aside her grief. "Just tell him to go away and I'll handle this alone, as usual."

"Susie, she's a police officer, your father's partner."

Maureen could not take her eyes off the photo, especially her former sister-in-law's face. An older version of the young woman who sat before the photo, Pam too had been beautiful and on that long ago late spring morning, she had been so radiant that she outshone the sun.

It broke her heart when Susie picked up the portrait and studied it for a few seconds, then placed it on the dresser, taking care to place it in the exact spot and angle.

Maureen sighed and left the room.

———————

As he walked to the house, Houston felt as if he were wading through a knee-deep swamp. Standing before the door, reluctant to press the doorbell, he kept telling himself there was nothing to worry about. After all, it was his daughter he was meeting, not some homicidal maniac. Before he could press the bell, the door opened and Maureen stood in the threshold.

"Not only are you late, but you look like you've just been through a meat grinder. What happened to your face and hands?"

Houston smiled and knew he looked sheepish. "Occupational hazard." He shuffled his feet. "Why do I feel as if I'm about to be thrown into a threshing machine?"

"You look as if you already have been." Maureen smiled and hugged him.

He returned her embrace, taking care not to put pressure on his bandaged hands, and grinned. "Yeah, but eventually I always show up."

"Bad pennies always do. Get in here."

Once Houston was inside, Maureen touched his arm and said, "It will be all right."

"That's easy for you to say."

Maureen led the way into the living room and paused. He hadn't visited his sister and her family for several years. His usual excuse was that he was too busy, but he knew that was not the reason. The truth was that he felt uncomfortable in Maureen's impeccable world. The living room was an example of her quest for perfection. It was beyond neat; it was spotless, with everything in its place, and not so much as a speck of dust was visible. *Typical Maureen*, he thought. Even when they were kids, her room had always been immaculate—a stark contrast to the mish-mash of sports paraphernalia and dirty laundry in which he had lived. He smiled and turned to face her. "You still paint all your interior walls every six months?"

"Oh, I'm not that bad." She gave him an impish smile. "Am I?"

"Well, I always thought you were the family's token obsessive compulsive. Hell, sis, compared to you, I was a feral child."

Houston walked deeper into the room, stepped over to the fireplace and stood mute, staring at the pictures on the mantle. The centerpiece of the display was a family photo; Houston was in his Marine uniform.

"Do you remember when that was taken?" Maureen asked him. "It was the morning you left for Somalia." The fact that she felt it was necessary to provide him with commentary was not lost on Houston.

"Dad died a year later," he said. "I couldn't make the funeral."

"That's a lot of bull and you know it. The Marines would have let you come home."

"The Marines had nothing to do with it."

"Most of the family was very upset with you. However, I knew the real reason you didn't come. You idolized him—and he you."

"I didn't want my last memory of him to be him in a coffin. I guess I thought if I never saw him like that it would be easier to pretend he was still around."

"Nothing ever gets resolved by running, Mike—or by hiding behind a macho tough-guy persona."

Houston sighed. Where his family was involved he had made a great number of mistakes—many of which could have been avoided. He took a deep breath. "Where's Susie?"

"In the guest room. Go up and see her. When you weren't here by one, I made something for us. I can make you a sandwich if you'd like."

"I'm fine." He looked at the top of the stairs. "I'll just go on up."

With each step up the stairs, Houston's apprehension grew. He could not forget his daughter's anger when he had visited her dormitory. Never in his wildest fantasy had he thought he would see a look like that on her face—at least not directed at him. He remembered her as a two-year-old daddy's girl and preferred that memory over the image of her as an angry adult. As he approached the closed door, each step seemed like a mile. He forced a smile, knocked on the door and opened it before she asked him in.

Susie sat on the bed and when he walked through the door, she stared at him, her face a mask of accusation and anger. Without a word, she got up, pushed past him and left the room.

"Susie . . ."

She ignored his call and dashed down the stairs.

Houston followed her. When he reached the living room, Susie stood beside Maureen. She glared at him as he descended the stairs. Maureen's back was to him as she tried to intervene, hoping to avoid another bad scene. "Susie, for all your father's faults, he does love you . . ."

"I'm sorry I'm late. The sniper struck again this morning and . . . well you know how it is."

Maureen turned and from her expression he knew that he'd said the wrong thing. Suzie's face reddened with horrific anger. "Stop it, Dad. You and I both know your job has always come first—it always has and it always will. Why are you here anyway? You've already told me Mom was murdered. Isn't there somebody who needs you to rescue them?" Her face torqued frightfully and she began to cry. Her tears made him feel that all he was to her was a symbol of loss. She turned away from Houston and wrapped her arms around her torso. "How could you leave me like that?"

He misunderstood her meaning. "You told me to get out . . ."

"I'm not talking about the dorm."

Houston stepped forward, turned her, and then draped his arms around his only child, keeping his injured hands from contacting her. When Susie pressed against his chest, he held her as she sobbed.

Fighting valiantly to maintain self-control, Houston swallowed the lump that stuck in his throat. Hot tears streaked his cheeks and he forgot about his damaged hands and pulled her snug against him. Ignoring the throbbing pain in his hands, he held his daughter. At that moment, Houston felt that maybe things would be all right between them. As quickly as it started, Susie's anguish burned itself out. She pushed against his chest and pulled free from his arms. His hopes were dashed when she curled her hand into a fist and confronted him. Then she stopped, her arm poised, like an angry rattlesnake ready to strike.

Maureen stepped between them. "No . . . there's been enough hurt and pain already. Don't add to it."

Susie's arm slowly dropped to her side. She spun away and flopped into a chair.

Houston backed up a step and sat in a chair across from her. "Susie, I know I was wrong and I made some poor choices. Now I'm trying to make up for all that. I came here because I thought you might need me."

"*I* might need you? Where were you for the past six years when I needed a father? You were off saving Boston. For you everything came before Mom and me. You didn't come for my birthdays or even my graduation. How could you not be there? I kept scanning the crowd, searching for you, but you couldn't—or wouldn't—be there for me."

She was right. He had not been there and, given the situation, to tell her that her mother had requested that he stay away would not help matters. It would only sound like an excuse.

"Susie, you're right. There's no arguing that I haven't been anything close to a father for a long time. But we can talk about that later. For right now, let's call a truce. I won't act like nothing has happened for the past six years . . ."

"Why shouldn't you—isn't that exactly what has happened for the past six years?"

"I screwed up. I won't deny that. But right now we have more pressing issues to discuss."

Susie stared at him. "I hope you haven't come here expecting to take over the funeral arrangements, because if you have you can just forget it. Aunt Maureen, Uncle Lee, and I have already made the arrangements."

"No, Susie, that's not what I meant. We need to talk."

"Okay, if you two aren't going to kill each other I'll leave you alone."

"Mo, you need to hear this too."

Maureen froze in place, a quizzical expression on her face. "I'm not sure I like the tone of your voice."

"Please, Mo, sit and hear me out."

Maureen sank into the couch across from the combatants. "I'm listening."

"What I have to say is going to make you angry and at the same time may frighten you, but you have to know. Two days ago a sniper assassinated four people on the Boston Common."

"That's been all over the news," Maureen said.

"The same person or persons killed Pam. The reason I was late getting here was because I met an old friend for breakfast—a guy I was in the Corps with. He had a list of former military snipers who live in this area. As he was leaving the restaurant, the sniper killed him and shot at me."

They stared at him.

"I think that whatever he's after involves me."

"What?" Maureen was aghast. "Oh my God, does this have anything to do with you being a sniper in the Marines?"

"We're looking into that. But . . ." he turned to face Susie, "he knows who you are."

He knew he had lost any ground he may have gained with Susie when her mouth opened and she paled. "And you came here? What if he followed you?"

"The house is under watch."

"That explains the police cruising past the front of the house for the past day and a half," Maureen said.

He turned to Maureen. "If he knows Pam and Susie, he may also know about you and Lee, Mo."

Maureen's face became ashen. She leapt from the couch. "The kids— they're at day camp . . ."

"Where?"

"At the church."

Houston walked into the kitchen, snatched the wall phone from its cradle and entered the number for Anne's cell phone. He waited a second and then said, "Hi, Anne. We got a problem. My sister's kids attend summer day camp at the First Congregationalist Church in Winchester. How soon can we get someone over there?"

"I can run over there, but it's going to take a while before we can get anyone on-site."

"Okay. Get there as soon as you can. In the meantime, I'll try another avenue."

"Like what?"

"Jimmy O doesn't have to deal with bureaucracy. He'll have people there in less time than it will take us to find out who we need to talk to."

"Mike, isn't that a bit extreme?"

"Under normal circumstances, I'd agree with you. But he's already in this up to his neck. I'll explain it later."

It took Houston less than a minute to get Jimmy O on the phone. He laid out the situation and felt instant relief when O'Leary said, "There will be someone there in fifteen minutes."

"Jimmy," Houston knew he had to be careful how he phrased what he had to say, "I doubt the church members will allow anyone they don't know near the kids. In fact, they'll probably be less than thrilled about any strangers walking in."

"Don't worry," O'Leary said, "they'll keep their distance. No one will even know they're there."

Houston replaced the phone and returned to the living room. "The kids are taken care of." Not wanting to deal with Maureen's objections to Jimmy O being involved, he said, "My partner is arranging for increased security at the day camp."

"I'm sorry, Mike, but I don't trust your so-called police security. I'm calling Lee at work. I want him and the kids to come home right now." She began to pace, shaking her hands as if they were dripping wet, a sign Mike knew well from their childhood.

Susie glared at Houston. "Are you saying that some creep with a grudge against you killed Mom?"

Houston turned to his daughter. "Yes, I'm afraid I am."

"You've finally done it, haven't you?"

Houston braced for the shot that he knew she was about to take.

"After all these years, you've finally done what you always said you'd never do—you've brought your job home."

18

"A sniper must remember that his camouflage need be so perfect that he should fail to be recognized . . . be able to be looked at directly and not be seen."
—*US Marine Corps Scout/Sniper Training Manual*

When Houston woke up it was early, barely daylight. He mechanically made his morning coffee. His meeting with Susie still disturbed him. There was no denying that the rift between them had grown into a chasm. He drank a cup of coffee and wondered if they could ever have any semblance of a normal father-daughter relationship. He paused, stumbling over the word *normal*. The truth was that he had no idea what it meant. Since his divorce, the only thing in his life that came close to approaching normalcy was his relationship with Anne—and due to the fact that they had to keep their feelings for each other hidden while on the job, calling that normal was a stretch.

His train of thought shifted and he began to think about the sniper. This case was complicating his life more than any other had. He paused and realized that he was deluding himself; his life had always been a complicated mess—his real problem was that this case was forcing him to face things he would rather avoid.

At six thirty, he left for the police station.

Arriving at the station, his first stop was at the copier. He made a duplicate of Drews's database. He knew that if he kept it out of evidence much longer there might be issues with the chain of custody. There was also the fact that if Dysart had it, he could assign additional manpower to check out many of the names in it.

He sat at his desk, studying the names. While he recalled many of those listed in the file, most were people he had never heard of. The list made him realize how quickly the years were passing by—it had been almost fifteen years since his discharge. A lot of marines had come and gone in that span of time. He leaned back and stretched, loosening the knots in his back. On a positive note, the list of names gave him a place to start.

Anne walked in at eight and sat down beside his desk. She placed a cup of Dunkin' Donuts coffee in front of him. "Don't tell me you've been here all night."

"Nope, I got in around seven."

"How'd it go yesterday?"

He picked up the coffee, held it to his lips, and glanced at her over the rim of the Styrofoam cup.

"With Susie," she said, "how did it go?"

"About as expected. I think she probably wishes the sniper had shot me instead of Pam."

"Oh, come on now, aren't you being a bit melodramatic?"

"You weren't there. Believe me when I say my daughter hates me more than anyone else on earth. In the next few days, should you get a call that I've been murdered, put Susie at the top of your suspect list."

Anne sipped her coffee and then placed the cup on the desk. "Well, Mike, I don't know what you thought her reaction would be, but it sounds to me like you got your eyes opened."

He stared at his coffee for a few seconds and then placed it beside Anne's. "I've been operating under a delusion. I always thought that she'd understood the way things were between her mother and me—obviously, she didn't."

"Mike, what do you expect? For six years, you've been out of her life. Now somebody shoots her mother down as if she were a fox caught raiding a chicken coop and you expect Susie to greet you with open arms. Come on, it took years for the relationship to degrade to this point and you can't expect to make it right with a single visit."

"I know that—I guess I wasn't prepared for her to hate me."

"I doubt she hates you. She's young and hurting and doesn't know who to blame—right now, you're the easiest and most likely candidate. Although I've never been a parent, it has always seemed to me that being the object of blame for everything lousy in a kid's life is part of the job."

"That sounds damned Freudian, if you ask me."

"Well, that's the way it is. I believe there are four stages in any parent-child relationship. The first stage is the child as child and the parent as protector, mentor, disciplinarian, and dictator. Second, in the child's teenage years, the parent becomes the enemy. Then, when the child is in his or her mid-twenties or early thirties, the parent and child become friends. Finally, the parent reaches old age and stage one repeats, only now the roles are reversed and the child becomes the parent and the parent becomes the child."

"It still sounds Freudian to me."

"I took a lot of psychology courses in college."

"It reminds me of something my mother once said. She told me we are all once an adult and twice a child."

"Well, I wouldn't worry about it too much. Susie will come around, but it's going to take time."

Houston leaned back in his chair. "I hate that . . ."

"What?"

"That *it'll take time* stuff. I want it now."

"As impatient as you are, how did you ever survive as a sniper?"

"That was different. A sniper without self-discipline doesn't survive."

"Maybe you should view your situation with Susie the same way. Be patient and let it happen in its own time. If you try to force it you could do more damage. There is one silver lining to this cloud though."

"And what might that be?"

"Kids are quick to condemn, but they're just as quick to forgive. Susie may yet realize that whether she likes it or not, she has only one parent now. That alone could have an impact."

Houston stared at her for a moment. "For someone who never had a child you seem to have a good handle on this. Where did you get so knowledgeable?"

"I spend a lot of time with a guy who's emotionally still a child . . ."

"Ouch." Houston leaned back in his chair and grinned.

Anne picked up her coffee, sipped it and pointed at the folder on his desk. "You find anything we can use?"

"Maybe."

She looked at Houston and waited for him to elaborate.

"Danny was meticulous in his record keeping. He compiled a list of every scout/sniper who's stayed in touch or ever gone to one of their reunions."

She sipped her coffee. "You know, I still never would have thought that ex-military would have reunions."

"Why wouldn't we? You keep in touch with students with whom you were close in college, don't you? For many veterans, military service was the most important thing we've ever done. We were young, many of us on our own for the first time, and we developed a camaraderie only people who have been in life threatening situations together can—kind of like you and me. Someone who hasn't shared the experiences you and I have would never understand our relationship."

Anne thought for a few seconds and smiled. "I can understand that. There are times when I don't understand our relationship. I assume that you mean they wouldn't understand why I put up with you?"

He returned her smile. "Exactly."

Houston continued reading the file. He flipped through the papers, turning to the section where the names were listed by state of residence, concentrating on the Massachusetts listing. Danny had four names listed in the Boston area; three of them were new to Houston, but the fourth he knew very well. "Here's a possibility. Steve Northrup lives at 1369 Mayflower Street."

Anne took her cell phone out of her purse. "Did he include a phone number?"

"Yeah." Houston read the number from the file and she punched it into her cell phone with her thumb, a trick he had seen her do many times, usually when she was driving. If he tried doing that, he would wreck the car.

She listened for a second and then said, "Sorry, wrong number." She turned off the phone. "It's the Belknap Foundation, a drug rehab center in Dorchester."

"It sounds as if you're familiar with it."

"It's one of the better rehab facilities in the Boston area. William Belknap was a high-powered criminal defense lawyer, right up there with F. Lee Bailey and Johnny Cochran." She put her cell in her purse and paused to sip from her coffee. "His son became hooked on drugs when he was in the army serving in Vietnam. Within a couple of weeks of coming home, the kid overdosed."

"There are people who can't deal with combat situations. I remember when I returned from Somalia, I went through a period of depression. Only rather than drugs, I turned to booze."

Anne looked at him with a level of interest he only saw occasionally. Before she could pursue this new topic, he said, "You were saying?"

"The boy was his only child and Belknap took it hard. When the old man died, he had no heirs he cared about, so he left millions in a trust to set up the foundation. Any addict can go there, but for down-and-out veterans there's no charge."

"You seem to know a lot about it."

"When I was in Family Justice Division, I dealt with a lot of young addicts and treatment centers. You want to go over there?"

"Sure do . . . and don't spare the horses."

Steve Northrup had gone through scout/sniper training with Danny and Houston. Houston did not remember Northrup so much for what he did or how good he was. However, he did recall that he was Edwin Rosa's best, and possibly only, friend. Houston definitely wanted to talk with Steve.

The triple-deckers that lined Mayflower Street in Dorchester looked old enough to have been around when Washington and his artillery scaled Dorchester Heights and drove the English from Boston. The buildings needed a coat of paint and landscaping was nonexistent. The narrow street was lined with cars, leaving just enough room for a single vehicle to get through. For the most part, the lawns were hardpan dirt with an occasional tuft of crabgrass. The street looked like somebody had dumped chemical defoliant on it. Houston and Pam's first house had a yard like these. He smiled as he recalled how Pam let the weeds grow the first year saying, "At least the weeds are green."

It was trash pickup day and the collectors had already been through, leaving empty cans scattered between the parked cars. Gusts of wind grabbed bits of paper and blew them around until the breeze pinned them to curbs or sent them spiraling like miniature tornadoes into the narrow walkways between the buildings. Houston looked at the run-down street and decided that even though the Belknap Foundation Trust was worth millions, they were not spending it on real estate.

Anne parked in a vacant spot by a fire hydrant across from the rehab center. Houston got out of the car and stood on the sidewalk, staring at the building. It was not as aesthetic nor as intimidating as most treatment centers. It blended into the neighborhood well, providing the one thing many recovering addicts sought—anonymity.

"Something bothering you?"

Houston nodded. "I was just thinking how close I came to ending up in a place like this."

She nudged him in the ribs. "Come on, I won't let them keep you."

"Thirty million unemployed comedians and I get you."

"Seriously, I think you're looking at it wrong, Mike. These places save lives."

"As long as insurance pays for it—it's all about the money." Houston stepped off the sidewalk and crossed the street to the short walkway that led to the house. From street level, the steps didn't look as if they would support Houston's weight, and he was wary as he climbed them. In spite of their appearance, the stairs leading up to the porch were as sturdy as new construction. At first glance, the farmer's porch that ran along the front of the house didn't inspire a lot of confidence either. Houston carefully placed his feet, watching where he stepped, certain that the rotting wood would break, sending him crashing through. Like the steps, the porch was surprisingly sturdy and curiosity got the better of Houston. He inspected the building closer. The structure seemed as sound as a five hundred thousand dollar house in the suburbs. It must have taken a lot of extra work to make the renovation look as dilapidated as the rest of the neighborhood. Anne was also appraising it.

"Amazing, isn't it?" he said. "This building is an architectural chameleon! It blends right in with the neighborhood, but the porch and siding can't be more than a few years old!"

"It's the perfect disguise. I can only imagine what it must look like inside." She pressed the doorbell.

The door buzzed and they entered the building. There had been no attempt to make the interior look like a rundown tenement. Everything, from the woodwork to the carpeting, looked new and clean and smelled of fresh paint. Anne looked around with approval. "What did I tell you?"

A foyer led them past a waiting room and reception area. On the wall, directly opposite the entrance, was a sliding glass window beside which was a beautiful decorative door. Houston slid his fingers along its surface. It was composed of heavy metal and was as strong as it was exquisite; nobody was going through that door unless admitted by whoever was behind the window. Houston turned to the window and a man who looked as if he spent hours each day in the gym greeted him.

"How can I help you?"

"I'd like to see one of your patients, Stephen Northrup."

"I'm sorry; the patients are not allowed visitors."

Houston held up his badge. "This isn't a social visit. It's police business."

The weight lifter became attentive. "I don't have the authority to admit anyone." He was unable to look directly at Houston—a sign that he was uncertain about what he should do.

Houston struggled to maintain his professionalism—he was not entirely successful. "Then, suppose you get off your ass and call someone who does have the authority, before I run you in for impeding a murder investigation." He glared at the man, giving him the look that Pam once said made him look like Charles Manson. He looked at Anne and saw that she was looking away, trying to hide her broad smile from the frightened muscle-bound receptionist.

The big man grabbed the phone and punched in a three-digit number. "Doctor Russell, I got a police officer here who wants to see Northrup. Yes, ma'am, right away." He gently placed the phone in its cradle as if he were afraid the doctor would take offense if he were to replace it too hard. "Someone will be right out. Please take a seat."

Anne and Houston strolled into the waiting room. They sat in a couple of plush easy chairs. For some reason that he could not understand, the room made Houston feel like he was a teenager picking up the daughter of the richest man in town for their first date. He realized he was picking at the chair's upholstery. He stopped digging at the fabric and slid his hand across the smooth surface of the chair's arm. *Nice*, he thought. *This must have cost more than I make in a month.* Several expensive paintings—most of them seascapes—hung on the walls, giving the room a relaxing tone. Houston realized he could wait in this room for hours and not be upset. Every doctor or dentist should see this place. How they got away with condemning patients to waiting rooms—many of which were as pleasing and comfortable as cattle pens—was beyond him. Invisible speakers played soft, relaxing music. Houston was engrossed, trying to locate the enclosures, when he heard the electric bolt open.

He turned toward the sound and saw a tall brown-haired woman come through the door, her hazel eyes appraising them. Houston was glad he didn't have to undergo the scrutiny that Anne did. The woman ignored him at first, concentrating on Anne. What she saw must have satisfied her. Anne, in turn, gave her the same scathing inspection.

Houston got the distinct feeling they were never going to be friends. There was something in the way they studied each other that reminded him of two wolves sizing each other up for a tussle. He thought the match had the potential of a successful pay-per-view event. However, rather than rising to the challenge, Anne, ever the consummate professional, whipped out her credentials and had them ready.

"I'm Doctor Lara Russell," the woman said, her eyes never breaking contact with those of Anne.

"I'm Detective Bouchard and this is my partner Detective Michael Houston."

Russell glanced at their IDs. "How can I help you?"

Houston said, "We believe one of your patients, Stephen Northrup, may have some information that could help us in a case we're working on."

She shifted her attention from Anne to Houston. "He isn't with us any longer."

"Oh?" Houston said.

"He was discharged two weeks ago."

"Do you have an address where we can reach him?"

"I'm sorry, Detective, but one of the most important components of an addict's recovery is anonymity. We're not at liberty to give out any information."

Out of the corner of his eye, Houston saw Anne tense and moved quickly to defuse the situation. He took the doctor by the arm and guided her to a remote part of the room. As they walked he decided that given the situation a small lie would not hurt. "Listen, Doctor Russell, I'm a friend of Bill W. myself and I was with Steve in the service. This is not exactly all business—you know what I mean?"

Mentioning Bill Wilson, the co-founder of Alcoholics Anonymous, took most of the tension out of her. She seemed to overcome the strain that for some reason had developed between her and Anne. She visibly relaxed and motioned for them to have a seat. She looked at Anne. "You'll have to forgive my defensiveness but it hasn't been one of my better days."

Anne accepted the doctor's apology. "That happens." She too seemed to relax.

"Getting back to Steve." Russell seemed tentative, still unsure of how much she should tell the police. "Well, his prognosis isn't as good as I had hoped it would be. We discharged him to a halfway house. This morning I got a call from Dave Kapoor, one of the counselors there. Steve's been acting strange lately, coming in late and leaving early. He's beginning to act as if he's using again—he seems to be regressing, exhibiting some of his old behavior patterns." Her eyes seemed to bore into Houston's. "And I don't have to tell you how dangerous that can be. In here, he was doing okay, but he seems to have started to slip right after an old friend suddenly appeared—"

"Do you know who this friend is?" Houston asked.

"Unfortunately, Steve is being very secretive—another bad sign." As she spoke, her hands were in perpetual motion. "Discharging Steve was against my better judgment. I didn't feel he was ready. His program is shaky—and that's when he works it. Nevertheless, when he agreed to enter the halfway house, I acquiesced."

"Where is this halfway house?"

"In Mattapan. I'll get the address from Charlie and give it to you." She walked to the window to speak with Mr. Universe for a few seconds, then came back with a slip of paper. She handed it to Houston, then looked at Anne. "Detectives, if there is any chance he has slipped please tell him we're still here for him."

Once they were in their car, Houston looked at Anne. "What was that all about in there?"

"I don't know. Have you ever met someone you immediately didn't like?"

"A time or two."

She put the car in gear. "So, what you say we go find Steve Northrup?"

———

As he had been doing for the past three days, the sniper followed Houston and the woman to the rehab center. He parked down the block, backing into a narrow driveway that separated two of the triple-decker houses. He rolled down his window and lit a cigarette. He settled back and sipped on a takeout cup of coffee—who knew how long Houston would be in there?

Less than twenty minutes later, Houston and the woman reappeared. He watched them walk to their car and drive off. There was no need to follow them; he knew where they were going. He drove out of the alley.

19

"... mobility multiplied the effectiveness of snipers in urban environments ..."
—Gunnery Sergeant Jack Coughlin, USMC

The halfway house's appearance was nothing like the Belknap Foundation's rehabilitation center. In fact, it was far from being the most impressive house on the block, yet it was far from being the least. Houston thought that a coat of fresh paint would do wonders for the place. As they approached the door Anne asked, "How do we play this one?"

"By ear. I don't think Northrup's going to buy any bullshit about my wanting to get together with an old comrade-in-arms. We were never that close and were never on friendly terms. Besides, if he's the sniper, he'll know why we're here."

An emaciated man answered the door. He was so gaunt and frail that Houston couldn't estimate his age, but knew that he was probably younger than he appeared. He wore a T-shirt that was way overdue for an appointment with the inside of a washing machine and a cigarette dangled from his lips. His eyelids closed to slits as they fought a losing battle to avoid the steady stream of smoke that rose along his face. When he said "Yeah?" the inch of ash that drooped from the end of his cigarette fell, bounced off his chest and he rubbed at it—grinding yet another gray smear into his filthy shirt.

Houston suddenly understood how Anne had felt with Lara Russell. This punk had only said one word to him and he didn't like him. He presented his badge. "I'm looking for Steve Northrup."

"He ain't here."

"Well, maybe you can tell us where he is."

"Sure, he walked down to the corner for a pack of butts. He's been gone about twenty minutes. I expect him back anytime now."

"We'll wait." Houston started to push past him. Before he could pass him, the man raised a scrawny, tattooed arm and pointed down the street. Houston's nose was on an even plane with his underarm and the musky odor told him the man hadn't showered since he had last laundered the grungy T-shirt. "There he is now."

Houston spun on his heels and looked down the street. Northrup wore a blue Patriots jacket, jeans and running shoes and shuffled toward the halfway house. The years had been hard on him. His hair was unkempt and a week's growth of beard made him look twenty years older than he was. Still, in spite of his appearance, Houston recognized him.

When he turned onto the street where the halfway house was located, the sniper immediately hit the brakes. Somehow or another, the cops had beaten him there. He saw Houston's familiar figure standing on the porch, talking to the loser who managed the place. Then he saw Northrup strolling along the street. When Northrup spun on his heels and ran into an alley, the sniper backed up and turned down the first street. He knew where Steve would come out and in which direction he would run. He had no reservations as to whether or not Northrup would spill his guts to Houston—after all, he was a junkie and everyone knew how untrustworthy they were.

The street passed through the parking lot that bordered an athletic field/playground complex. The sniper pulled into a parking spot that gave him a good view of the park's rear exit. He reached behind his seat, grasped his rifle and placed it across his lap.

Northrup turned into the walk, saw the people on the porch and stopped abruptly. Houston wasn't sure if Northrup recognized him or not, but he was positive that the addict's police detection system went off and he identified them as cops. He spun around and ran down the block.

Houston sprinted after him and Anne ran for the car.

Northrup turned into a narrow alley and Houston lost sight of him. By the time he followed him into the alley, Northrup was through the other side and out of sight.

Houston skidded to a stop before the narrow passage, trying to figure out which direction his quarry had taken. He heard the loud bang of garbage cans falling and ran toward the sound. He paused for a second and viewed the alley. Debris and garbage lay everywhere. Two garbage cans were on their sides, still rolling. Houston ran into the alley. He leapt over the rolling cans and concentrated on the lane before him. Either Northrup was in better shape than he appeared at first glance or he was scared out of his wits—the speed at which he ran surprised Houston. He accelerated, ignoring the stitch in his side. By the time he broke out of the alley, his breathing was labored. Just as Houston was about to give up the chase, he saw Northrup race through a small park and vault over a bunch of toddlers at play.

Houston was tempted to call out to him, but decided to save his breath for running. Seeing his target so close made him forget his pain and he put out another burst of speed. When he entered the park, he could see that Northrup was finally tiring. Out of a corner of his eye, Houston caught the flash of light shining from something in the parking lot alongside the softball field. When Northrup ran up some old wooden bleachers, he was able to close the gap.

Then Northrup made a fatal mistake. He might have gotten away if he hadn't paused and looked back to see where Houston was before jumping from the top row of bleacher seats. He coiled, preparing to leap when there was the unmistakable sound of gunfire. Northrup's arms windmilled and flapped like a baby bird attempting to fly for the first time. For a second or two he fought to maintain his balance, lost his battle against gravity and fell back, turning in the air.

Houston stopped running, took his pistol from its holster and quickly checked to ensure the kids were all right. He saw an adult herding the children away from the area. Believing that the kids were safe, he scanned the area, hoping to find the sniper's position. He noted a line of maple trees bordering the parking lot beside the softball field and knew that had been the sniper's location. He vacillated for a second, decided that determining Northrup's condition was the most pressing issue and then circled the bleachers. Northrup lay on the ground, blood pulsing from his chest as his heart pumped like a piston. Houston knew he'd be dead in minutes.

Houston ran to him. "Who's the sniper, Steve?"

Northrup stared at Houston, his eyes glazed with shock. When he smiled, frothy blood and sputum dripped from his mouth. Even if he wanted to talk, he couldn't. His lungs were filling with blood, drowning him. He coughed and another dark clot dripped from his mouth and stuck to his chin. Houston knew that Northrup understood what had happened and had come to grips with it. He gave Houston a mocking smile, hacked up another wad of blood and died.

"I'm exhausted."

Anne looked at Houston with concern. "You've been burning the proverbial candle at both ends since this case started."

He picked up the bill, glanced at it quickly and placed a credit card in the small plastic pouch in the folder. The waiter immediately appeared, scooped it up and walked away.

"It must be time to leave," Anne said. "They want the table."

"It's been another bitch of a day," Houston said.

"They all will be until we bring this guy down."

"I think we're close."

"I get the feeling this perp is playing us, making sure we stay close."

"I know," Houston replied. "He wants to ensure we stay on his trail. I only wish I knew what his agenda is."

"It's pretty obvious that you're his agenda, Mike. He's done everything he could to make that clear."

Houston stared out the window. It was dark outside. In the glass he saw the reflection of a man battling stress and fatigue. He turned away and faced Anne. "What bothers me is that he seems to show up wherever we are. His being in position to shoot Northrup was no coincidence."

"Are you implying that he's stalking us?"

"Nothing else makes sense. He's killed three people that we interviewed and could have had me any number of times. I'm starting to feel like a mouse that has been caught by a cat. He's toying with me and I don't like it."

Anne's eyes softened and she took a final sip of her margarita. "Do you think he has an inside source?"

"Inside what?"

"Inside the department. How else could he possibly know our every move?" She grew pensive. "I guess that doesn't make sense. Most of the time we don't know what we're going to do until we do it."

"Snipers seldom, if ever, work alone. It wouldn't surprise me if he has a network of accomplices. As for a source inside the department, I doubt it."

The waiter returned with the receipt, put it on the table and left. Houston reviewed the bill, added the tip and signed it.

"Maybe," he said, "we should be looking for them rather than the sniper. They might lead us to him."

———————

The sniper phoned at eleven o'clock that night. Houston picked the phone up on the second ring and heard the raspy voice. "Too bad about Northrup, huh?"

"You're a sick bastard."

"C'mon, Mike, let's be grown up about this. Calling me names isn't going to goad me into making a mistake. I'm too good for that."

"What's this all about?"

"It's about us. You and me on a private island I know about. I want to settle this the way we should have years ago—one-on-one, mano a mano. Think about it this way—at least you'll have a better chance than most people."

"I'm going to bring you down, and when I do you won't have to worry about due process either."

The sniper laughed. "I ain't letting go of this, old buddy. You'll come around, you'll see—even if I have to kill every friend and relative you have. Your partner and daughter for instance. So think it over, Mike. One way or the other you're gonna do it my way. If you don't believe me, turn on the local news. The shit is hitting the fan."

He broke the connection.

Houston hung up and turned on the television. Amanda Boyce stood in front of a hospital, the entrance to the emergency room behind her. "Son of a bitch."

"William Tyson, an appliance repair man was attacked and seriously injured by a mob of panicked residents of Dorchester, this afternoon. At this time, Tyson's condition is unknown. WBO news will keep you abreast of events as they occur."

The screen split, showing the in-studio anchor on one half and Boyce on the other. *"Amanda, has anything been announced as to what motivated the attack?"*

"Tyson was driving a white van. A witness to the attack told me that the mob believed the van was that of the sniper who has been terrorizing the city for the past several days, Paul."

"Thanks, Amanda."

Houston turned the TV off and called Anne to fill her in on the sniper's most recent contact.

"Did he say what he wants?"

"What we thought. Me—only he's got some crazy idea about us playing sniper on an isolated island."

"That's insane. You're not considering it are you?"

"Only as a last resort."

Anne detected concern in his voice. "What's wrong?"

"Nothing is wrong—I guess that's what's wrong."

"He'll make a mistake, Mike. They all do."

"Maybe what bothers me is that he hasn't yet."

The sniper hung up the phone and poured more bourbon in the plastic hotel glass. He gulped the whiskey down and picked up the bottle. He stared at the label. "Here's to Kentucky—the home of good whiskey, fast women, and beautiful horses." He barely recalled life there, one to which he could never return.

A local cable news channel was on the television; the anchors rehashed the story of Steve's death for the fifth time in an hour. He poured another glassful of alcohol and toasted the TV. "Here's to fallen comrades: past, present, and future."

He poured the liquor down his throat, flopped on the bed and stared at the ceiling. He hoped the sour mash would hit him and let him sleep without dreams of fire and agonizing pain—he hoped that, just once, he could have a night without reliving that part of his life. Eventually, he drifted off and in no time, he began to sweat and toss about.

As soon as he descended into REM sleep, they came back. The snarling black faces with yellowed teeth closed in on him, poked at his charbroiled body and tested his ability to withstand pain. The ghostly figures tormented him through the night as he twisted and struggled. . . .

20

It was going to be a lousy morning. Public hysteria had reached an all-time peak and everyone was screaming for someone's head on a platter. Captain Dysart called and ordered Houston and Anne to be in his office first thing. Houston knew that the purpose of the meeting was not to tell them what a fantastic job they were doing. They were barely in their seats when Dysart went on the attack.

"What in hell are you two doing? I got the mayor on my ass as well as the commissioner! In the three days you've been on this case, we've had a body count higher than Kandahar. Now, you go and get a potential witness shot."

"Come on, Captain," Houston protested, "Northrup wasn't a potential witness—if anything, he was an accomplice. The sniper knew we were after him and somehow or another got there in time to make sure we couldn't learn anything from him."

"Regardless, the top cop is tired of the media making us look like a bunch of bumbling fools, while the body count keeps going up. Now, we even got mobs stomping the shit out of anyone unfortunate enough to be caught driving a white van."

Houston knew Dysart was right. Having vented his frustration, Dysart walked to his office's sole window and lit a cigarette. He took a drag and exhaled the smoke through the open window. "It's a stupid goddamned law that won't let a man smoke in his own office." He tossed the cigarette out the window and stared after it. Houston would have thought Dysart was watching a close friend fall to his death. "Almost ten bucks a pack and I take two drags and throw it out." Dysart flopped into his chair. "All right, tell me what you got."

Anne deferred to Houston. "Tell him. After all, this seems to be about you."

"What?" Dysart leaned forward, his face inches from Houston's face. "What in the hell is she talking about?"

"Unfortunately, we believe the sniper is linked to my past. Our best suspect is a guy named Edwin Rosa."

"Okay. So what's being done to find him?"

"That's where we have a bit of a dilemma . . . Rosa has been listed as MIA for over fifteen years. One thing is certain though: whoever this perp is, he wants to go one-on-one with me."

"Look into it . . . don't overlook any lead, no matter how unlikely you may think it is."

"No one will be more surprised than me if Rosa turns out to be the shooter. However, we can't ignore the fact that two of the victims had history with me—Danny Drews and my ex-wife, Pam. And the victims near the Marriott were witnesses we'd interrogated just hours before they were shot. Then there's the fact that he's been calling me."

"This bastard has been calling you and you didn't report it?" Dysart looked at Anne. "I want a tap on his phone—*now*."

Anne stood but she stopped when Houston touched her arm.

"It won't do any good, Cap," Houston said. "He doesn't stay on the line longer than a few seconds and I'm sure he's using some type of untraceable phone—probably a disposable cell or pay phone."

"Like I could give a shit—I still want a tap on your phone."

"I think it's a waste of time and effort . . ."

"Since when does what you think matter? What's goin' on, Mike? Is your social life so busy that you don't want us listening in?"

Dysart cast a quick glance at Anne. Houston noted that there was the slightest suggestion of a blush on her cheeks.

"Then the tap goes on," Dysart said. "Now tell me what you got and don't leave anything out. I got to give the higher-ups something . . ."

Houston shuffled his feet.

Dysart saw that something was on Houston's mind. "Why do I feel that you're about to make my day even shittier?"

"Well," Houston said, "the shooter seems to show up everywhere we go. Some way or another he is keeping tabs on us."

"That may give us a chance," Dysart said. "I'm going to have our people on you two every minute of the day . . . maybe that will flush him out."

"On the other hand," Houston replied, "if he spots our people, he'll have more targets of opportunity."

Dysart flopped into his chair and a pensive look came over his face. "There is one other possibility," he said.

"We're listening," Houston said.

"A scanner—he's got a friggin' scanner and is listening in every time you update dispatch with your whereabouts or your next destination. As of right now, you stop using your radio when you go somewhere. I'd even be careful what you say on a cell phone, those calls can be picked up too."

As if on cue, Anne's cell phone chirped. Rather than upset Dysart any further, she ignored it.

The phone chirped again.

"Well," Dysart said, "answer the goddamn thing."

Anne flipped the phone open. "Bouchard . . ."

She listened quietly for a few seconds. "That's great, thanks." She closed the phone.

Houston and Dysart looked at her.

"We got an address for his Mattapan crib . . ."

The house in Mattapan was a wreck, located on yet another narrow street in another lower-class neighborhood. Houston would not have been surprised to learn that the city had condemned it. The outside hadn't been painted in years, the windows were so weathered it looked as if the slightest vibration would knock the glass out of its panes. The yard was so full of litter that it could have passed for a garbage dump. What little vegetation there was on the lawn resembled tufts of hair on a chemo patient's head. Houston and Anne stood beside their car about a half block away, drinking coffee.

"I don't see a van," Anne said.

"He's too smart to leave it out where we'd see it. In fact, it wouldn't surprise me if the son of a bitch didn't have several places to flop. If I were him, I'd have at least a couple of places."

The two-way radio in their car crackled and they heard a voice say, "SWAT three in place."

Houston cursed. "Goddamn it, we told them no radio traffic. If he's got a scanner he knows we're here. We'd better move."

He opened the trunk, handed Anne a Kevlar vest and put his on. "These won't do us much good."

"Oh?" Anne said.

"If he's in there, he's going to figure we'll be wearing armor and will go for head shots."

"You always were a cheerful SOB, Mike."

"I'm a realist—I've always believed in Murphy's law."

They saw several cops walking toward the tenement and went to meet them. Houston stopped beside Corso and Bullard, two of his fellow detectives, and nodded.

"We figured you two might need some help," Bullard said.

"Right, so how we going to do this?"

"It's your show. You call it," Corso said. He checked his pistol, reseating the magazine, and flipped the safety off.

"SWAT will go in first and we'll go with them," Houston said. "You two circle around and watch the rear."

"Well," Bullard said, "let's get to it. I don't want to be late for lunch."

Houston glanced at the detective's large stomach. "You haven't missed a meal in years, Elwood."

"Don't intend to either."

Houston and Anne followed two SWAT members into the dark building and up to the second floor. They positioned themselves on either side of the door to apartment 3. Houston waited for the SWAT team to indicate they were ready and then shouted, "Police, open up!"

There was no response. The SWAT team used a ram to bust the door open. It slammed against the wall and rebounded back. A SWAT cop pushed the door with his shoulder and they rushed in. Cops moved cautiously through the apartment shouting "Kitchen clear," "Bedroom clear," until they had checked the entire apartment. The SWAT team commander turned to Houston and then jabbed his pistol into its holster. "Looks like he got wind of us."

"More likely he's got a number of burrows." Houston walked into the living room and saw a sheet of paper taped to the TV screen. He bent down, without touching it, and read *Hey, Mikey. Sorry I missed you, but we'll get together yet.*

"Crime Scene Unit is on the way," Anne said.

"Probably a waste of time. I doubt they'll find anything."

"This guy seems to be charmed."

"I think he's good. Stealth is a sniper's greatest weapon . . . they must stay concealed if they're going to survive. He's probably got a number of hides and rotates where he sleeps—never in the same place two nights in a row."

From a safe distance, the sniper half-listened to the static squawk of his portable scanner and observed the activity around the old triple-decker. He watched cops scurry around the apartment building like roaches on a dirty plate. The police were getting closer. It was only a matter of time before they found his other warrens. It was time to escalate his plan. He moved the gearshift into drive and drove away. He turned the corner, making sure he used his turn signal. The last thing he needed was for some overzealous cop to pull him over for violating a traffic law.

———————

Houston and Anne spent the day at the Mattapan hideout, then went to his apartment. They spent the evening going over their files and notes on the killings. Somewhere, in the list of names and addresses Drews had provided, was a link and if they had to, they would visit and revisit every name in that file.

Houston was studying the files when Anne flopped down beside him on the couch. "Mike, what are you going to do about Susie?"

"That isn't up to me. I want nothing more than a decent relationship with her. However, I have no control over the situation. Susie has it all."

"Well, you need to control what *you* do. You need to start getting involved in her life. I'm certain of one thing—she needs you as much as you need her. Besides, I'm going to nag at you until you do it."

"Okay, I'll do what I can."

"Pam's funeral is tomorrow . . . seems to me that may be a good place to start."

21

"The sniper must be alert at all times. Any relaxation on a
stalk could lead to carelessness . . ."
—*US Marine Corps Scout/Sniper Training Manual*

Susie lay in bed, burrowed under the covers. She heard the sound of pots and pans clattering in the kitchen and knew her aunt was cleaning up after breakfast. The sounds mixed with the pounding of her cousins' feet as they ran through the house.

Her thoughts turned to her father. She knew that she had been hard on him, but there was a part of her that couldn't help but want to make him pay for deserting her. Still, she wasn't a child any longer and she understood that her parents' relationship was a lot more complex than it seemed.

She got out of bed, walked to the window and stared at the subdivision's perfectly manicured lawns. She absentmindedly watched a white van slowly pass by the house. It stopped for a second, as if the driver were looking for an address, and then moved down the street.

Houston turned his collar up against the drizzle and mist as he and Anne walked across the freshly mown grass. He always felt uncomfortable in cemeteries, but the prospect of facing O'Leary for the first time since

Pam's murder was daunting. Now Jimmy would be looking at him with the knowledge that he was the underlying reason for his sister's murder. He felt guilty enough.

Maureen and her husband, Lee, met them a hundred yards short of the mound of dirt that identified the grave. He shook Lee's hand and hugged his sister.

"You okay?" Lee asked.

"I've been better. I feel kind of like John Wayne Gacy, waiting for the hot needle."

"Well, we won't let anyone do that to you—not today anyway." Maureen smiled at Anne. "You must be his partner, Anne. How are you?"

"I'm as well as anyone who spends most of her time with your brother can be." Anne smiled and shook Maureen's hand.

"Well, I suppose we'd better go on down." Maureen looped her arm in Houston's.

"Where's Susie?"

"With Jimmy," Maureen said. "He picked her up early this morning."

"I think I'll give her some space."

"That may be the wrong thing to do," Maureen said. "Whether she knows it or not, she needs you. Besides, now more than ever, if you want to mend fences with her, you need to act like a father and be there for her."

"What if she doesn't want me there?"

"She does. She may not be able to admit it right now, but you're all she's got left."

Houston looked at the gathered mourners and located Susie. She stood beside her uncle, their arms intertwined. He tensed when he saw her and he felt Maureen tighten her grip on his right arm.

"Come on, hero," she said. "We'll help you through this."

They walked to the gravesite, where Maureen released her grip on his arm and urged him to stand beside Susie. Houston stood stoic. Afraid to look at his daughter, he concentrated on the coffin. He felt strangely safe with Anne on his left. Maureen stood on Susie's right and gripped her niece's hand.

The casket was under a canopy, protected from the rain, and suspended on a transom that hovered over Pam's final resting place. Houston didn't want to appear anxious, but was unable to keep from glancing at his daughter. He watched Susie from the corner of his eye, looking for any sign of encouragement. She appeared to be avoiding him intentionally.

Houston turned his attention to Anne and immediately relaxed. He realized what an anchor she was. No matter what, Anne was always there for him.

Jimmy O and Gordon Winter stood on the other side of Anne. Pam's death had shaken O'Leary and he barely moved his head when he nodded to Houston.

The priest began the graveside ceremony and Houston blocked him out, studying the people gathered around. Several of Pam's old friends stood by the grave, at least one of whom gave him a disapproving look. He did not dwell on those people and eventually he moved his observation to the surrounding gravesites. His eyes wandered away from the ceremony. Looking beyond the coffin, his attention turned to the slope of the land. His breath caught in his throat when he spied a white van parked on the hill overlooking the funeral.

For several moments, Houston debated whether to remain or to walk to the van and see who was in it. As much as his curiosity about the van ate at him, he knew that for him to leave at that moment would definitely exacerbate the situation between him and his daughter, so he stood fast. But he continued to watch the van. Just when he finally made up his mind to investigate, someone gripped his arm. He looked down and saw Susie's hand on his forearm. He reached across his body and patted it. Susie slid her hand down, grasped his hand and held it in a tight grip.

From the corner of his eye, Houston saw Anne looking in his direction. When she saw Susie holding her father's hand, she smiled.

Houston immediately forgot about the van and looked at his daughter. His knees went weak when Susie pulled closer, let go of his hand and intertwined her arm with his. He felt her body tremble as she struggled to maintain her composure. She wept silently, tears tracking down her cheeks. He gently freed her arm from his and placed it around her shoulders. Susie turned, pressed her face against his side. Sobs wracked her body.

Houston hugged her tightly and returned his gaze to the van. Anger and a desire to lash out at the sniper filled him. The van's window rolled down and Houston wanted more than ever to confront the driver and, if it was the sniper, kill him for bringing this tragedy upon him and his daughter.

The van's door opened and a man got out and walked to the back of the truck. He opened the rear door and began to unload a floral arrangement in the shape of a white cross, which he took to another gravesite. Houston watched the florist closely, wondering if it really was a delivery or just a ruse to cover his true mission.

The driver placed a large wreath on a recent grave and walked back to his truck. He paused beside the door, looking down at Pam's funeral. Houston castigated himself for being paranoid. Then the man raised his hand and waved.

O'Leary noticed Houston looking up the hill. He looked up to see what was so interesting and saw the van. Jimmy knew it wouldn't look good if he left his sister's graveside. However, there were no restrictions on Gordon Winter. When O'Leary nudged him and nodded to the van, Winter backed out of the small congregation, circumvented the gathered mourners and started up the knoll.

As soon as he was clear of the funeral, Winter began trotting up the hill, closing with the van.

The driver stood by the truck and watched Winter approach. When they were fifty yards apart, he waved again, got in the van and drove off.

As soon as the ceremony concluded, Anne walked to Susie, hugged her. "I'm so sorry."

Susie, still too emotional to speak, wiped tears from her cheeks and nodded.

Anne sensed Houston was distracted. "What's bothering you?"

"I need to check on something, I'll only be a moment." He turned to Susie. "Will you be all right for few minutes?"

"Don't be long, Dad."

"I won't even leave your sight. No more than five minutes, I promise." He looked over his daughter's head and nodded to O'Leary. As if synchronized, they started climbing the slope to join Winter.

As they walked up the hill, rain soaked their shoulders and their feet squished in the saturated ground. Once clear of the mourners, they ran up the hill, stopping on the paved roadway where the truck had been. Houston looked in the direction the van had taken and saw no sign of it. He dismissed it from his mind and walked to O'Leary and Winter. They were studying the floral display. "You get a look at him?"

"Nope," Winter said, "he wore sunglasses and his hat was pulled low. His license plates were coated with mud and illegible. There was nothing painted on the van that would indicate which florist he was from—if he was from one."

O'Leary pulled a card off the floral arrangement and handed it to Houston, who raised the fold and read it. All that was written on the card was a name: Michael Houston.

Houston and Susie sat across the table from each other. He was suddenly aware that he had no appetite. He couldn't take his eyes away from his daughter. In his mind, she'd always been an awkward child, yet a mature young woman now sat before him. He felt old and wondered where the years had gone. He had missed so much of her life that it was as if they were meeting for the first time.

"Why did you avoid me, Dad?"

Houston looked at Susie, trying to think of an answer that didn't make him sound cowardly or uncaring—nothing came to mind. He decided that telling her the truth was better than any excuse he could conjure. However, he had to take care not to denigrate Pam and use her refusal to allow him to come around as a reason. He decided to do the right thing and placed the blame where it truly belonged, on his shoulders. "I don't know, babe. After the divorce it felt awkward being around your mother, then I buried myself in work, and finally I started drinking heavily and was too ashamed to let you see it."

She reached out and took his hand. "Aunt Mo told me a lot about you."

"Really? What did she tell you?"

Susie seemed to be bursting at the seams so Houston listened. For once in his life he had no desire to talk; all he wanted to do was listen and look at his daughter. The skinny, uncoordinated teenager had turned into a beautiful, self-assured, strong young woman. He thought about the turmoil of their home during his final years of marriage and wondered if it was her mother or him who had given her the genes that made her so strong.

"She just told me stuff, about your military service and your life—I had no idea how much violence you've dealt with."

Houston stared at her, amazed at the person she had become. It struck him that she was much more mature than most girls her age were.

"She always loved you," Susie said.

"What?"

"Mom always loved you. She told me many times that she could never find anyone who could take your place. Nevertheless, she couldn't handle your job. She told me that waiting for the knock on the door bringing news of your death was more than she could deal with."

"She never said anything to me."

"That's how much she loved you. She knew being a cop meant more to you than anything else . . ."

"She was wrong."

"Oh?"

"You and your mother meant more to me than anything else. I guess I wasn't very good at expressing it."

"Dad, if you weren't a cop what would you be?"

Her question struck Houston dumb. He couldn't think of a single other thing he could do. Being a marine and a cop were the only things he had ever done or even considered. He believed he was ill-suited for anything else.

"You can't think of anything, can you?"

"Sure," Houston lied. "I can think of lots of things I could do."

"Really? Tell me one, just one."

"I could sell cars."

"Oh, riiiight." She laughed. "I can hear you now. 'Do you want the damned car or not?' If they didn't answer, you'd grill them. Face the facts, Dad, you're the only thing you can be—the only thing you've ever wanted to be. You'd go nuts if you had to stay in the same place all day."

"You got it all figured out, huh?" Houston smiled.

"Well, it's not like we're discussing quantum physics."

They fell quiet for a few moments, and then Susie looked toward the far end of the restaurant. "I like her."

"Who?" Houston asked.

"Anne."

Houston looked up and saw his partner walking toward them after visiting the ladies' room. After the funeral, she had tried to leave him and Susie alone, but they both insisted she join them for lunch.

Houston slid over and Anne sat beside him.

"It looks as if you guys have declared a truce," she said.

"We've ironed out a lot of things," Houston answered. "I have a lot of ground to make up."

"Dad, it isn't all that bad."

"That's not what you said a couple of days ago."

"I was hurt and scared. I mean, I don't see you for years and then when you finally show up, you tell me Mom's dead. What did you expect?"

"She's got you there," Anne said.

"I think having a grown woman for a daughter is going to take a major adjustment," Houston said.

Susie gave him a coy, yet confident, smile. "Dad, you have no idea how much I've grown up . . . nor do you have a clue about what you're in for."

Houston was taken aback by his daughter's answer and had no idea how to reply. He looked to Anne for support.

After the serious tone of the day, Anne took the opportunity to try to lighten things up. "Don't look at me," she said. "You're the one who opened this can of worms."

When the women laughed, Houston felt as if he had just become the victim of a coup d'état. Of one thing he was certain; his life was never going to be the same.

22

"Most enemy soldiers will camouflage themselves, their equipment
and positions to break up their distinctive outlines, so the sniper, while
observing, must be able to detect and identify an object by seeing
only parts or bits of it, and from unusual angles."
—*US Marine Corps Scout/Sniper Training Manual*

Included in Danny Drews's list were the names of several reservists
and Houston decided to check them out. He drove to the Marine
Detachment in Charlestown, parked in one of the lots used by the
tourists who visited the USS *Constitution* and walked into the naval yard.
He paused for a few minutes and scrutinized *Old Ironsides*, the oldest
commissioned naval vessel in the world. The vessel earned its nickname
in a sea battle with the British warship, HMS *Guerriere* during the
War of 1812. British sailors named the ship after they watched their
cannonballs bounce off the hull and do little harm to the ship.

It dawned on Houston that he had lived in Boston most of his life and
had yet to tour *Old Ironsides*. He determined he would do so as soon as this
case was over. He turned away from the ship and walked across the parade
ground toward the red brick rectangular buildings where the naval yard's
small contingent of US Marines and the local reserve detachment resided.

Being back on a Marine base, even if it was primarily a reserve outfit, made Houston nostalgic. It was as if he had stepped into a time warp. The buildings were in immaculate condition and the grounds impeccably clean, which didn't surprise him. Like Parris Island, the Charlestown Naval Yard was as much a tourist attraction as it was a naval base and therefore the military made sure it was always pristine. Houston knew, however, that inside the quaint colonial buildings, the work of keeping a Marine detachment functional was still going on and their interior would probably be identical to the offices he'd frequented during his time in the Corps.

Houston had called before leaving the precinct to make an appointment to speak with the commanding officer and was surprised at how easily he got an approval to meet with Maj. Francis Estes. A female Marine officer stood in front of the headquarters building. He admired her as he walked toward her. She was nothing like the female Marine officers he recalled. Rather than rough and gruff, she looked like something you would see on a recruiting poster. She was close to six feet tall and had the bearing the Corps strived to have in all of its marines. She looked elegant in her Class A dress uniform, a look which very few women were capable of. Her green skirt and tan blouse were so squared away that she would pass inspection by even the most critical sergeant major. She wore her light brown hair fashionable, but within Corps' regulations, down to her shoulders, without a single strand out of place.

As he neared her, Houston saw the golden oak cluster insignia of a major. "Major Estes?"

She offered her hand and Houston took it.

"I'm Michael Houston, Boston PD."

Her grip was firm, yet did not make him feel as if she were trying to impress on him that she was strong enough to be a marine. "How can I help you, Detective Houston?"

Houston knew that many Marine officers loved protocol and were extremely rank conscious. Not knowing her attitude, he corrected her. "It's Sergeant Detective Houston."

She smiled. "After your call I did some research. You're a former marine scout/sniper, served in Somalia, left our Corps and joined the Boston Police Department. Now, you're investigating the sniper attacks of the past several days."

Houston was impressed that she *had* taken the time and effort to do some rudimentary research into his background.

They walked inside the building, through a large open office. Several enlisted marines were busy typing and answering phones. They ignored Houston and Estes and went about their jobs with quiet efficiency.

"Would you care for some coffee?" she asked.

He nodded and she poured two cups of black coffee from the large metal coffeemaker that sat on a table outside a door, beside which hung a placard that read Major Francis K. Estes, Commanding Officer. She handed Houston one cup and didn't ask if he wanted cream and sugar. A marine would drink it black.

Houston couldn't speak for the other branches of the military, but he knew the Marine Corps ran on coffee. Marines would go a lot longer without food than they would without coffee. Even in a combat zone, they would come up with innovative ways to brew a cup. He sipped the steaming liquid and smiled. The coffee was as he always remembered it, strong and bitter. It was like coming home after a prolonged absence.

Estes stopped beside the door and beckoned him to enter first. Her office was laid out identical to every commanding officer's he had seen in the Corps. Centered high on the wall behind her desk was an eleven-by-thirteen-inch photo of the president of the United States, while below it and equidistant to either side smaller eight-by-ten-inch photos of the secretary of the navy and the commandant of the Marine Corps hung. Flags of the United States and the Marine Corps flanked the pictures. The major walked to a functional, gray metal desk before which were two metal office chairs with gray vinyl seats and backs. A cursory glance revealed no personal items on either her desk or the office shelves. It gave him the impression that Estes, like the office, was all business and she motioned him toward one of the chairs. Rather than sit behind her desk, Estes sat in the other. She crossing her shapely legs and smiled.

"Okay, now that we've observed all the necessary protocols, tell me why you're here."

"I have a file, a listing of scout-sniper trained personnel compiled by one of the vics . . ." It dawned on him that she might not be conversant in police slang and corrected himself. ". . . victims, that is. Daniel Drews was a friend of mine and one of the sniper's latest targets."

"What does that have to do with me or my command?"

"The file contains the names of two members of your unit."

"Really? I wasn't aware we had any scout/snipers here. If you give me the names, I'll see what I have."

Houston paused. He found it hard to believe that she was unfamiliar with the military credentials of any marine in her command. *Here it comes*, he thought. *Rally round the flag and preserve the sanctity of the Corps.* He steeled himself to deal with resistance. It seemed as if the major were hinting she was not going to tell him anything. Then she smiled in a way that told him maybe he had made a hasty decision. He decided to ride it out. "I'm interested in a Sgt. Lawrence Grey and Cpl. Richard Billips. According to my information, they're still members of your command."

Estes stood. "Let me check with my admin chief. I'll be right back."

She walked into the outer office and he heard her speaking with one of the enlisted men. Within seconds, he heard the rumble of a metal file cabinet door opening and a few seconds later, closing. In less than a minute, Estes was back with two military service record books in her hands. She placed the SRBs on the desk and then glanced at her watch. "I'm sorry, Sergeant Houston, but I've got to see about something in the armory."

Houston didn't know what was going on and prepared to be escorted out of the building. He assumed she wouldn't leave him alone in the office with the SRBs. He was wrong.

"I'll only be a few minutes, so finish your coffee. If you want, we can talk when I get back."

He stood up and unconsciously stood at attention. "Yes, ma'am."

She smiled at his involuntary action. "Amazing, isn't it?"

"Ma'am?"

It's amazing how old habits and Marine training never die." Estes picked up her cover, adjusted it so it sat on her head perfectly and paused at the door before leaving. "I don't believe any of my marines would do anything to bring disgrace on this Corps of ours. I hope you find the people responsible for these killings and bring them to justice." She smiled and left.

Once she was out of the office, Houston realized he was standing at attention and shook his head in disbelief. *She's right*, he thought, *the training never leaves you.*

It only took him a couple of minutes to get what he needed from the files. Grey and Billips were still on active reserve status and both lived outside Boston, on the north shore. Houston was surprised at how much they had in common. Even the towns they lived in were close together—Ipswich and Gloucester. He would be able to check them out in a matter of hours. Houston jotted down the addresses in his notebook. He had just put it in his pocket when Estes returned.

"I'm sorry about leaving you alone," she said with a smile.

"Not a problem," he said. "But, I should be moving on, so you can get back to work."

Estes held out her hand. Houston gripped it and she gave him a look that made him wonder if she was coming on to him. It was sort of a half-smile, half-invitation. He wondered if she had a hidden agenda. "Do you still shoot?"

"Only when my job requires that I do."

"Well, you should give me a call. We have a place up north. For obvious reasons, we call it the Brigade. A bunch of us get together up there every few weeks for some fun and war games."

"War games?" Houston was not sure he liked the sound of that.

"Sort of, more like paint ball wars. Have you ever tried it?"

"No, after Somalia and my years as a cop, I seem to have lost interest in running around the woods shooting at people."

"I doubt that. I'm told that once you've experienced the *hunt*, you're never satisfied with anything else." Estes finally released his hand.

He let it drop to his side, refusing to acknowledge that he thought she had been flirting with him.

Estes, too, played it cool. "There are a lot of places to shoot up there. We *do* need to keep our skills current. You know how it is—if you don't use it, you might lose it."

Returning to her desk, the major jotted a number on a message pad, tore the page off the pad and handed it to him. "If you ever decide you want to join us for a weekend, call me."

Houston swore there was a proposition in her eyes. If it had not been for the circumstances under which they met, he might have taken a chance. However, he didn't. Instead, he said, "I just might do that."

Back in his car, Houston was confused. Something about the whole scene with Estes did not ring true. She was too willing to help and should never have left anyone alone with the service record books. Then there was that little scene with the unsaid invitation—now *that* was bizarre. Houston glanced at the dash clock. He still had more than enough time to look up Grey and Billips. He drove out of Charlestown and onto the Mystic River Bridge, heading north on Route 1.

Ipswich and Gloucester were on the coast north of Boston. While Gloucester was a thriving seaport, home to one of the largest fishing fleets in the northeast, Ipswich was inland, nestled on the banks of the Ipswich River. The easiest way there was US Route 1 to 128, then 1A into Ipswich. From there it was a quick shot down Route 133 into Gloucester. Since Ipswich was the closer of the two, Houston decided to look up Sgt. Lawrence Grey first.

Grey lived on the outskirts of town in a white cape with black trim. When Houston slowed in front of the house, he saw a man wearing camouflage shorts and a green sleeveless T-shirt sitting on the front steps, drinking from a takeout cup of iced coffee. When he turned into the drive, the man stood and eyed the car with no small amount of suspicion.

Houston got out of his car and removed his badge wallet. He ignored Grey's visible hostility and studied him as he walked across the freshly mowed grass. Grey was tall, at least six feet five inches, and his hair was cut in a buzz cut with silver scattered through his dark brown hair. He was lean and muscular, with lines from too many hours staring into the sun reaching from the corners of his eyes like a cartoonist's depiction of sunrays.

"Lawrence Grey?"

"Yeah, you the cop Major Estes called me about?"

Houston knew Estes had been too eager to help. No doubt she'd called her men as soon as he had left her office. "I guess so. I'm Mike Houston, Boston PD."

Grey's eyes turned hard. "Estes said you're investigating that sniper that's been in the news."

"That's right," Houston said.

"So what brings you here?"

"Your name has come up in the course of the investigation."

He tensed. "You ain't pinning that on me."

His reaction intrigued Houston. Rather than show fear like most innocent people, Grey showed hostility and anger. "No one has even hinted about you being involved. But let's face facts, scout/snipers are members of a small elite society. Not many make it through the training."

"I heard you was one, in the Gulf."

"Nope, I did my time in Somalia. Seems like a lifetime ago."

Houston noticed Grey had some ugly round purple and yellow bruises on his arms and on his chest where the neck of his T-shirt dipped down. "Those are some nasty bruises you got there."

"Yeah, I play paintball. You give some and you get some."

"Mr. Grey—"

"Larry."

"Larry, let's cut to the chase, okay?"

"Hey, you're the one came to me."

"Do you have any idea who this shooter might be?"

"Nope." He drained his coffee and stood up. "If that's what you came to ask, you got your answer. Seems you made a long drive for nothing. You should have called first. It would have saved you some time."

He was right, but then Houston would have lost the opportunity to look him in the eye to see if he was lying and Houston was certain that if Grey wasn't lying, he was at least hiding something.

"No sweat," he said. "I wanted to see the country anyhow." *And*, he thought, *meet a certified flaming asshole.*

Gloucester had always been one of Houston's favorite towns. Over the years, it had maintained its old-time seaport feeling. As soon as they entered the city, visitors knew without doubt, how the residents made a living. One way or the other, if you lived in Gloucester, you owed your livelihood to the sea. Even the air smelled of the ocean; depending on what part of town you were in, the scent would come from either the hundreds of commercial fishing boats or the fish processing plants. Fishing was Gloucester; without it, the place would have dried up and blown away two hundred years ago.

Richie Billips lived in a small house not far from the waterfront. The door was answered by a frail white-headed woman who looked old enough to be Gloucester's first resident. She couldn't had been much more than five feet tall, possibly shorter, and craned her neck when she peered up at Houston. She squinted as she tried to determine if she knew him. At least two generations of your family had to live in small New England towns before they considered you a local and not *from away*. Houston knew she was trying to determine where he belonged on Gloucester's social ladder. "You ain't one of them Moonies are you?"

Houston knew she just placed him below the lowest rung on the social ladder. The followers of Reverend Sung Yung Moon had bought up quite a bit of real estate in Gloucester back in the 1980s and the locals had been more than a little upset over it—to be suspected of being a Moonie was not a compliment in Gloucester.

"No, ma'am. I'm neither. I'm here to see Richie Billips. Is he in?"

Inside the house, a talk show blasted from a television and for a second Houston wasn't sure if she'd heard him over the cacophony. However, she stepped aside. "Well, if you ain't a Moonie, come in. I'll get Richard. He's out back." The old woman elevated her voice so she could be heard over the blaring television.

Turning and walking, she didn't look back, talking as she went and taking it on faith that he followed. They entered a sitting room with a couple of armchairs, a couch and the television that polluted the air with talk show garbage. "Have a seat. You're lucky you came today."

"Oh, how's that?"

"Richard is going out tomorrow. He could be gone a couple of weeks or longer."

Houston agreed. He was lucky Billips was at home. When deep-water fishing trawlers went to sea they stayed out until one of two things occur: either, they filled their holds or their provisions and/or fuel dipped so low that they had to come back—a successful trip was one where you drifted into the dock with empty fuel tanks and a full hold.

A door slammed in the rear of the house and Houston heard a rough male voice say, "What is it, Grandma?"

The old woman answered, "You got a guest. Now before you go in the front room clean yourself up a bit. You don't want people to think you're a bum."

He grumbled something in a voice too low for Houston to make out what he said, but she must have won. Another door slammed and he heard water running through the house's ancient plumbing. The grandmother returned and asked if he wanted something to drink. Houston knew how these old women could be. The easiest way to deal with them was to say yes, even if all you asked for was a glass of water, which is what he did.

Houston got the water and a plate stacked three layers high with cookies and cake. He couldn't help but like Richie's grandmother—she was a food pusher par excellence, right up there with his own mother and grandmother.

When Richie Billips finally made his appearance, Houston was on his second glass of water, third cookie and was exasperated from trying to make the old girl understand he was not a descendant of General Sam Houston.

Grandma saw Richie and gave him a quick inspection to determine whether he was sufficiently presentable to receive visitors. Houston wouldn't have been surprised to see her spit shine her grandson's face and slick his hair into place. However, Richie passed the inspection and she excused herself so they could talk in private. She turned off the television and disappeared. After a couple of minutes, the talk show host's voice returned—this time from the interior of the house.

Houston turned his attention to Billips. Like Grey, he was big and obviously strong. He was a tall, wiry man, standing six-two, maybe six-three. But his muscular physique was that of a man who made his living doing grueling physical labor rather than that of an overdeveloped gym rat. His arms were sinewy and it was easy to see he possessed incredible strength. The physically weak don't cut it on deep-water fishing trawlers.

"Do I know you?"

"I don't think so. My name is Mike Houston. I'm a cop from Boston."

"How can I help you, Mike Houston?"

Houston tried a different approach with Billips. "I got your name from a friend of mine, Danny Drews."

Richie's eyes narrowed. "Danny's dead. I heard it on the news."

"Yeah."

Richie glanced over his shoulder to see where his grandmother was. "That shooter has to be one psychotic fuck, man—crazy as a rabid harbor seal."

"Be that as it may, we'll get him yet."

"Yeah, but you and I know that the only score that counts in the game those sick bastards like to play is who walks away."

"You talk as if you know this guy. Do you?"

Billips became suspicious. "Who knows you're here?"

"I got your address from Major Estes and I just talked with Larry Grey. Didn't she call and let you know I was coming?"

His face became pasty white. "I'm screwed."

"Why?"

"Grey is in it up to his neck—maybe Estes too. She has this not-so-hidden agenda . . . she's always trying to prove she's the greatest fucking marine since Chesty Puller. If they sent you to me then the shooter won't be far behind."

"Maybe you better tell me what you know."

"I don't know who's doing the shooting, but I heard there's this guy in town with a major league hard-on for someone. Rumor has it this is about some old garbage from years ago. All I know is he looks like a crispy critter."

Houston stared at him. He wasn't sure if he'd heard him right. "Say that again."

"I heard the guy is scarred worse than a patient at the Shriner's burn center. I've never laid eyes on him but some of the guys have told me that compared to this guy, burnt bacon looks good."

Houston's head snapped up. Disfigurement? Burn scars? He immediately thought of the smoldering ruins of the building in which he'd last seen Edwin Rosa. "You *heard*? From whom?"

"It's common scuttlebutt throughout the battalion. I heard some of the guys talkin' over coffee."

"I need a name or names."

"Look, I don't want to get anyone in hot water . . ."

"I understand that, but I need to know where you heard this."

"You already talked to him—Larry Grey."

"You ever hear anyone mention the name Edwin Rosa?"

"No."

"*I* sure as hell did." Houston wondered, *why would Estes and Grey get involved with a psychotic killer?*

"Estes has this hang-up about being a woman and not getting a combat command."

"Women have been in combat for several years now."

"As pilots and grunts, but no woman marine has ever commanded a combat unit. Estes wants to prove that she's as good as any male officer."

"What about Grey?"

"He's an asshole . . . he'd do it for kicks."

23

"The role of the sniper in an urban guerrilla environment is . . .
engaging dissidents/urban guerrillas when involved in hijacking,
kidnapping, holding hostages, etc."
—*US Marine Corps Scout/Sniper Training Manual*

Upon his return from Gloucester, Houston met Anne at the Union Oyster House, a block from Faneuil Hall. They sat in one of the more secluded tables in the old restaurant and Houston felt that the environment was safe enough for them to let their guard down. He reached across the table and placed his hand upon hers. He noticed her nervous glance around the room. "I'm at the point where I'd like to say screw the job; let's let everyone know how we feel."

"I'm sure there are people in the department who know," Anne replied. "Either they don't have enough proof to complain or they just don't care."

"There are times when I almost wish the brass would push the issue. I've been having thoughts of retiring."

Anne pulled her hand from under his. "What?"

"I'm getting tired of dealing with society's underbelly."

"Does this have anything to do with our discussion with your daughter over lunch the other day?"

"That could be part of it. There're other factors though. All my life I've been Mike Houston, marine sniper, or Mike Houston, Boston police detective. I wonder what it would be like just to be Mike Houston for a while."

"Where does that leave me?" Anne appeared to be cool, but Houston knew her well enough to see that she was concerned.

"Hon, that's up to you. There will be a day of reckoning when we both have to make a decision. We can try to keep on as we have, keeping up the façade of being in a professional relationship only—and I don't know how well, we've done that. Or we can come out and let everyone know and see how the chips fall . . ."

"That would be the end of our partnership."

"Well, I believe that our partnership has cost you. If you weren't tied to me, you'd be at least a lieutenant by now. Hell, you might even be in line for a promotion to captain."

"That was my decision, Mike. You know that."

The discussion ended when a waiter appeared and placed a glass of water and a menu in front of each of them. They studied the selections for a few minutes before Houston broke the silence. "You could leave the job too. I've been thinking of getting a place in either Maine or New Hampshire—someplace remote, away from people and all the chaos they cause. Or you can stay on the job."

Anne laid her menu down and stared at him. "Are you giving me an ultimatum?"

"No, anything but that. I'm trying—and not too successfully—to let you know that whatever decision you make, I'll support it."

"You sound as if you've already made up your mind."

Houston stared out the window for a second at the headlights on the cars driving along Union Street. "It's reached the point where the job has cost me too much . . ."

"Like Pam?"

"Like the chance to see my daughter grow up, to be there when she needed a father. Pam and I were doomed from the start." He took a drink of water. "Enough of this; let's eat."

"Oh, I gave Susie my key to your place. She said she wanted to spend the weekend with you."

"Did you call her?"

"No, she called the department asking for you and I happened to be there when Charley Davis took the call."

Houston and Anne arrived at his apartment shortly before nine and Susie was already there.

He stepped back and looked into the living room, where Susie sat on the couch and leafed through a magazine. "I can't believe how much she's changed. She's not a child anymore. She's—" He had a lump as big as an orange in his throat. He thought about all he had missed in the years since he and her mother had parted. "She's not my little girl anymore."

Anne said, "She'll always be your little girl."

Houston opened the refrigerator, took out a pitcher of iced tea and poured a glass. He leaned against the counter sipping it, unwilling to take his eyes off his daughter. He thought about what Anne had said about Susie always being his little girl and it made him feel good. Houston smiled, placed his glass on the counter, turned to Anne, and took her into his arms. He kissed her and she responded.

"I'm sorry. I know that's against the rules we've agreed upon."

"That's all right. It's just that we have to be careful."

"I know."

He turned toward the living room and stopped when she said, "Mike . . ."

"Yeah?"

"For what it's worth, I enjoyed it . . . maybe down the road, we could go away for a weekend—just the two of us. Far enough away that nobody on the BPD will see us."

"I'd like that. Let's not wait too long. Okay?"

"Go get acquainted with your daughter. I'll whip up some food and be with you in a minute."

Houston walked into the living room and stopped for a second. Looking at Susie, he couldn't help but wonder how many bad memories she had of him. He remembered the long battles between him and her mother and the times she had been disappointed when his job kept him from showing up for piano recitals, parent-teacher conferences, and PTA meetings.

Houston knew he had to make up a lot of ground. But what really ate at him was that he would have to go slow. He couldn't mend years of damage in fifteen minutes. It was going to take time—and taking time was something he had always hated. He wanted to make it right as soon as possible—if not yesterday, then now. Unfortunately, it wasn't going to work that way. It could take years to rebuild the trust and confidence he had betrayed and mend the invisible scars he had caused. That thought depressed him. He made up his mind that he was going to do this the right way and not push. It was an easy decision to make—after all, he had no other options. If he tried to control this, the way he tried to control things during those angry years, all he would accomplish would be to drive Susie away again.

The next day was Saturday. Houston woke up and rolled over. The sun blazed through the window and he felt hung over, only from lack of sleep, not booze. Swinging his legs off the side of the bed, he sat up and glanced at his watch. It was eleven in the morning! He had overslept. It had been around four when fatigue finally wore him down and he retired. Anne had left around one and Susie had dropped off around three thirty.

Wearing a pair of worn blue jeans and a T-shirt, Houston walked into the kitchen, put on a pot of coffee and then entered the living room. Rumpled blankets on the couch provided proof that Susie had slept there, but was gone. He knew that it was past the time when he should hit the streets, but could not bring himself to leave. Instead, he dropped into an easy chair and stared at the place where his daughter had slept.

The coffee maker popped, hissed and rumbled, telling him it was ready. He returned to the kitchen, poured a mug, and then leaned against the counter. Taking a drink of the hot brew, his eyes were attracted to a piece of paper stuck to the refrigerator by a magnetic miniature replica of the lighthouse at Portland Head. He sipped coffee while reading the note. It was from Maureen, she and Susie had gone shopping and if he wanted to join them, they'd be having lunch at twelve at a place they frequented in Quincy Market. Houston didn't have anything pressing so he took a quick shower, trying to clear the cobwebs from too little sleep.

Houston was toweling off when the phone rang. He assumed it was Anne and snatched it up. "Hey."

"Have a nice trip up to the north shore?"

The voice sounded muffled and disguised.

"Who is this?" Houston asked, although by now the gravelly voice was all too familiar.

"The game is afoot, my friend."

"Listen, asshole. I'm not playing any games with you—"

"Oh, you will, Mikey. Believe me, you will."

Houston fought back the impulse to make a childish threat.

"By the way, I think that little girl of yours is a real looker—"

"You stay away from my daughter."

"Then come and play with us when you're called, Houston. Otherwise we'll have to take steps to ensure that you do. By the way, it *is* a nice day for hanging out in Quincy Market."

The phone went dead.

Houston immediately punched the numbers to Anne's cell phone. Listening to the phone ring, he swore impatiently. After four rings, he got a message saying the cellular customer he called was unavailable. He cursed, left her a short message—Meet me at Quincy Market as soon as you can get there—and slammed the phone down. He grabbed his pistol and bolted through the door.

As he sped to Quincy Market, Houston tried to figure out how Maureen could have been so irresponsible as to take Susie to one of the most public places in Boston. The only reason he could fathom was that his sister and daughter were either unaware of or in denial about the danger they were in. When he arrived at North Market Street, he double-parked his car, leaving the emergency lights in the grille flashing.

Quincy Market and Faneuil Hall were two of Boston's most popular tourist sites. John F. Kennedy had announced his candidacy for president of the United States on the second floor of Faneuil Hall and shoppers could find just about anything they wanted in the market. Faneuil Hall's ground floor was a food court, offering virtually any kind of food a person could want. The rest of the market was full of small boutiques where shoppers could buy anything from embroidered hats to hot sauce. Houston skipped the food places and went straight for the shopping in the market's three buildings. His chances of finding Maureen and Susie were slim, but he had to try. First, he searched the North Market Building and, being unfamiliar with the interests of both his sister and daughter, checked out every shop he thought would be of interest to women. Not finding them, he entered the center building, Quincy Market itself. No luck there either. He was crossing the courtyard between Quincy Market and the South Market Building when he saw them strolling toward him. A guy dressed in camouflaged clothing was following them and, Houston thought, studying them more than a passing stranger should. He wore a soft Marine cover pulled low so it obscured his face. There was no doubt in Houston's mind what the stalker had planned. As the man closed with the women, he increased his pace.

Maureen and Susie had their backs to the stalker and had no idea that a would-be assassin followed them. Houston weaved through the stream of people, fighting his way toward Maureen and Susie. In desperation, he pulled his pistol out and screamed, "Police! Make way!"

People saw the gun in his hand and scrambled to get out of his way. The commotion attracted Maureen's attention and she had a surprised look when she spotted Houston rushing at her.

The stalker reached inside his shirt and pulled a handgun. "Maureen, get down!"

Maureen looked terrified when she grabbed Susie's arm, obeyed her brother and fell to the pavement, pulling the startled younger woman with her.

Maureen's action startled the stalker enough to throw him off stride and for Houston to get a clear shot at him. Houston shouted, "Drop the gun!"

The gunman turned his pistol away from the women and confronted the unexpected threat. Houston dropped to one knee and fired, hitting him in the throat. The man dropped like a sack of rocks. Houston ran forward and stopped beside the mortally wounded would-be killer. The dying gunman still gripped his weapon in his right hand and Houston placed his foot on the gunman's hand, pinning it securely to the pavement. He took the pistol out of the stalker's bloody hand. Houston holstered his firearm and squatted over the man. He pressed his hand firmly against the side of the dying man's neck, hoping to stem the flow of blood that gushed out with each beat of the stalker's heart and pooled on the sidewalk. The hollow-point bullet had ripped through the man's neck and Houston knew if he didn't get him to a hospital in minutes, he would bleed out. He didn't have to be a medical professional to know his attempts at first aid were futile.

The prone gunman stared into Houston's eyes. In minutes he died, a strange smirk on his face and his shirt saturated with his blood. It was only then that Houston took time to look at him closely. Through the smeared blood, Houston stared into Larry Grey's lifeless eyes.

In a second, Anne was beside him, her badge out. She pushed the traumatized spectators back, shouting, "Police, please, give us some room!" Turning to Houston she said, "I got here as soon as I could."

Houston ignored the hysterical screams and commotion around him and thanked her. Then he looked at his daughter's horrified eyes. Susie's terror had drained all the color from her face. Houston realized she was trying to understand and cope with what she had just seen her father do.

At that moment, Houston could not blame her for looking at him with disgust and terror. Thoughtlessly, he offered her his bloody hand and the fear left her to be replaced by revulsion. She spun away and disappeared into the crowd.

24

"Take advantage of any local disturbances or distractions that may enable quicker movement than would otherwise have been possible . . ."
—*US Marine Corps Scout/Sniper Training Manual*

Bill Dysart paced around his office. In his right fist he held a crumpled copy of one of the daily papers. The headline shouted out, *Gunfight in Quincy Market!!* Houston couldn't recall ever having seen his boss so incensed. Then, the circumstances under which he was meeting him were not conducive to a fatherly chat. Houston honestly couldn't blame him. The last thing Dysart needed was a shooting in the midst of another crowded tourist attraction.

Dysart was discreet with his anger though; he might have been ready to lock Houston up for fifty years, but he didn't make a scene in front of everyone in the building. The captain respected Anne too much and, rather than chew them out in front of the other officers, he took them into his office, where he then became unhinged. As soon as the door latch clicked behind them, Dysart said, "Bouchard, what the hell is going on?"

Before she could answer, he cut her off. There was more that he wanted to get off his chest. "You two are out of control! The body count on this case is going through the roof—and if that ain't enough," Dysart pushed a finger at Houston, "he shoots a guy in the middle of fucking Quincy Market—on a Saturday afternoon, for God's sake! There must have been a couple of thousand by-standers! What if you'd hit one of them? The entire city is hysterical enough without worrying about getting caught in the middle of a shootout between the Hatfields and the McCoys."

Dysart was venting and when the captain flopped behind his desk and glared at Anne, Houston knew things would settle down. Anne leaned back in her chair, grinned at him for a second, and then she looked at Dysart in a way that reminded Houston of his mother. When he would get mad and blow off steam she would sit and not say anything until he was finished venting. It was a look that said, "Okay, get it out and then we'll talk."

His need to unload his frustrations taken care of, Dysart opened the window of his office. Out of habit, he checked the door and lit a cigarette. He exhaled the smoke and blew it out the window. He tossed the cigarette out the window and stared after it. Dysart flopped into his chair. "All right you two. I'll handle the heat. Now tell me what you got."

Houston looked at Anne, hoping for a hint as to how much he should tell Dysart. He wasn't sure how the captain would react to learning that the object of the sniper killings was to get Houston alone to go one-on-one with him. Anne returned his look and said, "Mike, I guess it's time to lay it all out for him."

That's what they did.

Dysart listened as they told him everything. This time, however, they told him the complete version, not the toned down one they had written in their reports.

Dysart took it all in, saying nothing. Nevertheless, they knew, from the expression on his face that he was having a hard time with certain facts. He got up twice to sneak a smoke through his open window, observing his ritual of one or two drags then tossing the burning cigarette out the window onto the lawn below, which had so many cigarette butts on it that it was starting to resemble the bottom of a bird cage. Each time Dysart tossed one away, Houston listened for the indignant shout of someone hit by a burning butt falling from the sky. The captain was lucky—he did not hit anyone.

Finally, Houston finished by relating what he had learned in Gloucester, that apparently he was being enticed into a sadistic game of sniper versus sniper. Dysart finally reached overload and interrupted him. "Let me get this straight—these shootings are only preliminary bouts for some sort of championship shootout between you and this whacko?

Houston nodded. "That's what I've been told."

"Well, Houston," Dysart's voice elevated in anger, "for once, I'm going to ignore protocol and regulations. Please, make my life easy. Take this asshole up to Maine—hell, take him to Rat's-ass, Kansas, and expense the trip, I don't care—just get it out of my jurisdiction and do whatever you have to do to get the bastard!"

"Cap, you can sleep well knowing I'll do my best."

"I know some guys in SWAT. You want me to get you some back-up?"

"I don't think that's wise. People up in Maine may think we're an invading army."

Dysart didn't appreciate his attempt at humor.

"It's best if we do it his way—I have some experience with this."

"Yeah, right, only I seem to recall that was some time back."

"It's like riding a bike, Cap."

"*Sure*, it is." As Houston reached the door, Dysart added, "Mike, you be careful . . ."

"You know me, Cap."

"That's the problem. Now, get out of here—both of you. I've got to clean up the mess you've made."

As Anne and Houston walked through the squad room, they passed Corso and Bullard.

"Hey guys," Houston said, "you still sore for not getting lead on this case?"

The two detectives stared at him as if he were crazy. "With all the political bullshit going around this? No way."

"Are you working anything interesting?"

"Naw, just some gangbanger. They found his body in the marshes near Squantum. Somebody worked him over good. Pulled all his fingernails out."

"Yeah," Bullard added, "then cauterized the wounds with what looks to be a blowtorch."

Anne and Houston walked to a nearby diner for lunch. They ordered and Anne stared at him.

"Okay, out with it," she said. "What's eating at you?"

"Susie . . . I don't like not knowing where she is and I sure as hell don't like her being on her own right now."

"I thought as much."

"I haven't talked with her since—"

"Mike, give her some time. Do you have any idea where she's staying?"

"She's back in her dorm."

"I'll call her and offer to let her stay with me."

"Jimmy offered her a similar deal. She turned him down, saying her dorm was safe. Jimmy figured what the hell. She's at that age where they want to show that they're mature enough to take care of themselves."

"Jimmy just accepted that?"

"On the surface he did. He knows that it's bullshit and that she's still a kid. He'll keep his people on the job. What I keep remembering is the look on her face in Quincy Market. She was scared to death."

"Well, it was the first time she'd ever seen anything like that."

"That's not what she was afraid of."

"Suppose you tell me what you think she was afraid of."

"Me."

"Come on, Mike. You're her father. She knows you wouldn't hurt her."

"Does she? I'm not so damned sure. Her mother and I went through some scary times. First there was my return from Somalia then for a while I was drinking a lot and finally the job." Houston didn't have to tell her what he meant by *the job*. She'd been a cop long enough to know.

Anne sipped on her diet cola. "Suppose you lay it out on the table."

"Pam could never accept the fact that I had been a sniper. That the boy she'd dated in high school and the man she married could stalk and kill another human being in cold blood. I didn't help matters any when I returned full of anger and my head crammed to over flowing with bad dreams."

"So, a lot of veterans are in the same boat. Post-traumatic stress disorder is more prevalent than anyone knows. The mess going on in the Middle East is only going to make things worse."

"You ever wake up with someone choking you?"

"Can't say that's an experience of which I've had the pleasure."

"Well, it happened to Pam. Luckily, I woke up before I hurt her. She threw me out the next day. I went to work and when I came home, she had piled all my clothes on the lawn. The next time I heard from her was when her lawyer served papers on me."

"And you dove into a bottle."

"Yeah, I dove into a bottle. However, it wasn't as if I was diving off a cliff in Acapulco. I was already drinking heavy so it was just a short leap into the deep end of the pool."

Anne swirled her straw around and ice clinked against glass. "Do you think it would do any good for me to talk to Susie?"

"I don't know. That's the problem; she was thirteen years old when her mother took her away. Hell, she doesn't know me, only what Pam told her, and I'm sure that wasn't a stellar endorsement. If I'm correct, after the shooting at Quincy Market, she probably has me as being some-where between Jack the Ripper and Charles Manson."

"I think we were hitting it off pretty well. I'll see if I can have a woman-to-woman talk with her."

"I'm at the point where I'll try anything."

Anne stood up and grabbed her purse, "That's good enough for me. Now, all I have to do is see Susie. You got the tab?"

Houston nodded. "Good luck. I need all the help I can get."

She smiled and touched his arm. "You're sure that you're going to be all right?"

"Yeah, I got to go see Jimmy O."

"What for?"

"I need some tools of the trade."

"I'm not even going there," she said. "Here . . ." She tossed the keys to their squad car on the table. "I'll grab a cab."

"Are you sure?"

She nodded.

Houston snatched the keys from the table. "Thanks, kid. You're too good to be my partner."

"Everyone knows that—just as long as you don't forget it. Now pay for lunch and go get your tools."

25

"The USMC M40A1 Sniper Rifle is the finest combat sniper weapon in
the world. When using the Lake City M118 Match 7.62 mm ammunition
it will constantly group to within . . . one inch at one hundred yards."
—*US Marine Corps Scout/Sniper Training Manual*

Houston walked into O'Leary's office, waved his hands in front
of his face to part the smoke and flopped into the chair in
front of his desk. "Think I'll ever walk into this joint without
everyone looking at me like I was a walking syphilis epidemic?"

"Nope, not a chance."

Houston faked a hurt look, "I'll try harder not to look so much like
a cop."

"Speaking of which, what brings you back here? You need something?"

"Yeah, but first I got a couple things I want to say."

O'Leary smoked in silence and waited for Houston to get to the point.

"First, last night the body of a gangbanger—kid named Jermaine
Watts—was found in the marsh. Looks like someone worked him over
good. All his fingernails were gone, apparently yanked out, and his fingers
were burned, probably with a cutting torch. If that wasn't enough, someone

popped him in the head with a twenty-two. Don't suppose you'd know anything about it?"

"Nope. I just know what I hear on the street. He and some of his homeboys molested and killed a thirteen-year-old girl. I guess that maybe she had some relatives who took care of it when you cops did nothin'."

"Jimmy . . ."

"Your case?"

"No."

"Then ask me no questions and I'll tell you no lies."

"How many more bodies are going to show up?"

"Couldn't say, but you know how it is—what the cops can't or won't take care of, someone in the hood will. When you consider all the gang shit and drugs sold there, it doesn't surprise me people are taking things into their own hands. What's there been seven, eight murders there this summer?"

Houston knew he had gotten all the information that he would on the subject and dropped the line of questioning.

O'Leary lit another cigarette. "Now, what else you wanna talk about?"

"Pam."

"Pam . . ."

"Yeah, I know that you took our divorce pretty hard . . ."

"Let's finally get this out, okay? First of all, Pam was my sister and I loved her. You were like a brother to me and I loved you too, but you two just had bad chemistry together and everyone knew that. Everyone that is, but you two. Was I pissed about the divorce? Yeah, I was . . . but not as bad as I was when Pam went against my wishes and married you. Now as for her death . . . you didn't pull that goddamned trigger, Mike. Some psycho son of a bitch did that. Whether or not this goes back to your past I don't know. Why he shot her ain't all that important right now . . . the fact that he did is. Now we got to pool our resources, you and me, and bring him down. Once this puke is dead and buried we'll deal with our issues. Okay?"

"Okay."

"Alright, now what is it you need from me?"

"Just a few things. Like an M40A1 rifle with a Unertl scope, a couple hundred rounds of Lake City M118 Match 7.62 mm ammo. I want an A1, Jimmy, not the revised A4."

O'Leary remained silent for a few seconds, rolling his cigarette back and forth between his thumb and forefinger. "You wired?"

"What?"

"You heard me. Did you come in here wired? You ain't tryin' to hang an illegal gun beef on me are you?"

"No."

"Then why don't you get this shit from the PD?"

"I'd never get it in time. The fewer people involved in this, the better. Believe me, Jimmy, this is not a sting. I'll never let anyone know where I got the stuff."

"All right, I'll see what I can do. That's a pretty specific piece, only made by Marine armorers and not for public sale. What else?"

"A Ghillie suit."

"A Ghillie suit?"

"It's like a poncho, only made from jute."

"I'm supposed to know what in hell jute is?"

"Jute's what they use to make burlap, only it isn't woven like a sack, it hangs in strands that create corded netting. It allows a sniper to camouflage himself similar to his surroundings."

"So, you're going after this guy."

"Not if I can avoid it, even though I can't think of any other way to get him. Nevertheless, if he calls me out again I want to be ready."

"I hope you know what you're doin'. He's had a couple of chances to kill you already and has let you walk. This guy has the advantage of knowing who and where you are and when to strike."

"That's why I need this stuff as soon as possible. If I'm going to take him on, I want to be ready. I've got some practicing to do."

O'Leary looked at him as if he were out of his mind. "You're going to practice?"

"Yeah, I'm going to hone my skills."

O'Leary ground out his cigarette and scratched his head. "Are all ex-jarheads stubborn like you?"

"Pretty much."

"How in hell did we lose in Vietnam?"

"I don't know. As you might recall, I wasn't there. But I think the government tying the military's hands had something to do with it. So when can you have that stuff?"

"Give me a few days to get the rifle and the Ghillie suit. The other stuff I should have late tomorrow afternoon."

"See you then."

Houston stopped at the door and turned to O'Leary. "How much longer you think the hood will be policing itself?"

"Hard to say. At least until the last child molester is gone and the parasites that entice six-year-old kids to shoot drugs are off the streets. You're the expert in crime, you tell me."

"Sounds to me like it's going to be a long-term project . . ."

"On goin'."

———————

Houston went back to his apartment and broiled a couple of steaks with baked potatoes and all the fixings for Anne and himself. He turned the six o'clock news on and half-listened to the commentators give their opinions on world events, which in Boston usually meant the liberal point of view. The local news gave way to the national news and the steaks were starting to look like beef jerky. He paced the apartment for several minutes and then called Bill Dysart. Dysart told him he hadn't heard a word from Anne since they had left his office that morning.

Houston rummaged through the drawers of the small desk and took out an address book. He flipped it open to *H* where he had penciled in Susie's name and cell phone number. His hand shook as he held the phone and he had a hard time hitting the right sequence of numbers. The phone rang three times and then went to voicemail. He cursed with impatience as he referred to the address book and found the number to her dorm and punched the numbers. He breathed a sigh of relief when someone answered the phone.

"Yo," it was a male voice and Houston's paternal instinct kicked in. What in hell was a guy doing answering the phone in a girls' dorm room? Houston had bigger things on his mind though, like locating his daughter. Still, he made a mental note to ask Susie about it.

"Susan Houston," he said, trying to keep fear out of his voice.

"Hold on."

The guy dropped the handset, and the loud clunk it made banging on the desk almost deafened Houston. He pulled the phone away from his ear then quickly put it back. Houston forced himself to be patient and prayed until he heard someone pick up the phone. "Susie?" he asked before anyone had a chance to talk.

"No, this is her roommate, Melissa."

"Melissa, this is Susie's father. It's important that I talk with her—is she there?" He prayed she was and all that had happened was that she had decided to give him the cold shoulder after the trauma of Quincy Market.

"She was, but she left."

"How long has she been gone?"

"Let's see. I came in about two and she left not more than ten minutes later."

"Was she alone?"

"I didn't see anyone with her."

"Did she say where she was going?"

"No, but then I didn't think to ask."

"Does she have her cell phone?"

There was a pause and then Melissa said, "No, it's sitting in the charger on her desk."

He heard the door open and close. When he looked up Anne was standing in the door. Houston smiled and motioned he would only be a minute. "Melissa, have her call me as soon as she gets in."

"I'll leave her a note in case I go out too."

"Thanks."

Anne looked at him; the pallid cast to her complexion told him something was wrong. "No one has seen Susie since two this afternoon."

Mike grabbed the phone and punched in a number.

"Claddagh Pub."

"This is Houston, put me through to Jimmy."

O'Leary's staccato voice came on. "Mike, my guys lost her . . ."

Susie slammed the sociology textbook closed with more force than was required. She sighed in frustration and tried to deal with what was eating at her—her father and the way violence seemed to follow him no matter where he went. She recalled the Quincy Market shooting and an involuntary shudder raced through her. The shooting had bothered her like nothing she had ever experienced before. On one hand, she knew her father had saved their lives, but she couldn't get past the cold anger on his face as he muscled his way through the crowd and shot the gunman without hesitation.

The librarian walked by. "The Resource Center closes in fifteen minutes."

Susie nodded, gathered her books and stuffed them into her backpack. She decided she might as well head back to the dorm. Her state of mind made studying impossible anyway. She picked up the heavy bag and slung it over her left shoulder.

The evening was warm and pleasant so she opted to walk along University Road rather than take her usual shortcut. She was halfway to her dorm when the van pulled up beside her. An attractive, blonde-haired woman rolled down the passenger window and asked, "Can you direct us to Bay State Road?"

"Sure, it's easy," Susie said. Under normal circumstances she would be hesitant to approach a strange vehicle, but the presence of the woman gave her a sense of security. She walked over to the side of the truck and pointed north. "Follow this street until you come to the entrance to

Storrow Drive. Just before entering Storrow drive, turn hard right; that's Bay State Road."

She turned back to the woman to ascertain that she had understood and froze. The woman pointed a pistol at her. "That sounds confusing to me. Why don't you get in and show us?"

Susie fought back her urge to run. She knew there was no chance she could outrun a bullet. Before Susie overcame her indecision, the woman stepped from the van, the ominous gun never deviating.

"That was not a request. It's an order." She grabbed Susie's backpack, shoved her into the van and jumped in after her.

The driver turned and smiled at Susie, his face a hideous mass of burn scars. "Hey," he said, "I know you! I'm an old friend of your father's."

When he laughed a deep belly laugh, Susie wasn't sure if the distinct odors of smoke and burnt flesh that she smelled were real or imaginary. "We're gonna be good friends too," he said and laughed louder.

26

"Whenever possible, a sniper should work from a hide, since such a position affords a certain amount of free movement without the danger of detection and also protection from the weather and enemy fire."
—*US Marine Corps Scout/Sniper Training Manual*

Heavy dew covered the grass when Anne and Houston arrived. They got out of the car and Jimmy O walked to them. Houston glanced at Anne, hoping O'Leary wouldn't have his usual effect on her.

O'Leary nodded and offered them a thermos of coffee. "Hell of an hour to get up," he said. "Especially if you're nocturnal—which of course, I am."

Houston smiled. Obviously, Jimmy was going to be on his best behavior.

"I got your stuff in my car," Jimmy said.

"Thanks." Houston agreed with him about the hour. Six o'clock was early to be out in the woods. However, intuition told him that time was short and he needed to hone skills he had not used for a long time.

Gordon Winter unloaded the gear, piling it on a blue tarpaulin that he had spread on the damp grass. "Some weird-looking shit here," he said, holding up the Ghillie suit. "Looks like something Joe Shit, the rag picker, would wear."

Houston had not heard that expression in years—not since the Marines. "When were you in?" he asked.

"I got out in ninety-nine."

"What did you do?"

"Army Ranger."

"And now you work for Jimmy."

"Well, there ain't too many jobs you can do as an ex-grunt. It's kind of restricted."

"That's a lot of bull and you know it. You could've become a cop."

"Cops got too many regulations and shit . . . just like the military."

"I know where you're coming from."

Houston bent down and sorted through the equipment. He arranged things functionally. Weapons in one area, Ghillie suit in another, miscellaneous things, such as compass and topographical maps in a third. He saw several plastic masks that looked like the ones hockey goalies wore, except these had goggles covering the eye openings, and four jars of colored balls. He held up one of the masks and one of the jars and said, "What are these for?"

"I didn't think you'd want to use live ammo so I got these," Jimmy said. He held up a paint-ball gun. "I brought a mask for each of us. We wouldn't want to have someone's eye shot out, would we? There should be four different colors there, that way we'll know who shot who—neat, huh?"

Houston took one of the guns, inspected it for a few seconds and then screwed a CO_2 cylinder into the butt.

Anne took a red paint ball out of its jar and studied it for a few seconds. "These things look like they could hurt . . ."

"Only if you get shot," Houston answered. "The object of the game is simple: shoot but don't get shot." He saw doubt on Anne's face. "They may raise a bruise or two, but they aren't lethal."

Houston put on the Ghillie suit, letting it hang like a shroud, then took out a map and a compass. Once the paint gun's hopper was filled from a container of green paint balls, Houston charged it with CO_2.

"Give me a half hour, and then come after me." He spread the map and pointed to an elevation on it. "To simplify things, I'll be somewhere along this ridge. All you got to do is find me before I find you . . ."

Houston noted that Winter was grinning.

"Be like old times," Winter said.

Houston was surprised at how quickly old behavior and habits returned. He found an old logging road that led up to the ridge and followed it for just under twenty minutes. It would be at least a half an hour before his pursuit would arrive, and he needed that time to find a good hide.

Houston camouflaged his Ghillie by inserting local flora into its web-like covering. He wished he had a full-length mirror to see if he had distributed the material evenly. Deciding that given the situation, he had done as well as possible, he concentrated on finding a suitable location—one where he had a clear line of fire at the trail. Jimmy and Anne were city-dwellers, not used to moving through the woods, and he was confident that they would stick to terrain that they could traverse with minimal effort.

Winter would be his biggest challenge. Even though it had been years since he had been in the army, Rangers were highly trained and skilled. He would most likely avoid the easily traveled trails and come through the bush.

Houston found a fallen tree and approached it, checking for things such as hornet nests. The last thing he needed was to be attacked by swarms of angry stinging insects. Once he was sure there were no natural enemies to deal with, he backtracked and used a pine branch to brush away his footprints and any discernible signs of his passing. Satisfied all was as good as he could make things, he settled into his shooting position, pulled the Ghillie suit hood over his head and waited.

Twenty minutes passed before he saw Anne and O'Leary slowly working their way up the trail. Houston sighted in on Jimmy O and waited for him to get within the CO_2 gun's range. Jimmy's eyes were glued to the ground, searching for signs of Houston's passage. Then three things happened simultaneously. Houston shot O'Leary in the chest. The paint ball's impact stood Jimmy up, a large green paint smear on his protective clothing. Houston's new cell phone vibrated, breaking his concentration and Gordon Winter shot him in the ass.

Houston ignored the pain and fumbled through the loose folds of the Ghillie, searching for his phone. He wondered who could be calling. Only Anne and Susie knew the number. He pulled it out and looked at the caller ID but didn't recognize the number. He flipped it open and said, "Houston."

"Daddy?"

"Susie, where are you, babe?"

The familiar raspy voice came on the line. "Don't worry. She's in good hands, Mikey."

"You're a bastard."

"Calling me names ain't gonna help things one bit."

"What do you want?"

"You know what I want . . . directions to the killing ground are in your mailbox—and Mike?"

"What?"

"Don't take forever. I'll be looking for you in three days—no more. If you aren't there by then your little girl and I will play hide-and-seek. Am I making myself clear?"

"Crystal. I'll see you then. In the meantime—"

"She'll be fine. I don't have those desires anymore. It seems that at one time, my equipment got a bit overheated—another debt I owe you. Go check your mailbox. There should be an envelope there with detailed directions and instructions . . . follow them to the T or there will be consequences. Need I say more?"

"No, I got you."

After Houston ended the conversation, he looked up to see his companions watching him.

"The sniper?" Anne asked.

He told them about the call.

"When do we leave?" Anne asked.

"I'm leaving tomorrow, after the evening rush dies down. I don't want you going with me. This is no game."

"You're forgetting that I'm a cop too—not to mention the fact that I'm in far better shape than he is." She pointed to O'Leary.

"But you're not a sniper."

"The last I heard neither are they."

"This is going to be in the bush where you move a few feet in an hour. You crawl and hope you don't make a sound. It's the ultimate game of hide-and-seek—only, losing could be fatal. Other than me, the only other person here with the type of training and experience needed for this is Gordon."

Anne was not to be swayed. "Let me put it to you in the military terms you're so familiar with. Maybe then you'll understand. I'll go as your reserve. I can stay in the background until you send for me."

"And if I can't?"

"We can't allow him to get away. One way or another he has to go down. Besides, if you're hurt, Susie will need all the help she can get."

Houston sat back. "Sounds like you've made up your mind."

"It seems that way, doesn't it?"

"What are my options?"

"None. Like the old saying goes: when it's inevitable, relax and enjoy it."

Houston laughed. "I never expected to hear that from you."

Anne smiled. "I've been waiting years for the right chauvinist to use it on. Pack your stuff, John Wayne. We should let Dysart know that it's going down."

"No."

"Why not?"

"He'll want to throw all the manpower in the department into this. Can you imagine what the political repercussions would be if a bunch of armed cops invaded Maine? Hell, it would take more than three days to get the two states to coordinate—and then Maine would want to send in their people."

Anne remained silent.

"I'm not going to do anything that will put Susie in more danger than she's already in. I've got to do this his way."

27

"When you want to attack, you remain calm and quiet, then get the jump
on your opponent by attacking suddenly and quickly."
—Miyamoto Musashi, *The Book of Five Rings*

Winter felt over dressed. He wore a gray designer suit with a light blue button-down shirt and tie—not what one expected to see in a gin mill in this part of Roxbury. The suit had set him back almost a grand before the additional tailoring for his shoulder rig, which cost another hundred bucks. He sat at the bar and ordered tonic water with a twist.

He turned on his stool and studied the man sitting beside him. He was grungy, filthy as a street person. His dreadlocks were grimy and matted into a gnarled mess, which didn't even resemble hair; his knit cap was colored green, black and yellow, the national colors of Jamaica, and was saturated with gel and grit. The whites of his eyes looked brown and he smelled like carrion.

Winter turned back and watched the TV. The Sox were playing a day game and he smiled as he watched Big Papi hit a towering fly ball into the right field grandstand. "He sure can hit."

The other man glanced at the game then back to his drink.

"I'm Gordon." Winter held out his hand. The reggae junkie stared at his expensive clothes and ignored the proffered hand.

When the bartender slid the tonic water in front of him, Winter made a point of flashing his large roll of cash. He peeled a ten from it and put it on the bar. The junkie's eyes locked onto the roll of bills and widened. He didn't look away until it disappeared into Winter's pocket.

"Hey," Winter called to the bartender, "give my friend here a refill on me."

"I ain't your friend, cracker."

"Hey, man, don't get all bent out of shape, I'm just trying to kill some time before an appointment."

"An appointment in the hood?" the junkie chuckled. "You got an appointment around here, you either a narc or a pusher."

"Well, I'm sure as fuck no narc."

"You selling or buying?"

"Neither, not in here anyway. Is there someplace we can talk in private?"

"There be an alley out back—I meet you there in five minutes."

Winter finished his drink, paid the tab and walked out into the bright afternoon sun. It took several seconds for his eyes to readjust to the sunlight. His vision restored, Winter turned into the alley and followed it to the rear of the bar. He was walking into a set up and relished the prospect.

Before reaching the end of the alley, he drew a .357 Colt Python from his shoulder holster. When he rounded the corner, the reggae junkie grabbed him by his lapel. The would-be mugger's eyes looked like headlights when Winter pressed the barrel of the .357 magnum against his nose. "Now, you know my name. What's yours?"

The man's eyes crossed as they focused on the gun. His mouth opened and closed but nothing came out.

"Let me guess. I'll bet you're Shawnte Armstrong . . ."

A nod was all the answer he got. Winter backed up a step, grabbed Armstrong by the neck. He spun him around and smashed his face against the wall. Armstrong turned his head at the last second, avoiding a broken nose. "Jimmy O sends you his regards," Winter said.

"Who the fuck is Jimmy O?"

"He's the judge and the jury in the murder case of a thirteen-year-old named Latisha Worthington."

"What you talking about?"

"You been tried, Shawnte . . . tried and convicted. I'm your executioner. But first, you're going to tell me where I can find Andrew and Jamaal. . . ."

O'Leary drank from the ceramic mug and stared at Houston and Anne through a stream of smoke. "Your ass hurt much?"

"Only when I laugh. I never thought a wad of wax and paint could raise a welt that big."

"Gordon's very skilled at what he does."

"Either that or I'm out of practice. Where did he go?"

"I sent him to take care of something for me. I wouldn't feel too bad about Gordon sneaking up and shooting you in the ass. He's that good. Hell, Anne and I had no idea where you were until you shot me. Gordon had been watching you for at least five minutes before that."

"Well, he was trained by some of the best."

"Take him with you."

"I can't. Rosa wants me alone."

"So drop Gordon off someplace close. That way if you don't do the job, he can finish business and get Susie off that island."

"As I said this morning, I'm going too," Anne said. "Susie knows me— besides I can take Rosa into custody."

"You mean claim the body, don't you?" Jimmy said.

Anne glared at him.

Jimmy's cell phone rang and he answered it. "Yeah?"

He listened for a couple of seconds. "Give me a half hour."

"Business?" Houston asked.

"Kind of—you guys have a good time. I'll check in later." O'Leary turned to Lisa and pointed an index finger at the table. He moved the finger in a circle, indicating that Anne and Houston's bill was on the house.

"Jimmy?" Houston said.

"Yeah . . ."

"Is this another of those situations where the hood is taking care of its own?"

Jimmy backed up, holding his palms out in front of his chest.

"Ask me no questions . . ."

"Yeah, yeah, go on, get your sorry ass out of here."

"See you in a few hours."

O'Leary parked behind Winter's jet black Lincoln Navigator. Gordon and two other men stood alongside the truck. Jimmy stopped beside them and looked at the tenement across the street from them.

"Sheets in there?" O'Leary asked.

"Yep, he has Jamaal and a couple of his goombahs with him."

"They packing?"

"They usually are."

O'Leary turned to Gordon's companions. "Hey, Billy, Ed, how's it goin'?"

"Jimmy," the men replied in unison.

"Ed, you cover the rear."

"Got it."

They each took out a pistol and checked it. Assured their weapons were loaded and their actions were in working order, they waited for their boss to give the word for them to go about the business at hand.

O'Leary tossed his cigarette in the gutter. Thunder rolled, lightning flashed, and rain suddenly cascaded on them. "Looks like it might rain all night."

"Yup, can't ask for better weather for an ass-kicking."

Lightning streaked across the sky and when O'Leary smiled, his teeth shone phosphorescent in the electric flash. "Which apartment?"

"They're on the first floor, first door on the right."

"Well, let's get to it. Ed, we'll give you five minutes to get in position."

"Only need a couple. Sheets feels safe in there—won't be any lookouts."

"He never was the sharpest crayon in the box, was he?" O'Leary said.

Ed crossed the street, entered the shadows beside the triple-decker and disappeared from sight. The rain increased, becoming a steady downpour. O'Leary turned his collar up. "Let's go, this keeps up—I'm so sweet, I might melt."

Winter stepped off the curb. "Boss, you might be a lot of things, but I never would have thought sweet was one of them."

"There goes your Christmas bonus."

They entered the front door and paused before the apartment door. The hallway was dark, lit by a single bare lightbulb. The building was falling apart. Worn linoleum covered the floor and patches of paint hung from the walls. It reminded O'Leary of the dump where he had lived while growing up. The heady odors of marijuana, cooking oil, and fried fish filled the hall. Upstairs a TV blasted, trying to overpower the heavy thumping beat of rap music. "Another wonderful day in the neighborhood."

"Just like coming home," Winter said.

O'Leary nodded. He raised his handgun. "Let's get this show on the road."

Winter stepped back and seemed to coil like an overtorqued spring. He burst forward, slammed into the door with his shoulder and when it banged open, stormed into the apartment with Billy on his heels. There was a shot, followed by shouting. After a few seconds, the noise ceased and O'Leary heard Winter say, "Evening, Andrew. What's happening?"

"What for you bust in my place, asshole?"

"Just following orders, Andrew."

"Who give you that order?"

"I did." Jimmy O walked into the apartment and nodded at the body on the floor beside the couch. "Who's that?"

Gordon squatted over the body and grasped its face with his free hand. He rotated the head until it faced the ceiling. "Jamaal."

O'Leary nodded, and then without a word he checked the apartment, circling the room, holding his pistol against his side. He looked around and decided that business in the hood must be on the decline.

The furniture was curbside pickup, broken springs and frayed uphol-stery. The only thing of value was the entertainment center, which boasted a fifty-six-inch HDTV, equipped with a serious mega-watt amplifier and speakers to match. The kitchen was filthy; wallpaper hung in shreds and the sink overflowed with dirty pots, pans and dishes. The bedroom décor was early-nineteenth-century flophouse, sagging bed with no linen and greasy mattress and pillows. He opted not to see what state the bathroom was in. He returned to the living room and Andrew Sheets.

"You got no fucking right to come barging in here, shootin' people," Sheets protested.

"Jermaine Watts told me I should look you up," O'Leary said.

"Jermaine? That candy-ass motherfucker—he be dead."

"I know that. We took him for a swim in the harbor."

"You saying you kill him?"

"Yeah, I'm saying I made him dead . . . Armstrong too." O'Leary glanced at the body on the floor. "Now that Jamaal has departed us, that only leaves you to be dealt with."

Fear-induced sweat dripped from Sheets's ebony face and he smiled a wide, over exaggerated smile. His large teeth looked larger than a horse's. "You be shittin' me, right?"

"I wouldn't shit you, Andrew . . . you're my bas-turd. I'm here to settle accounts."

"What I owe you for?"

"Latisha Worthington."

Sheets bolted from the couch and ran through the kitchen and to the back door. He took one step onto the back porch and Ed's fist slammed into his face. His feet flew parallel to the decking and he slammed down onto his back. O'Leary and his men watched as the gangbanger tried to regain his feet and slipped on the wet wood. Trying to regain his breath, Sheets gasped, then rose up on his arms and saw a body lying against the railing.

"Som-bitch came charging out the door when you guys busted in. He ran right into my knife," Ed said.

Sheets saw a Bowie knife in Ed's hand; blood dripped from the blade.

Winter turned the body over. "Looks like his throat slid right along the edge."

Andrew curled up and covered his head with his hands. "I don't know nothing—never saw a thing. You let me go and I be in Bee-more by morning."

Jimmy knelt beside Sheets and pulled his hands away from his head. "I can guarantee you'll be someplace in the morning, but it's gonna be a lot hotter than Baltimore." He lit a cigarette and stared through the torrent of water that poured off the roof as he inhaled. After several seconds, during which the only sounds were the splash of run-off and Sheets's heavy breathing, he said, "Ain't it a crime how you can never find a cop when you need one, Andrew?" He nodded at his men. "Take out the garbage. Don't forget to bring the other two shitheads along."

They bound Sheets's hands and feet with heavy plastic tie-wraps and half-carried, half-dragged him to the back of Winter's SUV. Winter spread a waterproof tarp across the back of the truck and pressed the muzzle of his .357 against Sheets's nose. "You make so much as a squeak and I won't wait to pop a cap in your worthless fuckin' head."

Ed and Billy checked the corpses for anything that Sheets might use to free himself. Satisfied they were clean of weapons and cutting tools, they threw the bodies onto the tarp, tossed Andrew on top of them and slammed the hatch closed.

When Jimmy O turned to get into his own Lincoln, a woman stepped out of a dark doorway and walked around the vehicle and stood in front of it, barring his exit.

"Marian?" O'Leary asked. "What are you doing here?"

"I been watching this punk's crib all day."

The rain fell harder and O'Leary glanced skyward. "Well, you can stop watching and go home. We'll deal with him."

"He alive?"

"Yeah, he's alive—the others aren't."

"I want to go with you and see he gets what he got coming."

"Marian, you don't want to do that . . ."

"Yes, I do. I got the right, Jimmy. It was my baby them motherfuckers raped and killed."

O'Leary peered through the downpour and asked Winter. "What you think?"

"She's got a point, boss. If anyone has the right to see this piece of shit get what he has coming to him, she does. Hell, I'll hold the bastard while she does him if she wants."

"Get in the car, Marian." O'Leary held the door open for her.

They drove to a saltwater marsh on the outskirts of Quincy. Winter got out of his SUV, cursed and raised the hatch. "Either the asshole shit himself or one of them corpses did. I had to open all the windows. It better not be on my truck."

Winter pulled Andrew out of the Lincoln, letting him drop into the mud. Andrew's eyes were as big as pie plates as he watched O'Leary's men grab the edge of the tarp and pull it, dumping the bodies of his men onto the ground. He finally accepted the fate that awaited him and he began crying. "Don't be doing this, man. I didn't hurt the girl. It was Jermaine and Shawnte what done most of it."

"Were you there?" O'Leary asked. "Don't fucking lie to us; we'll know."

"Yeah, I was there."

"Did you try and stop them?"

Andrew shook his head. "She was just a horny little bitch from the hood, always hitting on Jermaine . . ."

Marian stepped around the car and charged at Sheets like an enraged pitbull. She punched him so hard his head turned and he shut up. "Mothah fuckah, don't you be calling my baby no horny little bitch!" She clenched her fists and hit Sheets again and again. Her arms wind-milling as she rained slaps and punches on his head. "You just a fuckin' coward, got no idea what it mean to try and make a living in the hood wit' no husband."

Blood dripped from Sheets's nose. He spat a wad of spit and blood at Marian. She rubbed the bloody spittle into her blouse. "I be keepin' that to 'member yo by."

"You better hope they kill me, bitch, 'cause I be coming for you next."

"I don't think she has to worry about that," Winter said.

When Sheets surveyed the grim faces of the people who surrounded him, he lost his air of bravado. He began to blubber and plead for his life again.

"It never ceases to amaze me how these assholes are such babies once you get them away from their pack," O'Leary nodded at Winter and Ed. "Do it quietly. We don't want to wake up the neighborhood. Better muffle his mouth . . . he's the type who will squeal like a pig in a slaughter-house."

Winter reached in the truck and grabbed the filthy rag he used to check his oil and a roll of duct tape. He shoved the rag in Andrew's mouth and secured it with tape. Once the gag was finished, he stepped away and held a hand out toward Ed. The Bowie knife suddenly appeared. Lightning flashed and reflected from the blade.

Andrew saw the twelve-inch blade and began to scream into his gag.

Winter took the knife, flipped it, caught it by the blade and offered it, handle first, to Marian.

"You want the honor of having the first slice?"

Marian took the knife. "I want all the slices." The huge knife looked like a scimitar in her small hand as she stepped forward and drove the blade deep into Andrew's stomach. She drove it home with such force that her small fist touched his stomach and the tip of the Bowie knife broke through his back—it was visible when lightning flashed. Andrew doubled over and they heard him puke, so Winter ripped the gag from his mouth. Blood covered Marian's hand and dripped onto the gangbanger's white shoes, where it mixed with the driving rain and washed away. When she pulled the knife out of his midsection, Andrew slumped to the ground and curled into the fetal position.

"Hey. Hey, Marian," O'Leary said. "Take it easy—make it last." He repositioned her grip on the knife. "Be careful, you don't want to cut yourself."

Thunder rolled and lightning flashed again making the scene look like a collection of still photographs. Sheets lay on his side. They listened to him inhaling loudly through his nose.

"Sounds like a damned beached whale." Gordon ripped a piece of duct tape from the roll and pressed it over Sheets face, cutting off the airway. "That's better."

For a minute or two, they watched Andrew struggle for air.

"I got twenty bucks that says he either suffocates or drowns in his own puke before he bleeds out," Billy said.

"I'll take some of that action," Ed replied.

Andrew died slow and Billy won the bet.

O'Leary guided Marian to his car and helped her in. He turned to Winter. "Dump 'em in the marsh. After that you guys can go home. We're finished for tonight."

II

THE ISLAND

"Whenever the word sniper is mentioned many of us automatically conjure up images of Germans and Japanese tied in trees or popping out of holes to shoot . . . In reality, nothing could be further from the truth."
—*US Marine Corps Scout/Sniper Training Manual*

28

"There was no second place in Vietnam—second place was a body bag."
—Gunnery Sergeant Carlos Hathcock, USMC

They left Boston at seven o'clock in the evening the day after the sniper's last contact, following I-93 north. As they passed through Concord, New Hampshire, the rain that had plagued them all day stopped and they maintained a steady sixty-five-mile-an-hour pace. In Franconia, they turned onto Route US 3 and followed it to Bethlehem, then took back roads to Route 16.

Hours of staring through the windshield made Houston's eyes burn with fatigue. The country road wove through Berlin and Errol and some of the emptiest country Houston had ever seen. This was a place where you could get as lost as you wanted. For the first time in his life, Houston wondered what it would be like to move to a place like this and leave city life behind forever. Houston thought that under normal circumstances, he could find comfort in the mountains. However, on this trip there would be no comfort.

The route Rosa had told them to follow led them deep into the woods of Maine's Oxford County—a place so remote that if the generator ran out of gas, there would be no daylight. It was an ideal place for them to play their deadly game unbothered for as long as it took to end it.

They had the night and the road to themselves, so far from civilization that they had not passed a single vehicle since stopping for fuel and coffee in Errol, New Hampshire. Houston's headlights cut a tunnel of light through the darkness that pressed in on all sides. A huge moth splattered across the already mired windshield. "At least we're helping with pest control." Houston checked his mirror to see if Winter and O'Leary were keeping pace. The trailer and boat they towed forced them to maintain a slower speed than Houston would have liked. However, the boat was crucial to their plan and was therefore a necessary evil.

Anne didn't respond to his comment. She stared out the side window and saw nothing but her own face reflected in the black background.

"What's bugging you?"

She sighed. "I've been thinking maybe we shouldn't have included Jimmy O and Gordon."

"What's wrong with them?"

"Mike, they're criminals. We shouldn't associate with them—let alone involve them in this."

"In spite of our differences, I trust Jimmy with my life—yours and Susie's too."

"I think you already have."

"I know you still don't completely understand what it is between me and Jimmy. Let me tell you some of our history."

"I'm all ears. There's nothing worth a damn on the radio."

"As you know, Jimmy and I grew up in Southie. My father was a hard worker who spent most of his life working as a baggage handler at Logan Airport. Jimmy's old man, on the other hand, was the Irish drunk that you've heard about. To compound matters, he was a violent drunk. When he wasn't drinking, Paddy O'Leary was a great guy—the problem was that Paddy was not often sober.

"By the time Pam was fourteen, she no longer looked like a gawky adolescent and Paddy was starting to take an unnatural interest in her."

"Why didn't her mother stop him?"

"By that time, Paddy had beaten Moira down physically and emotionally and she was barely able to take care of herself, let alone her kids."

"All she had to do was report him to the state. They would have intervened."

"This was the seventies, and women of our parents' generation didn't do that sort of thing. They had been raised by their mothers and the church to keep quiet, obey their husbands and be *good* wives. Back then anything that went on inside the home was always kept secret."

Anne folded her arms across her chest. "Hmmmmmph. Thank God those days are long over."

"I wouldn't be so sure about that. How many domestic violence calls have we been on where the wife refused to press charges? Instead, they insist that he's really a good man and it was her fault for making him so angry that he lost control."

Anne was staring out the side window again. After a few seconds, she faced Houston. "Do you ever get tired of dealing with the world's underbelly? There are times when I feel so dirty from dealing with the sewer rats we encounter that no soap is strong enough to make me feel clean."

"Yeah, I think that sooner or later all cops do. But getting back to Jimmy and me . . . He and Pam started hanging out at my parents' place. Pam and Maureen were pretty much connected at the hip and Jimmy and I fed off each other. We found it easier to show our wild side when we were together. They virtually lived at our house, which in its own way was dysfunctional too, but nowhere close to what they faced in their own home."

"That's understandable."

"It all came to a head during Jimmy's and my junior year in high school. That's a year I'd never want to relive. The courts had ordered the integration of the Boston schools and forced busing on us. Jimmy, Pam, Maureen, and I were assigned to the worst school in the city."

"I remember the Southie riots."

"That was nothing compared to what was happening in the schools. The black kids who were bussed into Southie and the white kids who were bussed into their neighborhoods had to fight for their lives every day. Not a day went by where Jimmy didn't get into an altercation over someone saying or doing something inappropriate to Pam or Maureen. Some of the fights were brutal—then there was Jimmy's appearance. His severe acne led to a lot of harassment."

"I can't imagine what that must have been like."

"Do you recall what you said when we walked into Jimmy's bar the other day?"

"That I felt like a Jew in Mecca?"

"Imagine spending five days a week feeling that way."

Anne pondered his words but remained silent.

"It was during that year that Paddy went crazy. In a drunken rage, he beat Moira so bad she had to be hospitalized for a couple of weeks."

"What happened to him?"

"Paddy disappeared. He just fell off the face of the Earth one night. He was seen doing beers and shots in a bar until shortly after midnight, then nothing. It was like he had been abducted by aliens. He's never been seen nor heard from since."

"Nobody has any idea where he went?"

"I've always believed one person knows Paddy's whereabouts."

Anne turned in her seat and glanced back at the headlights of the vehicle following them. "I think I know where this is going . . ."

"I've never been able to prove anything, but Jimmy was out and around that night and has never told a soul where he was. I've asked him about it any number of times and his answer is always his patented *Ask me no questions and I'll tell you no lies.*

"Shortly thereafter, he dropped out of school. Still every day when Pam, Maureen and I got to school, he was standing outside the school-yard making sure we were safe."

"Did he still visit your parents' home a lot?"

"No. Pam stayed close to Maureen and of course me. Jimmy drifted away and took care of his mother and Pam. He did that until Moira passed away and Pam and I married."

"Having all that responsibility must have been tough. Was he working? As a dropout all he'd get would be minimum-wage work."

"Jimmy has never worked for minimum wage. I'm certain that he joined Bulger's Winter Hill Gang. I know he boosted cars, ran numbers and did any number of things."

"Including hits?"

"Anything is possible, except there was one thing he refused to get into—drugs. He saw firsthand what addiction does to families and shied away from trafficking."

"I find that hard to believe."

"Well, it was true back then. I'm not too sure about now though. Let me tell you a story. It was the summer of ninety-nine, my first year as a detective."

———————

Boston was on the verge of exploding. It was the hottest, most humid day in the hottest summer since the weather bureau had started tracking that type of data. The temperature had hovered around 100 degrees for eight days and the humidity was a constant ninety percent; the heat index had been around 120 for seven days. Even darkness brought little relief to those without air conditioning; the city was at its breaking point and crime had escalated to an all-time high. Drive-by shootings were hourly events and gang-warfare erupted over minor incidents. Days and nights were so oppressive that the population started having fond thoughts of February's biting cold.

Houston was on his first stake out as a detective. He and his partner, Wilbur Addams, were parked out of sight in a dark alley, where they sat quietly in their unmarked car. Their shirts were soaked through with sweat and plastered to their backs. The ripe, sickening stench of rotting garbage filled the air.

"Smell is bad enough to gag a maggot," Addams said.

Houston glanced at him. "Now there's a visual I could have gladly gone without."

Jimmy O'Leary had told Houston that he suspected a large quantity of dope was going to change hands at one of his warehouses—estimated at over two million dollars street value. At first Houston was surprised that Jimmy O would sell out another mobster, but then it was drugs—O'Leary hated anything related to dope and the people who dealt in it.

They had been observing the warehouse, sitting in the oppressive heat and humidity for over three hours. During the time they had watched, Addams made several trips outside, ostensibly to inspect the area, or so he had said. Houston knew better. His partner was a drinking problem looking for a place to happen and the only thing he checked out was the scotch whiskey he carried in his ever-present flask. Houston was surly and it was not entirely due to the heat and humidity. More pressing issues drove him crazy—for instance the prospect of chasing a perp in the dark with a drunken partner as backup.

Addams straightened up. "Look," he said, pointing as a van turned the corner at the far end of the block.

The truck crept along the block of storehouses. It slowed, almost stopping in front of each building on the street, its driver peering out the passenger window, as though looking for an address.

"Let's get ready." Addams got out of the sedan.

Houston stepped from the car, avoiding a pile of garbage, and joined Addams in front. As the vehicle got closer, neither spoke nor moved. They remained as still as two statues until the Ford Econoline stopped in front of the building across from them. They watched the driver get out and unlock the door. He was cautious and looked in all directions before entering the building. Houston was glad they had parked back in the alley away from the ambient illumination of the streetlights. The driver seemed satisfied that he was unobserved and turned to the building. He fumbled for a key and then after a few seconds opened a door and went inside. An interior light came on, then a rusty latch ground in protest and the overhead garage door finally lifted—several times it caught on something in the tracks as it opened. The driver returned to the truck, and slowly drove it into the warehouse.

"Let's go," Addams said.

"Wait."

"Why?"

"Let's give it a few minutes. He wouldn't have to unlock everything if there were anyone else in there. He's waiting for someone . . ."

"All right, but this asshole better not get away."

Houston could barely discern the features of his partner's face in the shadows created by the dim light of the sole working streetlamp. He couldn't see the details of his partner's face, but experience told him all he needed to know about what was going on in Addams's mind and how he was going to act. "Will, keep cool," he said.

"I hate these fucking leeches," Addams said. "They suck the blood out of anyone who buys their shit."

Another truck rounded the same corner as the first and slowly cruised down the street toward their position.

"This could be them," Houston said.

He and Addams retreated to the rear of their car and squatted there, trying to minimize the possibility of the oncoming vehicle's headlights illuminating their faces.

The Chevy stopped in front of the open garage door and three men got out. In a manner similar to that of the first driver, they quickly scanned the area, looking for anything that might interfere with their business. Seeing nobody, two of the men entered the building, leaving the third as sentinel. Once his companions were safely inside, the guard reached inside the truck and retrieved an assault rifle that Houston thought was an M-16.

"I'll call for backup." Before he could grab the two-way radio's handset, Houston knew Addams was already on the move. Through the rear window Addams's bent figure disappeared around the corner of the warehouse that hid them. *Damn him*, Houston thought. He quickly called in their location, requested backup and then ran after Addams.

Before Houston could catch up with him, Addams had traveled the length of the warehouse, trotting as fast as he could without making unnecessary noise. In short time, Houston saw him reach the end of the building, draw his pistol and turn left, disappearing from sight.

Houston accelerated until he too reached the corner, hoping to overtake Addams before he bolted across the street. He was too late. He rounded the corner and saw that his partner had already crossed the street and approached the target building from the rear. Since he had been given no alternative, Houston followed.

Houston shadowed Addams down another narrow alley to the access road that served the warehouses from the rear. He peered in both directions and once he was certain that the way was clear, he continued until he too was behind the building where the deal was to go down. For the first time since he had left the car, Addams looked for his partner. When he saw Houston creep around the back corner, he raised his right hand and pumped it up and down—the infantry signal to hurry up. When he reached Addams, Houston motioned to him that he needed a few seconds to regain his breath. Addams nodded that he understood. Houston crept to the corner and ventured a look.

The lookout leaned on the van's left front fender, his back to Addams, cradling the assault weapon in his arms. He seemed to be enjoying the evening as he smoked a cigarette.

Addams grinned at him and Houston realized his partner was enjoying himself.

"Keep your cool, Will," Houston whispered, repeating the warning that he had given his partner earlier.

Addams didn't acknowledge the warning. Without a word, he slipped around the corner of the building, his pistol trained on the sentry. Houston barely heard him say, "Police. Don't move."

The lookout froze for a second and then threw his cigarette to the ground with a curse. "I'll be a son of a bitch!" He raised the rifle and Addams shot him in the chest. Before the gunshot had ceased echoing, there was shouting inside the building. Houston ran to the guard and bent down to check on the man. He placed two fingers on his carotid artery checking for a pulse. He was dead.

Houston crouched beside the truck and watched Addams holster his service pistol and pick up the discarded assault rifle. A shot rang out from the door of the warehouse. The round smashed through the front window of the van, spider-webbing it. Addams spun and fired. The bullet slammed into the shooter, who stepped backward and fell against an empty garbage can. The metal walls of the half-empty warehouse acted like a waveguide and amplified the sound of the gunfight. Houston heard cursing and people running inside the warehouse.

Houston ran to Addams's side and grabbed his arm. "If you weren't in such a rush to be a fucking hero, things like this wouldn't happen."

"Okay, no reason to go postal over it. I want these bastards." Addams turned his attention back to the building. "Cover me. I'm going in."

"You're nuts, Will. By now they've probably split."

"Maybe they have, maybe they haven't." Addams darted inside the door and another shot rang out.

Houston peered around the sedan, looking inside the raised overhead door and saw Addams laying on the floor, a pool of blood slowly forming beside his body. One of the drug dealers stood over him and another was beside the van with his gun aimed toward the doorway. He saw Houston and fired.

Houston raced inside and dove for shelter behind a pallet piled high with flattened cardboard totes. Bullets slammed into the cardboard, sending bits of confetti into the air.

When the echoes of the gunshots faded away, Houston heard someone running up metal stairs. He ran toward the sound.

Houston raced through the building, quickly searching the aisles of shelving. He heard the scrape of a shoe and spun around, his weapon poised to shoot. A young man stood in the aisle with his hands in the air.

"Don't shoot, man," the kid said. "I give up."

Houston rose from his crouch and slowly advanced. He kept watching the boy's eyes. Experience had taught him that if a perp was going to do anything, their eyes were usually the first thing to give them away.

Suddenly, the boy's eyes darted to the right and his right hand moved down, toward the waistband of his jeans. Houston shot him, then walked to the kid and removed the pistol from his jeans.

The boy was no more than sixteen or seventeen and was moaning and crying as he grasped his damaged shoulder. Houston grabbed the neck of his T-shirt and ripped it until he was able to inspect the wound. "That was a stupid fucking move, son."

He dragged the teenager down the aisle and across the floor to the Ford. He handcuffed his prisoner's uninjured arm, fastened it to the truck's side mirror and then reached inside and pulled the keys from the ignition switch. "Don't go anywhere. I'll be back."

Houston located the metal stairs and slowly started up. He wiped at his forehead to keep perspiration out of his eyes as he peered into the darkness. The catwalk provided access to six or seven doors. There were two more gunmen in the building and they could be behind any one of the entries. Creeping along the catwalk, he heard someone running below and froze in position. The dealers had him bracketed, one on the landing and one was obviously watching the stair, which to the best of Houston's knowledge was the only way down. He had gotten himself trapped.

Houston saw an armed man dart between two rows of pallets and turned to retreat down the stairs.

"Drop the gun." The voice made it clear he had no other option.

"I'm a cop," Houston announced, hoping it would make the man pause before shooting.

"So was he." The man pointed to Addams 's body. "It didn't do him any more good than it will you."

Houston vacillated, trying to decide whether he should take a chance and either run down the stairs or try to shoot the dealer before he was able to get a shot off.

"Use your head, cop. You won't make it ten feet before I kill you. Give it up."

Houston raised his hands and waited.

The gunman took Houston's pistol and nudged him down the stairs. When they reached the floor, another man appeared from the rows of pallets.

"Shoot him and let's get the hell out of here. This place will be full of cops in no time."

Houston glanced around, trying to find an escape route. Suddenly a car appeared out of the night, blocking the door and cutting off the dealers' avenue of exit. Houston and his captors tried to identify the new arrivals and stared into the harsh glare of the car's headlights. Doors opened and closed and seconds later, Jimmy O'Leary and three of his men walked in.

"Maurice," O'Leary said, "you pull that trigger and you're dead."

The drug dealers looked panicked. This development was not to their liking.

O'Leary reached over and took Maurice's gun from him. "You guys using my property for illicit purposes?"

"J-J-Jimmy, we was just transferring stuff from one vehicle to another."

"I had a feeling when you called and asked to use one of my buildings that you were moving smack. So I placed a call to an old friend. Ain't that right, Mike?"

Houston felt his tension and fear dissipate like a single drop of rain in the desert. "Yeah, Jimmy, that's right."

"Mike, why don't you put your hands down? You look kind of fuckin' silly standing there like that."

Houston looked at Addams. He bent over and checked for a pulse. "You may have lucked out, asshole. He isn't dead."

"Still gonna do time for something I didn't do—fuckin' Jules shot him." Maurice licked his lips, a sure sign of fear, and sweat—not entirely caused by the heat and humidity—dripped from his chin.

"Oh, I don't think you boys are going to do any time," O'Leary said. "I got other plans for you—I don't like it when you misery merchants try to put one over on me. You know I don't do the drug thing and by using my building, you may have involved me. I got to tell you, Maurice, that don't make me happy."

One of O'Leary's men stood beside the truck and looked inside. "The junk is in the van."

"Good, leave it there. Put Maurice and Jules in their truck and take them away."

"Where you want me to take them?"

"I don't care, as long as I never see or hear of them again."

"Jimmy, c'mon man, can't we talk about this?" Sweat soaked through Maurice's shirt and his eyes darted back and forth between Houston and O'Leary as he pleaded for his life.

"Maurice, you know how it is—if you fuck with a bull sooner or later you're gonna get gored. Get them out of here."

"What about the kid?" one of O'Leary's men asked.

Jimmy O looked at the frightened boy, still shackled to the door of the Ford.

"Him too."

Houston tried to intervene on the kid's behalf. "Hell, Jimmy, I doubt this kid is much more than seventeen years old. Why don't you give him a break?"

O'Leary looked at the youngster. That the kid was scared out of his wits was evident to everyone. "Can't do that, Mike."

"Why not?"

"There's a couple of reasons." O'Leary shook a cigarette out of his pack and lit it. "One, I can't let him run all over town tellin' people I was a rat an' sold 'em out to you. Two, there's an old sayin' he should know by now: If you can't do the time, then don't do the crime." He nodded to his henchmen and they dragged the kid toward the other dealers, where they dropped him in a heap.

When they tied his hands behind his back with heavy plastic tie-wraps, the kid began to shout in pain. "What the fuck is his problem?" O'Leary asked.

"Could be the fact that I shot him," Houston answered.

"That'd do it." O'Leary turned to the kid.

Like Maurice, the kid begged and pleaded for his life. "I won't tell a soul, Mr. O'Leary, honest I won't."

As O'Leary smoked his cigarette, he appeared to be considering the boy's plea. He flicked the cigarette butt out the overhead door. "Kid, let's face the facts here, okay? I let you walk and in a week, two at the most, you'll be back on the street, dealin' smack again and I'll just have to kill you then. We might as well do it now and save everyone the expense of havin' to find you again."

O'Leary motioned for his men to usher them into the Econoline. He pulled one aside, a big blonde-haired man of over six feet in height and at least 250 pounds. "Once you're a few blocks from here, let the kid out. But Gordon, make sure he understands that if I ever hear of him sellin' drugs again, his next trip will be to the quarry where he'll be fitted for a pair of concrete flippers and taken for a midnight swim."

Gordon Winter nodded, walked to the car and got into the driver's seat. O'Leary's other men jumped in, holding guns to the captives' heads. Within seconds, the car was gone and it was as if it had never been there.

Jimmy O turned to Houston and grinned. "Had you goin' for a minute there, didn't I?"

"Yeah, you're a truckload of giggles. Now I got to get an ambulance here."

"Go call your ambulance," O'Leary said.

They walked out of the warehouse. Houston crossed the street and got into his car where he made an *officer down* call. He hung up the radio, looked out the window at Jimmy O. "I should stop this. I can't just let you assassinate them."

"C'mon, Mike. What I'm doing is a public service. If you arrested those clowns it would be months before they got to court, then some assistant D.A. and a public defender will strike a plea bargain. In less than six months, Maurice and Jules will be back on the street sellin' slow death to kids. My way saves the state a lot of money . . . and it's a final solution. B'sides, it ain't like you got any say about it."

They heard sirens and O'Leary walked to his car. "You be careful, Mike. The neighborhood is a lot more dangerous than it was when we were kids." He pointed to the van sitting in the warehouse. "You guys are gonna be heroes for this bust—that's a lot of smack in there. With your partner shot up, you'll be okay. Once they see the dead dealer, they'll figure the others got away and will call it a righteous shooting."

As O'Leary opened his car door, Houston called to him, "Jimmy."

"Yeah?"

"Thanks. I thought I was a goner in there."

"Hey, no big deal. This is what friends are for. Maybe there will be a time down the road when you'll be able to return the favor. See you around."

"What happened to the dope?" Anne asked.

"I turned it in as evidence . . . wouldn't surprise me to learn it was on the streets in two days."

"Did you return the favor?"

"No. At least, not yet."

"How have you avoided arresting him all this time?"

"Lucky, I guess. The captain may have had a lot to do with it. I'm certain he'd shit if he knew Jimmy was involved in this."

"I wouldn't be so sure of that."

Once more Houston took his eyes off the road and looked at her. "Really?"

"I think Dysart would make a pact with the Unabomber if it would bring this guy down."

29

"On frosty mornings and damp days, there is a great danger of smoke
from the rifle giving the position away. On such occasions, the sniper
must keep as far back in the hide as possible."
—*US Marine Corps Scout/Sniper Training Manual*

It was after midnight when they passed through Harris Mills, Maine, and left Route 16. A couple of miles north of the town Houston turned onto an unpaved logging road and darkness and the woods closed in like a shroud.

Anne looked out at the night sky. Without the ambient light of street lamps, millions of stars were visible, creating an amazing spectacle. "Now I know how it would feel to fly through space."

"Yeah, it's remote." Houston glanced in the rearview mirror and checked that Jimmy and Gordon were still following. He was unable to see their vehicle, but could see the glow of their headlights through the cloud of dust his tires created.

The road suddenly turned north, angling west, back to New Hampshire. According to Rosa's instructions, they were to stay on this road until they passed a gravel pit and came to a small picnic area and campground.

Houston was drowsy and shook his head to keep from nodding off. Fatigue bore down on him and he knew that he couldn't go any further, when a deep gravel pit suddenly appeared in the beams from his head-lights. In the darkness, it looked like a lunar crater. Houston's exhaustion disappeared and he became alert. He studied the road, searching for the turn-off to the campground. Rosa had told him that the entrance was about a half-mile past the pit.

The entrance to the campground appeared out of the primordial dark-ness and they pulled in. Houston hoped that it was unoccupied and sighed in relief when his headlights swept around the camp site and revealed that it was empty. Hunting season was still a couple of months away and he didn't want nosy campers asking why they had all the weapons. He parked near a picnic table and shut off the motor.

Houston and Anne got out of the rental SUV and stretched. The engine ticked as it cooled and the whirring of flying insects and the chirping croaks of frogs seemed loud in the darkness. Anne walked around the car and stood beside him. Still fascinated by the stellar light show, she looked up. "I don't think I've ever seen so many stars in the sky."

When Winter turned into the gravel-covered parking area, Anne and Houston held their hands up to shield their eyes from the brilliant glare of the Lincoln's halogen headlamps. The SUV stopped, its lights went out and the engine shut down. O'Leary stepped from the Navigator and he too looked at the sky.

"Amazing, ain't it?" he commented.

Winter placed his hands against his lower back and stretched while he too looked to the heavens. "There's gonna to be a full moon the next few nights—that ain't favorable."

"Not a goddamned hotel within miles," O'Leary said. "I was never into this Boy Scout shit." He wrapped his arms around his torso. "Fu—" He cast a nervous look at Anne and amended his words. "Friggin' cold, too."

Houston said, "We'll just roll out some canvas and sleep on the ground."

Houston felt it wasn't necessary to be cautious and did not attempt to be quiet. There was no need to worry about Rosa—at least not until he got to the killing ground. Rosa wouldn't violate the rules of the game—after all, he had made them.

Houston grabbed his and Anne's sleeping bags and a lantern from the back of the SUV. He switched on the battery-powered lantern, found a level place, checked the ground and removed several rocks that would make sleeping impossible. Once he was satisfied that the turf was as smooth and free of obstacles as possible, he spread the impromptu sleeping mat. He held the lantern and watched while Anne prepared her sleeping bag. It was the first time he had seen Anne in a plaid flannel shirt and blue jeans, and he thought she was born to wear them.

Houston glanced at his watch; it was four in the morning. To the east, he saw a slash of bright sky split the darkness above the horizon. Houston was surprised to see O'Leary standing beside him.

"I always wondered where the expression 'the crack of dawn' came from," Jimmy O said.

"Now you know. We'd better get some sleep—even a couple of hours can make a big difference."

Jimmy O walked toward the SUV. "What I wouldn't give for a nice soft king-size mattress . . ."

Houston chuckled and flopped down on his sleeping bag. Once again, he realized that old habits return fast. In the Marines, Houston had learned to eat and sleep whenever and wherever he had the opportunity, because in combat you never knew when, or if, you would get another chance. Once he reached the island, he would be in a battle situation and sleep deprivation and cold meals would be the norm until the mission was completed.

———————

The sun shining on her face woke Susie up. She lay still and surveyed the cabin. It was bare bones, with everyday conveniences nonexistent. The decrepit shack didn't even have running water. They had brought her here yesterday, thrown her on the old bunk and tied her up. The bed was horrible, a musty, mildew-covered mattress and pillow that smelled of rodent droppings and years of accumulated sweat.

The woman sat at the rough-hewn table in the center of the room. She wore camouflage clothes, her face painted in green and black stripes; she looked like one of the amazon warriors Susie had seen in action movies.

"Good morning," the woman said.

Susie glared at her.

"Have it your way," the woman stood up and walked to her. "You need to use the head?"

Susie did not understand what she meant.

"The bathroom, do you need to use it?"

Susie nodded.

"I'm sorry, I didn't hear you."

"Yes."

The woman removed the bonds that held Susie to the cot and helped her up. "I hope you aren't too delicate to pee in the bushes."

"I'll make do," Susie said.

"Good. You just keep that attitude and you'll be fine. This will be over tomorrow and you can go back to being a student."

"I thought he wanted my father alone."

"He does, but snipers always work in teams of two. Also, in the event that fails he has a backup plan. If your father is anywhere as good a sniper as I've heard, he won't be alone either—he'll have at least one spotter with him."

The scarred man walked into the shack. "Where you going?"

"Head call."

"Keep a close eye on her."

"I will. When do you think he'll arrive?"

"I doubt he'll get here before tomorrow morning."

"I'd feel better if we'd brought along a couple of my men to act as sentries . . ."

"The last thing I need is a bunch of trigger-happy reservists running around and stirring things up. Besides, that would take all of the challenge out of the game—wouldn't it?"

"I'm not real comfortable with your referring to this as a game," she said.

"It's the ultimate game—one where coming in second gets you a body bag. Now take the kid and do what you gotta do."

The woman took Susie's arm and led her outside.

Houston woke at six. His eyes felt like burning coals and his back was stiff and damp from the heavy dew that covered everything. He knew there was no time to waste so he began gathering his gear for the trek through the woods.

The sound of him preparing his equipment woke Anne. She stretched in her sleeping bag.

"Good morning."

"Mornin', beautiful, time to rise and shine."

"I'll rise, but I'm not so sure about the shine part."

Houston rocked back on his heels and swept the area with his eyes. "There's something that I love about the early-morning light. Everything seems so clean and brilliant—not faded as it does in late morning and during the afternoon hours."

Anne sat up and reached for her boots.

O'Leary sat up, grunted and lit his first cigarette of the day. "How in hell is a guy supposed to sleep with all that chit chat going on?"

Anne stared at him, ready to go on the attack.

"Hey, lighten up," he said. "I'm just jealous, that's all. It's been a long time since someone greeted me in the morning."

Anne realized his comment had been meant as a good-natured barb and relaxed.

"Sorry, Jimmy."

"Don't sweat it, kid. It took my mother thirty years to get to like me—even then, I think she was faking it. I'm like a fungus—give me time and I'll grow on you."

Winter got up and walked to the boat. He reached inside and brought out a gas camp stove. "The least we can do is make breakfast. It's even better in the great outdoors. Anyone want to get some water? There's a hand pump over there. There's nothin' better than that first cup of coffee in the mornin'."

While Anne fetched the water, Houston and Winter lifted a large cooler from the inside of the boat. Winter lifted the cover and Houston saw enough food to feed them for the better part of a week.

"Gotta eat if we want to keep up our strength."

They cooked eggs, sausage and canned potatoes on the stove and sat quiet while they ate.

Finally, O'Leary broke the early morning silence. "What's our plan of attack?"

"The shooter gave me very detailed instructions. I'm to follow the trail that leads due east from here for about three hours, until I come to the lake where he's hidden a boat in some brush. I'm supposed to go north on the lake to the largest island. Once I reach the island, the game will begin."

Houston spread out a map. "There's no way we're going to be able to portage Gordon's boat three hours through the woods." He indicated a point on the Magallaway River. "It looks as if there's a boat launch here, you guys drive there and we'll meet on the south end of the third island this evening."

Jimmy stared at the map for a second. "Send Gordon and Anne back there—I'll stay with you."

"Jimmy, this ain't a stroll on the common. You got a three-pack-a-day habit and hiking through rough terrain is tough enough without that. I'll make the hike alone. I'm not so naïve that I think he's alone. He could have someone watching to make sure I didn't bring anyone with me."

"Why don't you come with us? We can use the motor boat to get there." Anne motioned to Gordon's boat.

"I'm going to follow his instructions to the letter."

Winter stood and peered into the trees around them. "Shit, they may be watching us now . . ."

"For some reason, I don't think so. But once I get to the lake it wouldn't surprise me if they were watching. That's why I want you guys to arrive at the island after dark—no lights on the boat."

Gordon Winter snorted. "All we got to do is navigate a lake I've never been on, to find an island that I've never been to, in the dark—should be a piece of cake." He poured the last of his coffee on the ground.

"That's where the full moon will help us," Houston said. "Besides, I'll have a small campfire going. You should be able to see it a long ways off."

"Won't the fire give away your location?" Anne asked.

"Possibly, that's why I'll camp on the south shore, away from the fourth island. Even if he does see the fire, he'll be expecting me to make a fire when I camp. The important thing is that he doesn't learn that I've brought you guys along as backup."

Winter rinsed the pans and coffeepot. "Well, looks as if we got a full day ahead of us—time to break camp."

Houston got his rifle from behind the backseat of his vehicle. He took great care when he placed the rifle on a blanket, unpacked the ten-power Unertl scope and securely mounted it to the rifle.

"That's a beautiful weapon," O'Leary commented. "I hope you appreciate what I had to go through to get it on short notice. They only made a thousand of them, and you'd be damned lucky to get one on the open market. In fact, I'd say it was almost impossible."

"It's accurate," Houston said. "Even though it's been years since I've been a sniper, I'm still more than capable of keeping a group in a two-or three-inch diameter inside two hundred meters."

Houston seemed to slip into another world as his hands caressed the rifle stock. He took out a bore-sighter and, with help from Winter, spent several minutes ensuring that the scope was properly aligned. He seemed more at ease than she had ever seen him . . . it was as if he had gone back in time to a place where no one would ever reach him.

Houston looked at O'Leary. "Thanks, Jimmy. What it set you back?"

"More than you can afford on a cop's salary—leave it at that. All I ask is that if possible you bring it back. I can probably resell it."

Houston raised a hand in the universal signal to stop. "I don't want to hear anymore, Jimmy. Remember, even though we're allies and brothers-in-law, I'm still a cop."

Houston took a box of ammunition from the truck and loaded the rifle. He opened the bolt and fed the integral magazine by pushing four cartridges into the breach one at a time. Once the last round was inserted, he closed the bolt and double-checked that the rifle was on safe.

When he gently placed the loaded weapon on his sleeping bag, Houston noticed that no one spoke and the camp was abnormally quiet. He looked at his companions. "I need to sight it in. I haven't fired any live rounds through this and I need to get a feel for the rifle and check the scope's alignment."

Anne picked up the rifle for him and was surprised by its weight. "That's heavy."

"Fourteen and a half pounds," Houston said. "That and the fact that it's bolt action is probably why it was never popular with the grunts." He saw the question on Anne's face. "The infantry call themselves grunts. This weapon would be too heavy to carry for hours on end and in a fire-fight it's difficult to gain fire superiority with a bolt action. It doesn't fire fast enough—accurate, but slow. We scout-snipers became accustomed to it."

"I don't know about anyone else," Winter added, "but I wanted more than five rounds in my magazine; then there's the problem of having to manually work the bolt action in the middle of a shit sandwich where gaining fire superiority means survival."

"I agree," Houston said, "but to a sniper it's all about accuracy."

"One shot; one kill," O'Leary said.

"It has an effective range of a thousand meters. At that distance you have plenty of time to work the bolt action." Houston took the rifle from Anne and picked up two boxes of 7.62 mm ammunition.

Winter walked to his truck, opened the door and motioned for Houston to join him. "I'll go with you and spot." He picked up a black plastic case and tossed it to Houston.

"What's this?" Houston asked.

"A Leupold Mark 4 Tactical Spotting Scope. All we need now is someplace big enough to sight in these weapons."

"That gravel pit we passed last night will be ideal." Houston placed his rifle, targets and ammunition into Winter's truck. "Shall we go?"

They reached the pit in ten minutes. While Houston cleared a shooting position, Winter used duct tape to mount targets to some plywood stands he had in the back of his truck, then paced off an estimated one hundred and three hundred meters, setting targets at each benchmark. He returned to the shooting position and stood beside Houston. He used a range-finder scope to measure the distance to the hundred-meter target. Winter sat on the ground and watched the target through the Leupold.

Houston got into a prone firing position and peered through the scope. When he was satisfied that he had good sight alignment and sight picture, he used his thumb to take the rifle off safe and fired.

"Low and to the left . . . bring it up one and right two," Winter said.

Houston turned the elevation knob up one click and the windage two to the right. He settled back in, worked the bolt to eject the expended cartridge and loaded a live round into the chamber. He took three deep breaths, exhaling slowly after each one. When the scope's crosshairs centered on the bull's-eye, he fired again.

"Bull."

Houston fired four rounds as fast as he could work the bolt action.

"Nice tight group in the bull," Winter said. "Do you miss it?"

"Miss what?" He removed a small spiral notebook from his hip pocket and recorded the scope's elevation and windage settings for the hundred-meter distance.

"The military—the high of going into combat with a group of guys you'd bet your life on and hunting an armed enemy."

"I did for a while. It's been over fifteen years since I was in and it fades." Houston fed another load of cartridges into the rifle's magazine.

"I hope I never get that way. I loved being in."

"Why'd you get out?"

"Wasn't entirely my choice. There was this sergeant who rode my ass from sunup to sundown. I finally had enough of it and took action."

"You get a dishonorable?" Houston asked.

"No, the members of the courts martial realized that the asshole had pushed me too far. Nevertheless, like everywhere, lifers always rally together and look out for each other. I got an honorable discharge under general conditions."

Houston glanced down range and turned his attention to the three-hundred-meter target.

It took a little over an hour for Houston to zero in the scope, record the windage and elevation settings for each distance and feel comfortable in his ability to hit anything he shot at out to five hundred meters.

Winter walked to his truck and returned with an assault rifle. He fired a full magazine of twenty rounds into the hundred-meter target. The barrage of supersonic rounds shredded the target and Winter smiled. "I don't think I'll be using this past one hundred meters—seems fine to me."

Houston stared at the target. Winter's volley had ripped it in half and the pieces flapped in the breeze like pennants.

"Not exactly a subtle weapon, is it?" Winter asked.

"No, I'd say it's about as subtle as a kick in the nuts."

"Can't beat one of these in a firefight though."

"Does Jimmy have you use that much?"

"No way I'm going to answer that. Who knows, once this is over we could be facing each other from different sides."

"If I know Jimmy as well as I think I do, I'd bet he does a lot of his own wet work."

"He believes in a hands-on managerial approach," Winter said. "Besides, his smoker's breath is lethal enough."

Houston laughed and packed up his equipment. As they drove back to camp, they passed the time chatting about their time in the military.

Once they were back in the campsite, Houston changed into camouflage coveralls and pulled out his Ghillie suit. He had chosen an oak color so he would blend in with the hardwoods that inhabited the northern woods. Once he started stalking, Houston would gather native flora, weave it into the netting, and tie the suit to his camouflaged coveralls. It was obvious to him that he was going to have to move through heavy brush and didn't want to worry about the suit snagging on branches and bushes as he moved. He carefully rolled the Ghillie up and fastened it with Velcro straps to the bottom of a backpack.

Once the sniper suit was secure, the backpack was filled with ammunition, beef jerky and canned cheese and crackers. He strapped two canteens of water around his waist and made a mental note to ensure the canteens were full at all times; all the camouflage in the world would do no good if his quarry heard water sloshing around in a half-full canteen. He poured a cup of coffee and, while drinking, conducted a mental inventory. *Damn it*, he thought, *it's been so long and there's so much to remember.*

Had the sniper not taken Susie, he would say to hell with it and return to Boston where he would be on familiar turf and could use conventional police procedures. He knew those thoughts were folly. After eight days and seven deaths, he was no closer to getting the shooter than he had been on the first day. It had to be done this way: using the rules that had been hammered into him and the assassin long ago. What bothered him most was that his quarry had obviously kept his skills honed, while he, on the other hand, had let his deteriorate.

Thus far, Anne had left him to his thoughts, but now that the time for the operation to commence was upon them, she broke her silence. "I don't like the thought of you going in without backup."

"It's no big deal."

"Still."

"Anne, don't worry. I've done this before."

"When you were a lot younger! It's been a long time since you were a marine, Mike."

"Like riding a bicycle . . . it never leaves you."

"Mike . . ."

"I'll be all right."

"This is nothing to take lightly." She knew Houston didn't want to debate with her in front of the others and glanced over her shoulder to see if either O'Leary or Winter were within earshot. "Fatigue raises the percentage that you'll make mistakes and you've only slept a few hours in the past two days. It could be fatal. What if you become exhausted on the island?"

"I'll deal with it." Houston was curt, ending the discussion. "I'll be all right. Trust me on this."

Jimmy stood beside Winter's car and called out. "Anne, we better get moving if we want to get to the island before midnight."

Anne wiped her hands on her jeans, reluctant to leave.

"Go on," Houston said. "I'll be fine."

She nodded, stood still for a second and then walked to the truck.

Previously, they had agreed that they would leave both vehicles at the boat launch, so O'Leary got into Houston's SUV. Anne paused, then turned and gave Houston a final look before getting in beside him. Winter waved out the driver-side window of his SUV and backed out of the campground.

Houston waited until they were out of sight, opened his backpack, took out the pistol belt that held his Glock 9mm automatic pistol with holster, and strapped it around his waist. He doused the campfire, slid the backpack over his shoulders, shrugged a couple of times to settle it on his back and started down the trail with the sniper rifle slung over his right shoulder.

O'Leary smoked a cigarette and flicked ashes out the open window. He finished smoking, dropped the butt into a disposable cup of cold coffee and glanced at Anne.

"It's going to be okay."

Anne stopped staring at the forest and looked at him. She made no sign of recognition.

"You don't like me much, do you?"

"Jimmy, I don't know you enough either to like or dislike you on a personal basis. It's what you *do* that's my problem."

"That's bullshit and we both know it. I can see it in your face every time you're around me. You aren't one of those broads who hate the fact that her man had a life before her, are you?"

"Not especially." Anne continued to glare at him. "Besides, Mike isn't *my* man. He's my partner."

"Either way, I know women like that. They think that everything that happened to him before they came along is a threat. Well, Anne, all I can say is this: Mike and me grew up together. Yeah, we've had our differences, but ain't nothing going to happen to him as long as ol' Jimmy O has any say in the matter. So what you say we bury the hatchet until we get beyond this—then you can go back to disliking me."

"Jimmy, as I said, it's not that I don't like you . . ."

"I know, I know. I smoke too much, I'm a chauvinistic asshole, I'm uglier than road kill, and you don't like what I do for a living—other than that I'm a prince. Ain't I right?"

Anne started laughing, in spite of herself. "Jimmy . . ."

"Yeah?"

"Mike and I . . . we're nothing more than friends and partners."

O'Leary looked at her. "Whether you know it or not, you mean a lot to him. I saw him like that once before. With my sister. Mike and Pam married young. Hell, as close as we were as kids, it didn't surprise anyone. Still, you ever know two people who were crazy in love, but at the same time were toxic to each other?"

"A few come to mind."

"Well, that was my sister and Mike. Pam had gotten her fill of craziness and violence when we was kids. All she wanted was a quiet life away from Southie and all the bad shit that happened to her there. On the other hand, Mike's like me. I guess you could say that we're adrenaline junkies. We need action. Things that are *normal*, if there is such a thing, bore the shit out of us. The only difference between him and me is the way we get our fix."

Anne remained quiet, mulling over what O'Leary had said.

"In her own way, Pam was as fucked up as we were. I done some reading and I think I know what her downfall as a wife was. After years as a helpless victim, she wanted to control the uncontrollable . . ."

"And by uncontrollable, do you mean Mike?"

"Yeah, no matter how much anyone tries to convince him otherwise, he's gonna do what he has to do. I know that and he knows that. Hell, I'll take it a step further—sometime down the road he and I are gonna come up against each other professionally. Well, I'll deal with that when the time comes."

Anne offered him her hand and when he gripped it she said, "Truce until this is over?"

O'Leary shook her hand. "It's going to be a nice day for a boat ride."

30

"At dawn and dusk, the flash from a shot can usually be clearly seen
and care must be taken not to disclose the position of the hide . . ."
—*US Marine Corps Scout/Sniper Training Manual*

The morning was warm, beautiful and sunny, and in no time Houston fell into the easy rhythmic ground-covering gait familiar to experienced infantrymen. He felt fortunate—giant trees sheltered the trail from direct sunlight and beneath the thick canopy the temperature was in the mid-seventies, while in direct sunlight it was most likely in the mid-eighties. In short time his muscles warmed, loosening the knots that had formed while he had slept on the cold, damp ground.

After he'd hiked what he estimated to be two miles, the trail downgraded from an old logging road to a footpath. After walking for two and a half hours, his leg muscles began to burn. He did a lot of walking on the job, but that was on paved city streets, a completely different thing from hiking through virgin forest. Houston knew if he ceased walking his legs would cool and stiffen, so rather than pause for a break, he pushed forward.

The trail followed a brook and sloped to the north. In short time, it became rocky and wet, making the footing treacherous. Rain had carved a narrow wash along the path, deep enough that an unwary or careless hiker could twist or sprain an ankle. Houston wanted to avoid any foolish accidents and slowed his pace, cautiously studying the terrain beneath his feet. Suddenly he stumbled and his left foot slid into the gully and rolled over as he slid forward. Pain lanced through his ankle. Houston cursed, held the injured foot out and dropped to his haunches. He removed his pack and gear and shook his head in a futile attempt to deal with the pain. It didn't help. Sitting on the edge of the gully, Houston removed his boot. His luck held; he was able to see that while he had rolled his ankle and it hurt, it was neither sprained nor broken. He replaced his boot and tightened the laces as much as he could to provide the ankle with enough support to continue on. He struggled into his backpack and used his rifle's butt as a crutch to get back on his feet. He hobbled down the hill following the brook, waiting for the exercise to diminish the pain.

Fifteen minutes later, he came to Aroostook Lake.

————————————

The sniper sat in front of the shack, smoking a cigar. The noon sun warmed his ravaged skin. He glanced at his watch. *Mikey should be gettin' close*, he thought.

"You think he'll come?"

"He'll come."

"What's to stop him from notifying the FBI of the kidnapping and sending them here?"

"His pride will drive him here—pride and anger will be his undoing. I'm sure that by now, he's thoroughly pissed off. I've killed his friends, his kid's mother and he's never gotten close enough to see me. I know that would grate on my ass. The truth of the matter is that he not only wants to see me dead, but he wants to be the one to do it. If the Feds get involved, they won't let him kill me."

"He won't be alone."

"He'd be stupid if he was. If he's shot, who's going to get the kid? You'll have your hands full too, Frankie. There will be plenty of opportunity to prove your marksmanship abilities."

"Don't call me Frankie. What is it between you two?"

"It goes back to ninety-three, in Somalia. I was a corporal and Houston was a sergeant and my squad leader. We had different ideas on how the war should be fought. He was too selective when it came to picking targets."

"And you weren't?"

"That wasn't my job. My job was to kill skinnies. It was God's job to keep the innocent safe. My ol' man was in 'Nam. He told me about how there were no civilians there. The guy who cut your hair in the base barber shop in the afternoon was the same one shootin' rockets and mortars at you that night. The gooks would have a kid hold a grenade—with the pin pulled—behind its back and walk into a bunch of our guys to beg for candy. When the kid reached for what the grunts offered, the grenade fell and killed the gook kid along with the Americans. If the enemy doesn't give a shit about their own, why should we?'

"So your philosophy was to shoot everyone."

"And let God sort out the innocent."

"That still doesn't explain why you hate him so much."

The sniper inhaled and removed the cigar from his burn-scarred lips. He stared at the burning tobacco. "Ever wonder how the fiery end of this butt feels? I know. I was on fire once."

Since Estes had met him, she had gone to great lengths not to question him about his scars. She remained silent as he told her what happened on that fateful day.

Houston stopped on the shore and stared at the massive body of water. When Rosa gave him his instructions, Houston had researched the lake, but he hadn't expected anything this rustic and beautiful. Before him, nestled in the forest, was 6,700 acres of clean water with a maximum depth of 160 feet. In the summer, the population swelled with the influx of people who own cabins—called camps by the locals—on the lake and its islands, places for seasonal "getting away from it all" rather than year-round living. Even then, the population was so sparse that no telecommunications or power company found it profitable enough to run phone and power lines beyond the general store and boat launch on the lake's southern shore. If a resident wanted electricity anywhere else on Aroostook Lake, he or she had to bring in a generator by boat.

Houston decided to take a break for a meal and let his weary legs and sore ankle rest. He opened a topographical map of the lake and its surrounding area and located his destination, which wasn't difficult, as it was the largest island in the lake. However, depending on the type of boat Rosa had left for him, it could take hours to get there.

Houston made a small fire and ate a hot lunch. It would have been faster to eat a cold meal, but he had no idea how long he would be on the water and unable to cook. His hunger sated, Houston dipped his mess kit into the surprisingly cold lake water. He scoured the metal dishes with sand and gravel. Once he was satisfied all was in order, he searched the shoreline, looking for the boat Rosa had hidden. When he found it, he knew it was going to take him some time to reach the island. "The bastard left me a canoe and a paddle!"

Houston hadn't rowed a canoe in years and would have to remaster it while underway. He threw his gear in the front, shoved the craft away from the shore and jumped in. He pushed out into the lake, dipped the paddle into the water on the left side of the canoe, and pulled it back as hard as he could. The small vessel angled to the left, and he realized he was going to have to use less force on the paddle and alternate sides if he wanted to travel in a straight line. In short time, Houston got the hang of keeping the canoe on a straight course and sliced through the water, his destination a dark bump on the horizon.

After an hour, the islands seemed no closer and his shoulders ached from the unaccustomed exertion. He muttered to himself and kept paddling. Suddenly a thought occurred to him and he smiled. Rosa may have made his first mistake. In his place, Houston would have left a motorized boat. The lake was so quiet that he would hear a motor miles before it reached him (something he needed to keep in mind when the others arrived). A canoe, on the other hand, was quiet and stealthy. Houston might gain the element of surprise. He wanted to time his trip so he would reach the killing ground around sunrise. Not that his arrival time mattered a whole lot. Regardless of when he arrived, Rosa would be waiting and watching.

The old man who ran the landing stood off to the side, smoking a pipe and admiring Gordon's boat. "Yuh, I betcha that baby'll handle big water. Looks sturdy enough for salt water."

"It's ocean-worthy," the big blonde fellow said.

The old-timer inspected the gear this strange group of fishermen had brought—if they were fishermen. Their equipment was better suited to hunting and it was almost two months until bird hunting started, three until moose and deer seasons.

"Where you folks say you was from?"

"Boston," the woman said.

"I knowed you was from away." He sucked on the pipe; a cloud of smoke rolled out of his mouth and formed a small cloud around his head before dispersing in the wind. He looked at the rifles the big, young fellow had loaded into the boat, one of which was one of them assault rifles he had seen on TV. "Gonna shoot them fish, are yuh?" He addressed the third and oldest member of this strange party.

When he got no answer, the old man ignored the man's surly silence and continued talking in his rambling manner. "Yup, don't get many folks in here. They like the more populated lakes like Sebago and Moosehead. I'll put our lake up against them anytime—once Labor Day comes it gets quiet out here, you know?"

The big young man walked onto the dock and patted him on the shoulder. "Keep an eye on our trucks, will you, old-timer? We'll be back in a couple of days and there may be a few bucks in it for you."

"Well, you should have a coupla good days fer it. S'posed to be clear, warm, and calm, although the feller on the radio outta Mexico says it could rain t'morrah night. You kids want to buy some fishin' poles and tackle? Game wardens here about don't like it when fishermen shoot at the fish . . ."

"Actually, we're here to take pictures of the wildlife."

"That so? You coulda knocked me down with a tamarack branch before I ever woulda figured that out. To me it looks more like you're huntin'."

"Well, we heard that bears and stuff can be dangerous so we thought we'd be careful."

"Yup, that's a fact . . . only they ain't much of a problem after spring. Once the cubs get able to fend for themselves. Looks to me like you folks are headin' up to the big island. You part of that bunch a damned fools that play soldier up there from time to time?"

"You got us figured out, old-timer."

"You know," the oldest man said, "it might be a good idea to have a couple of rods and some tackle. A mess of fresh fish would be nice."

The old man nodded once. "You got licenses?"

"We drove here, didn't we?" The older one couldn't keep the sarcasm out of his voice.

The old-timer either did not pick up on his tone or ignored it. "I mean fishing licenses."

None of them had thought about that.

"The state ain't got a lot of money these days and cops and game wardens are checkin' things close. Of late, they been handin' out a shitload of tickets." He held out his hand. "Name's Guy Harris. I own this place."

The woman gripped his hand. "I'm Anne Bouchard." She indicated to the oldest man. "This is Jimmy O'Leary . . . the big man is Gordon Winter."

Harris nodded his head. "Know a bunch of Bouchards, mostly good people. There's a bunch of O'Learys up around Allagash—some of the best guides—and poachers—in Maine. All I know of Winter is it's damn cold and harsh." His eyes crinkled at the joke.

"Cold and harsh," O'Leary said. "That's Gordon, all right. We don't have licenses. Anyplace close by where can we get them?"

"Just so happens I'm an authorized game inspection station and agent for the Department of Inland Fisheries and Wildlife. It'll cost you . . ."

Harris scrutinized the Massachusetts license plates on both SUVs and the boat trailer and kept to himself the fact that he thought it strange that they had two trucks for three people. "How long you plan on being here?"

"Two, three days at the most," Winter answered.

"A three-day nonresident fishing license will cost you twenty-three bucks plus two bucks agency fee—each. C'mon up the store an' I'll fix you right up."

O'Leary followed Harris into the small country store/snack bar/tackle shop and learned that he was owner and sole employee. He asked him what he thought they would need. For someone who looked like a backwoods hick, the man was a shrewd businessman; based upon his recommendations, O'Leary bought three fishing poles, some hooks and tackle and artificial bait. The bill came to $250 and change.

"I could buy a hell of a lot of fish for two and a half bills," he said.

"You think that's expensive, wait until you get one or two of them hefty fines the state hands out—not to mention havin' your boat and them fancy weapons impounded. Besides, I don't see how you can put a price on the trip of a lifetime." He handed O'Leary a paper booklet titled *Open Water and Ice Fishing Laws and Rules*. "Keep a tight grip on that. State's so friggin' broke they only print so many. Once they's gone, ain't gonna be no more."

"Thanks." O'Leary reached for his wallet. "You take credit cards?"

"Nope, don't take checks neither—I run a strictly cash business."

"Well, we got that in common." O'Leary counted out the money.

"Send the others in and I'll give them their licenses, unless you know their information."

O'Leary gathered his purchases and walked out of the store to the pier where Anne and Winter were standing beside the boat. "The old fart says you need to go in and get your licenses. I already paid for them."

Ten minutes later, Anne and Winter returned. Gordon got in the boat and held it alongside the dock with his hand. When O'Leary stepped off the wooden wharf and awkwardly lowered his body into the craft, it bobbed and started pulling away from the mooring. He almost fell into the lake. Once seated, he said, "I feel like a fuckin' cow walking on a frozen pond."

Harris chuckled. He helped Anne into the boat and tipped his hat to her. "Well, you kids have a good time. I'm always here from sunup until sundown. So if you get tired of roughin' it, just come on back. Oh, yeah, the state bird has been declared one of them endangered species, so don't hurt one . . ."

"What is the state bird?" Anne naïvely asked.

"Hell, young lady, I thought everyone knew what the state bird of Maine is—it's the black fly! 'Course, like the bears, they ain't much of a problem this late in the year . . ."

It irked O'Leary to no end when he heard the old man laughing to himself, apparently enjoying his joke, as he ambled up the pier toward the store. "What the fuck is a tamarack?"

Winter answered, "Beats me—probably some kind of tree."

Harris laughed harder.

The afternoon passed quickly. Houston lost himself in the rhythm of paddling the canoe across the placid lake. The water was cleaner and clearer than any he had encountered anywhere in the world. Several times, he scooped a handful and sipped it. It was sweet and cold. He wondered how many springs there were on the lake bottom. As they had on the drive from Boston, thoughts of leaving the hassle of city life for something simpler played in his mind. Maybe he was ready to put society behind him for the allure of the simple life. Not quite this simple, but something close to it where the tranquil environment would allow him to relax. He stayed that way until he passed the first island.

The sun was resting on the horizon when Houston came to the island they had designated as their rendezvous point. He steered the canoe to the leeward shore, the one away from the big island, and began scouting the area for a suitable campsite.

In a short time, he saw an open grassy area on the shore and beached the canoe. He pulled the boat out of the water, placing it securely on the ground. Knowing that the rest of the party would arrive soon and want a cooked meal, he set out to find firewood.

His arms full of deadwood and small branches, Houston returned to the campsite and built a fire. A small spring-fed brook that drained into the lake provided water for the percolator; he added coffee and placed it on the fire. All that remained was to sit back and wait for the rest of his party to arrive. In no time, the air was filled with the tantalizing aroma of perked coffee.

Houston sat beneath a large tree, resting his aching muscles and hoping to get a few minutes of rest. It could very well be the last chance to relax before he arrived at the killing ground. Once there, the hunt would consume all of his time and energy.

A large fish rolled on the surface of the lake. He wondered if it were a trout or salmon—not that he would know the difference. Still, Houston wished he'd brought along a fishing pole. Before he knew it, the sun dropped below the horizon and the downside of being in the wilderness showed itself. As the night overtook the day, flies and mosquitoes came out to feast. Houston coated the exposed parts of his body with a locally manufactured insect repellent. The stuff smelled so bad it would make a skunk back away, but the flying predators hated it and that was all that mattered.

The brilliant full moon had been up for a half hour, drawing the flies high into the sky, when he heard a boat. The surface of the lake sparkled and, due to the brilliant moon, visibility was almost that of full daylight. Houston peered at the lake and saw the phosphorescent wake of a boat plowing through the placid water on a course that would bring it to his camp. In the event that it was not his companions, he retreated beyond the firelight, stood in the shadows with his 9mm pistol hidden beside his right leg. The driver throttled down the motor and Houston watched as he exercised great caution as he approached the shore.

When Houston heard O'Leary say, "You sure this is the place?" and then Winter answer, "It's the only island with a fire burning," he put his pistol away and walked into the light.

The boat drifted to the shore and O'Leary stepped out into ankle-deep water. "Mike," he called.

"Yeah, come on in."

O'Leary walked toward the fire with a pistol in his hand.

"You can put the piece away," Houston said. "Nobody here but us."

Winter raised the outboard and locked it in place before he wedged the boat's bow into the sand and threw the anchor to the ground to hold it fast. He waited for Anne to disembark and walked with her to the fire.

"Is that coffee I smell?" Anne asked.

"Yup, just made it."

"Great, but first I have something to attend to."

Anne disappeared into the woods and Jimmy and Gordon flopped next to the fire. "Nice lake," Winter remarked. "Big."

"Ideal country for what we need to do," Houston commented. "I haven't seen a single boat all day."

"Probably be busier than rush hour in the O'Neil tunnel on weekends though."

In short time, Anne returned from the woods and sat beside Houston. "You guys have a definite advantage out here. All you need do is to locate a likely spot, point your thing, and let go—we girls need to find a place more suitable."

"Another disadvantage of open plumbing," O'Leary said.

"Another disadvantage?" Anne asked.

"Yeah, I can think of a few," he said with a grin. "Giving birth comes to mind . . ."

Houston grimaced and waited for Anne to explode. Rather than get angry at Jimmy's remark, she laughed. Houston gave her a quizzical look.

"Jimmy and I finally understand each other."

Houston shrugged. He was not about to upset the applecart.

They sat around the fire, drinking coffee and listening to water gently lapping against the shore. The croaking of frogs serenaded them from the darkness and they watched moths fly toward the fire's light before the rising heat swept them upward. Everyone seemed relaxed, each unwilling to break the mood.

Finally, O'Leary asked, "Okay, what's our game plan?"

Houston leaned back and rested his head against a fallen tree. "It's really pretty basic. I'll head for the island so that I arrive there right around sunup. You guys will come in later . . . hopefully by the time you arrive I'll have a fix on where he's keeping Susie."

"That's it?"

Houston grinned at Jimmy, sat up and picked up a wooden stick. "That's it, I believe in the KISS concept—Keep It Simple, Stupid." He stirred the coals for a few seconds and tossed the stick into the fire. "I think I was born a couple of centuries too late."

Winter stared at him through the flickering flames of the fire and nodded in agreement. "I could live like this too. The world would be a great place to live if it weren't for people."

"Yeah," Houston replied, "people do complicate the equation."

"Mike," Anne said, "there has to be more to the plan than that."

"Not really. You and Jimmy are going to take care of Susie. Gordon and I are going to hunt down Edwin Rosa, or whoever this sniper is, and kill him."

"That's it?" She was incredulous; he made it sound as simple as going to the corner store for a quart of milk.

"It's really quite simple, babe. My experience in situations like this is that the simpler you keep things, the less apt you are to screw things up. Before dawn, Gordon and I will take the canoe and head for the island. You and Jimmy will follow in the motorboat. You should wait until after sunrise."

"Doesn't sound so simple to me," Anne replied. "That's a big island."

"Maybe simple is a bad word. How does uncomplicated sound? It's no different from hunting an animal. You locate a spot to which you think it will come, get in position for a good shot and when it appears . . . bang."

"You make it sound so easy." She sounded unconvinced.

"It is. Whoever gets there the first-est, with the most-est comes away the winner."

O'Leary spread out a topographical map of the island. He stared at it for a few seconds then cursed. "Fuck, I can't read this thing."

Winter took the map and placed a compass on it, and aligned the map so north corresponded with the compass needle. "He's going to try and stake out the high ground. There's a ridge running through the center of the island." The map revealed a steep ridge that formed a spine that cut the island in half. He pointed on the map. "Here."

Houston bent forward and looked at the map. "Someplace on this island, there has to be some type of building. That's where they'll have Susie."

"Jimmy and Anne should probably circle around the island to the north. Sound really travels across water, so don't approach using the outboard motor; go in with the electric trolling motor and start sweeping south," Winter said.

"That's as good a plan as any. We'll go in here." Houston pointed to a spot on the map where the ridge was furthest from the shore. "Rosa will expect us to go in where the ridge is close to the water—at least that's what I'd do."

"How the hell do we use this trolling motor?" O'Leary asked.

Winter rolled his sleeping bag out and lay down. "Nothing to it. There's a foot pedal that turns it on, all you have to do is turn the handle until the boat goes in the direction you want it to. I'll show you in the morning. I'm going to get some sleep. Don't you kids be up all night. We got a big day ahead of us."

O'Leary tossed his cigarette into the fire and gave Houston and Anne a knowing leer. "It's time for me to get some sleep too. There ain't shit worth watching on TV."

Houston and Anne sat silent until they were sure Jimmy and Gordon were asleep.

"Let's take a walk," Houston said.

The brilliant full moon hung in the sky, and as they walked, they watched the surface of the lake ripple each time a fish rolled after a fly.

Anne stopped and stared across the lake. "It makes you feel insignificant, doesn't it?"

"That it does."

"I feel like I can reach up and touch the moon."

She let Houston guide her to a large rock and they sat on its flat crown. They said nothing for several minutes, each lost in their own thoughts.

"Mike?"

"Yeah."

"I'm scared."

"Me too. It's been years since I've done this." He paused, staring at the shimmering water. "Hopefully, by this time by tomorrow night it will all be behind us."

"As the saying goes: We have to get through it to get beyond it."

"I wouldn't be so damned nervous if Susie's life didn't hang in the balance."

"We'll get her out."

"Anne, promise me that no matter what happens, you'll be careful."

"I should be saying that to you."

"I've been here before and know what to expect. Still, it's different this time."

"Oh?" Anne replied. "How so?"

"This time we're up against a trained professional—maybe more than one."

She sighed. "I'd like to come up here some time—when I can truly enjoy this."

"I would never have thought you'd like roughing it." Houston stared at a loon as it swam through the beam of moonlight shining on the lake's surface. "Anne, there's something I have to say."

"Then say it."

"I couldn't have made it these last few years without you. I don't have to tell you that when we met I was going ninety miles an hour down a dead-end street. You've helped put purpose and direction back in my life." He looked into her eyes.

She was silent for several seconds. Her voice was barely audible when she said, "You give me more credit than I deserve. I depend on you for a lot of things too."

She guided him off the rock.

Houston turned and took her in his arms. When he felt her body respond to him, he held her tighter. Anne wrapped her arms around him. "Mike—"

"Yes?"

"We've held off making love all this time because we were partners and didn't want to complicate things."

"That's what we both agreed upon."

"Tomorrow, one or both of us could be dead."

"Don't think like that." He held her at arm's length and looked into her eyes.

"We have to consider it."

"What are you saying?"

"I want you—now—here."

"You're sure?"

She smiled at him. "I'm sure."

Before he could ask another question, she placed a finger across his lips. "If you ask one more question I could change my mind."

He swept her up and carried her into the trees.

31

"To overcome the difficulties of detection and to maintain security
during every day sniping operations, the aim should be to confuse the enemy."
—*US Marine Corps Scout/Sniper Training Manual*

Houston woke to the chirping of his watch, looked at the luminous hands and got up. He stepped around Anne's sleeping form and reached out to nudge Winter.

"I'm awake."

Houston nodded and began final preparations to shove off on the last leg of the journey within the hour. He took the Ghillie suit off his pack and put it on, snapping it to his coveralls. The previous night while waiting for Anne, Gordon and Jimmy to arrive, he had collected the assortment of local fauna he would need to complete his camouflage.

Once their preparations were complete, they packed their gear into the canoe. Houston returned to the camp and found O'Leary and Anne stoking the fire. Anne placed a coffeepot on the coals. "At least stay long enough to eat something and have some coffee."

Winter called to O'Leary from the motorboat. "Hey, boss, if you want, now's as good a time as any for me to train you on how to use the trolling motor."

O'Leary stood up and brushed off the seat of his pants. "A man's work is never done," he said as he walked toward the boat.

Anne got up. "I better get in on this too—just in case."

They ate a quick breakfast. During the meal, Winter checked his assault rifle. When he pulled and released the operating rod, he nodded to Houston. "I'm ready, we can leave whenever you want."

"It's time. There's only one paddle—we'll take turns."

"You okay with the boat?" Winter asked O'Leary.

"I'll let Anne drive. I've never been the nautical type."

Houston and Winter pushed the canoe out into the lake and got in. The paddle barely made a sound as Houston pulled against the water.

The surface of the lake was smooth as glass and Houston saw the reflection of early morning stars twinkling on the water. He wondered what it must have been like for early Americans to leave the safety of civilization to explore and settle the wilderness. He was afraid to do anything that might shatter the mood and remained mute as he concentrated on paddling the canoe.

Houston's reverie broke when a pair of moose—a bull with huge antlers and his cow—swam past the canoe on their way between islands. He became aware of the darkness and realized that they would have to be alert to avoid hitting anything.

It was six thirty, and daylight was just starting to push away the darkness when they came to the island. They placed their paddles in the bottom of the canoe and drifted while they stared at the dark silhouette.

"Now I know how the 1st Marine Division felt when they first saw Guadalcanal . . ."

The premise became even more sobering when he realized that, like the Solomon Islands, this one too was about to become a killing ground.

Houston wanted to err on the side of caution. He picked up the paddle and signaled to Winter. He slowly paddled around the island using the predawn darkness to hide their approach. As much as possible, he wanted to study the island's geography and hopefully find Rosa's boat at the same time.

The shoreline appeared primeval and uninhabited, as if the world had not yet discovered this place, or if it had had found it to be too remote. When dawn broke, they continued their reconnaissance, staying close to the shore, hoping to avoid detection in the early-morning light.

Suddenly, Winter tapped Houston on the shoulder and pointed to a small motorboat partially hidden in an inlet on the western shore.

Houston turned to Winter. "We'll row around to the eastern shore."

"Makes sense to me. Last thing we want to do is make it easy for him and walk into an ambush."

They caught a current and slid past the hidden boat, paying close attention to the trees as they drifted by. Houston was unsure how long Rosa had been in place and was not about to do the obvious by looking for him. Rather than tramp the island, exposing himself, he intended to find a hide and wait—for days if necessary. That would force Rosa into moving—and a sniper would be at his most vulnerable when on the move.

On the eastern shore, they beached the canoe and hid it in a copse of brush. They waited fifteen minutes for the woods to quiet down before unloading their gear. Houston loaded his rifle and checked his pistol. Satisfied with his state of readiness, he watched Winter finish his last-minute checks. They nodded in unison and slid into the forest.

The sniper sat in the tree stand, his eyes the only part of him that moved. His mind raced as a charge of adrenaline coursed through his veins. This was what he lived for—the hunt. In the distance, he heard the chatter of a boat motor coming from the south. He listened as the sound moved north and then diminished to silence—a fisherman, he decided.

He stared down the side of the ridge, seeking signs of movement in the forest. The only movement was the intermittent rippling of leaves as the wind blew through the trees. A calm day was preferable, but it was no big deal. He had done this often enough to know the difference between the breeze and human movement.

He settled back, breathed deep and felt the adrenaline subside—it could be a long wait.

Estes left Susie tied to the bunk and walked out of the shack. She glanced up at the morning sun, placed her hands on her lower back, and stretched. Looking back at the cabin, his orders about the girl ate at her. She was having a hard enough time adjusting to taking instructions from a corporal, but he was the expert sniper, so she acquiesced. His insistence on the kid not being harmed made no sense. After all, the kid's death was inevitable; Susie had seen both of them and heard their names. It would be suicidal to allow her to leave the island alive. She turned away and walked to the trail that led to the lakeshore. Why risk pissing him off? The kid's time was limited either way. About fifty meters down the trail, Estes turned into the brush. A fallen tree from which she could see the path provided an unrestricted field of fire and Estes settled back to wait. Two things were certain: Houston would not be alone and anyone he recruited probably knew little or nothing about military tactics. To ensure all was in ready, Estes rechecked her rifle, settled back and watched the trail.

Too bad that I can't document this operation. It will be historic, she thought. In the history of the United States military there had never been a woman sniper, even though Lyudmilla Pavlichenko, a female sniper, had scored more than three hundred kills as a sniper for the Soviet Army during World War II war in Stalingrad. Every marine knew the story of Carlos Hathcock tracking and shooting the infamous Vietnamese female sniper known as Apache. It would finally prove to the Corps that a woman was as capable of being a combat sniper as any man.

Estes's thoughts returned to the young woman in the cabin. He should have taken her advice and killed the kid yesterday—eventually they had to. His desire to cut the girl's throat while her father watched, helpless to stop it, was stupid. Once again she looked at the front of the shack. *Maybe, I'll just do it now. . . .*

Houston felt as if he were once again a young marine seeking out the enemy. There was more than a little truth to the adage "Once a marine, always a marine."

Winter's expertise impressed him. O'Leary's right-hand man knew how to move through rough terrain and bush. His eyes seemed to see everything, no matter how minuscule the movement. In no time, he and Houston had synchronized their movement, as if they were one. One thing that scout-snipers and army Rangers had in common was their need to operate unheard and unseen. Because of their training, it took them over an hour to move one hundred meters. They moved as silently as a pair of stalking tigers, taking care to step over dead brush and fallen tree limbs. They came to a small stream and settled in amongst some alders for a break.

"Christ," Winter whispered, "it's like I never left the army."

They drank from canteens, their eyes always on the move, watching, searching the terrain.

"One big difference though," Houston said.

"Which is?"

"We were young and immortal then. Now we're older and know we can die."

"There's only one thing about dying that bothers me," Winter said.

"Which is?"

"What if I'm good at it? I only get to do it once."

"Gordon, you're one weird dude."

"Yeah, my mother always said that."

"You got family?"

"Parents are dead—which is probably for the best."

"How so?"

"My old man was like you, a career cop. I doubt he'd find what I do for Jimmy easy to live with."

"On the other hand, if you'd grown up in Southie, the locals would probably call you a hero."

Anne and O'Leary left for the island at eight in the morning. They drove the boat past the large island and killed the motor when they were several hundred yards beyond the northernmost shore. He rummaged around for a few seconds, then handed Anne one of the fishing poles.

"What's this for?"

"In case they're watching. We're going to fish for a while. That way they'll ignore us."

Anne looked hesitant.

"Don't worry, we'll use artificial bait. I ain't too crazy about stabbing a hook into a worm either."

A surprised look came over Anne's face. "Are you squeamish, Jimmy? I never would have thought that."

"What?"

"That you'd have reservations about hooking a worm."

"I didn't say I had reservations, I said I ain't crazy about it—damn things are too slimy." O'Leary lit a cigarette and grinned. "Besides, I ain't ever hurt anything or anyone that didn't try to hurt me."

Anne chuckled. "Jimmy, the more I'm with you the less I dislike you."

"I told you that if you hung around with me long enough I'd grow on you."

They cast their lines into the water and let the boat drift toward the island.

"What are we going to do if we catch something?" Anne asked.

Houston heard a sound to their left. He froze in place scanning the area through the Unertl telescopic sight. He slowly panned the trees, looking for anything that broke the natural patterns of the forest. He forced his eye to seek out horizontal patterns; at scout-sniper training they emphasized that in the bush most humans missed seeing things because they lived in a vertical world and would look too high. Most unsuccessful hunters looked at a deer and never saw it; at its shoulders, a large buck would be only three to four feet high, but may have a horizontal length of over six feet long. Animals and experienced snipers looked for objects on the horizontal as well as in the vertical plane. Houston studied the area. He detected a shape in the scope and froze. It took him a second to identify a fully mature buck. He noted the full rack of antlers and knew he was observing a trophy whitetail. He centered the scope's crosshair just behind the buck's front leg. If he had been a hunter, it would have been a perfect shot through its heart. The deer froze in place, stared at the strange shape for a few seconds and then darted off into the trees.

Houston heard Winter exhale. "Good thing you're on the point. I'd have blasted it."

———————

At noon, they started scaling the slope that led to the top of the ridge. Houston and Winter took a short break and ate a lunch of crackers, cheese and water.

"We climbing all the way to the top?"

"I think not. I don't want to be silhouetted against the skyline." Houston pointed to a small plateau about three-quarters of the way up. "That looks like as good a place as we'll find."

"You're the sniper."

"We're going to separate."

"Is that wise?"

"It's not something a sniper team usually does. But then this isn't a typical sniper-op. The target is aware of us and he's waiting too. Whoever fucks up first gets the body bag. We won't be that far apart—we'll keep each other in sight. I'll go for the plateau. In the meantime, you find a place to watch my back. If he gets me first, take him out."

Winter looked uncertain. "What if he gets me?"

"Then I'll know where he is and I'll take him out."

Winter grinned. "Now there's a strategy. But, I get your point—either way one of us flushes the asshole."

"Exactly."

Houston waited until Winter had disappeared into the woods and then climbed for another hour before reaching the plateau.

He settled down and looked across the ravine that separated the ridge from a smaller one across the way. The field of fire was good and Houston settled in. It was time for the hunt to begin in earnest. It was time to see how patient his competition was. The shooter and he were now involved in a war of nerves that Houston felt confident he would win.

Houston melted into the brush and got into as comfortable a shooting position as possible. He unhooked the sling from the rifle's rear post and created a loop through which he slipped his left arm. Tightening the loop until it was almost as tight as he could without making a tourniquet of it, he wrapped the straight section around his arm. He placed his left hand against the swivel at the forward end of the hand grip, pulled the stock firmly into his shoulder and scanned the area through the telescopic sight. The tight sling held the rifle sight steady, creating a stable shooting platform. All was ready.

Once his stakeout site was established, Houston felt better. His opponent had several advantages, the greatest of which was that he had selected the terrain and knew it. On the other hand, Houston had an advantage of his own; he was damned good at waiting. He had been on many stakeouts and could wait for days if need be. However, this time there was one major difference. On previous sniper hunts, he hadn't had to worry about the target stalking him. This time, however, the target knew that he was the hunted as well as the hunter.

Houston munched on beef jerky and washed it down with water. The afternoon wore on and a couple of times he thought about moving, but fought back the urge. Successful snipers trained themselves to lie in wait with little or no movement for hours—if not days—on end. The primary problem they had to deal with was that although the body was motionless, the mind was anything but. Houston had always found maintaining mental alertness more difficult than maintaining physical alertness. As he lay motionless, his mind drifted in numerous directions, reliving his tumultuous marriage, wondering if he could have done anything differently. He recalled his own words: "Pam was by far a much better wife to me than I was a husband to her." His thoughts turned to Susie and fear gripped him when he realized that she might be dead. The sniper had said he wouldn't hurt her if Houston joined him in this psychotic game. Nevertheless, now that he was here, there was nothing to keep him from killing her.

Clearing his mind and studying the terrain, Houston searched for Winter. When he failed to find him, he was reassured of his abilities.

Of itself, that was not overly surprising; Army Rangers went through a rigorous training regimen, possibly more demanding than that of scout-snipers. Like scout/snipers, the washout rate for Ranger training was around eighty percent. Houston knew he could not have a better man covering his back door.

Susie struggled against her bonds, listening for the sound of anyone approaching the shack. She hadn't heard anything but the wind through the trees since Frankie and the scarred man had left to set ambushes for her dad.

Susie twisted her wrists, ignoring the pain as the coarse nylon bit into her flesh.

She had to free herself, to find some way of warning her father.

32

"Whoever is first in the field and awaits the coming of the enemy, will be fresh for the fight; whoever is second in the field and has to hasten to the battle will arrive exhausted."

—Sun Tzu Wu, *The Art of War*

Jimmy O watched the shore from the corner of his eye. From time to time, he ventured a look at Anne. "I can't say I like sitting out here like a floating target."

"The shore is only a few yards away."

"If they were watching us, I think they'd have made some kind of move already. Let's beach this thing."

They used the trolling motor to guide the boat to the shoreline. O'Leary jumped out of the boat into water that came halfway up his calves and pulled the vessel onto a grassy stretch of shore. Anne handed Jimmy a shotgun and checked the action of her pistol.

"There's a trail over there," she said.

"Well, I ain't a woodsman, but it's long been my belief that trails usually lead somewhere."

Anne jumped to the ground and started following the path.

When they entered the trees, leaving the blazing sun behind, the temperature dropped twenty degrees. Huge maples, oaks, and pines enclosed them like a cocoon; ferns and wildflowers leaned toward the trail in their perpetual struggle to reach the few shafts of sunlight that penetrated the canopy.

When O'Leary put a cigarette in his mouth, Anne shook her head and admonished him. "Don't . . . they might smell it."

His face reddened, but he realized the wisdom of her words and bit back his embarrassment. Anne smiled at him. "I wouldn't want anything to happen to you now that I'm starting to like you."

"Well, shit," O'Leary said, "that alone makes a little nicotine fit worth it."

They followed the trail for a quarter mile. It hadn't seen much use and ferns and saplings had started to regain their hold on the tread-worn path. Wind rustled through the trees and jay-like birds, gray and white rather than blue and white, chattered and thrashed loudly in the trees. "What type of bird is that?"

"I believe it's a Canadian or Gray Jay. Watch this." She reached up with her fingers touching as if she held a morsel of food and one of the birds jumped from its perch and flew to her hand. It flew close enough to her to determine there was nothing to eat and launched itself into the air.

"I'll be a son of a bitch," O'Leary said. "I never saw a wild bird do that before."

"The locals call it a Gorby bird. My father and grandfather were avid sportsmen and hunted the Maine woods on many occasions. Dad told me about them. He said they're camp robbers. You build a fire and in no time Gorby birds are around. He believed that as long as there are Gorbies in the area, no one should ever starve in the woods."

They turned away from the bird and continued up the trail at a cautious pace. Sunlight filtered through the trees and large flies buzzed around their heads, no doubt attracted by their salty perspiration. One landed on O'Leary's neck and he slapped at it. "Goddamned things take a big bite."

Suddenly Anne stopped. "There's a clearing ahead."

O'Leary peered up the trail. Before he could speak, a shot rang out.

———————

Estes remained in her lair. It had been quiet for hours, but she stayed vigilant. Her mouth was dry and her tongue seemed to stick to the roof of her mouth. She reached for her canteen and saw movement on the trail. *I knew,* she thought, *Houston wouldn't be stupid enough to come alone.*

Major Francis Estes, USMCR, pulled the stock of her rifle into her shoulder, sighted on her target and, for the first time in her life, fired at a human target.

———————

Houston heard the shot and believed it came from the north. He thought about Anne and his heart stopped. He didn't want to break cover, but when two more shots followed, he threw caution to the wind and slid out of his hide.

Although exposing himself was foolish and the smart thing to do was to remain in place, Houston turned toward the sound. The boom of a shotgun, followed by several pistol shots, rolled through the woods—a firefight was in progress.

He reached the bottom of the incline and found Winter standing beside a large fir tree, looking north. "Think we ought to check that out?"

"I don't know; it might expose us."

"On the other hand," Winter replied, "they may have got him."

"I doubt that. This shooter hasn't screwed up very often. It's more likely it's his accomplices and Jimmy and Anne."

"Either way, I think we need to find out . . . if for no other reason than to see what we're dealing with."

Houston thought about his options for a few seconds. "Common sense tells me we should stay put."

"What if one of our people is down?"

Houston thought of Susie and Anne.

"Okay. But, we maintain field discipline and we don't rush. It would be like this bastard to stake out any bodies hoping we'll get curious."

O'Leary was twenty feet behind Anne when she crumpled to the ground. He dove into a stand of bush as a bullet snapped over his head.

"Anne?"

"Yeah?"

He didn't like the raspy and strained tone of her voice. "Where you hit?"

"My left shoulder. I'm bleeding bad."

"Are you exposed?"

"No, the hole is small."

Jimmy's brow arched as he pondered her reply for several seconds and then he smiled. It took a special type of person to joke after being shot.

"I meant are you behind cover?"

Anne grunted in pain. "I'm good . . . there's an old log here and I'm pressed against it."

"Stay there. I'll get you out of here somehow."

Another shot ripped through the tree branches above his head. He peered in the direction of the gunfire and thought he saw movement.

"I think I see him," Jimmy said. "Are you able to get his attention?"

A bloody hand holding a pistol appeared above the log. Anne fired off two shots.

O'Leary dashed to his left, expecting a bullet at any second. He slid behind a downed tree and leaned against it, gasping for breath. "Fucking cigarettes."

He heard another shot, followed by the flat bark of Anne's pistol. The shooter had moved and was now abreast of his position. Jimmy slowly turned and crouched into a shooting stance.

A figure in camouflage clothes slipped around a tree, obviously trying to flank Anne. He stood up and raised the shotgun to his shoulder. "Drop it."

The shooter spun toward his voice. Jimmy saw it was a woman and froze for a split second—long enough for her to bring her rifle into play. The shotgun roared and bucked in his hands.

The twelve-gauge slug ripped through her chest, spraying the leaves behind her with blood. She stared at him in disbelief for a moment and then braced her feet to keep from falling. An expanding blood stain spread across the front of her blouse, but she still struggled to lift the rifle. O'Leary pumped the forward grip, ejected the spent cartridge and racked in a fresh one. He fired again. Another crimson hole appeared in her chest just below the first and she toppled backward.

O'Leary approached the woman cautiously and squatted beside her. Her eyes moved from side to side and there was a shocked look on her face. He picked up her rifle and threw it to the side. "I'll bet it never dawned on you that you could get shot too."

Estes stared at him, licking her lips. After a few moments, her eyes dulled and she let out a long slow breath. She relaxed and stared at a sky she could no longer see.

Stepping over the body, Jimmy darted between trees and through brush to Anne's side. A quick look was all it took to know that she was in serious trouble. There was a six-inch bloodstain on her shirt and she was unconscious, her face pallid. She was in shock. He ripped her shirt open and inspected the entry wound. It was about an inch above her breast and slightly smaller than a dime. Reaching under her shoulders to lift her he felt the warm stickiness of her blood.

Anne's eyes snapped open.

"I got to get you someplace where we can stop the bleeding, kid."

Anne gave him a weak smile. Blood splatters had peppered her face and she whispered. "I know, Jimmy." When she spoke, her chest rattled.

Fuck, O'Leary thought, *I think she's been lung-shot.*

Ignoring her cries, he lifted her from the ground and walked as fast as possible toward the clearing, praying for the strength not to drop her. When Jimmy staggered into the small meadow, he spied an old fishing or hunting shack. Mindless of the fact that there may be other shooters in the area, he struggled to carry his load onto the porch and kicked the door open.

Inside the shack were two rudimentary cots. Susie was tied to one. "Uncle Jimmy!"

He ignored her and placed Anne on the other. He placed a pillow under Anne's head, then went to Susie. He took a folding knife from its sheath on his belt and cut her bonds.

"You okay, baby?"

"Yes, just scared." She looked at Anne's pale face and saw the blood on her shirt. "Oh my God, she's been shot!"

"Get a grip, kid. I'm going to need your help. We got to work fast if she's gonna have any kind of a chance."

They leaned over Anne and O'Leary saw that she still had her pistol gripped tight in her hand. He pried her fingers from the gun and set it on the floor.

They cut Anne's shirt and bra off. "She ever finds out I did this, she'll shoot me," O'Leary said.

"Under the circumstances," Susie commented, "I think she'll understand. What can I do?"

"I'm going to need some hot water and the cleanest cloth you can find. There's a boat at the end of the trail, about a quarter mile. Do you think you can run there and get me the first-aid kit?"

Susie looked frightened and glanced through the door. As quickly as it appeared, the terrified look disappeared and a look of determination took its place. "I can do it."

"That's my girl. It's in the console between the front seats." He picked up Anne's pistol and offered it to Susie. "I shot the woman, but there could be others."

Susie pulled away, repelled by the weapon.

"There's only one more that I've seen," she said. "A creepy guy."

O'Leary put the gun in her hand and wrapped her fingers around its handle. "Take this and don't be a baby. Do you know how to use it? It's loaded and ready to fire, all you have to do is point it and pull the trigger."

Susie recoiled from his stern tone. Reluctantly she took Anne's pistol, hesitated for a moment and then cradled it under her arm. She held her hand up and saw Anne's blood smeared on it. She felt panic building, but O'Leary shouted, "Go! Do as I say, Susie." She blinked her eyes several times and then ran out the door.

After she had run from the cabin, O'Leary turned his full attention to Anne and tried to stem the bleeding. *Mike is gonna be pissed*, he thought.

The shooter heard the shots. *Houston must be at the cabin*, he thought. *I hope Frankie hasn't spoiled my fun.*

He slid out of his perch and slowly, methodically started toward the shack.

When they reached the clearing, Winter stayed in the trees and covered Houston as he approached the cabin. Houston was ten feet from the door when Susie stepped out and froze. "Daddy?"

Houston realized she couldn't recognize him in the Ghillie suit and slid the hood back. "Yeah, babe, it's me. You okay?"

"Dad, Anne's hurt." She looked around and he saw the pale look of shock on her face. "Uncle Jimmy is with her . . . he sent me to get some stuff from his boat."

"Then go get it, hon. Gordon, go with her. I'll take care of things here."

Winter stepped out of the brush and Susie started, raising the pistol.

Her father grabbed her hand and forced the gun down. "He's with us. Now go get the stuff your Uncle Jimmy asked for."

Houston rushed forward. When he stepped into the cabin, he saw Jimmy bent over Anne, trying to wrap bandages around her.

When Houston stomped into the shack, O'Leary spun, pulled a pistol from his belt and pointed it. "Jesus H. Christ, Mike. I almost drilled you."

"How is she?"

"It ain't good."

Houston covered the distance between him and Anne in two strides. He knelt beside the cot and inspected her wounds. "Thank God they used military ammo."

"Yeah, if they'd shot her with a hollow-point instead of a jacketed bullet . . ." O'Leary left the rest of the statement hanging in the air.

They were silent for several tense seconds, anxiously awaiting Winter and Susie's return. "What about the shooter—you get him?"

"Not unless he's had a sex change. It was a woman—some militant bitch. She's out in the woods."

Houston looked out the door.

"Don't worry; her shooting days are over. Where's Gordon?"

"He went to the boat with Susie." Houston noticed that Anne's breathing was shallow and her appearance made his stomach sink.

"She's still alive," Jimmy said. "But we got to get her out of here. She needs better care than we can give her."

It seemed as if time stood still and hours passed before they heard heavy steps outside and Winter and Susie burst through the door carrying a first-aid kit and some white cloth.

O'Leary opened the first-aid kit and dumped its contents on the cot. He sorted through the plastic packages until he found what he sought. He grabbed two packages marked *Dressing, individual, camouflaged* and used his teeth to rip the vacuum-sealed plastic wrappers off, then pulled the dressings out and handed them to Houston. Jimmy grabbed another package, with a label that identified it as a bandage, opened it and spread it out. He twirled the bandage until it created a strap and waited.

Houston raised Anne to a sitting position and pressed a dressing against the entrance wound. "A little help over here."

Susie rushed forward, took the second dressing and pressed it against the exit wound. While Houston supported Anne, his daughter held the dressings and O'Leary wrapped the bandage around her, tying it securely. Houston lowered her back onto the mattress.

"You guys have to take her and Susie out."

"We're over a hundred miles from the nearest hospital," Winter said. "I won't mention that we're hours from the boat launch. I got a CB radio in the boat, but they're only good for a couple of miles. If we get her to the old man's store we can call someone to send for an ambulance."

"Well, one thing is for certain," Houston said, "we got to stop ratchet-jawing and get to it."

"What we got that can be used as a stretcher?" Jimmy asked.

"We'll each take a corner of this cot; it will have to do."

They struggled to carry the improvised stretcher down the narrow path. On several occasions one or another of them staggered and almost lost their grip. Each time Anne cried out in pain. It seemed as if it took hours, rather than minutes, to reach the shore. They discarded the bed frame and placed the mattress with Anne on it into the boat. Susie wrapped Anne with the old blanket that covered the mattress. Once Winter, O'Leary and Susie were aboard, Houston pushed the boat into the water. Winter used an oar to pole them out to where the water was deep enough to lower the outboard motor and started it. Houston stepped back onto the shore.

"Ain't you coming?" Jimmy asked.

"I'd like nothing better, but there's business to be done. I'm not leaving here until this asshole is yesterday's news." He waved and turned back to the trail.

33

Houston watched Winter shift the motor from reverse to drive and then spin the boat around in the water. He saw its bow point upward and heard its hull slap the surface as it raced away. Once the boat was out of sight, he walked to the clearing for a closer look at the cabin. On the way, curiosity got the better of him and he crept into the woods, looking for the sniper's partner.

He followed the trail until he found blood sign, which he presumed to be Anne's, and then stepped into the woods. The sounds of buzzing flies and something rustling in the brush led him to the body. He found her lying in a small copse. Two huge crows picked at the corpse and flew off when he approached. Their loud cawing filled the afternoon stillness. He crouched beside the cadaver and recognized Estes. She was not as squared away and pretty as when they had first met. Even though it had been less than an hour since she'd died, scavengers had already been at the body, eating away portions of her face. The foragers he scared off had already eaten her eyes and the bloody sockets seemed to look through him. No one, he thought, deserves this. He stared at Estes's body and wondered how many more marines in her outfit were involved in this escapade. He was still crouching over her when a taunting voice called, "You've become lax, Mikey! I could have nailed you already."

Houston crouched lower and spun toward the voice. He raised his rifle and peered through the trees, hoping to locate where the shout came from. "If that's so, why didn't you?"

"That would have been too easy. Here's the rules. You and me hunt each other until one of us is dead."

"You're fucking nuts . . ."

"Maybe I am, but when this is over there will be no doubt as to who's the best."

"Who are you?"

"A friend from your past . . . your worst fucking nightmare. Too bad about your friend getting shot, but it seems to have evened things—we both lost spotters today. I guess that's the breaks, huh?"

"This is only just beginning, asshole."

"Ain't that the truth? Sorry we had to snatch your kid, but it was the only way I could get you up here."

"Well, you know how that old saying goes."

"There's a lot of old sayings, dipshit. Which one are you talking about?"

"The one that says be careful what you ask for because you just might get it."

The sniper's laugh rolled across the forest. "Yeah, that's a good one."

"Why don't we just cut to the chase? We'll meet by the shack and end this right now?"

"Who do you think I am, fucking Wyatt Earp? No way, José, we'll play it out just like we were trained. Well, I gotta run, Mike—see you around the campus."

"You're not thinking of taking off on me are you?"

"I wouldn't think of it, buddy. Either one or none of us is leaving this island alive. I sure hope your friends don't send a bunch of goddamned cops up here—I got nothing against them and it would serve no purpose other than to run up the body count. What was that old song? I remember. Catch us if you can."

Houston waited for five minutes, hearing nothing but the leaves rustling in the breeze. Convinced that the shooter was gone, he set out to find him, circumventing the clearing.

Houston stayed below the skyline and in the trees, following a course parallel to the shoreline as he searched the island. He stopped at the shooter's motorboat, removed the fuel tank and carried it into the woods. He buried it under leaves and loose sediment. Houston would return to the canoe and disable it. *Then, asshole*, he thought, *I'll know you aren't leaving.*

He left the shore and avoided the trail, moving through the woods. If it took him the rest of his life, he was going to find this guy—and he would turn over every rock on the island to do it.

Winter kept the throttle wide open. The boat bounced across the water like a skipping stone. Each time the hull slammed into the water, Anne bounced and grunted in pain. O'Leary and Susie knelt beside her to keep her from tumbling off the mattress.

O'Leary cursed. He had been broadcasting constantly on the citizen's band, trying numerous channels, but all he heard was static. He turned his head to avoid the constant spray that the boat's bow sent flying over them and saw that Susie's head was bent slightly forward and her eyes were closed in what he believed to be prayer.

They were five miles from the boat landing when Winter spied another boat racing on a course that would intercept them. He angled slightly, hoping to avoid a collision, but the oncoming craft also corrected its course. A uniformed man stood in the boat and waved for them to stop. Winter reduced the throttle and when the boat decelerated and the bow settled into the water, he shouted at the intruding boatman. "I got an emergency here and I don't have time to waste."

The fiberglass boat drifted alongside and a muscular man wearing a green uniform with black stripes running down the legs and a gold badge said, "I'm Marvin Marsh, game warden for this wildlife management district—"

"Thank God," Winter said. "I've got a severely injured woman who needs to get to a hospital as soon as possible."

The warden leaned over and looked inside Winter's boat. He took a quick look at Anne. "I got a report of some shots being fired on one of the islands and I'll bet dollars against donuts that if I looked under those bandages I'll find a gunshot wound."

Susie held a wallet toward him. Marsh took it and when he opened it and saw a badge and police ID his level of urgency ramped up. He removed a two-way radio from his hip. In seconds, he was talking with his dispatcher and requested that a medical evacuation helicopter meet them at the boat launch on the south shore of Aroostook Lake as soon as possible. He stopped transmitting and turned to the people in the boat. "A Coast Guard chopper from Portland will meet you at Guy Harris's place."

Winter cast a nervous look at Anne. "We really don't have time to be bullshitting."

"Understood." The warden pushed away from Winter's craft. "Follow me." He pushed forward on the throttle and raced south. The two boats stayed abreast, bouncing as they raced across the lake's surface.

In twenty-five minutes, they were within sight of the boat launch and Winter rocked back and forth in his seat, as if he could coax another knot per hour out of the roaring outboard. He cut the motor at the last second and the boat's nose dropped down into the water. They had decided that it would be easier to unload Anne from the bobbing boat if they stood in the water, using their bodies to hold the vessel steady while they hefted her out. The craft slid onto the sandy gravel near the dock and Susie leapt into the water and held the small vessel steady. It took all of the strength that O'Leary and Winter had to lift the mattress and wade ashore. Once they were on land, O'Leary began coughing and hacking. Susie ran forward and helped Winter support the mattress as they lowered it to the ground.

Harris appeared in the door of his store. "You fellers sure seem to be in a rush." He strolled toward the dock.

When he was halfway to the pier, O'Leary shouted at him. "You seen a helicopter?"

"Nope, but then I ain't been lookin' fer one. Onliest time I ever see one is when there's a 'mergency—you got one?"

Harris noticed that Marvin Marsh was with them and his brow furled. "Hey, Marv, what brings you here?"

"Guy, there will be a chopper landing here any minute. Make sure there's enough room in the parking lot for them to land."

The old-timer stared at the mattress lying on the gravel-covered landing. He saw the woman. She was wrapped in an old woolen army blanket and it and the mattress were covered with what he thought was blood. "Jaysus, what you fellahs been up to?"

"Just get out of our way," Winter said.

Harris shuffled aside. "I got a couch in the back of the store . . ."

The sound of rotor blades beating in the sky attracted their attention. "Looks as if her ride's here," Marsh said.

A Coast Guard HH-60 helicopter appeared over the trees. It hovered over the parking lot. The pilot swung the tail around 180 degrees and slowly settled to the ground, its rotor blades creating a windstorm that swept dust and dirt before it. O'Leary and Winter turned away from the aircraft and bent over the mattress, shielding Anne from as much of the detritus as they could. The rotor blades decelerated and the helicopter settled onto its landing gear. Two crewmen, wearing flight helmets with visors down that made them look like bipedal insects jumped from the rear door and ran toward them carrying a folded stretcher. "We got it from here. Why don't you folks get aboard?"

They moved Anne from the mattress to the stretcher and carried her to the helicopter. The instant they were aboard with safety belts on and Anne's stretcher secured, the pilot increased rotor speed and lifted out of the parking lot.

O'Leary slumped in exhaustion and doubled over in another fit of coughing as the aircraft lifted, hovered as its tail spun around, then the nose dipped forward and they sped toward Portland. He watched the two EMTs feverishly work on Anne.

Winter and Susie were crammed into a small space behind the medical crew, each staring out the window at the seemingly endless wilderness speeding past below the aircraft. The pilot motioned for Winter to put on the headset that hung on the bulkhead beside the compartment door. Once he had done so, he heard her metallic voice. "We should be at the hospital in thirty to forty minutes. The state police are waiting there. I'm sure they'll have a lot of questions for you."

Winter raised his right hand and acknowledged her with the thumbs up, letting the aviator know he understood. He put the headset back on its hook and sat back. He looked at the sun setting and wondered what was happening on the island.

Marvin Marsh used his right hand to shield his eyes and watched the Coast Guard HH-60 turn in midair and head for Portland. He walked into the store. Guy Harris stood behind the counter, dipped his thumb into a container of Red Top snuff, lifted a mound of red powder with his thumbnail and placed it between his lower lip and teeth. He picked up his pipe and lit it. The air between them filled with the strange combination of wintergreen and cherry blend tobacco.

"Guy," Marsh said, with a knowing grin, "you know it's against the law to smoke in a public establishment."

"Then," Harris said, "as of this minute this ain't no public establishment. I own this place and ain't no damned Democrat with the government in Augusta gonna tell me what I can and can't do in here."

Marsh grinned in spite of himself. "You got any i-deer what in hell is goin' on in the north islands?"

"Nope. Them people from away come yesterday an' said they was goin' fishin'. Only thing was, they didn't have a single fishin' pole among them. Fact of the matter is, they had to buy licenses and tackle from me. Only a damn city fool from away would bring along his boat, but forgit all his gear, don't-cha think? They sure as hell had enough guns to start a war though. Now, you know me, Marv, I don't give a good goddamn what folks does, so long as it don't bother me. But, like I said, them fellahs looked like they was goin' huntin' not fishin' and, considerin' the kinds a guns they had, they weren't huntin' no animal I know of."

Marsh turned to the door.

"Marv, you ain't thinkin' about goin' up there, are you?"

"Yup, I agree with you—somethin' about this situation stinks."

"Ya better go armed . . . like I said, them fellows was all packin' some heavy ordinance. Looked to me like they wasn't huntin' nothin' that walks on all fours. In fact, if I was goin' to stick my nose in there, I'd want at least one long gun with me. A man might even want to consider takin' a machine gun."

34

"The sniper must be camouflage conscious from the time he departs on a mission until the time he returns.... He must master the techniques of hiding, blending, and deceiving."
—US Marine Corps Scout/Sniper Training Manual

Night fell with no sign of his quarry. Houston settled on the side of the ridge, in a small copse of alders nestled in a grove of large, gray-barked beech trees, munching a cold meal. It was the last of his food and he would have to live off the land until this was over.

He wondered if Anne had gotten help in time. He was not a corpsman, but he had seen enough wounds to know a serious one. The way she rasped when she breathed and the blood that seeped from the corner of her mouth was disturbing, both symptoms of a lung shot. He forced his mind to more pressing matters.

Houston stared up through the trees at the moon and knew the brilliant orb was both a blessing and a curse. The spots where openings in the trees allowed the moonlight to penetrate were lit up almost to the level of daylight and it would be easy to see anyone attempting to close in on him; on the other hand, it also made him visible. It was a night best suited for staying put.

He sat back against a tree and fell into a light slumber.

Noise in the woods woke Houston. He glanced at his watch: 5 a.m. He didn't move, but strained his ears for the sound that had awakened him. He heard a grunting noise to his left and slowly shifted position so he could see the source. In the early-morning light, he saw a black bear and her cubs. The cubs cavorted in the trees and brush while their mother ripped apart an old stump, digging for ants and bugs. Houston let the unsuspecting animals entertain him for more than twenty minutes. Suddenly the mother bear stood on her hind legs and turned, looking up the ridge. She sniffed the air for a few seconds then dropped down onto all four legs and herded the cubs out of the area.

Houston froze, wondering what could make the bear react in such a manner. Surely, it wasn't another animal. It had to be the shooter and, some way or another, he had gotten behind him.

Houston dove to his left and a hole appeared in the trunk of the tree where he'd been sitting, immediately followed by the sharp crack of a supersonic bullet passing close by and the bark of a rifle.

A second bullet slammed into the maple and Houston drew back further behind its protective bulk.

Houston ventured a look, peering around the tree and detected a slight movement. He sighted in. Through the scope, he saw an unnatural line in the flora, maybe two inches of a human arm.

He fired.

The shape disappeared and Houston knew he had scored a hit—albeit a minor one.

Houston studied the terrain, hoping to see movement. All he saw was the intermittent oscillations of branches and bushes as the breeze blew across the ridge. He crawled toward the spot where Rosa had been. Without warning, the ground beneath him gave way. He rolled into a copse of alder bushes and silently cursed in frustration. As quickly as his anger had exploded, it waned and he lay still studying the area around him. The bushes swayed in the gusting morning wind and all he heard

was a sound similar to a cat wailing. It took him several seconds to identify the sound—it was nothing more than a tree rocking back and forth.

Houston had no idea how long he had been hidden in the alders. Certain
that Rosa had departed, he crawled until he found the spot from which
he had shot at him. In seconds, he found blood splatters on some leaves
and verified that Rosa had indeed been hit. Knowing he'd scored a hit,
no matter how superficial, felt good. Rosa could make mistakes too. He
followed the blood trail, looking for marks left behind when Rosa had
crawled away. The trail led higher, up the ridge.

Marsh was familiar with the island and spent the night in the cabin.
Knowing that the nearest officers available for backup were several
hours away, he came to the island alone . . . a mode of operation not
unusual for Maine game wardens. Soon after arriving on the island he
was convinced that he had found the right place. First he had found
a discarded bed frame near the shore where there were signs of a boat
being launched, and then there was the blood sign. This was where
the wounded woman had been shot. The ravaged carcass of another
woman meant that something very wrong was happening on the
island. He tried to ignore the wasted state of the body as he searched
it for identification. He found a US Marine Corps identification card
and read it. The first thing he noticed was that the card was green,
indicating that at the time of death she had been on active duty. Then
he read her name: Francis K. Estes, USMCR. Her rank was listed as
a major. Marsh rocked back on his heels. "What in Christ is goin' on
here . . . World War III?" A military assault rifle lay partially hidden
by underbrush. He picked it up and read the information engraved on
the barrel. It was an M-16A4, the model currently used by the armed
forces and capable of automatic fire—which made it illegal for use
everywhere except on military bases. "Guy hit the nail on the head,"

he muttered. "This sure as hell isn't a hunting rifle—not unless these people are hunting men."

He slung the rifle over his right shoulder, then hefted the corpse into a fireman's carry and carried it into the clearing. He had placed Estes's remains in the small shed behind the cabin and latched the door so that predators would be unable to damage it further.

35

"Doctors all agree that the only place on a man, where if struck by a bullet instantaneous death will occur, is the head. (Generally, the normal human being will live 8–10 seconds after being shot directly in the heart.)"
— *US Marine Corps Scout/Sniper Training Manual*

O'Leary paced around the waiting room. Anne had been in surgery throughout the night. The only thing the medical staff had told him was that her prognosis was not good. She had lost a lot of blood, and the bullet had, in fact, nicked her right lung.

A tall man walked in. "Are you Jimmy O'Leary?"

"Yes."

"Duane Saucier. I'm with Criminal Investigation Division One, Maine State Police. You want to tell me what the fuck is going on here? How does a cop from Boston get herself shot in the Maine woods?"

"It's complicated."

"I can handle it." Saucier took out a notebook and sat in one of the chairs that lined the waiting room walls. "Go ahead, tell me this complicated tale."

"Are you aware of the sniper shootings in Boston?"

"It's been on all the news, even up here in the sticks."

O'Leary poured a cup of coffee and sat down. "There's these two guys …"

Houston was hot and sweaty. His knees and elbows were raw, scraped and bleeding from hours of creeping and crawling on his belly with no sign of Rosa. It had become a war of wits and nerves. After hours of nonstop tension waiting for the shot that would end it all, fatigue was now a major factor. So far, all he had achieved was to get a worm's-eye view of the island.

By late afternoon, Houston had nestled into a copse of trees overlooking the cabin. He had searched every inch of the island and his quarry had eluded him. At first, he thought that Rosa could have circled back to the boat, found the gas tank and left. He rejected the prospect, believing that if Rosa had fled the island the motor would have been loud enough to hear. No, Rosa was still on the island. However, would he be stupid enough to return to the cabin? Probably not; that would be a huge mistake. To this point, Rosa had not made many.

Houston looked at the clearing; his eyes followed the trees until he came to the trail where Estes's body had been. He wondered if it was still there. He remembered the bears he had seen that morning and shuddered. Bears were carrion-eaters; by now they would have picked up the scent of the decaying body … He forced his mind back to Rosa and his current situation.

Houston settled back and decided he would stake out the shack. If Rosa did not appear by morning, he would move out, continuing his search.

O'Leary recounted the events of the past few days.

Saucier, the Maine State Trooper took copious notes and when he finished, the cop said, "You have any idea how crazy this sounds?"

"Hey, I told it like it is."

Saucier opened his cell phone and punched a speed-dial number. "I need a SWAT team and helicopter . . ."

O'Leary saw a doctor enter the room and he tuned out the cop. "Mr. O'Leary?"

O'Leary saw the look on the doctor's face and his stomach sank.

"We did all we could . . ."

"She's dead?" he interrupted.

"No, but there's nothing more we can do. It's up to her and God now. Who administered the first aid?"

"In a way, we all did."

"Well, if she does pull through, she owes her life to you. If you hadn't stemmed the bleeding, she would have surely bled to death. All we can do now is wait . . ."

"Do you think she'll make it?"

"At this time all I can tell you is that she's stable, but on life support. Only her higher power knows at this point."

Jimmy sat down and hung his head.

"Are you a religious man, Mr. O'Leary?"

"No, not really."

"Well, if you know any prayers that work, say them." The doctor walked out, turning sideways to allow Winter and Susie to pass him. They saw the dejected look on O'Leary's face.

"Any news?" Winter asked.

"It's up to Anne now."

"Are you Gordon Winter?" Saucier demanded.

"Yes."

"I'm going to need you to guide us to the scene. I have SWAT mobilizing and helicopters to take us up there."

Winter looked past Saucier's shoulder at the darkening sky. "Tonight?"

"No, only an idiot would fly up there at night. We'll go first thing in the morning."

36

"A stroke of the sword that does not hit its target is the sword stroke
of death; you reach over it to strike the winning blow."
—Yagyū Munenori, *The Book of Family Traditions on the Art of War*

For the better part of the afternoon, Houston observed the
shack and saw no sign of activity. Like him, Rosa would spend
the night in concealment. While adjusting his equipment for
the move, something caught his eye and he peered through his scope.
A man clad in a green uniform came out of the woods carrying what
was obviously Estes's body and walked toward the cabin. There were
patches on the shoulders of his sleeves and Houston was able to read
them through his telescopic sight. He saw Department of Inland
Fisheries and Wildlife embroidered on it. It was a game warden.

"Where the hell did he come from?" Houston whispered softly to
no one.

He maintained his observation post until the warden had settled
into the cabin. About a half hour later smoke drifted from the stove-
pipe chimney and it became evident that the warden was not leaving
the island that night. Houston thought about the food that the warden
was probably cooking and his stomach growled. He shook his head in

frustration and hoped that the warden would leave the island in the morning because if he didn't, Houston would have to look twice before he took a shot. The last thing he wanted to do was to shoot another law enforcement officer. His opponent, on the other hand, would have no such restriction.

———————

Houston slowly made his way down the ridge. He paused at the edge of the clearing, hesitant to expose himself. It was dark, but he didn't know if Rosa was equipped with night-vision goggles. Houston dropped onto his belly and crawled through the tall grass until he was within yards of the cabin. Vaulting to his feet, he covered the short distance and, without knocking, dashed into the cabin.

The warden sat at the small table, his service pistol disassembled before him as he cleaned it. The officer leapt to his feet, knocking over his chair. "What the—"

Houston aimed his rifle at the startled man. "Relax . . . I'm a cop."

"State or local?"

"Boston PD."

"Last I heard, Maine hasn't been part of Massachusetts since eighteen twenty. Is that some new uniform that I haven't heard of?"

"No." Houston lowered his rifle and slid his hood back. "It's a Ghillie suit."

"Snipers wear them."

"Yes, we do. I'm here to bring one down."

Marsh picked up his chair and dropped into it. "Suppose you sit down and tell me what in the hell is going on."

Houston looked toward the coffeepot warming on the wood stove. "You got anything worth eating?"

The warden stood once again. "I can throw something together for you."

"Great, I'm starving."

Marsh walked to the bunk and opened his pack. "I think I met some of your friends this afternoon."

"Is Anne all right?"

"If you're talking about the wounded woman cop, she was medevaced to Southern Maine Medical Center. Other than that I can't tell you anything."

"But, she's alive?"

"She was when I saw her last."

"Any of the others hurt?"

"Not that I could see." Marsh placed a small black iron frying pan on the stove. "Beans okay?"

"Right now the south end of a north-bound skunk would be good."

Marsh poured coffee into a blue metal cup. "I hope you like it black. I don't have any cream and sugar. Now what about this sniper you're after?"

"Have you heard about the sniper killings in Boston?"

"Of course. It's been in all of the newspapers."

"Anne, my partner, and I are the investigating officers. But there's more to it than that."

Marsh stood up, retrieved the frying pan from the stove and poured the beans into a metal mess kit. He slid the food in front of Houston. "My name is Marsh, Marvin Marsh. I'm the game warden for this district."

Houston offered his hand. "Michael Houston."

"Okay, Michael, tell me about it."

Houston scooped a spoonful of beans into his mouth, chewed two or three times and swallowed. "You got radio communications?"

"Yeah, I can reach our regional headquarters in Gray. They can link us through to any other law enforcement agency in the state . . . or nation, for that matter."

"You may want to do that—after I'm gone."

"After you're gone? What if I tell you to stay here?"

"It wouldn't do you any good. The guy I'm hunting is a highly trained killer. He can hit a moving target at over a thousand meters and will kill you with no reservation. I need to be out in the bush if I'm going to get him."

Sometime after midnight a series of squalls rolled across the island. Houston hunkered down beneath a large pine. Raindrops hit the ground, popping loudly when they hit dead leaves and sediment on the forest floor. The noise was further amplified by the primordial darkness. Knowing that the moisture would make movement quieter was small consolation for the discomfort of being soaked. Shivering and wishing for a hot shower and warm bed, Houston wistfully recalled the warmth of the cabin and shook his head to clear it of the distracting thoughts.

Thoughts of Anne momentarily distracted him from his miserable state. Marsh had used his radio to get an update, but all they were able to learn was that she had come out of surgery alive. However, she was still listed as critical. Houston muttered a short prayer asking God to intervene and save Anne's life. His thoughts shifted in a direction he didn't like, a course he had been ignoring since he watched the boat carrying her damaged body disappear from sight: what was he going to do without her? He cradled his rifle in his arms, taking care to keep its working parts out of the rain. Tomorrow, one way or the other, this ends.

His eyes grew heavy and without being aware of it, he dozed.

Houston woke to the sound of crows cawing. He opened his eyes and he tried to ignore the burning sensation in his eyes—an obvious symptom that the lack of good sleep was bringing on fatigue. Water droplets fell from leaves making loud pops when they hit the sediment and dead foliage that littered the forest floor. The wind had calmed after the frontal passage and he heard birds calling and the explosive sounds of squirrels as they foraged for food. Finally, hearing no alien noises, he stretched.

Houston drank some water and realized he was hungry again. He needed food. The easy alternative would be to go to the cabin and join Marsh for breakfast—but the easy alternative was not always the smartest one. It would be better to eat off the land.

He left the protection of the woods, bound for the stream. There might be berries along its banks. They were not his food of choice, but would have to do.

Despite the effects of numbing fatigue, Houston felt more alive than he had for years. The three-day ordeal was already toughening him. His stomach seemed flatter and harder and his wind was much stronger. The fatigue that had caused his legs to cramp two days before was gone. For the first time since he had set out on his quest, he felt capable of doing what he had to do.

Marsh left the cabin at first light. He would give Houston half the day and then if he hadn't found his quarry, he would bring in reinforcements. He arched his back and felt the knots and kinks of sleeping on the narrow, thin mattress loosen. Following police procedure, he checked his sidearm to ensure it was in good working condition and started for the door. The dead woman's assault rifle leaned against the wall and he picked it up. It might come in handy.

Not wanting to stay at the cabin where he would be an easy target, Marsh followed a trail leading to the top of the ridge. The ridge was covered with hardwood trees beechnut and oak predominated with a healthy maple and evergreen population. The ridge would be ideal habitat for the diminishing whitetail deer population. Who owned the island? Would they consider making it a game sanctuary? He turned his thoughts back to the matter at hand and decided to climb to the top of the ridge for a better view of the surrounding forest. Halfway to the top he heard the first shot.

Houston squatted in the forest, studying the stream. His eyes methodically surveyed the area as far as he could see. The sound of water cascading down the side of the ridge enticed him. His mouth was pasty with thirst and his stomach rumbled. The craving urged him to rush forward, to drink until he was ready to burst. However, his resurrected discipline made him cautious. His quarry was not stupid; he, too, would know that streams were magnets, attracting animals and men alike. To a sniper, a stream was analogous to a kill zone.

Houston crouched and duck walked through the trees, following a course that was anything but straight. As much as possible, he avoided the dead foliage that littered the ground, using trees and bushes for cover. The ground in this section was littered with layers of dead pine and fir needles that made movement easier and much quieter. He found a pine whose boughs hung low to the ground and over the stream. He dropped to his stomach and crawled to the water.

Pushing aside debris from the trees, he lowered his face to the stream and drank. The cool water tasted faintly of pinesap; still, given the situation, it was the best water he had ever drunk. His thirst abated, he sat back on his haunches. Now, he needed something to eat.

Movement up the ridge caught his eye and he dove to the side as a bullet thudded into the pine tree. He rolled behind an exposed tree root and scanned the area through his scope. Seeing nothing, he decided to go on the offensive. He gathered himself and ran across the shallow stream into a stand of brush on the opposite shore. Another shot rang out and he dove behind some dead fall and fired an answering shot in the direction of the last one. Houston crouched, considering his situation. What he needed now was mobility, not stealth. Houston removed the cumbersome Ghillie suit. He worked the bolt and replaced the round he had fired, poised himself as he gathered courage and then rushed up the incline.

Five minutes of frenetic scrambling had him squatting in the place from which Rosa had fired at him. There were scuffmarks on the ground and he found two ejected cartridges. He wanted to end this now, for the last time. It was time to flush Rosa out.

Houston tensed and then dashed through small bushes and trees, knocking them out of his way with his left arm. He cut left along the face of a small outcropping when his enemy stood up to his right.

Houston almost panicked and blew it. However, he quickly got himself under control. He took a quick half turn, raising his rifle for a shot, but before he could cradle the weapon in his shoulder, a tremendous force hit him, followed by a loud crack.

The shot came from Marsh's left, and he changed his course in that direction. He held the M-16 in both hands, ready to bring it into action. He struggled to maintain his balance while descending through the dense brush and deadfall. The rain the night before had soaked the foliage and the fallen leaf sediment of past season, making walking treacherous and traction tenuous. His feet whipped out from under him and he tried to keep the rifle free of dirt by holding it over his head as he landed on his left hip and slid down the slope. He smashed through a small stump that was in an advanced state of decay. The old tree butt exploded in a cloud of soft rotten wood and slowed his descent enough that he could brace his feet and use them as brakes. He lay still for several seconds, listening to determine if his fall had attracted any unwanted attention. After several moments, he felt the chill of wet leaves and moist dirt soaking through his uniform and he sat up. Other than the sounds native to the woods, everything seemed quiet. Taking care not let the rifle come in contact with the ground, he struggled against the slippery slope and gravity to regain his feet. Back on his feet, Marsh checked his weapons to ensure they had not gotten fouled during his uncontrolled descent. Satisfied all was in order, he stood still and listened for the telltale sounds of human movement.

The bullet hit Houston when he was a quarter into his turn, most likely saving his life. If the bullet had hit him square, it would have severed his spinal cord. Instead, the round slammed into his left shoulder and exited just below his left shoulder blade. He fell to the side and tumbled through dead foliage and brush. He rolled down the ridge.

Rosa saw Houston spin and fall from sight as the bullet's impact drove him back and he lost footing. It was all Rosa could do to refrain from shouting in victorious excitement. He watched Houston roll down the slope and started after him. This was one kill he wanted to verify personally.

He stopped about twenty meters down the slope and scanned the area through his telescopic sight. He saw Houston scrambling for cover behind a large fallen beech tree and fired.

The loop sling did its job as Houston tumbled down the steep incline; the rifle stayed in his hands the whole way. He slammed into something hard and unyielding and was dazed. He opened his eyes and saw he had hit an old downed tree. He scrambled under it a second before a bullet slammed into the rotting wood, inches above his head. He spun around on his stomach and heard the dull thud of yet another bullet crashing into the dead tree followed by the sharp bark of Rosa's rifle.

Pain lanced through Houston when he tried to bring his rifle to bear on the ridge. Unlike the rifle, the telescopic sight had not survived the tumble down the ridge. It would not have helped him if it had. His hands shook like an earthquake measuring seven on the Richter scale. He gritted his teeth and realized he was going to have to shoot the rifle without the benefit of sights. One of the modifications made to the Remington 700 by the Marine Corps was the removal of the M40A3's rear sight and front sight blade. He studied his hands and hoped he could control the shaking that his adrenaline rush, brought on by stress and fear, caused; failure to do so would be fatal.

Even though the bullet had hit him hard, at first he felt no pain. Now that the shock of the full metal-jacketed projectile passing through him was wearing off, pain took over and he knew he was in bad shape. He lay under the fallen tree and felt as if a hockey player had collided with him at full speed. Suddenly, his vision blurred and he felt warm wetness spreading across his chest and down his back as well. Houston knew, without seeing it, that his wound was severe.

He hoped Rosa would want to finish him up close and come looking for him, even if it were only to gloat. The smart thing for Rosa to do would be to stay hidden and let Houston bleed out. That is what a trained, disciplined sniper would do. His only hope was that Rosa's hatred was greater than his discipline

Houston saw movement and knew he was lucky. Rosa wanted to revel in his victory so badly that he cast aside his training and was coming to count coup. Rosa would want him to live long enough to taunt him.

Houston fought off a blackout. He realized that in his confined shelter, there was not enough space to allow him to use the rifle. If anything, it would get in the way and he needed to get rid of it. The last thing he wanted was to have the useless weapon interfere with what little movement there was. He ground his teeth to keep from grunting and groaning with pain while sliding the sling off his left arm, all the time watching the ridge. The terrain and every-thing in it was a blurry mishmash, almost like a modern painting in which the artist intermixed hundreds of colors into an explosive blob with no definite borders. Once again, something moved—this time descending the slope. He would not be able to testify in court that it was Rosa; but only a human being would be walking upright as it threaded a circuitous path down the incline. Pushing his rifle out of the way, Houston freed the Glock from its holster, pointed it up range and waited.

Rosa was good. His descent was almost soundless, which did not surprise Houston. After all, several times Rosa had gotten on top of him without making a sound.

He saw Rosa appear, standing with the sun in his face—a big mistake. Houston saw Rosa's shape squat down and check the ground for blood sign. After several seconds, he stood up and looked down the slope. Houston guessed he was about twenty-five meters from his hiding place, still too far for an accurate pistol shot. However, he was weakening fast and needed Rosa close, real close. He was losing a lot of blood and he knew he would only have one chance—he had better make it good.

Marsh saw an armed figure appear out of the brush and walk slowly down the incline. The gunman wore a Ghillie suit similar to the one Houston had worn the previous night. The suit was camouflaged with bits of flora interspersed throughout it. The figure looked like a pile of leaves with legs. When the gunman raised his rifle to his shoulder, Marsh took a shooting stance and yelled, "Stop right there!"

The rifle spun toward him . . .

Houston started to sweat, yet he felt cold. He did not know how much longer he would remain conscious, "Come on, you sonuvabitch—" he whispered.

Rosa started forward, cutting the distance in half, still moving cautiously.

He followed the signs of Houston's slide and after what seemed an eternity Houston saw his feet outside of his shelter.

"Mikey, are you in there?"

Suddenly the warden appeared out the trees and shouted, "Stop right there!" Rosa turned and aimed his rifle at him.

Houston rose to his knees, staggered to his feet and said, "Hello, Edwin."

Rosa forgot about the warden and spun to face Houston. It was impossible for his severely scarred face to show expression. However, his cold, pale blue eyes widened in surprise when he found himself staring into the barrel of Houston's 9mm pistol.

Houston widened his stance to compensate for his shaking hands and fired . . .

. . . and fired again.

The first round hit Rosa in the stomach. He doubled over and the second bullet smashed through his face. The heavy slug drove him back a step, where his foot slipped on the berm of a small ravine. Rosa tumbled into the ditch and came to rest at the bottom.

Houston staggered forward; the pain from his mangled shoulder filled his eyes with tears. Walking on the uneven ground was difficult, but he urged his wounded body forward. Houston slowly approached the berm and looked inside the gully.

Rosa rested in a quagmire of mud and blood and decayed sediment. From ten feet away, Houston saw that his head was lopsided and the 9mm bullet had blown out a large piece of his skull. He would never make another kill.

Even though Rosa had identified himself, Houston needed to confirm the identity and he slid down the gully. He knelt beside the body and rummaged through its pockets where he found a pair of old dog tags. Houston grimaced as he turned the tags to see the name punched on them. The sniper with the horrific burn scars on his face was indeed Edwin Rosa.

"You all right?"

Houston stood and looked up at Marsh, the stock of an M-16 rested on the warden's hip, muzzle pointed at the sky. He raised his hands so that his pistol was in plain sight and pointed at the sky and then threw it on the ground at Marsh's feet. "I'm sure as hell glad you're here." He slowly dropped to his knees in the chilly debris-and blood-covered water.

37

"But for me it is over. I have passed my rifle and scope to others
who are also gifted at this arcane and secret craft, and there is no
one left for me to shoot. . . . I will never fight again."
—Gunnery Sergeant Jack Coughlin, USMC

Houston woke up and saw Jimmy O'Leary sitting beside his bed. He thumbed through a magazine. Unable to speak, he lay still staring at Jimmy.

Jimmy glanced up from his magazine and saw that Houston's eyes were open. "Welcome back to the world."

Too weak to control his head, Houston let it roll to the side. A nurse walked in and stood beside him. She checked his pulse and felt his forehead. "Fever seems to have broken."

Houston tried to talk, but all he was able to do was make a dry croaking sound.

"A bit dry are we?" The nurse held a glass with a straw before his mouth and he sipped. The water felt wonderful as it cooled his mouth and lubricated his tongue and throat.

"Enough?"

He nodded and the glass disappeared.

Houston looked at Jimmy and whispered, "Anne?"

"Gonna make it." O'Leary pointed at Houston's heavily bandaged shoulder. "You two are something else. Name me another couple with his and hers gunshot wounds."

Houston's eyes felt heavy and he forced them to remain open. "Susie okay?" His voice was hoarse and it hurt his throat to talk.

"She's fine. Turns out she has as much of her father in her as she does her mother."

The nurse straightened the sheets on his bed. "Damned lucky for you that medevac got there as soon as it did. You would have died otherwise."

"I don't remember."

"Wouldn't matter if you did; it wouldn't have changed anything. You're one popular man."

"Oh?"

"There are Maine state cops and people from the Department of Inland Fish and Wildlife waiting to talk to you. Marvin tried to clarify things, but the state police want you to personally explain why a Boston cop is in Maine killing people."

"Nurse," Houston said, "I'm not up to that right now."

"I know that," the nurse replied. "Hell, the doctor and I already told them it would be at least three days before you'd have enough strength to be interrogated." She smiled. "Then I'll feed you to them." She finished fussing with his bed, turned her attention to recording his vital signs on his chart. "You're much stronger than you feel."

"You could have fooled me."

A man dressed in pale green scrubs walked into the room, closing the door behind him. "Hello, I'm Doctor Hayward. How are you feeling?"

"Not bad, all things considered."

"Well, if it's any consolation, you're going to live." He looked at Jimmy. "Could we have a minute?"

"Anything you have to say to me can be said in front of him," Houston said. "He and I go back a long way."

"You're one lucky man, detective. If that bullet had been a couple of inches to the right . . . well, quite frankly, it would have ripped your heart apart."

The doctor stayed with them for several minutes, checking Houston's chart and then left. O'Leary looked at the door to ensure they were alone. "I want you to know that this ain't changed nothin'."

Houston gave him a questioning look.

"About us," O'Leary said, "Now that you got the bastard, it's back to business as usual . . . you're still a cop and I'm still what I am."

Houston smiled. "I never expected anything else."

O'Leary took out his cigarettes and shook one out before he remembered where he was. He coughed and shoved the cigarette back into the box, which he put back into his pocket.

"You got one thing wrong though, Jimmy."

"Which is?"

"I'm through as a cop."

"I'll believe that when I see it."

"This case has opened my eyes. The job cost me my wife and almost my daughter and my life. I don't want to lose anything else, man. I'm done as a cop."

O'Leary walked past Houston's bed and stared out the window. He studied the Portland skyline for several moments. "I always wondered if you were ever gonna realize that there are times when the price of staying is higher than the cost of leaving." He turned toward the door and, as he walked toward it, he looked over his shoulder at Houston. "You need a job, there'll always be a place in my organization for you."

"We both know that will never happen." Houston winced as a stab of pain ripped through him. He exhaled deeply. "Truth is, I'm burned out on living in the city. I kind of took a liking to Maine."

"You, living in the fuckin' woods? That I gotta see."

"I can live in the country just fine. Besides, even if I can't I'll never admit it."

"We are a couple of stubborn micks, aren't we? You going to be all right?"

Before Houston could reply, Susie pushed Anne's wheelchair through the door. Anne's appearance rattled him. Black circles surrounded her eyes and she had lost so much weight that she looked gaunt and frail.

Without taking his eyes off Anne, he answered O'Leary, "Yeah, I'm gonna be just fine."

Susie bolted around the wheelchair, bent over and kissed her father. "I love you, Dad."

"I've always known that, kid. Although I'm sure I haven't always made it easy."

Susie hugged him and when he grunted in pain, snapped back. "I'm sorry."

"No problem, babe."

Susie stepped aside, giving him a clear view of Anne. Houston smiled at his partner, trying to hide his nervousness. How was he going to tell her that he was leaving the cops and Boston?

"Getting crowded in here—think I'll go have a smoke." He nudged Susie.

Anne turned and looked up at Susie. "Would you please push me over to the bed?"

Once Anne's wheelchair was beside the bed, she took Houston's hand in hers. "I heard that you got him."

"It's more like we got each other . . ."

Susie and O'Leary looked at Houston and Anne, whose physical pain seemed to fall away as they held hands, ambivalent to anything else. "I'm outta here. You guys got things to talk about," Jimmy O said.

"Help me up," Anne told Susie.

"Are you sure? The doctor doesn't want you standing yet."

"Just help me up."

Anne used Susie's shoulder to raise out of the chair. She stepped beside Houston's bed and said, "Move over you big lug."

Houston made room for her and she lay down beside him. Houston winced as he let her settle in and put his arm around her, pulling her against him.

Susie looked at her father and Anne and then turned to her uncle. "They're so cute at that age."

"Christ, before you know it, you'll all be kissing and bawling. C'mon, kid, they don't need us right now." Jimmy O and his niece walked out, closing the door behind them.

ACKNOWLEDGMENTS

O f all my work, *Sniper* took me the longest to write, just over ten years. I owe thanks to many people. To list a few: My late wife and soul mate, Connie; cancer took her before she could read the finished manuscript and, after seven years, I still miss her terribly. At the same time, Connie was my most devoted fan and also my most valuable critic—she was always willing to tell me what I needed to hear, not what I wanted to hear. On those occasions where I wanted to give up writing, she was the one person who gave me the strength of purpose to struggle onward.

To be successful, a new writer needs a strong critique group of writers who are willing to read the bad stuff and to be strong enough to give the writer constructive, honest criticism. I have been fortunate to be involved with two such groups. First is The Monday Murder Club group where I truly learned *how* to write. Thanks Paula, Steve, Andy, Margaret and Jim. Second, the *Breathe* group in Maine. Thanks are also due to Wendy, Heather, Vince and Larry for their invaluable feedback and input.

Thanks are also owed to Brian Thiem, formerly commander of the Oakland, California Police Department Special Operations and USA retired, for pointing out correct police procedure and updating this old jarhead on current military weaponry.

Thanks are owed to my agent and excellent editor, Paula Munier, who has had faith in this novel since its inception in 2002 and to Constance Renfrow and Jay Cassell of Skyhorse Publishing for their excellent editorial assistance.

This book is a work of fiction and any mistakes within are entirely the fault of the writer. That being said, I would like to cite the following works for aiding me in learning about the world of the sniper:

1. *Shooter, The Autobiography of the Top-Ranked Marine Sniper* by Gunnery Sergeant Jack Coughlin, USMC, Captain Casey Kuhlman, USMCR, with Donald Davis, St. Martin's Press, 2005.
2. *Marine Sniper* by Charles Henderson, Berkeley Publishing Group, 1986.
3. *Silent Warrior* by Charles Henderson, Berkeley Publishing Group, 2000.
4. *US Marine Corps Scout/Sniper Training Manual* by Scout/Sniper Instructor School, Marksmanship Training Unit, Weapons Training Battalion, Marine Corps Development and Education Command, Quantico, Virginia 22134. Desert Publications, 1994.

I sincerely hope that this work of fiction is not construed as a condemnation of a group of honorable, skilled marines.

Hoo-rah!
Vaughn C. Hardacker
USMC 1966 to 1974

PERMISSIONS

1. *Shooter, The Autobiography of the Top-Ranked Marine Sniper* by Gunnery Sergeant Jack Coughlin, USMC, Captain Casey Kuhlman, USMCR, with Donald Davis, © 2005 Reprinted by permission of St. Martin's Press. All rights reserved.

2. *Marine Sniper* by Charles Henderson, Berkeley Publishing Group, © 1986. Reprinted by permission of Charles Henderson. All rights reserved.

3. *Silent Warrior* by Charles Henderson, Berkeley Publishing Group, © 2000. Reprinted by permission of Charles Henderson. All rights reserved.

4. *US Marine Corps Scout/Sniper Training Manual* by Scout/Sniper Instructor School, Marksmanship Training Unit, Weapons Training Battalion, Marine Corps Development and Education Command, Quantico, Virginia 22134, Desert Publications, ©1994. Reprinted by permission of Desert Publications. All rights reserved.